Massen

Also by C P James
Rescue Charlie
Goliath
Picket
The Crossing

Coming soon:
Unleashed
The Dustbin Man/Over the Wall

Massen

Massen

Chapter I

It took me two days to realise what was wrong with the counterweight.

The light of the distant sun cast ever changing shadows across the boulder's rocky surface. They never seemed to be the same twice, so I rarely saw the odd oblong outline I'd seen on the very first day of my voyage back to the Maw. And that was after staring at it for several hours a day. I confess there isn't much to do in the tractor's cramped cabin.

"Shit," I said when I finally caught a glimpse of it again. Of course it was gone as quickly as it had appeared, lost as the counterweight span around the tractor, casting it into shadow once again.

It was definitely there. An oblong shadow. Like a doorway. On a rock hundreds of millions of kilometres into space, orbiting the gas giant Oberon. The light so thin it barely brought any warmth with it.

Impossible. Absolutely absurd. Yet there it was.

Unless I was mad. I had to concede that possibility. A week of staring at the arse end of the roid I was shepherding to the Maw, with nothing but the slow wheezing of ancient air scrubbers for company, would drive anyone mad. And the counterweight, don't forget that. That was something else to look at. True, the view of Oberon was awe inspiring. It was a giant swirl of oranges and yellows, the odd purple blemish toward the poles. Tute and Sweet came into view ever now and then. The giant planet's closest and largest moons. They were little more than faint dots against the emptiness of space. Besides that was the Shatter, the ancient debris of two other, unnamed, inner moons that had collided a very long time ago. Breaking apart to form a ring of rocks varying in size between a mountain and my fist. They were the very reason I was here. Harvesting the debris for precious minerals was very lucrative.

OK, there was a lot to look at. Still, few tractor drivers lasted long out here. I'd been here longer than most. Two years. And in that time I'd seen two drivers head off into the black never to return. Their tractors discovered weeks later, abandoned. Their interiors smeared with blood, faeces and who knew what else.

Losing one's log was common amongst drivers. Perhaps it was just my turn.

"Bollox." I pulled myself up to the stern observation hatch and stared at the counterweight. I was effectively hanging from the ceiling here, my arms quickly shaking from the exertion. The oblong shadow didn't return.

I cursed again as I let myself down clumsily against the driver's couch. It didn't take me long to contemplate my next course of action. In fact I was doing it before I came to a decision. I was slipping into my air reclaimer when I realised I couldn't let this lie. I simply had to know what the shadow was. There was no way such a regular shape was natural. Next came my helmet and then my gloves. Fortunately I pretty much lived in my pressure suit. Every tractor driver did. These machines were old and often sprang leaks. If it took me too long to get into my suit I was dead. It was as simple as that. Safer to live in it.

The tractor was too small for an airlock. I depressurised the cabin and clumsily yanked on the hatch's locking handle. Something flapped past me as the last of the cabin air dumped into empty space. I didn't see what it was. Clearly something I hadn't secured properly. I clipped an impact drill to my belt and followed it with a bag of carabiners. Once I was on the other end there would be nothing to hold onto.

I didn't come out here often. There was no reason to and hanging on the side of the tractor in mid space was risky. One small mistake and I could become detached. Then I could take my time watching the tractor slowly recede into the distance. I clipped onto a railing and crawled clumsily towards the tow cable. Once I'd clipped to that I balanced myself and looked upwards.

The cable was as thick as my wrist, made up of hundreds of steel wires twisted together. As old as it was some of those wires had split, springing loose from the cable. Any one of them would rip a hole in my suite. So, I had to make my way across the eighty or so metre span without making any contact with it, apart from the carabiner I had clipped to it. If I did, I was very likely dead.

Yep. This was a very bad idea indeed. Still, if I arrived at the Maw with something questionable in tow there would be questions. The Jane had no sense of humour. They had the power to imprison and interrogate me at whim. Or to remove my tractor licence. Once that happened back to Reaos I went. To my family and cheating spouse. I'd rather stay here in this horrible place.

I could cut the counterweight loose and coast the rest of the way to the Maw. It was only a few more days. Which would, in itself, raise questions.

I crouched on the tractor's dented yellow hull, gauging my leap. Simply jumping wasn't going to work and I knew it. The tractor and the counterweight were spinning around each other, held together by the cable. That spin generating artificial gravity on either side. The only thing that made this trip even slightly tolerable. Still, there were complex forces at play. Which, as I'd set up the dance, I was very familiar with. A tractor driver did need to have a rudimentary knowledge of trigonometry.

There's a trick to this.

I leaped in the direction of the tractor's travel, allowing my tether to snap me back to the cable. I met it with the soles of my boots, and ran up it. Grunting with concentration I kept the cable underneath me, well aware that one slip could snag my suit on the ancient cable. It was hard work.

As I neared halfway the pressure against my boots faded and I found myself floating away from it. The tether snatched me back again and I allowed my momentum to carry me the rest of the way.

"Shit." I landed awkwardly, banging my helmed against hard stone. My breath knocked out of me, I waited a moment, half expecting alarms to sound in my helmet. Glass cracking or a seal shifting under the impact. There was nothing but the slight hiss of air from the rebreather.

Lucky.

There was gravity here too. The same force I was accustomed to on the tractor. I sat down for a bit, looking up at my trusty vehicle hanging overhead. Shadows were twisting around it now. It was an ugly affair. Thick drive unit with a simple cabin bolted to it between two stubby fuel cells. Beneath were the two grappling arms, which were folded out of the way, their claws hidden from my perspective. All of this had once been painted yellow, with black lines and lettering. All of that was long faded and scratched, revealing stark steel beneath. I didn't know how old it was, nor who had built it. I did know it was a long time ago. If you were to say it was a hundred years old I wouldn't be surprised. No one built these things anymore. I don't know when they ever did. They had simply always been here, servicing the Maw, shepherding roids from the Shatter into its processing fields.

It was home. As near as anywhere was.

The counterweight itself was simply a rock. One I'd chosen with two criteria in mind. Firstly, it had the correct mass to offset the tractor. Secondly, it looked like it would stay in one piece when I tethered the two together and set them spinning. Other than that it was of no interest to me. When I reached the Maw I would simply let it go on its way. It was far too small to be worth feeding into the processors. It would need to be a thousand times the size to be worth that. Something like the rock I was shepherding towards the Maw, its own orbit of Oberon broken when I set carefully positioned charges on its surface. Giving it the odd nudge from the tractor to fine tune its trajectory. Nudge. I'd used the grappling arms to secure the tractor to it before lighting the main drive, leaving it running for twelve hours before shutting it off. That was how much force it took to nudge something of this size.

My magnetometer claimed there were some juicy metals in that roid. Well worth the trip. Maybe sixty or seventy thousand C's. Enough to pay off the lean on the tractor and fuel for the next trip out. With that lean gone everything I earned from then was pure gravy.

If I could steer clear of the Jane. If they took an interest in me all of that was at risk. So, I needed to know what was off about this counterweight.

It looked like a rock. No different to the other billion or so others out here. Grey and boring. Some jagged edges I had used to anchor the cable. It also had some sheer faces, probably from the catastrophe that had ripped the moons apart all those centuries ago. As a result it had a relatively high albedo, making it easy to spot out here in the dark. All in all pretty mundane. Apart from that odd shadow.

I drilled in some clips to attach the carabiners to and started making my way around it. The further I moved from the tethering cable the steeper the side became until I was clinging to a near vertical cliff. Nothing but emptiness beneath my boots. I slipped more than once as I made my way around the counterweight, searching for the elusive shadow. Every time I did I decided this was a really stupid idea and should go back. But every time I found myself continuing. Perhaps I was just stubborn.

And then there it was. A regular shape against the jagged edges of the counterweight. A shadow deeper than it should be. Depths impenetrable to the feeble light from the sun. I steadied myself with a few extra clips drilled into the rock and slid down towards it.

It was oblong all right. It wasn't natural either.

"Shit." I hung next to it, all my weight on the line, staring at it. It was a doorway. A door in a rock a million kilometres from anywhere. "Shit," I said again.

I swung in, grabbing hold of an ancient locking handle to steady myself, my headlamp bright on the metal. It felt brittle, like it would come away in my heavy gloves if I pulled too hard. There were some markings on it. Impossible to read now. And a symbol, barely visible. A circle inside a triangle. Other than that nothing but for tarnished metal.

I could open this and see what was inside. Something long lost. From before the Fall perhaps. That was two thousand years ago. A long time for secrets hidden behind doors lost in the Shatter.

I turned and looked behind me. Not an easy task in a restrictive suit. There was no one else out here. No one would ever know what I was doing here. The Maw was still days away. It was safe to take a look.

I had to take a look. I couldn't enter Maw space with this door closed and the tractor still attached to the counterweight. Perhaps the Jane would never see it, the counterweight lost to space when I set it free. But what if they did? What if they did and there was something …. illicit behind here? It was very possible someone was using the Shatter as a place to hide smuggled goods. Banned technologies. Secret information. It could be anything. I mean, it had to be secret, right? Otherwise why would someone put it out here?

It was only then it occurred to me someone other than the Jane might take an interest. Someone who had put this door here. Someone who would want to know why their asteroid had moved, and who had moved it.

Double shit.

I ran my gloves around the door jamb. It seemed to be sealed tight. But, I discovered as I tried the locking mechanism, the handle was loose. It wasn't secured. It was unlocked.

I hesitated still. My mind in turmoil. But then, I realised, it was too late for all this indecision. My mind had been made up the moment I depressurised the tractor. I hadn't come all this way to leave the door closed. Was I going to turn around and go back? Leaving it like I found it?

Like hell.

Careful of the brittle metal I took a firm hold and turned. It stuck for a moment before swinging free. I yelped, catapulted into space, the handle still in my hand.

"Bloody shit." I steadied myself against the counterweight and peered into darkness.

There was light coming from somewhere. Reeling out the line I ventured in, my headlamp casting weird shadows into the oblong passage beyond the door. There was a little bit of dust here, coating the walls and floor. Whichever they were, it was impossible to discern the passage's orientation. That light was not a light as such. More like a patch of slightly less dark darkness. It was on the other end of the passage, as if it opened up into a dimly lit room.

Or, I realised, the other side of the counterweight. An opening in the other side of the rock out of view from the tractor.

I wedged myself against a wall to steady myself and studied the light. The counterweight's motion threw me to the side slightly. It took no more than a few seconds for something to swing into view. A tiny moon. Toot perhaps.

Well, that was disappointing.

I let out more cable and ventured further in. There was an indistinct shape on the floor. (ceiling?)

"Ah, shit."

It was a corpse. Long desiccated by exposure to hard vacuum. I couldn't tell if it was a man or woman, its skin was sunken until it was little more than a skeleton tightly covered by brittle leather. There was no hair. It had either fallen out or the person had been bald. No eyes. Just dark sockets where they had once been. It was dressed in some kind of coverall. Grey perhaps. Or it had been once. No insignias of any kind.

Shit.

Tractor drivers tended to be a hard, unimaginative bunch. We had to be. Still, I didn't like this. Dead bodies in space, floating around for who knows how long. It wasn't right.

I nudged it with a boot. It was surprisingly light. With nothing to keep it in place it was a wonder it was still there. There was nothing to stop it from sliding out the opposite end of the passage to vanish into space.

It was only when I started searching the body in earnest that I discovered a metal pin protruding from its chest. It looked like a very large nail. It was this pin that kept the corpse motionless. Someone had nailed the body to the wall.

I cursed for a moment before continuing my search. Whoever that killer was they were not here anymore. They were probably long dead themselves. Still, I checked over my shoulder again. No one.

There was a bulge in a pocket. Something square and hard. I hesitated for a moment before trying to pull it out. My gloves were too big to get into the pocket but a utility knife quickly parted the material.

A box. Also metal. Square, about three or four centimetres to a side. I pocketed it and turned the corpse over to see if there was anything else of interest. There wasn't.

I ventured further into the passage. There was nothing else there either. Just more passage. This had clearly been part of a larger complex before the moon it was built on was ripped apart.

I had decisions to make. What now?

Which was no decision really. I yanked on the desiccated corpse, trying to free it up. After centuries exposed to vacuum the material of its clothing was brittle, tearing easily.

"Shit damn." I fell backwards as it came free suddenly. Almost tipping me out of the doorway. A long dead face banged against my visor as it passed me by. It had already vanished into the darkness of space by the time I twisted around to look behind me. I was about to wave it farewell when I realised some of it remained behind.

I might have sworn then. The ancient body had torn in two, leaving its pelvis and legs stuck to the floor. I used a boot to kick it free. Disrespectful perhaps, but I wanted as little to do with this thing as possible. Like a piece of old driftwood it was stiff and brittle. One of the legs seemed to snap as I kicked it. Still, it slid free and started skittering down the passage towards open space at the other end. Happy to see the last of it I aimed my lamp down the passage to ensure it kept on going. It did, quickly vanishing into darkness like its upper half had done.

I saluted it jerkily. It was the least I could do. Probably more than had been done for it in a very long time.

Chapter 2

The rest of my journey back to the Maw was uneventful, if slow. I was used to that though. That was the nature of the business.

I didn't look at the counterweight again. There was a small nag of guilt over how I had unceremoniously tipped the body into space. It deserved more than that. We all did. I'd lost companions before – tractor drivers all – who had disappeared into the Shatter. Their bodies never found. Who could say that wouldn't happen to me one day? My body left to orbit Oberon forever. Frozen and timeless. Still, I'll admit the Jane scared me, and what they would do when they discovered I had been hauling an ancient corpse around. In honesty I didn't know what they would do, which made it worse.

Comfortable in the driver's seat I put the box I'd fished from its pocket onto the controls before me and studied it. It opened easily, displaying some very odd contents. A small sphere, about the size of my little finger's knuckle. Glass perhaps, with the slow swirl of something inside. It glowed eerily. A faint bluish light from a power source I couldn't discern. It wasn't natural, it was a made thing, using a technology I couldn't guess at.

I scooped it up carefully and weighed it in my palm. It felt light. Almost as if it was hollow. Even if I kept it, hiding it from the Jane when they inspected the tractor, what would I do with it? Sell it? Who would have an interest in such a thing? And for how much? What was it? It was an exquisite bauble, that was true. But what then? Someone could keep it on their desk to look at perhaps.

Still, it was important. That … person had thought to keep it on them when catastrophe overtook the moon, that was clear. No one built random passages in asteroids, one end sealed by a door, the other open to space. Why should they? No, I believed that passage had been built when the asteroid had been part of something much much larger. A whole moon. Before the collision that created the Shatter. I didn't know how long ago that was. Thousands of years. Before the Fall certainly, and that was two thousand years ago. That people had lived here, colonising this moon so far out on the edges of the system, was a miracle. Who would have believed it? True, we knew little of those times, all that knowledge was long lost. What else had there been out here? Certainly a far larger installation. A city perhaps. Destroyed when the moons ripped each other apart and cast rubble into space.

This jewel, or whatever it was, came from a time before that, which would make it precious to the right people. Whoever they were.

The Meranti Familia perhaps. They collected ancient curios dating to before the Fall. Art works. Ceramics. Those kinds of things. People did also find the odd piece of technology from time to time but the Jane soon confiscated them. Pre-Fall technology was proscribed. The penalty … well, who knew what that was? The penalty was disappearance.

Was this a technology? A machine of some sort. I didn't know. I couldn't. It didn't look like it and even if it was, how did it work? Its surface was glassy and featureless. No scratches of blemishes at all. It was only the interior that made it interesting. The glowing swirling shapes were quite mesmerising.

I shrugged and put the bauble back in its box and secured that box in a locker. I was not qualified to answer any of those questions. This was just a distraction. True, I had nothing else to do, but it would only succeed in driving me crazy.

The rock I was shepherding to the Maw was mid-sized, I guessed. About a kilometre on a side and roughly oblong in shape. The longest side possibly a kilometre and a half. It would fit neatly into the Maw, which could accommodate rocks at least three to four times the size. I'd chosen it for two really good reasons. Firstly, it drove my magnetometer crazy. There was clearly some heavy metals inside. A lot of them. It was also not too large, meaning I could keep my fuel expenditure down. Fuel was money in this business. I would need to spend some more when we got closer to the Maw. We weren't currently aimed directly at it, but rather a few dozen kilometres to the side. A safety precaution in case the Maw was busy with another load or if someone else was blocking the entrance. I would only fine tune our approach when Maw Control gave me their permission. Anyone approaching without that permission would be fired upon while they were still a long way away. Nukes did light the sky up nicely. I had only seen that once, an inexperienced driver making a mistake they would never repeat.

Because I liked my privacy, and a bit of peace and quiet, I tended to coast the tractor and its attendant counterweight in the lee of the rock, keeping it between me and the Maw. It also meant the rock would take the impact should we wander into any debris. There was a lot of that out here.

As I neared the Maw I pulsed the tractor's motors in time with my orbit about the counterweight. Causing the assemblage to drift to one side. It slowly nudged me out of the rock's shadow and into sight of the Maw. Once in the clear I fired a LOS comms beam towards the Maw.

I cleared my throat. "Maw Control. Tractor MFB 1018, Massen."

I was greeted by nothing but silence, forcing me to repeat myself. Eventually an annoyed sounding voice responded. "I read you, 1018."

"I'm at 2024K, 20 degrees high. ETA eight hours fifteen."

"Stay on course. Recontact when at 200K. MC out." The line went dead.

200? Seriously? I refrained from airing my feelings at the dark comms station. I never did trust it. I didn't trust the Jane weren't eavesdropping on drivers and keeping secret records of what went on in their tractor fleet. One of the reasons I cruised in the rock's lee where comms were impossible.

If I adjusted our trajectory for the Maw now I could do it with little more than twenty minute's thrust. The later I left the manoeuvre the steeper the angle of approach, requiring more fuel. At two hundred kilometres I would be firing the motors all the way in. Almost two hours at full thrust.

Fuel was money.

Of course they wouldn't care about that. There was probably an earlier consignment still in the entrance way. The rock would be coming in fast as it needed to to engage the grinders. It was that very momentum that set them tearing the rock apart. A rock of this size going this speed carried a lot of energy. Like a bomb going off in the entrance if it struck something it shouldn't. A big bomb. So, while I understood it, I wasn't happy about it.

I aimed the docking camera towards the Maw and zoomed in as far as it would go. At this distance I could make out a blurry spot but nothing much else. If there was something in the entrance I couldn't see it.

I set an alarm and crawled into my bunk. It was little more than a strip of foam with a pillow at one end. Barely long enough for me to stretch out on. There was no blanket. I didn't need one. I slipped a frozen pre-packaged meal into the little microwave built into the cubby and thumped its already dented side a few times for luck. I don't think it helped, but it made me feel better. The thing was old, like everything inside the tractor. Sometimes it worked, sometimes I ate half frozen chicken curry. Today was about standard. One half lukewarm, the other still frozen. I ate it anyway, the icy crystals crunching between my teeth. It was probably unhealthy but who cared? It was sterile, so I wouldn't be getting a stomach bug from it.

I'll have to be honest with you, the life of a tractor driver is not glamorous. The tractor's cabin was tiny. There was space for a control couch up against the fly-eye canopy, with a narrow bunk almost directly behind it. The bunk itself was ringed by storage bins and a kitchen unit. Alongside the rear hatch was an ablution unit, which was nothing more than a zero g toilet. Which, if I need to be more precise, was an array of two suction hoses. One for each job. It was lucky there was only enough space for one person in these things, as you wouldn't want to share those hoses. The smell inside was something else altogether. I don't think I'll even try to describe it. I half pitied the inspectors when they boarded the tractor after I docked, checking for contraband. I wasn't sure what kind of contraband they expected to find, but there you go. Everyone had a job to do.

This was my life right now. A few days at the Tongue for rest and recuperation – along with any repair work that needed doing to the tractor, then back into the Shatter. It was a hard life, as I've mentioned before drivers don't tend to last all that long. There was a supply ship back to Reaos once every three months, opportunity for any driver who couldn't hack it to escape. Bearing in mind they would have to work for the company for the rest of their lives if they bailed early, paying off the transport fees to the Maw and back. A contract lasted four years, most of which went to paying off the OMC loan every driver took out for transport, board on the Tongue, and hire of their tractor. Once that was paid any proceeds were the driver's to keep. If you could survive the four-year tour they went home wealthy.

The Tongue was the crewed part of the Maw structure, housing its engineering facilities, docking bays and living spaces. It orbited the Maw itself, which was a very strange assemblage of machinery indeed. The machinery that ripped apart asteroids and processed them for their valuable metals wasn't actually machinery at all. But rather a string of electromagnetic and gravitational fields wielded by accelerators along the rim, that ground down the asteroid as it passed between them, before filtering different minerals into collectors set along its length. The gange, as it was called, was all the dust and small rocks left over from this process. It was allowed to spew out the back of the monstrous machine.

Operations had been ongoing long enough that that cloud was starting to build up. In a few more centuries Oberon would have a beautiful system of rings.

As the tractor moved closer I grew bored and crawled out of the bunk. I could see flashes inside the Maw. The machinery was clearly working on a previous meal. The odd radioactive element sparked, creating the flashes I could see from here. It looked like lightening seen from a distance. Like a storm hovering on the horizon. I sincerely hoped that tractor driver had flagged the radiological readings from their roid before they sent it into the Maw machinery. If they hadn't, the Jane would be knocking. If the concentration or purity of the element was too great it could be quite catastrophic.

Still, while radiological elements dangerous, they were valuable, so worth the risk for any tractor driver. If anything I was envious.

At 200 kilometres I flagged the controller again. "Maw Control. Tractor MFB 1018, Massen."

"I read you 1018."

"Passing the 200k marker, Control. 40 degrees high. Awaiting instruction."

"You are clear to approach, 1018. Specify details of payload."

They didn't often ask that. It could only mean the previous driver had missed some crucial details out. I no longer envied them. "Twenty GT, Control. No radiologicals. Iron, titanium, hydrogen, platinum and gold. Other traces."

"Proceed." They cut the connection.

Radiologicals were generally not a problem. Generally. That depending on the type of material they were dealing with, as well as its purity and mass. The forces applied through the Maw were enough to propel sufficient quantities to critical mass. While the Maw itself was robust enough to ride out any kind of nuclear blast, the radiation sweeping the Tongue could be lethal. Not to mention the damage caused by the electromagnetic pulse. The driver must have been crazy or completely inept to drive a radiological payload into the Maw without giving prior notice.

The Tractor rattled as I fired up the thrusters again. There was a bang behind me. Something was clearly working loose. Something else to be checked back at the Tongue. More money. I detonated the firing pins keeping the counterweight attached to the tractor. I didn't look at it as it sped away, quickly lost in the darkness of space. I'd had enough of it, I think.

I squirted more fuel to the thrusters to cancel the momentum donated by the counterweight as the connection was cut, careful not to tangle the tractor in the cable as I reeled it in. Once it was secure I positioned the tractor against the roid, the claws outstretched to firmly anchor the two together. Once the craft was settled I jetted fuel to the main drive. Only a little at first, slowly ramping up the power once I was confident the claws were firmly set against the roid's side. The tractor began vibrating as I eased the regulator to full power. That didn't worry me. This old heap always vibrated. I would worry if it stopped.

"On our way," I said to myself.

I fished the tin from the cubby and regarded it for a moment. I couldn't keep this thing. The tractor would be searched and serviced upon docking. I might have to pay for the tractor's use, refuelling and service, but I didn't own it. It was owned by the Oberon Mining Confederation, I was simply leasing it. They would want to take a look at it after I docked. They would also be interested to know whether I had smuggled any illicit cargo aboard. There were valuable jewels out here. Diamonds and the like. Valuables the tractors sensors easily found against the backdrop of empty space. The OMC owned the rights to anything I brought back and so would take umbrage at any attempt to smuggle something past them.

"Down the hatch." I opened the tin and quickly swallowed the ball. I gagged on it for a second in my dry mouth before it slid down my throat. The x-ray machines were offline the last time I passed through offboarding. I hoped they still were. The tin went into the refuse hatch to be expelled on the next cycle.

I won't give you all the mundane details of manoeuvring and docking procedures. They are pretty dull and time consuming. None of it was easy to achieve, and involved a lot of laborious laser telemetry checks and inevitable re-adjustments. Each one meaning I had to manoeuvre the tractor to a different part of the roid before firing the main drive again. Often with Control shouting at me over the LOS. They were getting nervous as they observed the roid getting closer and closer. If it struck any part of Maw machinery it could cause immense damage which would result in it to being out of operation for some time. I ignored their entreaties. It was their fault I was coming in at such a steep angle. Once the roid in my care was aligned with the Maw I allowed it on its way. Retracting the grappling arms, I squirted fuel to the manoeuvring jets again and headed for the Tongue. I didn't look over my shoulder at the roid as it passed through the Maw's outer ring. I'd seen enough of it. I didn't want to look at it ever again.

The Tongue was a tube of rock five kilometres in length, the centre hollowed out to allow living space on its inner surface. The whole affair spun to simulate gravity within. The station walls were about five hundred metres thick, themselves riddled with power generation nodes and atmosphere processors. The north end, as it was known, held the docking facility and command and control areas. Most of the docks themselves were aligned with the centre of the roid's axis, meaning they were virtually gravity free. They were reserved for transport, logistics and VIP access. The ring around it was for the tractors, heavy steel girders linking airlocks and fuel lines to facilities buried beneath grey rock. The 0.01G was miniscule, barely enough to be an annoyance when docking. Dozens of tractors were already parked. Most identical, some in various stages of disassembly, either being scrapped or repaired. Bright spotlights were set into the rim of the facility and aimed inwards, casting deep shadows beneath the vessels docked there. As I neared I saw small groups of engineers floating around the vessels, their headlamps picking them out in the shadows.

Maw Control assigned me a cradle and I eased the tractor into it. There was a slight bump and a sigh as I deactivated the vessel's internal systems.

There. That was it. I sat while the docking bay crew connected the tractor to air and power conduits, before connecting an expandable tube to the hatch. I was in their hands now.

There was a sharp clang on the hatch as a docky rapped on it with a wrench. They tended to let drivers open their own doors, in case we were engaged in a last-minute wank or something, I don't know.

I'll admit to a certain reluctance to leave. You get used to these ancient, dented and stained walls. The hiss of the air recycler and the smell of your own body odour and a slightly malfunctioning toilet. It was safe. Out there there were people. Lights. Noise. People making demands of you. It could be intimidating. I'd known more than one driver refusing to leave their cab. One even welded the hatch shut to prevent anyone getting her out. The dockies left her in the cab after uncoupling the power and air supplies and powering down the drive from outside. In the hopes of driving her out, to be fair. Not to kill her. She still died though. Suffocation, hyperthermia. Who knew? It was all the same in the end.

The docky rapped on the hatch again, breaking my reverie. It was getting harder for me every time I left this tiny space. I wasn't there yet. Not yet.

With the tractor attached to the ring the gravity wasn't what I was accustomed to, so it took me a moment to orient myself and claw my way to the hatch. Cool air blasted in when I cracked the seal.

"About bloody time, thought we'd be cutting you out," the docky grumped as he moved aside to allow me past. He was a stocky man with a bush of unkempt, wiry hair. It floated about his head in low G.

"Sign this. Fifteen thousand litres of fuel remaining. You were cutting it tight. It'll cost you." He pushed the clipboard at me.

I signed it without really looking at it. My tanks weren't empty but they could have been so much better.

He swept away from me, scooping up his clipboard. "Leave your suit."

I hesitated, looking down at myself. Of course I didn't own the pressure suit either. That was also property of the OMC. I'd been wearing it so long I had forgotten about it. I wrestled with the fastenings and slid out of it, shedding it like the second skin it had become. I felt vulnerable without it. My creased grey OMC singlesuit felt so insubstantial I may as well have been naked. Once I'd dumped it back inside the tractor I was ready to leave. I'd be back of course, once the vehicle had been serviced and I was ready for the next assignment. I couldn't afford to leave just yet. Not that I was sure I wanted to.

And that was that. I was back. There would be no welcoming party or debrief, my job was too mundane for that. No one cared. There were guards posted at the torus, a narrow walkway leading deeper into the Tongue. They maintained a scanner to check for contraband, and I was relieved to see the machine still had wires hanging from a half open cover. An engineer had clearly had a go at repairing it before leaving the task half completed. Possibly awaiting on spare parts. Things moved slowly around here.

And I was through the entrance. The jewel, whatever it was, was mine. The guards completed a perfunctory search of my person and the rucksack containing personal effects, but they clearly didn't care for the task. It was so distasteful they wore gloves. I didn't think I smelled that bad. But then I wouldn't know, I'd been smelling myself for days.

There was an elevator to the residential level, hoops set into the deck for your feet to slip into. Keeping you in place while accelerating from near weightlessness to 1G. face it, most people are idiots. Left to their own devices they'd float into the elevator and punch ground level. Then wonder why they wake up in hospital with a concussion, or worse. Which was the reason the ramps had been sealed off, forcing workers to use the elevators. Too many came out at ground level with a momentum they just couldn't control, and collided with a wall, window or another traveller. At least this way travellers were safely enclosed in a small steel box. There was only so much damage they could do, and that mostly to themselves.

There was a small observation lounge at the foot of the elevator. There wasn't much to see, so few tarried here. One wall was thick pressure glass, allowing a view of the docking ring and a slight glimpse of the Maw itself. Every now and then Oberon came into view, which was worth looking at if I hadn't seen it so many times before. It was a massive shape from this perspective, filling most of the view with its swirling orange and grey clouds.

This was where the steel of the docking bay gave way to the rock of the Tongue itself. Materials were not wasted here. If a floor could just as easily be smooth rock, smooth rock it was. No one bothered with niceties like flooring or wall panels. A string of lights were clipped to the ceiling, running alongside a simple aluminium tube – a ventilation duct. There were a few carts pulled up alongside the lift doors, should anyone be hauling anything particularly heavy down the access tunnel. They were all but useless now, the floor had become rutted after centuries of use.

"Mas, that you?"

I turned to see a driver hurrying to catch up to me. He was pulling a cart behind him, the ancient wheels rattling and squealing in despair over the rough surface. Arden. He liked comforts in his tractor, rigging curtains and pillows. I heard there were even candles. Candles? In a tractor? He must be insane.

Hence the need for the trolly. He wasn't finding it easy going.

"Arden. What are you doing?"

He drew level with me and paused a moment, out of breath. "I've been suspended for three months. The Jane."

That surprised me. "Oh? Why?"

He shrugged. "My trajectory was a bit off. Like less than one degree. They threatened to cancel my contract and send me back. Shiiit." He was a short man, his stature ideal for driving tractors. They did not have large interiors, particularly once they were full of clutter. He usually kept his head bald but a red fuzz was starting to grow out after weeks in space. I could smell him, I realised. It was not a nice smell. Sweat and faeces.

"So you're the reason my approach was delayed?" I turned my back on him and continued walking.

"Wait. Wait. It wasn't like that." He huffed as he caught up to me. "The roid was off balance. Diamonds ... I hope. They didn't register on the mag ... mag ... shit."

"Magnetometer."

"Yeah. Don't make me run, man. I'm having a shit day as it is."

I stopped and faced him. "You cost me, man. I had to come in steep with you blocking the entrance. I'll barely make even on my roid and it was heavy in metals." I continued walking.

"Shit. I'm sorry. Listen, if it's diamonds I can make it up to you. I swear." He followed on behind.

"Diamonds? Shit. I've only ever heard of one driver bringing back diamonds and they weren't worth shit. It could just as easily be an air pocket throwing you off balance. That's why we spin them on the way in, so we can gauge their stability. You didn't spin it, did you?"

"Shit man. I'm sorry."

I ignored him as he rattled his cart behind me. Grunting in frustration as a wheel caught on a rut and almost tipped the contraption over. Drivers were a solitary breed. We needed to prefer our own company. We were alone in the dark for for weeks on end. No contact with anyone at all. Not even via LOS.

As a result I didn't particularly want his company. I wanted to be left alone. Perhaps when I got to the Garden later I could enjoy some tequilas and female company. But not right now. And definitely not with the man who had cost me so much.

"Listen. Listen. Stop dammit." He panted as he caught up with me. I might have sped up my pace a bit. "There's more out there. A fucking mother load, man. There's one big bastard. Too big for me to bring in on my own. It'll fit into the Maw though. At least its short axis, and that's all that matters. I can show it to you, I memorised the co-ords."

"You want my help bringing an oversize roid in? You know you have to get permission from Control to bring something like that in? They won't grant it. Not for someone who can't even bring a standard roid in straight."

"Yeah." He was silent a moment. Apart from his puffing. I hadn't slowed down. "That's why I need you. You've never had trouble with the Jane. Nor with Control. You follow the rules and you do it right. They'll grant it to someone like you."

"And that's why I won't do it. Besides, what's in it for me? That roid will have to be better than twice the standard size to be worth it since we'll be splitting the proceeds. You know what's in it? You checked the boards?" Demand for raw materials fluctuated. Sometimes heavy metals brought in the cash, sometimes carbonates. Sometimes diamonds, yes. But that was rare. It all depended on what industry back on Reaos demanded at the time. If you brought the wrong roid in at the wrong time it could bankrupt you. It was always wise to keep an eye on the boards and hunt the right roids. Which in itself was always a risk. The boards could have changed or you might have misjudged your roid. Metals were always valuable, I tended to stick to them.

"Ive only just gotten back," he grumped. "Diamonds are good sellers."

No. They weren't. "Besides, you're grounded."

"Only for three months."

"Will you be able to navigate to that roid after three months? The Shatter changes you know. Nothing stays where it is."

He shook his head and said nothing, concentrating on keeping up with me. I couldn't believe I was starting to feel sorry for him. The feeling didn't last long once I reminded myself how much he had cost me in fuel. And then the feeling returned when I realised the Jane would have confiscated his roid too. The notion that he would cash in on diamonds in his roid was mere bluster. He was probably broke.

Damn.

"Listen. I'll be at the Garden later. I'll get you a drink and you can tell me why you think this roid is your payday. You'll have to convince me."

"Really? Shit, man. I'll be there."

I cursed myself for being weak. The man was a fool. A dangerous one at that. He shouldn't be out here at all. He needed a friend. Someone who would tell him to give it up and go home. At the very least someone to guide him right so he didn't kill himself. Or worse, wreck the Maw. Which would kill him just as dead. Even if he survived the incident, he wouldn't survive the Jane.

He stopped and leaned against his cart. Panting. "You go ahead. I'll catch up later."

I hesitated and then shrugged, continuing my walk down the access tunnel. It was fortunate very few people were ever in a rush in the Tongue: this tunnel was long. There was a railway tunnel linking the Garden and the docking facilities a few metres away, but it was only used by important people. Certainly not tractor drivers. The odd steel door linked the two, should a train break down. Obviously those doors were locked. I could hear the rumble of steel wheels on ancient tracks when one passed by. They rarely did as there weren't enough important people in the Tongue to warrant a regular schedule. They powered up the rails only when it was needed.

I did eventually reach sunlight. I say sunlight, what I mean is the light from the strip, a bright beam of light running through the cavern's axis, stretching from one pole to the other. I couldn't say what powered it, the science was beyond me. I did know it was a wonderfully pleasant light, almost as good as a bright sunlit day on Reaos. It was even warm. It conveniently dimmed in the evenings, allowing the Garden to go dark. It never went out completely though, it was always there even in the middle of the night. A faint glow against the opposite floor of the Garden.

The Garden was a tube hollowed out in the centre of the Tongue. A few kilometres in length, and just over a kilometre in diameter. Gravity was exerted on its inner surface by the spin of the asteroid, keeping everything where it was put. This was the habitation area of the Tongue. residential blocks ringed the space, walkways allowing access through them to the precincts on either side. The spaces were filled with leisure facilities. There were bars and clubs. That was where most of the drivers spent their down time. You would rarely see them venturing into the gardens proper, to enjoy the trees and fountains. Drivers were simply not the type.

The north end cap wall was the administration building. It was so tall it almost met the strip in the centre. Gravity on those higher levels must be very limited. I wouldn't know, I'd never been there. Some said there were laboratories of some kind there. Doing who knew what kind of research. I doubted it. The southern end cap was wall of condominiums. Living quarters for the administrators and other VIP's. I had heard there was even the odd swimming pool to be seen there. I'd never seen them myself. Not because they were hidden, but because I simply wasn't interested. I'd never made it through the park to take a look.

There were perhaps five or six thousand people living here. Most of them were engineers, who maintained the facilities themselves, the tractors, or the Maw. There were only a few dozen drivers and they were in space more often than not. The remainder were shop keepers, bar tenders and prostitutes. As a result the Garden felt empty much of the time.

Rock gave way to metal for the last few hundred metres. It was showing its age, marked by rust and some interesting orange stains here and there. There were machines hidden behind these walls. Air scrubbers, generators, sewage treatment and water reclamation plants. There was even a hydroponic farm here somewhere. I'd never seen that, but I understood it was quite an impressive sight. They allowed the operations here to be largely self sufficient. The only shipments required from Reaos were heavy machinery parts and replacement personnel. Although, I understood, many of the personnel had been born here. Generations of people had lived and died out here, never to set foot on a planet's surface. Never to see sky. I supposed they didn't know to miss it.

I paused, enjoying the warmth of the sun on my face. The Garden's aroma washed over me. Grass, cooking and … pepo. The latter was unmistakeable. It was a drug smoked in a pipe. Very popular on the Tongue. I didn't know who grew the stuff, but there was always a ready supply. I'd tried it once and didn't enjoy what it did to me. I remember having a conversation with one of the hookers in Barnaby's, and every few seconds I forgot what I was talking about, and so changed the subject. So – I rambled to her for about half an hour. I think she gave up on getting any business out of me and left halfway through, I didn't notice. The loss of focus disturbed me. I didn't like losing control like that, so I never touched it again.

The tunnel exited in a courtyard. It had clearly been rebuilt several times as it was ringed by a mishmash of styles. There were odd plinths here and there, as if there had once been trees or fountains dotting the space. The buildings felt old. Not weathered, as there was no weather here, but dilapidated. Poorly kept up. The odd windows were missing shutters. Some were missing glass completely, the rooms beyond long deserted. Here and there doors were not hanging straight, as if a drunk handyman had given up halfway through the job. This was all pretty much cosmetic, you understand. None of this really mattered to the functioning of the Garden or the Tongue itself. All of those critical machines were in perfect order, properly maintained by a legion of engineers. Priorities being what they were.

To the left was the entrance to Jupiter House. It was the first and largest blockhouse, a triple storey building that stretched overhead and then ran down the opposite side, to meet itself again on my right. Its walls were bare stone, hewn from the Tongue itself. A garden was planted on its roof. Once it might have been a pleasant space of grass, hedges and trees, but now it had become overgrown. A tangle of bushes and trees, some of them leaning precariously over the roof, their roots ripping up the stone of the walls. Some sections had died out completely, the watering channels becoming blocked over the years, allowing those sections to dry out. They were little more than dust bowls. Skeletal trees and mats of dried out grass and bush. Once again this was cosmetic damage, so no one really cared. True, the foliage served the purpose of trapping carbon from the atmosphere, but the loss was minimal. Barely noticed by the machines purring under our feet.

I waited for a goat to get out of the way before I could enter the building. Yes, we had goats. They kept a lot of the undergrowth in check. We also had rats, because of course we did, as well as a colony of cats. Not to mention the odd hawk that had become very adept at navigating the variable gravity of the spinning habitat.

"Massen, 1018," I said to the wizened old woman who sat behind the counter of Jupiter House reception.

She stared at me over her ancient, dog eared, ledger. "You tell me that every time, Mas. Do you think I'm stupid? Every time you come in here and give me your name and designation, like I haven't been doing this job for a hundred years. Like I don't know every one of you scruffy tractor drivers," she ranted as she filled out the ledger. "You insult this old woman, you really do. I cry in the back sometimes."

I couldn't help but laugh. "Of course you do, Heli. I don't believe it's been a hundred years though. More like a hundred and fifty, maybe a hundred and seventy-five."

"Asshole." She scowled as she pushed a pen in my direction. "Sign your smelly name right there." She jabbed a finger at her ledger. "Now go away so I can cry."

"What room is it?"

She shrugged, pushing some ancient and massive keys in my direction. "Guess."

"You have to be kidding me." I knew which room those keys belonged to.

"Don't sass me next time and I might give you a better room. Now get out of here."

"Come on, Heli. Have a heart."

She threw a pencil at me. "Scram."

Muttering I mounted the stairs. There was no arguing with her when she was in this mood.

So, I say Jupiter house has three floors. That's primarily as anything above that becomes uncomfortable. Too close to the strip it gets a bit warm and everything starts to feel light. Not to mention the fact you wake up nauseous because of the faint Coriolis forces that acts on you in your sleep. On the third floor you can just about ignore it. On the fourth, you can't. So no one builds that high.

Apart from some enterprising soul who built a retreat atop Jupiter House some years ago. It was meant to be private, out of the way of everyone else. There was plenty of room, as the roof top was empty apart from trees and bushes. It was a good construction to be fair. The stonework was better quality than that of the main building. Power and plumbing had also been run into it. It should be have been a great pad for whoever stayed there. Should have been. Everyone who slept there woke up ill. And I do mean everyone.

As part of my contract I was guaranteed a residence in Jupiter House when I was in the Tongue, however that contract didn't stipulate what kind of residence it should be. Today it looked like it was to be the penthouse. Damn. That just meant I would be spending more time in the Lucky Roundhouse, the local drinking establishment. Known as the 'Roundy' by drivers and locals alike it was where most people spent their off-duty hours anyway.

I'll have to be honest, the penthouse was a good room. In fact it was more of a suite. It had been a labour of love and few stayed here these days, meaning the fittings had not been worn out and the walls weren't marked by who knows what - let's just say never take a black light into one of the standard rooms. The state you wake up in is its one and only downside. It was not pleasant. And this coming from someone who spent a lot of time spinning about a counterweight, which had to be closer than the strip. Making me wonder whether it was the Coriolis effect after all. Perhaps something to do with the proximity to the strip itself? I didn't know. I wasn't a physicist. I just knew the end result.

I looked around the suite before dropping off my bags. It was as I remembered it. It was an initiation rite for new drivers to spend their first night here. Perhaps so a trip in a tractor didn't feel so bad. That felt like a long time ago. I had vomited next to the bed. And in the small bathroom. And near the front door. Damn.

"Shit." I threw down my satchel and stalked out.

I realised why I was in the penthouse the moment I walked into the Roundy. It was full. I hesitated in the entrance, allowing the rumble of conversation to wash over me. I had never seen it this full before.

"What's going on?" I asked a driver I recognised.

"Hey, Mas. You back? Yeah, The Jane aren't signing work permits. They haven't done for about a week now. Everyone's stuck here. Unless they're out already," Sersh said. She was one of the old timers. One of the real old timers. She'd completed three tours already and was working on her fourth. I doubted anyone had been here longer than she had. She was a tall, almost skeletal woman, wearing simple grey coveralls. She was lounging on a couch just inside the Roundy's entrance. Another driver I didn't recognise had her hand inside Sersh's coveralls, idly paying with her breasts-it looked like. She ignored me, taking out her hand to lick her fingers before sliding it back in. Sersh looked like she was ignoring her too. I decided that was a good strategy.

"The Jane? What's the flight schedule got to do with them?"

Sersh shrugged. "Dunno. It was ever since Hanno the Fourth got back with his roid. The Jane took him away. Haven't seen him since. Next day we were locked down. Losing a lot of money we are, sat here like this."

It was driver habit to shorten names. They called me Mas, even though my name was Massen. Well … Eli Massen to be precise. Sersh was Sershesewa. Hanno the Fourth was … Hanno the Fourth. He insisted that was his name and refused any contraction.

"Reckon he found something out there?"

She looked up at me. "Tell you what, Mas. Why don't you go and ask the Jane? They might actually tell you what's going on. I mean, they haven't said shit to us. But you, hey…"

I frowned. "Sure, Sersh. I'll do that." I left her and her friend and headed for the bar.

"I reckon they found something," Dal, a driver I barely knew, said as I seated myself and ordered a beer.

"Like what?" I pushed over a credit chit and cradled the chilled glass. This was going to taste good and I wasn't going to rush it. These things took time.

"Dunno. I hear they didn't push Hanno the Fourth's roid through the Maw. They kept it."

"Nah, it went through the Maw all right," another voice interjected. I glanced down the bar, it came from a thickset woman in janitor's coveralls. I didn't know her. Well, I guess they could come in here too. "They just switched it off. The roid is parked on the dark side of the Tongue. All in one piece like."

Dal grunted. He was a hairy man. Hairy head, hairy face, hairy arms. The prostitutes claimed he was hairy every else as well. All you could really see of him were slices of skin between beard and fringe, punctuated by some of the bluest eyes I had ever seen. "What would you know?"

"I know some engineers," the janitor said. "They were on duty when it came in. They reconfigured the Maw to keep the roid intact, and let it pass through to the other side."

"So, what did they find? What was special about this roid?" I asked her. I took a delicate sip. I simply cannot explain to you how good it tasted. Like icy liquid pleasure. I let it slide down my throat and took another. It was even better.

The janitor shrugged. "The weight was off. Like it was hollow or something."

"A hollow roid? What bollox," Dal said.

A thought made the third sip go stale in my mouth. A hollow roid. As in it had passages inside it or something. Passages like the one I had discovered in my counterweight. Or something passages might lead to. Chambers of some kind.

Which was not entirely impossible. We didn't mine the Shatter in a disorganised, haphazard way. We were assigned areas, all the drivers picking an area clean before moving on to another. There was a lot of space out there so we very rarely saw each other while out prospecting. Still, whatever my counterweight was attached to would have been relatively nearby. Close enough for Hanno the Fourth to stumble onto it.

And the Jane took him away for it. Shit.

I began debating whether I should stick my finger down my throat and rid myself of the jewel. It was the only evidence that I had stumbled onto anything unusual.

"You know how excited MC gets when a roid is unbalanced. Burns out projectors in the Maw. I hear they were all thrown out of synch by that roid. That's never happened before, and will only happen if the roid is pretty much hollow," the janitor said.

"So, what did they found inside it?" Dal asked.

The janitor shrugged. "Dunno. The Jane have it locked down. Only they are going inside. I hear a shuttle is coming up from Reaos full of science types. Just to get inside the thing."

"Rubbish," Dal scoffed. "What's going to be inside a roid out here?"

"Some artefact. Maybe people have been here before. Building things."

"Bollox. We're the first ones out here."

Which I knew to be false. I'd found a passage, after all. A passage leading who knew where. I remained silent. I needed to get this jewel out of me. I was starting to doubt I would ever get anything for it.

Fool, I told myself. I was a fool.

I needed a lavatory. I was going to stick my finger down my throat and flush the thing away. It might be pretty but it would never amount to anything. Nothing good anyway.

"We boring you?" Dal asked as I stood.

I didn't respond, walking quickly to the lavatory and locking myself into a cubicle. Lavatories looked the same the world over. And in space too, it appeared. They were all equally as disgusting, no matter how often they were cleaned, and these were not cleaned often at all. I dropped to my knees and contemplated the rancid bowl. I'd never done this before.

As it turns out making yourself throw up is not as easy as you would have thought. I gagged on my finger no matter how far back I pushed it. Nothing happened.

"Save some for me." I heard a woman's voice comment. She probably thought I was making use of some kind of drug, even though none of us bothered visiting the lavatory to do that. No one cared who used what out here. As long as drivers were sensible when they boarded their tractors, and remained so during the trip. What they did on their downtime hours was no one's business.

"Shit." This wasn't working. Perhaps my stomach was empty. I hadn't eaten anything in hours.

I kept trying anyway. I had to get this thing out. The only result of my efforts was saliva all over my hands and a very sore throat. Damn.

Perhaps the jewel had passed too far along to come out. That was always possible. What then? I just had to hope it passed out the other side quickly. Before the Jane took an interest in me.

You know, I hadn't thought about that either. About fishing it out of the other end. Now that wasn't a pleasant thought, particularly as I'd never know when to expect it, so I would have to check every time.

What a fool.

I washed my hands and headed back to the bar. My half-finished beer was still there. It was warm and flat. Dal was deep in conversation with another driver. The janitor had left, possibly to start her shift. I didn't recognise the new driver, a newcomer maybe.

"Not to Reaos they don't," the newcomer was saying. He was drinking what looked to be some kind of cocktail. It was pink. Very odd. No one drank cocktails here. I didn't think they served them. "I worked two tours on the OCC. We didn't pass as many slugs as you would expect. And they need guiding in so we see all of them. So they hit a desert someplace and not a city, see. In that year I think we saw …" He shrugged. "Half as many as we send from here."

"No way. The Maw launches a slug every day. Sometimes more than one a day," Dal said.

"Not to Reaos they don't," the new driver insisted.

"There's nowhere else to go."

He shrugged again.

The Maw condensed the raw materials it collected from roids, ejecting the junk and creating metallic slugs from the valuable stuff. They were pretty big, each weighing thirty or so tonnes. They were accelerated to the inner system and forgotten about. I'd always assumed their destination was Reaos. As Dal had observed, there was nowhere else for them to go.

"Maybe whoever they're sending them to doesn't need them anymore. So they shut down production," the new driver continued.

"Mate, we've been at this for decades. We'll be doing it decades more," Dal said. He turned to me. "You're an old hand. What do you think?"

I shrugged. "I've only just come back. I have no idea what's going on."

"They took your roid though?"

"Yeah. Made me wait some, so I wasted a shit load of fuel. Something to do with Ard's roid being unbalanced. He was hoping it's diamonds but I reckon he's full of shit."

"Ard?" Dal turned to face me dead on. "You saw Ard?"

"Yeah. About an hour ago."

"Shit. Did he say anything?"

"How do you mean?"

"I heard the Jane were waiting for him. They got him. Can't be long after you saw him."

"Shit. What for?"

It was his turn to shrug. "Don't know. Maybe they found something in his entrance scan."

I shook my head. "It ain't working."

"Yeah it is. Fixed last week. Hagga told me. She fixed it."

"Hagga?"

"I was talking to her when you so rudely walked off."

Oh. I'd taken her to be a janitor. The coveralls looked similar. "Shit. It's working?"

"Yeah. Why? What has you so worried?"

Damn. The scan would have found the jewel. There was no way it hadn't. But why hadn't they stopped me? It made no sense. They should have arrested me on sight. The Jane were a blunt instrument. There would be no letting me go to see what I did with it. It would never occur to them.

I felt ill. My stomach roiled. Not helped by a diet of warm, flat beer and no food.

"What's with you? You're not usually this quiet when you get back. You've not even had one hooker yet and you've been here an hour."

I shook my head. "Been out here too long, I think."

"Been smearing shit on bulkheads have you?"

"What?"

Dal smiled and went back to her drink. "It's what people do isn't it? Lose their log and smear some shit."

I shook my head. I was a long way from that. "I lost a lot of cash on this last trip and I've not heard what my roid is worth yet."

"They will still be processing it, you know that. It will take days for your dividend. In the meantime, drink up and get laid."

"Yeah." My heart was not into all that. Even a fresh beer didn't seem appealing.

"Let me get you another." Dal waved to the barman.

I didn't get as much as the opportunity to lay eyes on my fresh beer. Even as the barman headed over a quiet fell over the Roundy. A few chairs groaned as they were moved aside. I frowned and turned around. The Jane.

"Eli Massen. Come with us."

Chapter 3

They left me in some sort of holding cell. Or perhaps it would be better to call it a dungeon. The walls were ancient, water stained rock. There was a simple platform on one wall that, I imagine, was supposed to be a bed. There were some blankets on it. I have no idea how old they were. Their smell was indescribable and they came apart in my fingers. I opted to brush them aside and sit on bare rock. The floor looked to be dirt, but on closer inspection I discovered it was simply compacted faeces. Decades, perhaps centuries, of accumulated shit. Dried and walked on, to make a floor. It was so old it didn't smell any more. The only light came through a yellow, age stained, glass panel in the ceiling. It was out of reach some two metres above my head. I couldn't even reach it standing on the platform. There were no toilet facilities – hence the floor – and nothing to drink.

They hadn't asked me any questions or laid any accusations against me. The two thickset Jane who led me here had barely spoken to me on the walk down into the bowels of the Tongue. Their only words instructions to hurry up. I didn't argue. They had batons and stunners on their belts and I knew they would not hesitate to use either.

"Shit," I said to the simple steel door that was the only way out of the chamber. Like everything else it looked ancient. It also sported some interesting black stains on some of the rivets that held it together. Blood perhaps. Was that a bit of scalp attached to one of them? I shuddered and looked away.

As my eyes adjusted to the gloom I realised there were markings on the walls. Graffiti left by previous inmates. Most of it was painted in some medium I didn't want to think about, while some had simply been carved into the rock. I couldn't imagine what implement was used, as the Jane had searched me before pushing me through the door. They hadn't left me with anything hard, certainly no belt buckle or shoes. The only things I had left to make an impression on the stone were my fingernails.

I couldn't read much of it. What I could read made no sense. 'Suffer the … something'. 'Bonus 1064'. Something that looked like 'persimilous' or 'persmian'. Something like that. I didn't know what that meant. 'Remember 20 10 1764'. Was that a date? If so it was over two hundred years in the past. People had always wondered how long the Maw had been operational. The only conclusion anyone had ever come to was that no one knew. It felt like a very long time, bearing in mind the state of some of the machinery. But it couldn't be all that long, surely? The first person to make it into space had been Colonel Antionette Shane in 1821. And she had died there, her suit malfunctioning, dumping all her oxygen into space. It was a further twenty years before anyone followed her, since the Clutch Invasion had put paid to the then Alliance Space Treaty Organisation efforts to reach orbit. ASTO, as they were known, failed as an organisation when the Clutch took over their research facilities and burned it all. The Clutch hadn't liked that kind of technology, as they considered it heretical. What remained of the ASTO had become the Federal Group before anyone ventured to orbit again. This time the two pilots managed to return alive, even if their pod landed in enemy territory, where they were promptly executed for spying.

Space travel did not have a great start.

Anyway, enough of the history lesson. My point is that, if that was a date, it preceded the first person to space by sixty odd years. Never mind that it would be over a hundred years before anyone made it this far out into the system. So it simply couldn't be a date.

I looked away from it and tried to make out more of the writing. I couldn't. Well, that was a nice two minutes I'd whiled away. Now what?

"Shit."

At the very least my career as a tractor driver was over. Even if they found no transgression I would not be returning to my tractor. Those taken away by the Jane never returned. Ever. Potentially because the Jane had a reputation to keep, or more likely because when the Jane took interest in you they always found something. Whether it was to be found or not.

Damn, I needed not to think about this. That was not an avenue of thought I wanted to pursue at this time. Not if I wanted to refrain from trying to claw my way through the walls with my nails. Some of the marks on the walls made it look like that had been tried before, and whoever it was had been very unsuccessful.

I think I might have spent some time staring into space then. I didn't know. It was impossible to tell time. It could have been ten minutes, it could have been two hours. I had no way of knowing. My mind was blank. I don't think it was on purpose, but rather because I simply could not form a coherent thought out of my swirl of emotions.

I stood and started pacing over the compacted excrement. Three steps, right turn, two steps, right turn. That went on for a while until I realised my heart was beating so loud I could hear it. I was driving myself into a panic.

I might have sworn then. I forced myself to sit down again, trying not to think about what constituted the dust covering my bare toes. I took a deep breath and tried to steady my nerves. There was nothing I could do about any of this. I was here. There was no way I could get out. I had to let it happen.

It was then something very strange happened. A voice. I couldn't see a communications grille anywhere, and the door had not opened to allow anyone to speak through it. It was calm and measured. I couldn't tell if it was male or female.

"Initial communication attempt,' it said.

Startled I stood and put my back to a wall. "What? Who is that?"

"Communication successful. Progress authorisation requested," it continued.

"What the hell?" I must say this was not what I had been expecting. I had expected interrogation. Torture. Shit. But what was this? "What?"

"Progress authorisation requested."

"I don't know what that means. Who are you? Where are you?" I walked in a tight circle, studying the light, the door, the bench. There was no way a voice would be coming from any of those avenues. And certainly not this clearly. It was as if someone was standing in the cell beside me. I looked over the walls again. Nothing but those odd dates and scratches.

"Progress authorisation requested."

"Seriously? What does that mean?"

There was no reply and the voice did not repeat itself. I stood silent for a time, waiting for it to speak again. When it didn't I studied my cell more closely, searching for where the voice had come from. As before there was nothing. No gap, no grille, no speaker. Nothing.

I sat on the bed and rubbed my forehead with my fingertips. Was I going mad? This place could do it. The stains on the wall proved that. Still, I hadn't been here long enough surely? It was a few hours if that.

I pulled myself onto the bench and rested my head on my knees. I could handle this. I spent weeks on my own in a smaller compartment that this. This was a few hours. The Jane wouldn't leave me here. What would be the purpose of that? They would either charge me with something and toss me out of an airlock, or send me back to Reaos on the next shuttle. Obviously the latter was the preference even though I dreaded the notion of going home. I was here for a reason after all. I didn't think either my wife or Gerad would appreciate my early re-appearance. It would be an embarrassment to them. Gerad was not a man who tolerated embarrassment.

My mother. It has all been about my mother. She was the daughter of the dread warlord, Captain Taam. Taam rose to the ranks in the Artigade Authority military. Back when the Authority was a group of aligned city states along the eastern seaboard of Versima. Which had been quiet and peaceful, until Taam's uprising and ultimate coup. He and his loyal lieutenants assassinated the council members and formed their own government. He ran it as its warlord, its dictator. Under his rule the army grew in strength and they invaded a number of nonaligned states along their borders. His empire grew.

Lieutenant Massen was one of his henchmen. An enforcer, if you will. You can probably predict the story. He and my mother fell in love while he was assigned to protect the Spires, the defacto capitol of the Authority. They married without my grandfather's consent and I was the ultimate result. My grandfather was enraged when he discovered this and had my father thrown from a rampart. A rampart that is still known today as the Massen Fling. Lovely.

Still, my grandfather loved my mother, as most of his subjects did, and so could not bring himself to get rid of me. A child barely out of diapers at this time. She never spoke to him again and he never visited the Spires after that day. He was ultimately assassinated by my uncle, Gerad's father. While my mother remained alive I remained in favour. I'll be honest and admit that I never wanted for anything. I even married the most beautiful woman in the Spires, Van Ken. I was happy, as happy as anyone could be in that world, isolated from what was really happening by my wealth and family connections.

Then my mother died. A brief illness that took her life all too soon. In that moment I was out of favour. Van no longer cared for me as I was beneath her station. I was an embarrassment. Still, she couldn't divorce me when she started a relationship with Gerad. That would have resulted in even more embarrassment.

So I was sent here. Out of the way. Better that than an unfortunate accident. Which was all they could do to me. There was still some affection left for my mother, enough to keep me from outright assassination. This was middle ground, as it were.

Going back there was not my preference.

So, it was death by spacing or death by unfortunate accident. Of which there were plenty opportunities in the Spires. They might even name a spire after me. Eli's fall. Awesome.

I paced. Three steps, turn right, two steps, turn right. It wasn't helping. Shit.

"Secondary communication attempt."

"What? Seriously?" I might have sworn a bit and sat down on the ledge. Damn, this was getting irritating. Was the Jane trying to play some kind of game with me?

"Communication successful. Progress authorisation requested."

I groaned and rested my head on my arms. I didn't need this. Just stop it.

"Progress authorisation requested," the voice tried again when I didn't respond to it.

"I don't care. Do you want something from me? What do you want from me?" I searched the chamber. There was nothing – no one – there. There couldn't be. Not until the Jane came through that door and dragged me away to whatever fate awaited me.

"Progress authorisation requested."

"Shit. Whatever you want, just do it. You need authorisation from me? Go ahead. Do it, see what I care." I half expected the door to blow open and the atmosphere to get sucked out of the chamber. Or spikes to come down from the ceiling. Something.

"Authorisation received. Initial recombination process begun."

I giggled. "Really? What the hell does that mean?" The voice did not return. Whatever it wanted it had now gone away. Hopefully for good.

I stood and paced again. This time I didn't stop. Not until the door creaked open and two Jane entered. The same two Jane as before. One raised a stunner baton and I fell to the floor.

Chapter 4

I vaguely remember being dragged through dimly lit passages. One Jane on each arm. The moment my legs started recovering they pulled me upright. They were damned if they were going to carry me if I could walk myself.

I'm not sure what I did could be called walking. It was more of a stagger. Still, we arrived at out destination and I was dumped behind a table. The interrogation was to start.

The Jane trooped out and locked the door behind me. I was left on my own.

Groaning I lay my head on the metal table. I felt terrible. Every nerve in my body was on fire. I didn't know why they had stunned me. Probably simple bloody mindedness. Or to soften me up for the interrogation. I dashed dust out of my hair, trying not to think what was in it. What was the point in having a floor of faeces in a space station? It couldn't be that hard to put in some decent plumbing. But I supposed it wouldn't have the same effect.

The door open softly and someone entered. It was done so quietly I almost missed it.

Grunting I forced myself upright. I struggled to focus for a moment.

Mission Commander Asey Hayes. Not Jane at all. She seated herself and placed a pad on the table between us. She was wearing Mission Command coveralls. Purple with yellow insignia on breast and shoulder. She was the one who assigned missions to drivers. She was OMC – Oberon Mining Confederation. The company we all worked for. Even the Jane. They were its muscle.

"Good afternoon, Mas. I have to say, you do look like shit," she said bluntly.

I focussed on her face. "It's afternoon is it?"

She nodded slowly, consulting her pad, as if it had supplied that information. "Do you need anything? A drink?"

I hesitated. A bathroom would be preferable to be honest. I hadn't reached the point of adding my waste to the floor yet. "A drink would be good."

She raised a hand to an unseen observer. I realised there was a camera on the wall behind her. We had an audience. She waited while a Jane entered and placed a glass of water on the table before me. I just stared at it.

"Go on."

I gave in and drank deep. The water was lukewarm but I didn't care. I quickly finished it. Hayes moved the empty glass out of reach. Perhaps she thought I might throw it at her.

"So, your debrief," she said. "You were assigned to sector 23b, subsection 12. Correct?"

I frowned. "Yes."

"Did you deviate?"

I shook my head. There was no deviation. It was not allowed. Deviation meant losing your licence.

"For the record please."

"No. No, I didn't."

She nodded as if satisfied. "You returned with a metalleo carboniferous roid. Two hundred and twenty thousand tonnes. About mid range in value." She smiled. "Perhaps the lower end of that range."

"There were metals," I said. "Magnetometer readings were strong."

"Indeed. Some iron, copper ..." she checked the pad. "Aluminium. Anything else?"

I hesitated. "How do you mean?"

"Anything else to report? Anything out of the ordinary?"

I opened my mouth to speak but nothing came out.

"Go on."

"No." My voice was a bit high pitched. I cursed inwardly. That sounded like a lie.

"You sure? According to your tractor telemetry you exited the cabin for three hours mid traction. What was that for?"

"I ... er ... I wanted to check the counterweight. It seemed a bit off."

"Expand on off."

"Its weight. It was lighter than I expected." Which would be true enough. A big chunk of the counterweight had been missing, a hole was drilled through it.

"Aah. We noticed that."

I frowned.

"We track all objects coming into the vicinity of the Maw. Your counterweight was one of them. After you released it, of course," she explained. "It didn't follow the trajectory we expected."

"That makes sense." I shifted uncomfortably in the seat. "What am I being charged with?"

"What makes you think you are being charged with anything?"

"Well ... I'm here."

"You always have a debrief after a mission, do you not?"

"Yes, but ..."

"But?"

"Well, I haven't been escorted by the Jane before. Or kept in a holding cell." Or stunned.

"You heard about the incident with Hanno the Fourth? You heard about the roid he sent us?"

I nodded. "Of course."

"So perhaps we want to be cautious. That roid could have caused a lot of damage. We simply cannot allow that kind of risk."

"What happened to him?"

"Who?"

"Hanno the Fourth."

She shrugged. "Let's focus on your case for the moment."

"Case?" She didn't respond to it. "Yes. I had a look at the counterweight. Took me a while, I was out there a few hours as you say. I didn't find anything." I don't know why I was denying it. The entrance scan would have picked up that I had swallowed something. She would have the report on that pad.

"So you didn't notice anything odd about the counterweight?"

"Odd? It was a roid. Underweight for its size but no. I couldn't see anything odd about it. What do you mean?" In honesty I don't think I was being convincing. I was sweating and I think my hands were shaking. I had them pressed against the table where they were inevitably leaving pools of sweat. There was no way she wouldn't notice.

"No unusual features on its surface?"

Of course they had seen something. Chances are they had reeled it in to take a closer look. I couldn't trust my voice so I just shrugged.

"Verbally please."

"No." It came out as a croak. "No."

She said nothing for a long moment, simply sitting still and studying me. Her lips were pursed. I don't think she believed me. Why hadn't she asked about the odd shadow in my stomach on the entrance scan? There was no way they could have missed it. But I wasn't going to offer up that piece of information. In honesty it was because I was scared. Yes, the Jane scared me. A lot.

"OK. So, I don't believe you. Let's just put that out there. I have seen pictures of your counterweight, and I don't for a moment believe you didn't notice anything odd about it. Particularly as you spent some hours outside the tractor having a look at it. Why would you risk that without good reason? Drivers don't leave their tractors. It's an unwritten rule. You just don't. Ever. But you did." She watched my reaction. "Explain."

"There was a weird shadow."

She waited for me to continue before asking, "what kind of shadow?"

"Oblong. It was an oblong shadow. I didn't think it was natural. But it had to be, right? I mean, a roid out in the Shatter. There's nothing out there but ice and roids. What could there possibly be?"

"Ah, so you lied. I don't like liars, Massen."

"I …" I had nothing to say to that.

"So, you had a look at it. What did you find?"

I hesitated. Should I continue lying? How could I not? Could I admit to finding a long dead corpse? Desiccated after exposure to vacuum. A corpse with an odd tin in their pocket. An even odder jewel inside of that. One I chose to swallow.

Damn. Why hadn't I simply ignored the whole thing? I couldn't even get the jewel out now either. It was blocking everything up inside me somewhere. I'd probably never see it again. And what if I did? I couldn't do anything with it.

"I … I couldn't get to it. It was down the side. I decided it was too dangerous trying, so came back."

"Really?" She sat back in her chair and regarded me silently for a moment. Then she sighed and raised her hand again. The door opened and a Jane stepped in. "You know, I just don't believe you. So Sergeant Mitte is going to hurt you for a while. Let him know when you've had enough."

With that she stepped out.
I don't think I need to describe to you what happened next.

Chapter 5

I had to wait two months for the next shuttle. Fortunately they moved me to a new cell, one with an actual floor and toilet facilities. I imagine they didn't feel the need to punish me further after Sergeant Mitte satisfied himself that I had nothing more to add. I think that was because he didn't actually ask any questions. If he had I am sure I would have admitted to just about anything. Just to make him stop. Oddly he didn't enquire about the jewel. The door scanner clearly hadn't picked it up.

It still hurts when I cough, and the jewel never made an appearance. I imagined it to be blocked up somewhere.

The shuttle trip back to Reaos took a further two months. Fortunately it was one of the big cargo shuttles, large enough to have a rotating crew and passenger torus. Meaning it had gravity. My original outward trip had been on a smaller vessel that had no gravity. I remember vomiting a lot. Two months of free fall was not something I wanted to experience again.

As the trip neared its end I spent some time in the forward viewing lounge, sat with my boots up against the visiplex viewport as I relaxed on a threadbare bench, watching Reaos growing larger. I've mentioned I didn't want to go back, so I won't belabour the point. As a passenger I was allowed access to the comms room, and I sent a courtesy LOS to Van, my wife. Letting her know of my early return. I didn't detail as to why. I imagined she would guess.

The response was brief. 'Send your ETA to Gerad. He will send a car.' No regards, and certainly no love. In fact it was unsigned, only the comms log giving away who had sent it. Julio, the comms officer asked if I wanted it printing. I walked out without replying.

Interestingly neither Hanno the Fourth nor Arden were aboard. Arden might have escaped the interest of the Jane, but I knew Hanno the Fourth hadn't. That meant he was currently orbiting Oberon somewhere without the benefit of either tractor or a space suit. I didn't know what to think about that. I knew it had happened before and would again. Hanno the Fourth had been a bit odd but otherwise I had enjoyed his company. Friend? No, I wouldn't say that. I didn't wish him harm though.

There were two other tractor drivers aboard. They had finished their rotations and were heading home, looking forward to spending their earnings in Ships no doubt. I barely knew them. Neither had been aboard the Tongue while I was there. Sometimes rotations just don't cross. They didn't really speak to me, preferring to keep their own company. I didn't mind that at all.

Other than that there were only four crew members aboard. Two pilots, an engineer/communications officer and captain. We took turns preparing meals in the narrow galley. They didn't really talk to me either. They had actual jobs to do.

I leaned forward and breathed on the visiplex, making the hard surface mist up. With a finger I drew a sad face. I think that was me. Mister feeling sorry for himself.

"Shit." I wiped it away.

Massen

I was heading home with nothing. I had just about broken even on the last trip out. I had only succeeded in paying what I owed to the Oberon Mining Confederation. Passage to the Tongue and back, boarding, gear and lease of the tractor.

I had seen Commander Hayes just before boarding the shuttle. She pushed some papers in my direction and asked for thumb prints. One was a receipt for the remainder of my credit. Essentially all I had earned while on the Tongue. C6000. That was a month's earnings at the dosser pits. Digging out ancient garbage that had long been compacted into a sort of clay. Fuel for the furnaces, and I understand they made a very smelly lubricant out of it too. Six thousand lousy credits. And those two tractor drivers were both returning with in the excess of a million. As I should have been.

I did swear a lot just thinking about it.

A claxon sounded. Captain Peerse's voice came over the intercom. He coughed and said, "Deceleration in ten minutes. Please go to your cabins and strap in. Secure anything not tied down. That means everything folks. Once had a woman who got impaled by her tea mug. How does that even happen? I'm not cleaning brains off a bulkhead today, so strap in. Out." After a moment. "Further warnings at five and two minutes. Out."

I didn't move, my gaze still on Reaos. The shuttle was not atmosphere capable, so we would be slowing and inserting ourselves into orbit. Meeting with either an orbital or Sky City - where we would connect to the elevator. Or neither. The elevator handled mass cargo. It was easier to simply drop personnel into the atmosphere in a pod, which could from the shuttle directly. Cheaper too. The elevator touched down on the equator in Dunn, some eight thousand kilometres from where we wanted to be in Ships. There was also a small civil war going on in Pachesse, where any connecting flight would touch down. The cost of a drop pod was far less than that of a secure flight from the elevator to where we were contracted to go. An odd state of affairs, you would have thought, but such was the state of modern Reaos politics. Besides, the pods were simple affairs. Little more than a pressurised, heat protected shell and a parachute. The shell itself could be recycled upon arrival.

I headed to the passenger compartment on the five-minute warning. We didn't get our own cabins, but rather a curtained off bunk and a locker. The bunks themselves could be reconfigured to become acceleration couches, keeping its occupant's organs from migrating too far when the Shuttle's main engines fired. The cabin had eight berths, only two were occupied. They already had their curtains drawn. I sidled into mine and cranked the handle to form the mattress into an acceleration couch. It got about halfway before the mechanism froze. I was struggling with it when the two-minute warning came and went. By the time I realised I was wasting my time it was too late to find another berth.

I think I swore a bit. This was going to be uncomfortable.

The OMC 15BDC, as the shuttle was creatively named, turned its main drive in the direction of travel and lit it up. It wasn't a gentle increase of thrust, but rather a hammer blow in the kidneys as we went to 6G in under a second. My harness snapped around my neck as I slid towards the footwell. Gasping I clung to it, trying to prevent myself from being garrotted. A loose piece of cargo crashed somewhere. Glass shattered.

It was loud. Engines roared. The shuttle vibrated like a ground car racing over a corrugated road. My vision blurred. Stars appeared as it started to darken. I would have cursed it I could. As it was I could just about breath. Gritting my teeth I clawed my way higher, easing the pressure on my neck slightly.

The shuttle jumped suddenly, throwing me towards the tiny cubicle's roof. The harness snatched me back again just as the shuttle span, bouncing me at the restraining curtain. My nose crunched against it. Blood spurting over my face and down the back of my throat.

At least the movement reoriented me in the couch slightly, easing the strap against my neck. Fingers slippery with blood I pulled myself up further. I managed to get an arm over it so I could take the strain off my quivering arms.

I think I'll have to write a sternly worded letter to the OMC board.

No, I don't think I'll do that. I just wanted to disappear.

I fingered my nose delicately. It felt like it was broken. I spat out some blood. It splatted against the footwell, making a pretty red pattern on the faded grey material.

The session of full thrust was due to last about half an hour. It felt like a lot longer than that. I clung to the strap all through it, the material digging into my armpit. The vessel bucked twice more, bouncing me between padded wall and curtain. I kept my chin tucked into my chest, protecting my beleaguered nose. It kept on bleeding throughout. The interior of the compartment was a pleasant speckled red by the time the drive switched off.

I lay there for a while. Glad it was all over. The shuttle did twitch a few more times as the pilot adjusted its trajectory slightly.

The captain came on the intercom again. "A few more minutes now. We're almost at Amirite Station. Sorry about the rough ride, there were some satellites we had to avoid. You can get up and walk around now. All of the hard manoeuvring is done. Out"

I heard movement outside the compartment as the two other drivers exited their berths and sorted out their belongings. They spoke in quiet voices. I couldn't hear what they were saying. I didn't want to. In honesty I couldn't even remember their names. It just didn't seem important. I stayed where I was until they were gone.

Even though this was one of the larger vessels serving the Maw, it still wasn't very big. All of its inhabited spaces were within the pressurised occupation ring. It could carry thirty or so passengers in its cramped compartments. Many of them were dual purpose, with sleeping pods to one side built into one bulkhead. Even the galley could be repurposed as berthing facilities. There was plenty of space now as there were only three passengers, but I couldn't imagine it with a full compliment. It would not be pleasant.

Even though the control spaces were on the opposite end of the ring, I could still hear what was going on when I finally exited my berth. There was loud talking, the captain having a disagreement with one of the other crew. I ignored it as I wiped blood off my face and gingerly fingered my nose. It hurt. I had a spare jumpsuit and started pulling it on. The current one needed a good wash.

"What happened to you? You should have buckled in." I heard a chuckle as one of the other tractor drivers returned to the compartment.

37

"Yeah, thanks," I muttered, belting up the coveralls.

"Hurry up, we're getting into the pod." She picked something from a locker and headed out.

"We not docking?"

"The ship is. We don't need to. We'll get the same return trajectory launching now, so Able and I are heading out now. You're welcome to join us." She didn't look around as she exited the cabin.

That did make sense. We were headed down in a pod regardless of whether we set out now or later having passed through the station first. In fact we'd likely be in the same pod. Our original arrival time at the Ships field was 6 in the morning. If we left now we'd touch down much earlier. Possibly in time for a decent meal and a hotel room.

Real food. I did long for that. C6000 might last me a few days in Ships.

"Hold on, I'm coming." I picked up what meagre belongings I had and hurried after her. I didn't have much. Some clothes, that was all. Everything else had disappeared while I was incarcerated.

The pod bay was barely that. It was little more than a hatch alongside the control spaces. There were two pods docked to the occupation ring, one on each side to balance their weight. As the ring itself was not terribly large you tended to get thrown off balance a bit if you moved along it too quickly. Which I, foolishly, did. I grimaced as I jarred my injured nose trying to fend off the bulkheads as I lost my footing. The arguing grew louder.

"Try to re-establish comms."

"LOS is projecting. Nothing on the return though. The reflectors are fine," Julio complained.

"Impossible," the captain scoffed. "You got it lined up correctly?"

"Of course. It's locked on fine."

Communications in space relied on laser technology, or Line Of Sight. Which meant bouncing lasers off the other vessel's receptors in order to ensure they received the signal. Fiddly, certainly, but not impossible. Every tractor driver could do it. If they couldn't no one would ever see them again. Once that alignment was achieved it did tend to be pretty reliable.

"We can't dock without confirmation," Peerse observed.

"I know."

"Then sort it out."

I peered into the cramped compartment. It was lined with screens and control stations. It boasted the largest visiplex window in the vessel, a virtual wraparound of the compartment apart from the rear and sides where it connected to the ring. It allowed good visibility during manoeuvres.

"What's going on?" I asked one of the tractor drivers. Able, I guessed.

He shrugged. "Their problem. We're leaving. You with us?"

"Sure."

He swung open the connecting hatch to the pod and waited for his companion to climb through. "Go on then."

The first driver was stowing her luggage beneath one of the five cramped seats within the pod when I swung inside. I grunted an apology as I got in the way. She ignored me, not bothering to ask where my luggage was. One of our infrequent conversations had already covered off that topic. They both knew I had been ejected from the Tongue early, which meant I was not someone they wanted to affiliate themselves with. They didn't know why and they didn't care. They just knew I was bad company.

"We cleared to jettison, Cap?" Able asked the captain once I was out of the way.

Peerse waved over his shoulder absently. "Sure. Go ahead."

"What the hell is that?" I heard someone in the control room ask as the driver swung the hatch shut. Able didn't wait for an answer to the question. He didn't care about that either. He had sealed the hatch and was attending his own gear when something struck the shuttle.

I felt rather than heard the bang through the metal of the connecting collar. The pod was thrown to one side, the driver's rucksack colliding with the couch alongside me, instantly splitting open, disgorging its contents into the cramped cabin. I heard a yell as Able landed on another couch. Bones crackled as they snapped. His yell was cut off abruptly.

The pod spun around and around. Lights flickered and died, replaced by emergency illumination. One of the drivers screamed, the other oddly silent. I simply clamped my teeth together and held on, waiting for it to end. I didn't know what was going on outside the pod. There were no windows. There were more bangs against the pod's hull a if it was being struck by something. Debris maybe.

My vision started going dark as I realised the spinning would never end. Whatever we were connected to was simply taking us with it. It couldn't be the whole shuttle. There was no way it could spin like this without breaking up.

We needed to disconnect.

My mouth open in a silent scream I clawed my way against the spin. For the second time today I was being thrown around, for the second time today I was fighting against my own weight. Which was probably equal to that of a dozen tractor drivers.

There was a control alongside the hatch. A simple lever allowing the pod to disconnect and start its pre-programmed deorbit burn. I needed to pull it. Just that. Nothing else. Until I did that we were going wherever whatever we were attached to went.

It was just one lever. It should be so easy.

Muscles straining I got my fingers around it, I clung to it and pulled as hard as I could. Something clunked and we were thrown free.

I think I screamed as I was flung into a bulkhead face first. Fresh blood exploded from my nose. I might have lost consciousness for a moment.

"What the hell? What the hell?" I dimly heard a voice. "Shit. Able … Able … you ok?"

I discovered I was crumped upside down in an acceleration couch. The spin had stopped, replaced by silence. The pod vibrated slightly as its motors aimed it at the planet below.

"Shit. I think he's dead."

"What?" I pulled myself upright, trying to get my feet beneath two of the deck hoops. I just wanted solid ground. Ground that didn't move around.

She was pulling her companion upright, trying to settle him in a couch. His head was lolling to one side. His eyes were open but unseeing. His neck had clearly snapped. I remembered hearing the crackle of breaking bones. That would explain it.

"His neck's broken," I said. I found a loose t-shirt and tried to clean up my face. The contents of a rucksack were scattered all over the pod's interior. Underwear and shoes were everywhere. I remembered the bangs against the pod's hull and hoped they hadn't caused damage. If they had this would be a short ride. A hot one.

"You'd better strap in," my companion said as she did so herself. "This is going to be bumpy."

"Something happened to the shuttle." I followed her advice, my fingers sticky with dried blood.

"Something hit it," she agreed.

"Or they hit something."

She shook her head. "I was army before all this. I know what a missile strike feels like."

"You were army?"

"We all have a previous life you know. No one would want to shoot me down because of it though, and I know no one would want Able dead. He was a plumber before all this. What about you? Anyone want you dead?"

I hesitated. "No one who has access to missiles." That was a lie. Gerad had easy access. In fact he was probably minister of war by now. And the Authority was more warlike than most nation states. It would be no challenge at all ordering the shuttle shot out of orbit. But would he?

Yes, of course he would. He wouldn't hesitate killing everyone on board if it meant preventing my return. Particularly if the incident could go unexplained. A sad accident in space.

Shit. I should have anticipated this.

Vibration grew as the pod touched the atmosphere. It twitched a few times as it settled its orientation – heatshield down. We had no control. We wouldn't know how to if we did. We could do nothing but sit, teeth clamped, and hope the heatshield wasn't damaged. Or the parachute. And that the guidance algorithm was taking us to the right location. Not the middle of the ocean, hundreds of kilometres from shore.

In honesty I barely registered much of it. My thoughts were consumed by Gerad and his willingness to slaughter the shuttle's crew and passengers just to get to me. And what he would do when he discovered I was still alive. Clearly he would make another attempt. At least now I was expecting it, as I should have been before.

It also occurred to me we would all have been dead had it not been for the impatience of my driver companions. We would still have been in the observation lounge when the missile struck. If that's what it was. We would have perished with everyone else. I think it's safe to assume they were dead. The shuttle a shattered ruin.

It grew warmer in the pod. The roar of air rushing past outside grew until it was impossible to hear anything else. The pod jerked as the parachutes opened and it grew still. My companion unbuckled herself and crossed unsteadily to the hatch, quickly working on the handle.

"Wait, I wouldn't."

"It's safe now," she said without turning. Hinges creaked and the door eased open. Fresh air billowed in. I could smell rotten seaweed. The sea was nearby. "At least we're in the right place. Hold on, this will be bumpy." She sat in a couch alongside as we hit the ground. The pod lurched as if the parachutes were about to drag it but then it settled.

We were down.

"Shit. I'm out of here." My companion threw open the compartment beneath a couch and extracted her rucksack. Without a further word to me she was out of the hatch and into sunlight.

I sat, listening to seagulls. There were voices. A team was coming to check over the pod and ensure everyone was out.

I was back. Back on Reaos. A world I had been trying to escape. It was a strange thing to say that I preferred the icy darkness of the outer system to this warm, well worn world. A world where you could buy a decent beer. At least out there I had a bit of privacy. Here only the rich could afford that. Which I was not.

"What the hell is all this?" A tech said after she'd wheeled a stair up to the hatch and peered inside. "I'm not picking this up. And what's with him?"

I shrugged. "Rough ride. I think his neck has snapped."

"Shit. On my watch too. Who is he?"

I hesitated only for a moment. "Massen, I think he said his name was." I started picking up Able's belongings and stuffing them back into his rucksack. The buckle had come open on impact but it was undamaged. Everything went back in.

"Same as happened to your face?"

I fingered my nose delicately. "Yeah. Something happened to the shuttle. Do you know what it was?"

She shrugged. She was perched on the hatch's lip, as if hesitant to enter. "Pass. I'm field tech. You want control for that. I heard they lost contact with it just before it docked at Amirite Station though. That's all I know. Looks like it hit some debris, judging by the shape of your pod. You're lucky. Another few centimetres and a manoeuvring thruster would have been hit."

I allowed her to talk, using the time to pat down Able's pockets. I removed his ident and credit chit. I hoped she didn't notice me pocketing them and produced my own to pass over. "Here. I don't know much about him I'm afraid."

She didn't look at the ident. It wouldn't have made any difference. Idents differed from country to country. Some didn't carry either photographic or biometric information. States like the Authority didn't waste money producing high end ident chips. It was little more than a card stating some basic personal information. As long as you looked roughly like the person described no one bothered checking further.

"You want customs. That way." She pointed as I squeezed past her. She sighed and entered the cabin. I could only imagine the paperwork involved in processing dead bodies.

Ships Airfield was pretty much just that. A field. A blank space no one really cared about, where it was safe for vehicles to crash should they malfunction. It was a few dozen kilometres on each side, the southern end a swamp that led to the Sollen Delta. It looked like a few vessels had indeed crashed here. There was the odd crater marking the field. Only one wreck was still in situ, and that was slowly being dismantled by a group of scavengers. It looked like it had been an atmospheric shuttle once. I could see stubby protuberances that had once been wings. Most of it had already been cut up and carted off.

"Shit." I stopped and looked around me. Apparently I as supposed to walk to the terminal building, a squat concrete affair some kilometres away. There were a few cars scattered about, similar to the one the tech had driven up to the pod. None were designed for passengers though. My pod mate was already a few hundred metres in the terminal's direction. She had wasted no time in humping her gear towards it.

The field didn't look busy. Apart from the pod there were only three other craft currently landed there. All were small civilian vessels, only one orbit capable. It was possible the military used a different field, somewhere they could control access. As I walked, my legs quickly tiring from lack of exercise, a flatbed rumbled over the uneven ground. The crane on its bed swung as the vehicle bounced, chains rattling against its dented side.

"Hey! Get in!"

I jumped as a groundcar whirred up, its electric motors virtually silent. The field tech drew level and pulled the brake so I could board. I could see she had the body of Able draped over the back seats like little more than luggage. I didn't hesitate, not fancying the long walk to the terminal. I wasn't used to that kind of exercise. I tossed Able's rucksack beside him and swung into the empty front seat.

"You finished back there?"

The tech shrugged. "Bodies take priority. They want it logging in. They smell in the heat." She laughed. I didn't know how often this happened to her, but she didn't seem overly concerned having to handle a dead body.

"Sure," I agreed as the groundcar picked up speed. It was an ancient, dented utility vehicle. I couldn't see what colour it had been when new, all its paint had long been scratched off. Few of the gauges in front of the driver seemed to work - those that were still in place. There were a number of empty gaps where others had once been. The machine worked well enough though, apart from its suspension that was far too spongy for the terrain.

"Sorry! No more room!" The tech yelled at my tractor driver companion as we bounced past. She shouted something back. I couldn't tell what it was, but it didn't sound polite. "There's some guy at the terminal wants to check out the body," the tech continued. "Seemed very interested when I called it in."

"Oh. Who is he?"

She shrugged. "Some diplomat from the Authority. He some kind of bigwig." She managed to indicate the body with a hand while guiding the goundcar around a pool of foul-smelling water. Rainwater collected in an old crater.

"What's the Authority want with him then?"

The Artigade Authority was officially an ally of Ships. On paper. However in reality the relationship was somewhat different. Ships was little more than a city state, a few million in population, some natural resources and sitting right on top of the cross roads of two major strategic communications routes. One of which was known as the Hub, a network of fibre optic cables that fed into the datasphere and global communications systems. Any war here would risk it being damaged, which was the only reason the Authority had never sent in the tanks to take over. It did leave Ships as little more than a vassal state however, as their neighbour surrounded them on three sides and could easily enforce an embargo. The only side they didn't control faced the Lantic Ocean which was rife with Authority sponsored privateers, so it may as well have been Authority territory. They certainly acted as if it was.

"I look psychic?" She asked.

"What?"

"Hey, you can still walk."

I decided it prudent not to reply.

"What do psychics look like anyway? They got big heads or something? Weird antennas?"

I shrugged.

"They look different to ordinary folk?"

"I wouldn't know." I was regretting the conversation now.

It was warm. I could feel the sun burning my exposed skin. My nose hurt. I mean it really hurt. So did my armpit from hanging onto the seatbelt earlier in the day. I was thirsty and had a headache. I really didn't feel like having this conversation. I might picked up the whiff of alcohol on her breath. Was she drunk?

It occurred to me I didn't want to go all the way with her anyway. She was meeting a representative of the Artigade Authority. It was unlikely I knew them but it was not worth taking that chance.

"Stop here," I said.

"What? Offended you have I now?"

"I feel like walking. Been in space a long time."

She shrugged and stopped the groundcar. We weren't all that far from the terminal building now anyway.

"Hey, take your bag!"

I'd almost forgotten it, bearing in mind it wasn't mine. I waved her goodbye and watched the goundcar bounce past the last crater before entering a relatively flat section of ground around the terminal. Clearly no one landed this close to the building. I hefted the bag and followed behind. It occurred to me all the underwear in the bag probably needed washing. I shuddered at the thought. Perhaps I'd discard that and buy new. Now that I had a shiny credit chit in my pocket with who knows how much on it.

I had a slight tinge of guilt that I had stolen the chit. It didn't last all that long. The man was dead, he wouldn't be using it. Besides, I needed it to disappear.

The terminal building was in keeping with much of the architecture of Ships, in that it had been built in the appearance of an upside-down boat hull. The sweep of tarnished metal was broken here and there by glittering windows that reflected the afternoon sun. Control towers and communications masts sprouted from its keel. To one side was a monorail station that served the city itself, while the other was a wide, squat building. A hangar of sorts. Its doors were half open, revealing the needle nose of a high-speed jet.

A fuel truck rumbled past me, heading for one of the vehicles parked on the plain. The driver gave me a jaunty wave. I gave a half-hearted saluted back.

What can I say about Ships? An odd name, certainly. A descriptive name. That was because, in essence, the city of Ships was just that – ships. It was situated on a river delta, the Sollen, a waterway that drained almost a quarter of the Markan Continent. When it reached the delta it was a swollen, slow moving mass of water two kilometres wide at its greatest. Easily navigable for hundreds of kilometres upriver. A communications and trade route for many of the larger, more developed cities in Marca. In the days before rail and air travel, it was the only reliable and safe means of traveling between them. The countryside between rugged and filled with pirates who would predate on the unwary. Most of those had been based in the Spires, and were my kin.

After the Fall the vast majority of the world's remaining ships had gathered here. Naval, commercial and civilian alike. A refuge perhaps. Concealed in the swamps and forests of this area for decades, they avoided the malaise that spread around the world during the Dark Ages, a time when the sun grew dim and crops all around the world failed. It was then most of the people in the world starved. The ships had maintained what little knowledge and civilisation they had and became all but self-contained. Venturing out only to fish in seas that were suddenly empty of all other vessels. I'm no historian, so couldn't say what caused that Fall, that Dark Age. I understand historians themselves don't entirely understand it. I do know that Ships retained the torch of civilisation for hundreds of years when it went out everywhere else in the world. Ultimately, it failed here too. Their power waned just as the local warlords were gathering their own. A thousand years ago Ships finally fell to the army of King Goode. He lost most of army doing it, drowned in the estuaries or predated by crocodiles and freshwater sharks. Still, he ultimately raised his banner over the Smoke Stack, the tallest tower in Ships. Only to find the victory hollow indeed. There were no riches there. There were no magical machines he had grown up hearing about. Those had all seized and turned to rust. In a fit of pique he burned much of the city, including the university libraries, which – at that time – were still the richest source of knowledge in the world.

Oddly that was probably the best thing to ever happen to Ships. Their legend in tatters no one bothered with them again, allowing them to rebuild what they could. As the centuries passed they became a trading hub, taking advantage of their strategic position at the mouth of the Sollen, a gateway to the world. The rebuilt their libraries and were in fact the first nation to generate their own electricity and light their streets at night. That technical edge was maintained into the present. Which was why, when the oceanic data cables were laid, they went right through Ships. Some of the data centres were stationed within the city itself.

A city which, largely, still floated on the waters of the Sollen. In ships.

I had been here before. Van and I came through here on our honeymoon. A cruise line was based here, so we spent a few days here before heading out to sea. I was interested in the city itself, so spent much of my time taking in the sights. Not something she had ever been interested in, so stayed in our penthouse suite at the Ships Continental. To be fair she could see many of those sights from its balcony. Should she care to look – which she didn't.

What amazed me was that the streets were made of metal. Which, as they were aboard ships, made sense in retrospect. The city plan could also change, one vessel sliding past another to reconfigure the precincts. This was an easy way to add to the skyline. The city engineers didn't need to build tower blocks in situ. They could build them off site, where their work interfered with no one, sailing the vessel into the city and parking it in its allotted slot once the building was done. One of the wonders of the world was within the city. Two of the original ships still existed, their origins lost before the fall of civilisation that preceded the Dark Ages. Their hulls were not metal, in fact no one knew what material they were made of. No modern technology could mar their surfaces to collect samples. Both were museums of sorts now. If a government palace could be called a museum. There were sections where tourists could touch the original hull, marvelling that they were touching something so perfect and so old. Almost two thousand years old, yet still silky smooth. Of course I went there and touched the hull. It was a hull, I didn't know what else I should have expected.

The interior of the terminal was deliciously cool. I dropped the rucksack beside a security desk and passed over my pilfered ident. There was a scanner alongside it the desk for the usual perfunctory checks, I presumed. I wasn't concerned about it. I'd passed through the scanner on the Tongue without issue. Although I did think about the jewel for a moment as the officer behind the desk checked the ident against a manifest and typed something into his terminal. I'll have to admit, I had not sieved through the contents of the toilet every time I visited, on the off chance it would make a re-appearance. Half of me didn't want to see it again. The other half firmly believed I never would. Smuggling was not something taken lightly in Ships. If they caught someone trying to get contraband across their borders they could expect a lengthy jail term. I don't think I had anything to worry about though.

"You were on shuttle 15BDC," the guard commented.

"Sorry? Oh, yes, I was." I had to think about that.

"We'll have to detain you for debrief. The OMC wants an inquest and you were a witness." He gazed at me levelly over his desk. "Shouldn't take long."

"I didn't see anything."

"You can tell them that, then." He smiled and pushed back my indent. "Someone will be here for you in a moment. Care to wait over there?" He indicated a waiting area.

I groaned. I wanted to lay down somewhere and sleep. Maybe clean up my face – something the guard didn't seem even slightly interested in. I mean, it was covered in blood after all. Maybe get a beer and a decent meal. Perhaps this was just a formality. I noticed someone approaching. Perhaps this was them.

"Hey, Mas. You know, I heard the weirdest thing. I heard you were dead."

I groaned. Caitlin. Gerad's driver.

Chapter 6

I didn't have that interview. The appearance of an Authority functionary put paid to that. Around here the Authority was respected (feared?) more than the OMC. Instead Caitlin led me to a limousine and we headed north, away from Ships and towards the Spires.

She didn't ask questions. She wasn't paid for that.

"We missed you at Founder's Fair last year," she said over her shoulder. The privacy partition between the driver and the cab was down. "Cully opened your stall for you but his sweets weren't as nice. I don't think he got them from the same place you do."

"Liquorice. I get it from Barkand," I said. The stall had always been my mother's pet project. I ran it the year after she died, just before I headed towards Oberon. It hadn't felt the same. Sweets are for the kids, she said. But then everyone was a kid at heart, so everyone got some. It cost a lot of money importing it all from Barkand, which was a long way from the Spires.

"He had sours too. I didn't like them." She turned around to look at me. I winced when she took her eyes off the road. "Hey. The fair is only a month away. You should run the stall again. They're trying out the kites this weekend. You'll get to see them."

"Might be a bit late. It took months to import it all last time." I pointed. "Watch out for the truck."

She laughed. "New car. Road guidance. Don't worry."

"What?"

"Watch." She swerved into oncoming traffic and took her hands off the steering wheel. I distinctly heard hooting from other road users as the car smoothly guided itself back into the correct lane. She laughed. "Hardly need me here."

"Shit. Can we just get there safely, please?"

She shrugged. "Ade's got a kite in the running this year. Made it herself .... With a bit of help from me."

"Isn't that cheating? You were an engineer in JE." Joussan Aerospace. An elite task force that operated both in space and on land. You had to be insane to join. I understand they were trained to re-enter the atmosphere in nothing but a heat ablative pressure suit and glide wings. This will tell you a lot about Caitlin, and also what her role in Gerad's organisation really was. She might drive his car but she was not his driver. Ade was her daughter. She must be about ten now.

She turned to look at me again. I really wished she wouldn't do that. "Who's going to tell? You?"

"You're safe." She scared me. I'll be honest about that. She was shorter than me, taking me up to my shoulder. Still, I had seen a protestor lunge at Gerad with a knife once. The way she moved had not been natural, and what she did to the man was nothing short of brutal. It had been reflex, she hadn't even stopped to think. A knife was produced and less than a second later the man was on the floor, bones broken and concussed. The man should count himself lucky. He had survived the incident. Only to be jailed to be fair. Still, she hadn't killed him.

We didn't talk much after that. I spent much of my time looking out of the window. I was amazed at how bright everything was. Even as the sun dipped beneath the horizon as we approached the border it was still brighter out there than it was in Oberon's orbit. As evening drew in we left the swamp lands to the north of Ships behind, replaced by grassland with the odd hill poking above it. The moon was already in the sky, casting its baleful light over the vast open stretches. The plains were interrupted every now and then by farmsteads and small towns. The I249, the interstate that was taking us north, didn't deviate for any of them. It simply left them in the darkness behind us. A few other vehicles flashed past. Most were commercial, busses and heavy goods vehicles.

About midnight we pulled into a service station and Catlin got out to change the batteries. A car of this size carried two powerplants. It needed them. As it would take hours to recharge them it was more effective to drive the vehicle onto an automated service station, the machine unloading the old battery to replace it with a new one. Hydrocarbons were in short supply on Reaos. The only reliable sources were from the dosser pits, and even then only in small amounts. Everything extracted from there went into lubricants and the chemical industry to produce plastics. Ground and air vehicles alike were powered by batteries. Some ran on hydrogen but they tended to be military.

I ventured into the shop and plugged the credit chip into a vendor. My eyebrows rose at the balance printed on the screen. C2 548 391. Able hadn't done badly for himself. I picked up a sandwich and a drink and headed back to the car. I didn't bother trying to escape. Caitlin would be watching out for that. I didn't think for a moment she was fooled by my efforts to evade detection at the landing field. She was simply too polite to bring me up on it.

"Didn't get me one, I see?" She looked up from the battery meter as she finished paying.

I shrugged. "No vegetarian option." And got back into the car.

She made a rude comment and headed inside herself. Leaving me to watch a heavy freight vehicle pulling into the loader a few metres away. Larger vehicles had a dedicated depot as their batteries were a lot larger. Mechanical arms reached out from beneath the vehicle and removed the spent cell. There was a puff of air as it blasted dirt and grit off the connection plates before lifting another cell into place. The cells themselves were impressive technology. They were almost larger than some of the smaller ground cars I'd seen pulling in behind us. The driver headed for the bathroom, leaving the machinery to finish servicing his vehicle.

I could drive one of those, I decided. The controls were similar to a tractor's. If anything they were a lot simpler as they operated in only two dimensions. The controls would still be active to allow the recharging to complete. It wouldn't take more than a moment to slip out of the limousine and into the truck. I could be gone before Caitlin returned.

And she would hunt me down. The limousine was a lot faster than that truck.

I finished my sandwich instead. While I was waiting I discovered the liquor cabinet and helped myself to some of Gerad's brandy. The limousine rocked slightly as my companion slid back into the driver's seat. We slotted in behind a convoy of military vehicles as we re-joined the road.

"The army looks busy," I commented.

"Manoeuvres. Just a training exercise," Caitlin said as she steadied the steering wheel with her knees as she unwrapped her sandwich.

"Who are we trying to impress?"

"No, seriously. Gerad has been busy while you've been away. If we want to get into the League we need to get away from our reputation of a rogue state. Means no picking fights with neighbours. Free and fair elections. You wouldn't recognise the place."

"Elections? Are you mad?" The League of 8 was an organisation of the eight biggest economies on Reaos. Peacekeeping, trade, development and aid, that kind of thing. Between them they were the most powerful trading block – and military – on the planet. By a very long way.

"Seriously. The elections are next Second. The candidates are announcing themselves this Founder's Day. I think Gerad might be announcing. That would be amazing, wouldn't it?" The Second was the second month of the year. We had ten months, all named as you can imagine - bearing in mind the name for the second month.

"Yeah. Sure." No it wouldn't. Not even slightly. "What's he do now? He was head of Spire Security when I left."

"Minister of the Interior. It's great for my paycheck, I can tell you."

My enemies were growing decidedly stronger while I was becoming weaker. Enemies? Were they my enemies? I didn't actually know if he was behind the missile strike on the shuttle. He was certainly no friend, however. He had made it quite clear I was no longer welcome on the Spires, which had ultimately led to my original decision to leave.

"You've not asked about Van," she observed.

No. I hadn't. Even hearing her name caused my stomach to clench. I didn't want to see her. Not now, not ever. I never wanted to think about her again. I couldn't bear to even think ... I pushed the thought aside. Not now.

"How is she?" I think my voice might have squeaked a bit.

"Aaah, well. This is awkward." Caitlin glanced at me in her rear-view mirror. "I shouldn't have brought her up."

"Why?" I was suddenly worried. "She ok?"

"Oh, sure, sure. It's just ..." She hesitated a moment longer. "Well, to be blunt, you're dead. At least officially. No one thought you'd be coming back, so you were announced dead last year. It got around a lot of ... awkward embarrassment. She and Gerad are engaged. They're getting married during the Founder's Day celebrations."

"Shit." My eyes burned as I looked out of the window. Noticing the government plates on the limousine an outrider for the column waved us past. The engine purred as Caitlin guided the heavy car alongside the armoured vehicles. I tried not to look in her direction. Embarrassed.

"Yeah. Listen, I'm sorry. No one could have predicted all this. It does mean no one can see you on the Spires though."

"Which is where you're taking me," I observed.

"The Spires yeah. But to Gerad's compound on Tellus Spire. No one's to see you."

"So, how did I die?"

"Accident of some sort. It's dangerous out there. It didn't surprise anyone. We had a funeral. You would have liked it."

A bark of a laugh escaped my lips before I could stifle it.

"You've changed," I heard her comment. Yes, perhaps I had.

We had been within the Authority for some time, the border was a long way behind us. All of this here was Authority territory. Stretching all the way from the Bay of Bascal in the tropical south, briefly interrupted by Ships, to continue all the way to the frozen north. There wasn't much beyond the border in that direction, the population was too low to be called a country. Those territories were known as the Freeholds. Communities of wandering reindeer herders with few permanent settlements, and those were nothing more than trading posts. The Authority dominated the eastern side of the continent, stretching inland to the vast grasslands that dominated much of the interior. Beyond the grasslands were mountains and the only two states not to owe allegiance to the Authority. Tondo to the north and Cali to the south. There had been the odd border conflict over the years, most ending in favour of the Authority. Inevitably leading to those states ceding more territory to their eastern neighbour.

As a result the Authority was vast, with a population upward of a hundred million. It was also pretty much self sufficient when it came to resources. Not because it harboured any particular mineral deposits, but because it had a burgeoning recycling industry. All the materials anyone could ever want had been unearthed and deposited on the surface at some point in the distant past. Some had been combined into complex alloys and so it was difficult to extract their constituent metals from them, but the Authority had perfected some very efficient techniques in this area. So much so it was a net exporter of refined metals, which made it one of the richer nations on Reaos. Possibly the one and only reason the League was even considering allowing the Authority to join their number. They would get access to the Authority's resources and the technology. As a bonus, it would ensure the Authority never turned its formidable military on any of them.

The Spires were still some hours ahead of us, located about a hundred kilometres south of the Wetten, a mountain range cutting through this part of the continent. They were situated in the Parcis Flats, about twenty kilometres from the city of Parcis itself – after which the flats were named.

I'm not entirely sure how to describe the Spires, other than to say they are not natural, although I couldn't imagine what technology had been used to create them. It was as if slivers of the planet's crust, each several kilometres in length, had been pulled upwards, drawing them out of the ground around them. Their sides were sheer cliffs, rising between five and eight hundred metres above the plains. Apart from some of the topsoil that had collapsed over the years, their summits retained the grasslands of the plains below.

Although, with height comes a slight change in environment, so the undergrowth had changed over time. If anything it was lusher that the plains below. Water pumped from deep underground supplied the people who had taken to living on the plateaus, fortresses overlooking the vast plains below. A refuge, if you like, for those escaping the barbarism of the Dark Ages.

There were towns up there now, built of native rock, supported by a number of farms that were perched alongside them. Each spire was joined by soaring bridges, allowing easy access and trade between them. Even though the Spires had been besieged by enemies several times over the centuries, no one had successfully conquered it. It was simply impossible to access the top if those living there resisted. Even with modern weaponry it was a very difficult position to effectively engage. The opposite was not true. The residents of the Spires enjoyed a strategic position above the plains, able to come and go at will, striking anyone venturing near. Which is perhaps why banditry had been the occupation of choice of many of its residents. The leader of this community known as the Warlord, which went some way to cementing their reputation as thieves, robbers and murderers. In time nearby communities found it better to pay off the warlords than to suffer their regular predations. When that began the warlords became the defacto rulers of this part of the world.

It was home, if I actually had one.

"I need a pee," I informed my companion.

"You what?"

"I ... I need to go to the bathroom." My sudden outburst had surprised even me. I could do with visiting the facilities, true enough, but I couldn't say it was urgent.

"Why didn't you go back there?"

Now that I had said something I was forced to continue down that avenue. "Didn't need to then."

"Shit. Actually, no, you haven't changed." I heard her muttering something about a two-year-old. "There's a station coming up," she said more clearly. "You'll have to hold it in. Don't you dare pee on that seat."

"I won't. I won't."

"Shit."

I admit to feeling somewhat humiliated. I could not, in all honesty, say where that sudden outburst had come from. I sat silently while Caitlin found the next service station. They were quite regular on here as many of the smaller vehicles had limited range. Battery storage was universal problem. We were also approaching the more built up part of the Authority. There were two cities in our path before we hit the Flats. The first was Philia, which was only a few kilometres north of us. We were already passing through its suburban outskirts. The road had widened and was getting busier. Even at this time of night.

"Here. This OK?" She guided the limousine into a service station and stopped in the car park. "Two minutes."

"Sure. Sure." I entered the brightly lit establishment and headed to the rest rooms. Like all restrooms the world over they smelled of stale urine, no matter that there was a clipboard on the wall claiming it was cleaned twice a day. There was a small frosted window about shoulder height on the far wall.

I had to bear down on the window's latch to get it to budge. After a groan it allowed me to open the window wide. It was just about big enough. With a foot up on a sink I clambered up and squeezed through. I didn't want to think about all the gunk I was getting over my freshly liberated clothes. The windowsill itself didn't look like it had been cleaned in years.

It was dark beyond the window. I could just make out some rubbish bins and discarded pallets. With a finesse that surprised even me I managed to slide out of the window onto me feet. I did knock over some bottles that skittered away into darkness. Cursing I froze.

Luckily no one had heard it. I headed out of the alleyway towards a darkened side road and freedom. I had money in my pocket and an ident card I could still pass off as my own. I needed to disappear and that was my plan.

"Mas, Mas. I am disappointed in you."

"Shit." I was startled as Caitlin stepped in front of me just as I approached the road.

"Shit is right. Where are you going?"

"I can't go back, Caz. There's nothing for me there."

I just about made out a shrug in the gloom. "Not my problem. I have orders."

I stepped back from her. Debating my chances should I run for it.

"You are coming with me. It's up to you if you're conscious or not."

"Shit, Cas …" I sensed her move long before she knew she was going to do it herself. Her weight shifted. A kick was coming, I was sure of it. A kick that would have me laying on the tarmac. In reflex I stepped aside, her boot missing me by millimetres. I lifted an arm and helped it on its way, throwing her off balance. With a grunt she recovered quickly and came at me again.

I was already responding. The heel of my hand slammed under her jaw. Hard. I felt something crunch. Teeth shattering or jaw cracking. I didn't know. With a sigh she collapsed to the ground.

"Shit." I stood over her, staring at her body. I was relieved to find she was still alive. In fact she was only dazed. I had moments before she would be up again.

How could I do that? I stared at my palm. It hurt, but I'm sure nowhere near as much as her jaw did. This was Caitlan. I knew how fast she was. There was no way I could beat her. Yet I had. Easily. It was almost as if she had been moving in slow motion. It was all reflexes, as if my body had been running on automatic. I hadn't decided to do any of this. If I'd had the time to think about it I would have given in. Allowing her to take me away.

Those reflexes were screaming at me again. Run. Run now. I had to leave. Quickly.

"Shit." I looked around me. There was movement in the dark. Perhaps someone had witnessed this.

"Hey!"

Startled I turned. The butt of a rifle cracked into the side of my head. It was my turn to grunt and fall to the floor.

The shadow moved over me. "Never heard of backup, asshole?"

Chapter 7

The rest of my trip to the Spires was not as comfortable as it had been in the back of the limousine. It couldn't be further from it, in that it was in the back of some dusty troop transport. Tied up with a gag around my mouth. It was loud and bumpy, as the vehicle was made for navigating rough terrain, not an interstate. There were also a half a dozen other people in the back, our knees zippered together as we faced each other, backs to the vehicle's armoured sides. Soldiers all. All armed. None looked at me. I didn't know which one had struck me down. It didn't really matter.

I closed my eyes and tried to sleep. The noise and vibration made it difficult. As did the ache in the side of my head. I couldn't reach it to see if it was bleeding. It certainly felt like it was.

It had been worth a try, I thought. Escaping that is. Climbing through that window and taking on Caitlin had been a very odd feeling. Like I was a passenger along for the ride. As if I didn't have control over my movements. I didn't understand how I had beaten her. I don't think I was a coward when it came to physical violence, although I'd never really had a reason to find out. I certainly wasn't trained and would have no idea what to do in a fight. She was the opposite. She was a fighter. That was what she did. She was exceptionally good at it.

And within seconds she had been on the floor, all but unconscious. It didn't make sense. I have to admit, I was troubled. The only way I could make sense of it was believing it was some kind of accident. I got lucky. It was as simple as that.

I slept a bit. If you can call it sleep. I dreamed fitfully as the troop carrier headed into the dawn, leaving the cities behind and heading out onto the flats. My dreams were strange. As if I was fighting something unseen. Some presence I couldn't identify. A faceless shape. It was trying to get through to me, to talk to me. But that was the last thing I wanted. I pushed it away stubbornly, keeping it at bay until bright morning sunlight leaked through a thick armoured visiplex window. It succeeded in waking me as a beam of light focussed on my face.

Feeling awful I groaned and opened my eyes. Everything hurt. My nose. My head. My wrists where I was bound. My arse where I had been sat on a plastic bench for hours. I was thirsty and hungry, and this time I did need the bathroom. These soldiers would not be stopping for me.

Fortunately we were almost there. I did manage to see that out of the window as we turned a corner, casting the sunbeam onto someone else.

Home Spire was the largest. It was seven kilometres long and three wide, almost completely flat on it's upper surface. Trees lined the edges, all of them imported at some point in the distant past. They were certainly not indigenous to these grasslands. The town of Spires itself was not visible from the ground, being situated somewhat away from the cliff edge. A ramp had been chipped into the rock some centuries ago, curving around the outside of the spire, one side open to the elements as it headed towards the summit. There were a dozen places where it could be sealed should anyone unwanted try to use it to access the town. None of them were in use now. Instead there was a check point at the entrance where a guard verified our identities before waving us past.

Up we went.

This part of the trip was reasonably smooth, even though it was at almost ten degrees inclination. This section of the road had recently been repaved. In fact it felt good, only in that my weight was now settled on a different part of my behind. I closed my eyes and tried to rest. I still felt exhausted.

The vehicle banked a number of times as the road curved around the spire, and abruptly it was on level ground again. Still, we didn't stop. This wasn't our destination. Tellas Spire was, and Gerad's compound. A fortress within a fortress. There were a number of them up here, each belonging to the families that called this place home. There had been regular conflict between them over the centuries. Sometimes open warfare. Fortresses were necessary.

Tellas Spire was on the far western edge of the Spires. Taller than most, it looked down on those around it. There was only one way to access it, and that was from Home Spire itself, across a sturdy stone bridge that spanned the chasm between spires. It met up with a tunnel on the other side which lead up to the surface. A tunnel that could easily be closed off to prevent access in times of conflict. That tunnel culminated just beneath the fortress itself, the last hundred metres overlooked by tall walls on each side upon which defensive platforms had been built. There was also a line of arrow slots in the walls themselves, where defenders could pour fire into anyone wanting to gain access. Those chambers were long unused now, I think they were storerooms or something. There had been peace between the families for generations. All of this was just for show now.

We stopped in an underground garage. I could hear the faint sounds of other vehicles stopping beside us through the armoured steel.

Hydraulics wheezed the back door open and Caitlin looked in. "He's with me," she said, pointing.

I was shuffled out of the vehicle and she took me by the bindings about the wrists to lead me away. I tried to mumble an apology but she ignored me. Her voice, when she spoke, was thick, as if she had a swollen tongue. Which, noticing some dried blood at the corner of her mouth, she might just have. I felt a bit guilty. She had only been doing her job.

The fortress was a sprawling affair. In fact it was more a town surrounded by high stone walls. Beyond that was farmland and the odd homestead. To the north, on a section of slightly raised and rocky ground, was a forest. A hunting ground reserved for local gentry – such as it was. Within the walls were plazas and narrow, winding avenues. Houses, shops and warehouses lined them. The Spires had tried very hard to put its lawless past behind it. It almost looked respectable.

Caitlan didn't lead me through the town proper. Gerad's offices weren't far from the gate house, and that was where we were headed. There were a lot of stairs and narrow passages. She remained silent through all of it, barely looking at me and certainly not taking her hand from my bindings. She wasn't going to risk me fleeing again.

Gerad's official offices were in Tarontville, the capitol of the Artigade Authority. His official residence was there also, this was just his family home. Still, he had an office here too, equipped with an aide in an outer office to keep visitors at bay. He just waved us in.

"You're expected." He looked over his glasses at us, taking in our state with pursed lips.

The inner office was little more than a wood panelled study. Cluttered with bookshelves and a suit of raider's armour inside a glass cabinet in a corner. A light above it setting off its blood red leather panels and helmet. The only metal on it was in the sabre scabbarded at its waist. Metal had been a precious commodity in those days.

Gerad was a big man. He seemed to fill what was left of the study. A head taller than I was, with broad chest and thick arms. He was dressed in hunting garb. Tan coloured breeches and shirt with sturdy black boots. Caitlan looked tiny alongside him.

"What the hell happened to you?" He looked up from some papers he was studying when we entered.

"This asshole jumped me," Caitlan said, pushing me forward.

Gerad laughed. "Mas? Mas landed a punch? Are you joking?"

"No, boss." I could almost hear her teeth (what were left of them) gritting in humiliation.

"Shit," he said. He looked me up and down, raising an eyebrow. "You look like crap too. Take that thing off." Caitlan pulled off my gag and unlocked the shackles. "What happened to you?"

I rubbed my wrists before gingerly touching my brow. It was slightly sticky. "Someone shot down the shuttle while I was on it."

"Why would they do that?"

"I rather thought you could tell me." I didn't care anymore. I wasn't going to hold my tongue.

"Ah." He nodded. "Go see the doc, Caz. You look like you lost a few teeth there."

"A few, boss. What about him?"

"He's not going anywhere."

I think she was glad to be away from me. The heavy wooden doors closed quietly behind her. Unbidden I sat on a chair opposite his desk. Glad to be on something comfortable.

"So, someone shot you down?" Gerad reached for a decanter and filled a glass before pushing it in my direction. "Water. It's too early for anything stronger."

I took it thankfully, trying not to think about my bladder. "Are you going to lie and say it wasn't you?"

He blew out his cheeks. "Well, that would make me a liar now, wouldn't it? But it wasn't for the reason you suppose."

"Nothing to do with Van and the fact I'm already dead?" I put the empty glass down again. My headache was dwindling somewhat. The water was helping already.

"Caz told you that? That's a pity. Actually, no. I shot you down because someone asked me to. There's a feud going on at the moment, you see. Between the OMC and Dynamique."

"You're on the board of Dynamique," I observed. Dynamique Industries ran a large chunk of the Authority's recycling programmes. An industry diametrically opposed to the OMC and its mining concerns in the Shatter. He had had an opportunity to kill me and inconvenience the OMC at the same time. I'm sure the thought had filled him with a great deal of satisfaction.

He smiled. "Of course. How did you escape, if I may ask? Want another?" He nodded towards the glass.

"No, thank you. We were leaving in a drop pod as the missile hit. Two of us made it to the ground. The other broke his neck."

"Aah, the other driver. You tried to steal his identity. Shrewd move."

"So, you're going to try and kill me again?"

He smiled. "Try?"

"You failed the last time." I had no idea where this bluster came from. I didn't have this much courage.

Gerad laughed. "So I did. No, I am not. Van would be unhappy with me if I did. She wouldn't want you harmed. Despite everything." He opened a drawer, took out a credit chit and pushed it over the cluttered desk. "Two million. Yours if you go away and never come back."

I looked at it but didn't pick it up. "That from her?"

"Does it matter?"

No. It didn't. I could go a long way with an additional two million. "She thinks I'm dead?"

"Van?"

I said nothing.

He shrugged. "I haven't informed her otherwise. What for? She would be angry at me if she ever found out I had something to do with your death, however."

Ever practical was Gerad. "You're getting married?" I said.

"Aaah. Caz talks too much which is very unlike her. She's slipping. Talking too much and getting beaten up by a civilian all in one day. Yes, we are. At the Founder's Day celebrations." He studied me silently for a moment. "So, are you going to take it?"

I shrugged. "What choice do I have? There's nothing for me here anymore. I either take that or you kill me." It wouldn't be hard for him to do away with me. Not here. He owned everyone here. No one would come to my aid.

He sighed and looked out of his window. There was a courtyard beyond where a number of cadets were going through their morning drill routine. Marching up and down, up and down. Stopping, starting. All very repetitive stuff. I could hear their drill sergeant's bark from here.

"Tell me. Why are you back? If memory serves you're two years into a four year contract. I rather thought I had another two years to make the necessary arrangements."

What could I say? In honesty I didn't know why the OMC had voided my contract. I knew what they could have used as a reason, in that I had smuggled contraband onto the Tongue. But I didn't believe they were aware of it. Which was fairly miraculous. So, what was their actual reason? "They would say breach of operating policy," I said.

"And what does that mean? Exactly? I know enough about them to suspect they would have spaced you if they caught you breaching operating policy. Which leads me to think they suspected you of something but couldn't prove it. So, what was it?"

I hesitated. "There were some irregularities in payloads. Effecting a number of drivers. We were prospecting the same grid. A previous payload was ..." I shrugged. "Irregular. They had to pull it from the Maw. They wouldn't take any risks with the Maw so everyone prospecting that grid was pulled." Which, in a sense, was the truth. Even though Hanno the Fourth was operating hundreds of kilometres from my location, it was the same grid. There was every chance he had come across whatever had once been on the opposite end of the passage I found.

"I take it that guy was spaced?"

"I don't know. I was not informed."

He nodded slowly. "I understand it's a myth that people explode when spaced." He poured himself a glass of water and took a sip, swilling it around his mouth for a moment as he looked out of the window. "It's still not a nice way to die. Suffocation. Tender parts of your anatomy rupturing. You shit yourself." He studied me for a moment. "To be blunt. It's cold out there but you don't freeze straight away. You would swell up though ... like a balloon. But you probably wouldn't explode. You could survive for a few minutes. Painful, I would have thought. Do you know if this is true?"

I frowned. "I'll have to be honest, I've never tried it."

He smiled. "Of course." He put down the glass. "I was curious so I looked it up. There was a blowout at Percival Station a few years back. Two survived."

"OK."

"I see I'm boring you." He stood abruptly. "There's a bathroom behind you. Go clean yourself up. I'll get some clothes for you. Meet me outside, we're going for a shoot." He opened a concealed door set into a bookcase, revealing a small bathroom. "I won't be a moment." He left his office.

I sat for a moment, watching the cadets doing star jumps. Punishment for being out of step, possibly.

That was a weird conversation. I muttered a curse under my breath and stepped into the bathroom. It was appointed with a small shower which I made use of. I didn't know when I would have the opportunity again. The hot water felt good - after it stopped stinging.

When I stepped out I found that Gerad had left some fatigues folded up on his desk, along with some combat boots on the floor. They all fit snugly. His aide, Thomas, knocked politely on the door as I was lacing them up.

"They are waiting," he said.

"Coming." I was surprised how good I felt. The pain I had felt earlier was receding rapidly. Even my nose no longer throbbed. I know a good hot shower was great at easing aches and pains but I had never experienced this. I was not going to complain.

Thomas led me to a courtyard – not the one the cadets had been marching in. Two open top all-terrain vehicles were waiting there, a number of people gathered around them. Most were dressed as I was. There were a few shotguns in evidence, making me think we were off grouse shooting. Birds were the only wildlife that could make it up here and without natural predators their numbers quickly became unmanageable. Regular hunts were held to thin their numbers a bit - not to mention for entertainment. They started mounting up as we approached.

"You look better," Gerad commented as he swung into the driver's seat of the lead vehicle. "Get in."

I joined him and studied the boxes of shotgun cartridges he had collected on the metal dash before him. They were all birdshot. A relief. I don't know what I would have done had any been designed for use against people. "You do this a lot?"

"Go shooting? Only on weekends. We're short on beaters. I presume you don't mind helping out? Unless you fancy shooting?"

I had been on hunts before. My grandfather had always been a keen hunter and took me with him when I was younger. I can't say I ever took to it. "I'll beat." If he wanted to shoot me it wouldn't matter where I was standing.

Driving through the town was a bit of an affair. Gerad was clearly popular here. A number of people waved as we passed. A group of youngsters, some dragging colourful home-made kites behind them, ran alongside, cheering. He laughed and complimented their kites, all while guiding the groundcar through the cobbled streets. I was surprised we didn't hit anything.

I just sat and watched. This was a world I had been born into but had never really belonged in. This was my grandfather's world. My father's too, even though I never really knew him. Certainly my mothers. She had been adored by these people. Virtually their queen – or perhaps princess. Beautiful and talented, she loved her people. Opening soup kitchens for the poor and day care centres for children. She even sponsored a number of university places for local youngsters who couldn't afford the tuition fees. I think those places were still open, probably funded by Gerad now. It certainly looked like he had picked up her mantle. The kids loved him just like they had loved her. Driving through towns with her had been just like this. We'd been the centre of attention wherever we went.

Part of me couldn't blame Van really. Gerad was a big man in stature and presence. He had a way about him, making everyone in his company feel at ease, as if they were the centre of attention. Just as my mother had before him. He was also rich and powerful. And who was I? Some scrawny whelp who lived off the reputation of his mother. Useless at pretty much everything.

I looked away from him as we bounced into the countryside, hoping he didn't notice as my face grew red. Why was I thinking like this? I needed to stop.

I fingered the shape of the credit chits in my pocket. There were three there now. I could escape this place and disappear. The world was big and I had money. I considered a number of options as we headed towards the forest at the edge of the spire. It was about twenty or thirty acres of trees and bush, a place where grouse congregated at this time of year. They would be breeding soon so it was a good time to take out some cocks.

A couple of other vehicles were drawn up at the boundary. Handlers with their dogs along with some local youths who would help with the beating. The dogs were beautiful animals. Big and strong they stood almost to my waist. They had been bred for this. They were excited at the prospect of the hunt, barking and pulling on their leads. Their barks grew louder as they caught sight of our approach.

"Who's after pie for dinner?" Gerad asked as we pulled up and he slid out of the driver's seat. He was met by an outcry of approval.

I grimaced and watched them huddle around him. I so wanted to dislike him. I had good reason to. Over and above Jan. Specifically, the downing of one OMC shuttle, and the deaths of all those aboard. To make it worse he clearly didn't care. Not to mention his casual attempt to kill me. He would try again, I was convinced of that. Regardless of what Van would think about it. She probably wouldn't even know. She thought I was already dead.

And would she care anyway?

I shook my head and climbed out of the ground car. A number of cooking implements had been gathered in a pile. I picked a frying pan and a ladle from it. I could make a lot of noise with that. I waited patiently while the shooters organised themselves and were allocated their zones. Each was assigned a specific arc of fire, ensuring they didn't cross over into the territory of a neighbour. The safety briefing consisted of: do not shoot at a bird below the horizon. Flying birds only. It wouldn't do for anyone to get shot. I stood with the beaters as they were briefed. Most had done this before so weren't really listening. They knew not to get too close to the shooting line. They didn't want buck shot in their legs either. Some were wearing protective goggles to shield their eyes. A good idea, I thought. I wasn't planning on getting that close. In fact, I might just stay as far from the others as possible.

"Nate, you want to go with Able here?" Gerad indicated a young boy of about twelve. "Nathan's an old hand, he can show you around," he told me.

It took me a moment to realise 'Able' was me.

The boy seemed to deflate. "Aw, do I have to? Skaz has got his trumpet too. We were going to practise." He held up a trumpet, which he was clearly going to use to drive the birds. No kitchen utensils for him.

"Practising for the fair?" Gerad asked him.

"Yeah. We're part of the parade."

"Today you get to do a special favour for me. Tell you want, if you do this for me you can fly my kite at the fair for me. I'm needing someone who knows what they're doing."

"Shit, really?"

"Language, young man. And yes. Of course."

"Sorry." He blushed slightly. "Sure. What's your name?" He looked at me.

"Able," I repeated what Gerad had claimed. Clearly Caitlin had briefed him.

"Stay with me, old man." He grinned.

"Old man," I grumbled. "Don't blow that in my ear."

"You're going to use that?" He looked at my implements.

"Sure. These might look like a frying pan and ladle, but they're actually tried and tested bird scaring equipment. You couldn't cook dinner in this."

"You're weird."

I couldn't disagree.

It was still early. I didn't know what time it was as I didn't have any kind of timekeeping equipment on me. All that had disappeared when I was incarcerated on the Tongue. I could only guess. Mid-morning, maybe. A bit late for shooting grouse, but I imagine Gerad had been waiting for my arrival before heading out. It felt a lot later to me, as I had been awake most of the night. The grass was still a bit damp as we tramped into the bush, leaving the sounds of excited dogs behind us. Nate shushed me, even though I hadn't intended on talking, as we headed out. It was too early to scare the birds. That came later.

The beaters lined themselves up towards the far end of the forest, within a stone's throw of the edge. I admired the view while we waited for the signal to start beating. I could see two more spires from here. Sammar and Kinnertop. Both slightly lower in elevation. Smoke rose lazily from Kinnertop. It was where a number of industries were based. Beyond that was empty space and the Parcis Flats beneath. They were hazy in the distance. I could barely make out smudges that were towns, lakes and rivers. The city of Parcis itself was visible from here, its skyscrapers jutting into the horizon. They glinted in the morning sun.

"Airship," I pointed to my companion.

He shushed me.

I ignored him. "What's an airship doing here?" A dirigible was lazily cruising around the Spires. It looked military. There were machine gun nests along its spine and gun emplacements in its side.

Nate rolled his eyes. "The president is coming for Founder's Day. They're protection detail. Now pay attention. Shit."

"Language."

He muttered something under his breath. It sounded like it ended with 'off'.

President Farnathanan would have been known as 'The Warlord' in times gone by. He had taken the position on the death of my grandfather some ten years ago and had held it ever since. If there were elections coming I can only imagine he was looking to retire. Something unheard of for a warlord. They typically died in post. I'd never actually met him, even though he grew up a few kilometres from my home. That was long before I was born though, and had spent most of his adult life engaged in politics away from the Spires.

A trumpet blew and the beating started. My companion lifted his own trumpet and blew with all his heart. Without looking in my direction he started stamping his way towards the shooters, making as much noise as he could. I heard other beaters nearby making their own racket, depending on their own implements. Already startled birds were taking to the skies and fleeing the noise.

I followed at a more leisurely pace. My heart was not in this at all. Shooting birds for sport did not appeal to me. Even though they would make it to dinner plates later in the day, and even though they would get out of hand if they were not culled. They were still living creatures.

I headed closer to the edge and watched the airship instead. It turns out there were a number of them, each slowly orbiting the Spires. Their electronic sensing equipment no doubt scanning the ground beneath to ensure no one was approaching who shouldn't be. I heard the pops of gunfire behind as the birds flew at the shooters. It sounded like they were having a good day.

I sat down and drowsed in the sun. I think I might have fallen asleep. It had been a long night.

"So this is where you are."

I started, sitting up quickly. "What?"

"We've been looking for you." Gerad walked up to me, holding his shotgun in the crook of his arm. He'd donned a floppy marine beret and a pair of sunglasses since I'd last seen him.

I groaned and stood, my joints stiff from immobility. "You finished?"

"Yeah. Plenty for the pots tonight." He walked towards the edge and looked out himself. "Quite a spot."

"It's a good view." I agreed.

After a long moment's silence he turned and looked at me. "What am I going to do with you?"

I said nothing, wondering whether his shotgun was loaded. It would be so easy for me to disappear now. I could go over the edge where no one would ever find me. These cliffs regularly shed rubble, forming quite a scree at its base. My body would get covered in time and that would be it.

"I guess I'm just in the way," I said. "An inconvenience."

His jaw clenched as if he was annoyed. "We all loved your mother you know. She was such an amazing woman. You lived under her protection for a long time, whether you knew it or not. Face it though, she belonged to the past. A past we're trying to move away from. We're not criminals up here anymore."

"Missiles and shuttles," I said.

He ignored me. "We're trying to build a future. We have big plans and none of them involve you. I'm afraid to say."

I looked away from him. I could hear barking somewhere. The dogs would be gathering up the kills and delivering them to their handlers. "Well, here's your chance," I said. "The edge is right there and you have a gun. I have … these …" I lifted the pan and ladle.

"Fuck. What do you think of me?"

"Missiles and shuttles," I repeated.

"Shit. That was business."

"I imagine it's easier to kill five people when you don't have to look into their faces."

"Five? There were four on the shuttle."

"Able broke his neck on the way down. That counts as one of yours too."

He shook his head and looked away from me. "You're a gutsy shit, you know that? I never thought you had it in you. Here we stand, on the edge. Everyone thinks you're dead. It would be so easy. And you provoke me."

"Well, now's your chance."

A chance he never got to use. Barking grew suddenly louder as one of the gun dogs cantered towards us, a grouse in its jaws. It whined in excitement as it saw us and only ran faster.

Gerad swore and threw aside his shotgun, reaching out for the dog's collar as it bounded up to him. Unable to stop it skittered towards the edge, almost yanking him off his feet as he stopped it short. "Stupid thing." He froze, staring at the shotgun at my feet. I made no move to pick it up.

"You know, Ger.."

As I started speaking the ground rumbled beneath his feet. Dirt slipped on rock, tipping it all towards the edge. With a shout he pushed the dog away from himself, towards safety. His arms windmilled as he teetered. He had gone too far, he started falling.

Without thinking I grabbed a hand, trying to yank him back. More dirt gave way, collapsing under him. He slid foreward, his feet heading towards empty air. I gasped, reaching for a branch behind me to stop myself going after him. Muscles creaked but they held.

His weight completely off the edge he scrabbled with his feet and free hand, trying to gain purchase. Only causing a bigger avalanche as more dirt went off the edge.

"Shit," he said, looking back up at me.

For a long moment we were frozen like that. Me holding his full weight from going off the edge. To a kilometre of free fall before the rocks below. A branch creaking in my grasp as it bent alarmingly, the tree it was attached to shivering under the stain. He looked up at me, his eyes on mine.

He knew then. It would take nothing for me to let go. I would be stupid not to. There was no way I could pull him up. He was a big man and I was just a skinny wretch.

"I wouldn't blame you," he said calmly.

I think I was in shock. At the turn of events. At how calm he was, even while looking certain death in the face. There was no fear in his eyes. None at all.

"Fuck," I said. And pulled. With every muscle in my body I pulled him upwards.

"You can't … shit."

I don't know how I did it. Adrenaline maybe. But I pulled him upwards, all his weight hanging from my one hand. With a heave I threw him towards firm ground and collapsed to the dirt myself, careful not to let go of the tree. My muscles quivered from the strain.

He sat there, staring at the edge. More dirt collapsed over it but we were far enough away to be safe.

"Why did you do that?"

I shook my head. "I don't know."

"How did you do that?"

I looked at my hand. It ached from the exertion. "I don't know."

"Shit. This changes nothing."

"I know." He dusted off his clothes and stood before scooping up his shotgun and checking it quickly. It was undamaged

"We'd better go."

"Yeah."

I followed as we headed back towards the others. The dog had gone, still gripping its prize in its mouth. As we neared the others we could hear voices through the trees. Laughing. I recognised one of them.

Van.

I stopped, unable to walk further. Gerad had stopped also.

"She's not supposed to be here," he said.

I said nothing.

"She can't see you."

"Yeah."

"She doesn't know you're here."

"Yeah."

"Go that way." He pointed. "The other beaters will drive you back. I'll get you picked up."

I started walking away, my legs wooden. Every laugh was like a knife in my stomach.

"Mas ..."

I paused, looking back.

"I was tempted, you know. Just now." He pointed back to the cliff.

"Yeah." That had been pretty obvious.

"But now ... I don't know."

"Yeah." I kept on walking. The sound of laughter followed me.

Chapter 8

I slept fitfully. I dreamed again. The same dream as the night before. Someone was trying to get through to me, to talk to me. I resisted. It didn't feel right. I didn't know who they were and they felt … wrong. They were insistent, but the more they insisted the more stubbornly I resisted.

I didn't know what this was, but I didn't want it.

I hadn't seen Gerad for the rest of the day. Nor Van — for which I was grateful. The beaters drove me back into town and dropped me off at a boarding house. Gerad's instructions apparently. There was a room with Able's name on it and I curled up on the bed. Asleep without even bothering to remove my boots.

It did occur to me on the drive back that some of these kids — and most of them were — should recognise me. If only because I had once been associated with my mother's work with the children of the Spires. I couldn't remember any of them, but then I had met a great many children during that time. Surely at least one would remember me? She'd only been dead three years after all. Did people get forgotten so quickly?

None of them did. I was a stranger, accepted only because of Gerad's instructions. Eli Massen was no one to these kids. I suspected he was no one to their parents either.

I did wake long enough that afternoon to source something to eat before retreating to my room again. There was a message for me on the front desk, written in Caitlin's neat script. Gerad was inviting me to breakfast the following morning. He wanted to talk apparently. I screwed the note up and threw it away.

It was late at night when I awoke again. My head ached.

Groaning I fumbled for the side light before stumbling into the en-suite bathroom for a drink of water. I didn't notice a figure sitting silently beside the window. The curtains were open, allowing in the glare of a streetlight outside. The window was open too, allowing in a slight breeze.

"Shit!" Startled I discovered the visitor when stepping out of the bathroom.

He held up a hand. "It's OK. Sorry for creeping in like this. I needed to see you without anyone else around."

"Shit." I switched on the overhead light, the sidelight wasn't very bright. "Daise? Is that you?"

"Yeah. Switch that off." He stood quickly and crossed to the light switch to switch it off. "It's been a while. I was surprised to see you'd come back. What with the wedding and all."

My eyes hurt where the sudden bright light had seared them. My head didn't feel good at all. I sat on the bed and looked up at him. Daise. He had a first name but he hated it — Grodroft - so no one used it, primarily because no one knew what it was. He was always just Daise. I knew it because I had known him a very long time. Since childhood in fact.

"I thought you went to the army," I said.

"I did. I left." He shrugged as he switched off my side light also. "We don't need light for the moment."

"How did you know I was here?"

"I saw you earlier. Driving through town sat next to Gerad. Are you insane? That guy wants you dead and he's not afraid to act on his impulses."

"Thanks, I know. He's already tried to kill me."

"You're lucky. He rarely has to try twice. Listen, we have to get you out of here."

I leaned back against the headboard, closing my eyes. "Can't say I really want to be here. But I doubt he'll let me leave."

"Not through the main entrance, no."

"What are you suggesting then? I can't fly so there's no other way down."

"Well ..." He sat in the chair again and pulled the curtains closed slightly, peering through the gap. "I don't think he has you under surveillance. He doesn't need to. He controls all the access points."

"So I'm stuck here."

"Well, I think there is one way off he won't be watching." He paused. "I think."

"You think?"

"Well. Using my amazing powers of deduction and observation, I have reason to believe he has built an emergency back door for himself. The Spires aren't as impregnable as they once were, you know. Someone could still hit them with a cruise missile. Or they could drop something onto them from orbit. Or use a nuke. Gerad is nothing if not cautious."

"If you want me to jump off the edge in a paraglider you are very mistaken. I'm not doing it."

"No, no. He will have built something a lot more civilised than that."

"You think? You don't actually know?"

"I am fairly certain. Look, if you stay here he will have to deal with you. He only knows one way of doing that. He might try to pay you off but that will only be a distraction to get you to drop your guard. As long as you remain alive you remain a potential embarrassment. You've known him long enough yourself, do you think he will take that chance?"

"No," I admitted. "No, he wouldn't."

"Neither would he risk his life. Think about it. These Spires are great as a defensive position. It's damned hard to get up here if you're not welcome. But they're also a trap. It's also damned hard to get off if there's someone hunting you. As you admit yourself, he's shrewd and cautious. Would he allow himself to be trapped up here during an armed conflict?"

"What armed conflict? The League of 8 are even considering allowing the Authority to join. Who's to threaten the Authority then?"

"He shot a shuttle down."

"What? The OMC? The Jane?"

"The OMC has powerful backers. Under what circumstances do you think Gerad would be willing to fire a missile at an OMC vehicle in orbit? That's a declaration of war, there's no way around that. That is military action against an OMC asset, resulting in the loss of a valuable vehicle and a number of OMC personnel. They will not allow that to stand. Those OMC backers I mentioned ... the Jane ... they have militaries of their own. They are a military. With cruise missiles. Nukes. I think we've already seen the opening shots of a shooting war."

"Shit." My headache was becoming the least of my problems. "If they hit the Spires it will mean war. A war like we've not had in decades."

"Exactly. So, under those circumstances, do you think Gerad will concern himself about getting rid of you?"

"No."

"And do you think he will leave himself without a back door?"

"No."

"Good. So." He stood and opened the curtain. "We go then?"

I stood and looked out of the window. It must be late – or early. The street outside was empty. The sky was dark. The moon was not out, and neither were the stars. "Do you know where it is"

"I have a very strong suspicion."

That would have to do. I pushed the window open and looked down. We were only on the second floor. There were a number of steel brackets attached to the wall beneath the window, used during festivities when lights were strung over the avenue. I'd helped string similar lights before. They were heavy so I knew those brackets would take our weight.

I didn't have anything to take with me and I was already dressed so out the window I went. I was soon on the pavement beneath, Daise beside me. "Why are you helping me?"

"We're friends aren't we?" He waved. "Come, this way."

We headed towards Gerad's compound in the centre of the town. It was where the cadets were barracked. They formed a small part of the self defence force stationed on the Spires. Every family contributed recruits and equipment to support them. The last remaining vestige of a force of a very different kind. Centuries ago these recruits had raping and pillaging to look forward to. All youngsters joined up, even I had. I was never any good at it and I didn't like guns so it never became anything more. Not so for Daise, who went on to join the Authority Army. He'd shipped off for Turquoise the last I heard. His battalion destined to take part in exercises in the frigid north. Neither of us had been very good at long distance communication so we'd lost contact.

In fact I couldn't say we had ever been very good friends. Not enough for him to take this risk with me.

"You have family here?" I asked. "Shouldn't you be trying to get them off instead?"

"They can leave any time. My sister works in Alahan and my father died last year. Heart attack."

"Oh, I'm sorry."

He shrugged. "Too much ale, I think. Only my mother lives here now. She's due to visit my sister for a while. So they're ok."

"What about Senhan?"

He laughed. "Shit, we broke up years ago."

We slowed down as we approached the compound. Part of cadet training was to take part in guard duty so there would be watchful eyes even at this time of night. Daise took me to a side entrance. It was unlit. There was a small keypad set into the wall beside the door. He put his back to the wall and peered around the corner.

"68911."

"What?"

"The code. 68911. Key it."

I did as instructed. A light flashed green and the door clicked. "How did you know that?"

"Inside," he instructed. "I saw someone key it in. They thought they were shielding it with their hand but they weren't very good at it."

"I've seen this before," I said as I closed the door behind us. "I've been here." I couldn't remember when. I hadn't spend much time on Tellas Spire. We had been hosted here once or twice by Rafael, Gerad's father. I always suspected that was how Gerad met Van but could never be sure.

"Just keep moving."

The passage beyond was dimly lit. It led to a freight dock of some kind. Empty now but for one truck pulled up against a platform. I could hear voices somewhere. Cadets possibly.

"That's it. My mother's seventieth birthday. Rafael hosted a party for her. Shit, Van and I were late." We'd had a disagreement over something, I couldn't really remember what. We argued a lot in those days, even though we'd only been married a few months. Gerad had paid her a lot of attention that night, I'd been too drunk to care.

Damn. You know I think this was all my fault. I should have seen this coming.

Waster, she had called me. It still hurt now.

"That won't help us now. Keep moving. Why have you stopped?" Daise urged me on. He was little more than a deeper shadow in the dark. I could see his eyes glinting.

We went down some stairs, moving quietly and keeping to the shadows. Fortunately there were few people around. We did hear the odd voice or footstep in the distance but that was all.

"What time is it?" I whispered.

"I dunno. About two, I think. Does it matter?"

I shrugged, aware he couldn't see it. "Not really."

"I think we're just about there." He paused at an intersection, taking his time to study the options.

"We're in the middle of his compound. Unless he has some super-secret teleportation device there's no way off the spire from here."

"You've been watching too many science fiction movies. This is a lot more practical. And I think I know what he did. Here, this way." He led me down a wider passage. It looked new and functional. Cement floor, walls and ceiling. Strip lighting, now dark. There were no side passages leading off it. At least for a hundred metres or so. Very odd.

"I noticed his drill square had been disturbed. The sand had been turned over, so I figured he'd built something important right in the middle of his compound. Something he wanted to hide," he continued, sounding proud of himself.

"What is it?"

"You'll see."

"Shit." I didn't like surprises.

"This looks promising." We came to a steel door at the end of the passage. It was closed and locked. There was a locking handle that refused his attempt to open it when he tried. Other than that there was nothing. No lock or keypad. Just steel. He ran his hands over it for a moment, studying the shape of the panels.

"Here. Put your hands here ... and here." He guided my hands.

"Why don't you do it?"

"Just ... do it. And push upwards." Something clicked. The door swung open. "Ah-ha! I thought so! It would need locking to stop anyone getting in. But Gerad would need to get in at short notice. A key might get lost and a code could get forgotten. So, secret switches. Clever."

"Awesome. What the hell is this?"

It was dark beyond. I could see absolutely nothing. I heard Daise ease the door closed behind us. Its hinges were new and silent. He found a light switch and clicked it.

"What is this?" I scanned the chamber, unable to recognise what it was for. It was roughly square, about a dozen metres on a side. There were racks on the walls holding what looked like slim backpacks. Twenty or thirty of them. Strangest was what sat in the middle. It looked like a well.

"Ah-ha!" Daise chuckled to himself as he walked around the well, studying it. "I suspected as much."

There were steps leading up to it with a hand railing beside them. A grid sealed it off although it looked easy enough to open using a handle conveniently located in its centre. He leaned down quickly and pulled off the grid, peering into the darkness beneath.

"I'm always tempted to drop something into holes," he said. "Or spit."

I looked down myself. The sides were smooth rock, perhaps slightly ridged as if the hole had been drilled. "What is it? Are you expecting me to jump in there? If so you're going to be disappointed."

"That's exactly what I'm expecting." He grinned at me. "But using one of those." He pointed to a backpack. "It's a drogue."

I knew what a drogue was. A skydiver needed a large parachute to control their descent because air could move around it. However in a confined space like this it couldn't, meaning the arresting chute could be a lot smaller. About two metres, judging by the diameter of the well. We'd still be moving pretty quickly. I said as much.

"Doesn't matter. There's water on the other side."

"How do you know that?"

"Well, where do you think the Spires draw their water from? There's underground lakes beneath each of them. They were created when the Spires were."

I shook my head. "That makes no sense. Have you seen them?"

"No, he admitted. Look, some sort of anti gravity ... or gravity reversal device ... like the one used in the Maw to rip roids apart ... was used here. Long ago. Long before anyone lived here. It created the Spires by pulling them out of the ground. But that leaves a gap underneath them. Which gets filled with water."

"How do you know this?"

He shrugged. "It's obvious when you think about it."

It wasn't to me. "And how do you know about the mechanism used in the Maw? You've definitely never seen that."

Daise sighed. "Listen, you're going to have to trust me. Gerad plans on using this in an emergency. He's not going to break his legs at the bottom. And I'll be right behind you."

"Shit." I looked into darkness again. I didn't like it. I did put on one of the backpacks though. It fit snugly with multiple straps keeping it firmly attached to my back. A rip cord hung from the left hand side.

"It's easy. Just jump in and pull that."

"Easy my arse. Do you know how high up we are?"

"Doesn't matter. You'll be moving fast but not too fast for the wat- ... What was that?"

The ground rumbled beneath our feet. As we looked around us — as if that would tell us anything — it rumbled again. Harder this time. Something fell over in the darkness and shattered.

"What the hell was that?"

"I suggest you go," Daise said, pointing downward.

The ground jumped, almost throwing me down the well before I was ready. I clung to a railing to stay on my feet.

"Go!" Daise pulled my hands from the railing and gave me a shove.

"Bastard!"

I don't think he heard me — I was already in the shaft. Air roared around my ears. I bumped against the sides as I went, a glancing impact that knocked me into the opposite wall. That impact was hard, knocking the wind from me. Which then bounced me back again. Cursing I tried to fend it off, almost dislocated my arm in the process. It hurt.

Pull the cord. I fumbled with the pack, trying to find the pull cord. The light had long vanished above me, leaving me in complete darkness. The cord was nowhere to be found. Starting to panic I made the mistake of trying to brace my arms against the tunnel walls. The walls tried to rip them off.

"Ow. Shit." That really hurt. I clenched my arms to my side until the throbbing eased slightly. I didn't know how far I had fallen. A long way at this speed. I needed to pull the cord.

I fumbled for it again, finally discovering it flapping around my ear. I pulled hard.

The drogue spilled out, snapping rigid against the airflow. Straps yanked at me, slowing my descent.

I cursed as I held my throbbing arms across my chest. Fortunately the drogue seemed to keep me in the centre of the well so I didn't come into contact with the side again. I was still in the dark though, I had no idea where I was.

As it turned out I had only just started my journey. The drop went on and on interminably. Now that the rush of air had eased I could hear rumbling above me, followed by regular thumps. As if someone was pounding on the floor with their fist. I looked up, trying to see past the drogue. There might be light up there, I couldn't tell.

I didn't know what was happening behind me. Had Daise known something? Some rumour or tip off from someone in the army? And who was firing on the Spires? The Jane? While I could understand their feelings towards Gerad and – possibly – Dynamique, I couldn't imagine them doing this. Could I? They had little respect for life, that was obvious. But openly attacking a rival in this way? That seemed a stretch. And like this? I could only imagine what weapons were being used to bombard the town. Certainly non-nuclear which was a relief. Jumping down this hole wouldn't have saved me from that.

All those people … shit. There were over five thousand people living on Tellas Spire alone. Men, women and children. That vast majority were civilians. Clerks, farmers, artisans. Shopkeepers. Why would someone murder them all?

Van.

I shuddered, suddenly feeling chill. Van had been up there. Only Daise and I had made it to the well. I doubted anyone else would have the chance to get there in time. She was up there in the town, under fire. I couldn't imagine what was happening. The town burning, being struck by who knew what.

That imagine stayed with me the rest of the way down. I just couldn't shake it.

I presently passed into the open. Still in the dark I didn't see the well vanish, leaving me in a vast open space. The drogue shuddered a bit as further flaps opened up, increasing its wind resistance. It felt cold here, almost damp.

There was a light below. I peered down, trying to make out what it was. It looked like a number of lights strung about some kind of platform hanging in space. It didn't make sense. Obscure shapes were collected around it. They were lost in the gloom. It was approaching quickly.

It was a pontoon of sorts with lights strung over it. It was floating on water so clear –

I hit the water hard, knocking the air from my lungs. I flailed, trying to make my way back to the surface. Something clung to me, wrapping itself around my legs and holding me down. The more I struggled the more it got twisted. The drogue. It was pulling me deeper.

71

Lungs aching I forced myself to calm and pulled at the straps holding me to the drogue. The backpack slipped off and dropped beneath me, taking the drogue with it. I pushed for the surface, relieved when I made open air.

I didn't want to do that again. I trod water as I looked about, searching for the pontoon. It was some way off to my left. I started swimming.

The water was cold. It couldn't be more than a few degrees above freezing. It was hard to believe Gerad would drop into it on purpose. It wasn't the most dignified way of making your way off the spire. An elevator would have been infinitely better, although I imagine that would have been subject to power failures should something untoward happen. This was simple technology. Simple was always best in an emergency.

"Took your time." I heard a voice greet me as I pulled myself onto the pontoon. I lay on it for a moment, enjoying its stillness. There were no waves on the underground lake to make it rock.

"Typical you'd beat me down," I commented as I eased myself upright.

"They steer," Daise said over his shoulder as he studied the controls of one of the boats moored to the pontoon. Boats – that was what the shapes had been. That made sense.

"What?"

"The drogue. Once you're out of the tunnel you can steer them."

"Shit." I stood unsteadily and watched what he was doing. He was wet too but had no doubt come down within a few metres of the pontoon itself. Then a few strokes to escape the freezing water.

"Have a look in there," he pointed to a locker set into the boat's side. "There might be towels or blankets."

Shuddering from the cold I joined him on the boat and opened the locker. The vessel was some kind of speed boat, big enough for five or six passengers at most. There were others moored alongside of different shapes and sizes. Gerad had clearly intended saving a number of people.

I pulled out a towel and started drying myself, ignoring Daise's suggestion to strip my clothes first. I wasn't in the mood.

"I think we head that way. You drive while I look around some more." He pointed into the darkness.

"Why that way?"

"I can see lights. It could be a tunnel or an exit or something."

I nodded, throwing off the mooring lines before settling myself behind the controls. They were simple enough. After checking he wouldn't be thrown overboard when I accelerated I pushed forward on the throttle. Like most engines it was electric. The batteries showed they were fully charged. I left the pontoon behind and aimed in the general direction he had indicated. I couldn't see anything yet. As we left the lights behind and my eyes became accustomed to the gloom I could just about see a light there. He had better eyes than me.

"There's some food. A change of clothing," he said.

"No one came down after us."

He was silent a moment. "No. I think it happened too quickly. They just didn't have the time. I don't know what it was. Cruise missiles perhaps. Or orbital bombardment."

"The OMC? The Jane?"

"I don't know who else it could be."

I shook my head. "There were civilians up there. Children."

"Yeah."

"Children! Who would do that? Why would they do that?"

"I don't think they care," he said softly. I barely heard him.

"Van was up there!"

"I know."

I said nothing more for a long while. I didn't look in his direction so he couldn't see my face. I didn't want him to know how I felt. I know I had already lost her. She thought I was dead and she was marrying someone else. I had lost her long before that. Driven away by my carelessness, driven towards someone who did care. Someone she could respect. Did I still love her? After all that?

Yes, of course I did.

There was a tunnel set into the side of the cavern. Its lower half was flooded so I couldn't see its floor. A line of lights were bolted to the ceiling, leading off into the distance. Clearly this was the way we went.

"We're headed north," I said. There was a compass set into the controls. "We're headed towards Kinnertop."

"The route might just use the cavern lakes. Saves on drilling tunnels," Daise commented. "Do you think it's getting warmer?"

"Warmer?"

"Yeah."

"The sun might be coming up."

He shook his head. "Won't make any difference down here." He was settled onto a bench in the boat's bow, his feet up on the cushions. He had changed out of his wet clothes when I wasn't looking. He was now dressed in an army jumpsuit of some description. Drab olive green. "It would take quite a thermal spike to heat all of this water," he continued. "It must be hot up there for us to feel it here."

"I can't feel it." But then I hadn't seen the tunnel either. It did feel somewhat cooler as we swept into the tunnel though. The humming of our motors echoed off the rock walls, accompanied by the sound of rushing water beneath the bow.

"Maybe we should speed up," he said.

"Why? I don't know where we are going."

"Well, that thermal spike I was talking about-"

"I couldn't feel it."

"OK. But humour me. What do you think is holding the Spires up?"

"What?"

"Well, some science fiction weapon was used here a long time ago. Reversing gravity or something. Pulling up these spires."

73

"You said that."

"Sure, sure. So what do you think keeps them from falling back down again?"

I must admit I had never thought about it. In fact I hadn't thought about any of it until tonight. The Spires were just ... the Spires. "I'm sure you will tell me. Friction?"

"Yes. Friction. Friction between the wall and the part of the Spires that are still under ground. That's all that's keeping them up. Against billions of tonnes of rock and dirt pushing down from above. And what happens when you heat all that up? Particularly where those points of friction meet?"

"The rock would expand at first, increasing friction."

"Clever bastard. What when it gets hotter still?"

"But it won't. All this water will absorb the heat."

"As I say, humour me."

"Well, they can't fall down again. There's water down here now."

He sighed. "It's not the water I'm worried about. It's us. On this boat. On top of the water."

"Shit."

"Shit is right. Rock melts at over a thousand degrees, depending on the amount of silicate and iron it contains. That's hot. I don't think it will get that hot, not this far down, not with this much water. But it doesn't have to. It will become plastic and lose its integrity long before that."

I didn't feel in the mood for a science lesson. "You think they used nukes?" It would take nukes to generate that kind of heat.

He shrugged but said nothing.

We swept out of the tunnel into another cavern. Kinnertop was long and narrow, about two kilometres wide and about six in length. At this speed we should be at the other side in a quarter of an hour. There were lights bobbing on the surface here, keeping us on track.

It was definitely warmer in here. Daise made that observation.

"Not enough though?"

"How hot is it up there?" He pointed towards the rock above our heads. "I think we should speed up."

I eased the throttle further forwards. The engine hum increased, Daise had to raise his voice to be heard. "If the spire collapses into this space we're in trouble."

"Yeah, thanks."

Something splashed in the darkness. "What was that?" I couldn't see anything. There might have been a ripple on the water.

"Something hit the water," he stated the obvious.

"Something"

"Like a rock. Speed up some more please."

I pushed the throttle to its stopper. The boat's bow rose above the water, motors thrumming. Air whipped past us.

"We have to get off the water!"

"What?" I couldn't hear him over the noise of our passage.

"If it comes down!" Daise shouted, pointing towards the darkened ceiling. "All this water has to go somewhere!"

Even off the water we wouldn't be safe. We had to be out of the entrance and well away from it before the surge of water came our way. There was a lot of water down here. If the Spires fell it would have nowhere to go. Nowhere but down the escape passage.

"This might not have been a good idea!" I shouted.

"Rather be up there?"

I didn't. There was another splash nearby. Big and close enough to throw water over the boat. I cursed but didn't deviate on our path. I couldn't. We were possibly halfway now. At full speed it wouldn't take long.

"Shit. I saw that one," Daise commented as the boat skipped over a wave thrown up by a splash. The rocks were getting bigger. "I think it's starting to shift."

I heard a crack behind us as a large part of the ceiling broke free and fell. It collapsed into the lake, throwing up a wall of water. The impact of the water on the boat almost threw me overboard. I clung on, desperately trying to keep the little boat aimed where we wanted to go. I could no longer see the path. The cables for the lights had been ripped out. I just had to hope it was the right direction.

"You still there?" I yelled as the boat righted itself.

"Yeah! Keep going. A little to the left."

"You can see the tunnel?"

"I think so, about two hundred metres."

It became impossible to steer a straight course. Boulders larger than ground cars slammed into the water all around us. Splashing water over the boat and knocking it from its path. I couldn't see them coming in the dark. I could only hope one didn't hit us directly. I was almost thrown from the boat again and again as water struck the little craft.

We bounced off the tunnel wall as a wave knocked us sideways at the last moment. I heard fibreglass shriek as it caved in, a long crack developing below the water line. Water began squirting in.

"Just keep going," Daise said. "We can't stop now."

At least the water was calmer here. Nothing was falling from the ceiling. I put my foot against the crack, trying to slow the leak. It didn't help. Water just shot up my leg instead. The lights were back. Clearly this circuit hadn't been interrupted.

"I think we're almost there." He pointed to a wharf ahead of us. There were a few boats already tied up. Left there for servicing Gerad's back door perhaps. "Don't slow down. Just hit it. Then get out and run!"

This was going to hurt but I saw his logic. It would take too much time to slow down and dock properly. Time we didn't have.

"The lights are going out behind us. Don't look! Just keep going!"

I felt a rush of damp air on my back. Something was blowing it towards us.

This was going to be close. I urged the little boat to go faster as it faltered, the weight of all the water rushing onboard slowing us down. We were almost sunk. I braced for impact.

We struck the dock squarely. Wood and fibreglass crackled. I was thrown from my feet, took a glancing blow off the crumpled bow and bounced onto what remained of the dock. Daise shouting at me to run I scrambled to me feet and bounded up a short flight of stairs to a wooden door. I didn't take the time to open it, simply crashing through.

"Go. Go. Go." Daise pushed me from behind.

I could hear a roaring from somewhere. Air beat at my retreating back. There was another door. I burst through that too. Beyond was some kind of loading dock. A few cars were pulled up before the shuttered doors.

"Wait. A car!" Daise shouted as I headed straight for the doors.

"What the hell? We don't have the time!" The roaring was growing louder. I could barely hear him.

"We have to!"

Cursing I slammed the palm of my hand on a door control. The shutters creaked as they began opening. I slipped into the driver's seat. "Why don't you drive some time?"

He yelled something unintelligible and pointed to the exit.

Water blew out of the passage, knocking the car alongside us out of the way. It tumbled into the slowly opening shutters, tearing them from their brackets. The dim light of dawn flooded in.

This car didn't need keys either. I didn't argue, simply slamming my foot on the accelerator and aiming for the newly formed exit. Motors screamed as the car slewed sideways, water catching on the wheels. I clung on, aiming for dry ground. Something hit us from behind, tossing us through the doors. Somehow we managed to stay upright.

"Keep going! Let's get out of here." Daise peered out of the windscreen. "Taylor."

"What?" I think I said that a lot around him.

"We're in Taylor. Take a right and head for Cobs Hill."

"Why?"

"High ground. We have to get out of the valley."

Cobbs Hill was the only high ground in the vicinity. The town of Taylor wasn't very big, it was barely a village. A village built around the old windmill sitting atop Cobbs Hill. It might be dwarfed by the spires that loomed over everything for kilometres around, but it was the tallest hill in the vicinity.

"What the hell?" Daise was craning his neck to look out a mirror.

I looked behind us. "Shit."

Water was jetting from the ground behind us. The building we'd emerged from was gone, ripped from the ground and thrown into the air. As I watched the torrent grew in size as it eroded the passage we'd escaped through. Rocks and other debris were flung high above the town, disappearing into the early morning sky. I didn't want to know where they would come down. I hope they didn't hit a house.

"Watch it!" Daise pushed on the steering wheel. Distracted I'd misjudged a corner. Metal shrieked as we bounced off a wall.

"Thanks!" Waves of water flooded the village behind us. Bowling over walls and surging through doorways. I wanted to stop and warn people. To tell them to get out. To run. But there simply wasn't time. Even racing as we were a flood of water beat us to an intersection. It battered into the beleaguered car, knocking us off our path.

"It's OK. Take the next left. It takes us there too." Daise pointed.

Up the hill we went. We clipped some of the low stone walling in our haste. I didn't care. I only allowed our pace to slow as we broached the brow of the hill, the tyres kicking up gravel as we slewed to a halt at the base of the windmill.

Lights were blinking on in the houses alongside, residents alarmed by the noise and vibration. Sleepy eyed they stumbled into the streets to stare at the geyser of water where the centre of their town had once been.

"Are we safe here?" I was drenched in sweat. I think it was sweat. It could just have been water. I climbed out of the car and watched the village disappear below us. I doubted anyone had escaped in time. It had simply happened too quickly.

It was only then I noticed the Spires. They were gone. Where the towering structures had once risen into the skyline to the south was now a jumble of burning rubble. I could almost feel the heat coming off them from here. Steam billowed around fissures in the rock where water had escaped onto the half molten surface. There was little flame. Anything that could burn had already been consumed. Instead there was an evil red glow coming from the rock itself.

I couldn't imagine what kind of weapon had done this, but its power was frightful.

"Daise, you saved my life."

He turned from where he was watching the horror himself, looking slightly uncomfortable. "It's nothing. You would have done it for me."

"Thank you."

He said nothing, turning back to watch instead. Presently he pointed to the sky. "Look. Airships. They're looking for survivors. There won't be any."

I saw the dirigibles myself, tiny in the distance. They floated above the chaos, like flies looking for a place to land. I don't think they knew what to make of all of this either.

A building crashed nearby, its foundations eroded by the water. It could be my imagination but the geyser seemed to have slackened somewhat. That or the water already on the surface was slowing its exit. Most of the village was submerged. Only houses near the top of the hill were still standing, and some of those were starting to disappear beneath the water. I didn't know if we were safe here. The water might keep on going, flooding even this spot. There was just no way of knowing.

I could do nothing but sit and watch.

Chapter 9

The water receded quickly. This was a plain after all, there was nothing to keep it dammed here. The initial flood surged through fields, ripping up the summer's crops. It felled trees, undermined roads and railroads and knocked down communications towers. If anything it caused more damage than the initial attack on the Spires. While that damage had been catastrophic, it had been quite localised. The flood, on the other hand, effected hundreds of square kilometres of prime farmland. Swamping a number of towns as it went. It even ripped through the outskirts of Parcis itself, knocking down houses, schools and factories. The worst loss of life happened when the water hit Pontus Excavation. A dosser pit extracting minerals from a rich seam twelve kilometres from the village of Taylor. The night shift had still been underground, and with power and communications knocked out they had scant warning before the water roared through the works. Fifteen hundred workers had been underground. Fifty made it out.

In all, eighty thousand people lost their lives that morning, although it would take weeks for that final number to be settled upon. Weeks before rescue workers managed to dig out the stinking mud and rubble to find all the bodies. Some would just never be found.

Of the Spires themselves there was nothing left. The destruction was complete. Kilometres of rock had been seared before collapsing into the chasms beneath them. The remaining structures shattering at the impact, throwing rubble into the air. No human remains were ever found. Not one bone or tooth. The only comfort was that it had been quick. The weapon had killed just about everyone before they even knew they were under attack. The vast majority would never even have woken up.

There was no trace of the weapon. It was not nuclear as there was no residual radiation. None of the early warning systems had detected missiles of any kind approaching the Spires. To add to the conundrum, there had been no stations or satellites within easy striking distance of the Spires at the time either. It was almost as if the attacker chose that one moment when the sky above the Spires was relatively clear.

No one saw anything.

Of course that didn't stop the accusations. Against the OMC and the Jane, against Tondo and Cali, against all the members of the League of Seven. The Authority was hurting. It had lost a lot of people, some of them senior military and government officials. It had lost much of the year's crop in that region. The damage to its infrastructure was considerable. Worst of all it lost face. A typically bellicose nation state had been struck, and struck hard. With no one to blame. The national humiliation was intense.

People wanted someone to pay for it and they didn't particularly care who it was. Tensions were high and appeared only set to increase. Daise had not been wrong about the start of a shooting war. It was inevitable at this point.

We travelled west with all the other refugees on the backs of military transport vehicles. The trucks bounced through muddy fields, their massive tyres sometimes getting bogged down in the quagmire. The only vehicles that didn't get stuck were those with caterpillar tracks, and they were kept busy pulling their beleaguered companions free when they ran into trouble. The going was slow, particularly as the column kept deviating to visit flooded village after flooded village looking for survivors. There were always families huddled on farm roofs with their livestock collected about them. The animals they couldn't fir onto their roofs were everywhere. Cattle, sheep and horses washed up against what remained of the roadway. Their bodies quickly bloating in the heat. Swarms of flies were crawling over everything.

The refugees Daise and I shared the back of our truck with were strangely quiet. They simply sat and watched the devastation as it passed. They were in shock. The lives they had known were over. Many had lost most of their families. They had lost all their worldly belongings apart for what they were wearing when the flood struck. As a result many were still in their nightclothes.

Helicopters and dirigibles, military and civilian alike, cruised overhead, searching for survivors. The drone of their engines was a constant background noise.

"We should head west," Daise said. "Once we get out of this."

"Don't you want to get to your family?"

He shrugged. "I'll give them a call to let them know I'm OK." He didn't talk about his past much, about what he had been doing since we last met. He didn't mention his family at all. I got the impression something had happened, something he didn't want to talk about.

To be fair I didn't talk much either. I didn't really want to. Fortunately he didn't seem inclined to enquire. As a result much of our time was spent in silence.

It took almost two days for the convoy to reach ground unaffected by the flood. By then the sodden ground was drying in the early spring sun. The army unloaded us at a bus terminal. A small tent city had been set up there to accommodate refugees. After identities were checked, we were free to leave if we had somewhere to go to. The army either didn't have the resources or interest to look after us further. Daise and I took a train west, using the cash credit chip Gerad had given me. I was wary of Able's as it was tied to his identity. I didn't know if he had been reported dead or not. It might raise questions. Fortunately the army hadn't cared who I identified myself as. The name went on a ledger and that was it. They didn't check it.

We stopped at Permiset, an ancient city on the banks of Lake Iger. Much of it was a squalid slum. A shantytown of ancient buildings built so close to each other you could pass something to a neighbour through your window. Still, despite its dilapidated state and the ever-present stench of open sewers, it had its charm. There was an energy here I couldn't quantify. The narrow streets were always busy, there was always the sound of music coming from somewhere. Smoke from cooking fires wafted through the air, carrying with it the aroma of a dozen different spices. Unfortunately they were not quite up to the task of covering the underlying stench of the sewers. There was rubbish everywhere. It blew around underfoot when a welcome breeze penetrated the tangle of buildings.

The old quarter was where the rich lived. It was walled off from the city proper, armed guards keeping the poor out of their well-manicured streets. Here were the ancient marble edifices built in the time of the Lafayette Kings, when this port city had controlled a vast kingdom. That was a long time ago now. The kings were dead and the kingdom had fallen to foreign invaders. The railway station was situated just beneath those walls, allowing the first-class passengers to turn left and head straight for the closest entrance. Everyone else turned right.

We followed the crowds.

Holding my valuables tight I ignored the vendors trying to flog us food on sticks as we hit the street. We couldn't walk on the pavement, it was too crammed with stalls and rubbish. No one seemed to bother with it anyway as everyone walked in the streets. Which forced the rare groundcar to drive slowly as it wound its way through the throng.

The noise, heat and dust assaulted my senses. I'd spent too many months in the relative silence of space to easily deal with this. "I'm not convinced," I said.

"It'll be fine. It's not as dangerous as they say. Just don't buy food on the streets. And only drink bottled water. Oh, and stay away from the hookers." Daise grinned at me as he pulled me out of the way of a slowly moving police car. "Don't try the drugs. And don't shake anyone's hand. It's considered an insult."

"I'm not planning on touching anyone." I picked up the clear stench of sweat whenever anyone got too close. I doubted bathing was a daily ritual around here.

This was just a stopover on our way west. Our intention was to leave the Authority behind. The coast of Cali held a certain appeal. I could easily disappear there, and the money held on the chits in my pocket would last a long time. Beautiful beaches and palm trees. Tall drinks and women. Yes, I was being shallow, but I didn't care. Daise seemed content to tag along. I didn't object. I enjoyed his company and he had saved my life after all.

The desert sat between us and that objective. A thousand kilometres of sand and stone with desperately little shade or water. We needed to gear up and join one of the caravans. They regularly ran the trail through the bad lands to the hills beyond, and then the ocean beyond those. The trailmasters were known to run drugs and guns through the pass, we wouldn't be noticed.

"We need a Hub," I said, looking down the busy street. I had noticed an increase in military presence just about everywhere I went. It was no different here. I could see three squads from my vantage point on the kerb, the soldiers warily eying the throng about them, fiddling with their weapons nervously. The locals parted around them.

"There's one behind you," Daise pointed.

I turned around and found the brick building he was indicating. There had once been a 'Hub' signboard above the door. It had long been ripped off, leaving only the faint outline of the words. I waved my companion on and we entered the sweltering interior. Clearly their air conditioner was down.

The Hub was a communications franchise. Once we had our temporary login cards from a woman sitting in a steel cage at the entrance we went in search of empty terminals. Most were busy, locals and visitors alike engaged in voice or video communications with loved ones scattered around the world. It was a noisy place, everyone trying to get their words across to their audience over the racket around them. There was a couple of cubicles open at the far end and we took those.

I didn't want to talk to anyone. I wanted to check on whether Able or I were registered as deceased. These consoles were linked to the Datasphere, allowing access to anything that was in the public record. I ignored what Daise was doing – that was his business.

Eli Massen was dead, the record stated. Deceased aboard OMC shuttle, 15BDC, while on approach to a transfer station. Technical fault leading to catastrophic systems failure the report stated. No mention of a missile. No survivors. The OMC file investigating the incident was closed. I wasn't sure what I felt about that. I was officially deceased.

I re-read the file a few times, hoping to glean some additional insight. There was nothing I hadn't caught on the first reading. I felt a bit bereaved. As if I had lost a member of my family. Except that member was me.

I moved on and checked on Able. I slipped out his ident card and typed in his full name. Ardent Occilomb Able. What kind of a name was that? No mention of him being deceased. As he was considered alive the record keepers were concerned with his privacy, and so little information about him was accessible. Last occupation: contracted tractor driver for the Oberon Mining Confederation. Now released from contract, obligations fulfilled. That was all.

Well, at least Able was still alive. I tried to check on next of kin but the system was unforthcoming. I did feel a twinge of guilt over his family wondering where he was. It seemed unnecessarily cruel. Not that I could tell them anything without revealing the fact I was travelling under his identity.

I leaned back in the chair, the ancient wood creaking alarmingly, contemplating my next steps. At least now I was free to make use of both credit chits in my possession. Four million and some change. Plenty to disappear for good. I could probably buy a new identity. Someone not Able. I didn't like masquerading as a dead man.

Out of curiosity more than anything else I logged into my own mail account. There was a red banner marching across the top, indicating the mail owner was deceased, and asking additional security questions so next of kin could access it. I knew enough about myself to be able to get in.

I heard a cough from Daise. "What are you doing?"

I shrugged. "Just checking."

"Would a dead man check his own mail? You have to act dead."

"I'm logged in as next of kin. Besides, who cares? Gerad's dead. No one's looking for me."

"Shit." Realising it was too late anyway he leaned forward in his own booth and minded his own business.

I had mail. One unread entry above the OMC employment mails I had received months ago, notifying me of the cancellation of my contract. I didn't need to look at those again. It was the unread mail that drew my attention. It was from Van.

"Shit." I stared at it. I felt suddenly cold despite the heat of the room. Why would Van mail me?

It was dated the afternoon of the grouse hunt.

I swore again. I wasn't sure I wanted to know what was in it.

It was a video file.

"Mas ..." She looked dishevelled, her eyes red as if she had been crying. "Mas ... I ... I saw you today. After the hunt when the beaters were leaving. I didn't want to believe it was you but I'd recognise you anywhere. Are you alive? I want you to be alive. Gerad tells me you died in some shuttle accident. I didn't tell him I saw you. He'd deny it anyway." She hesitated for a moment, looking away from the camera as if trying to find the words. "I wanted to say I never wanted any of this. I didn't want it to happen this way. I'm sorry. You never deserved this. If you're out there be careful. I don't know what Gerad's intentions are. He scares me sometimes. Be safe and go somewhere he can't find you. Just don't trust him, OK?" She hesitated again. "That was all. I hope you're ok." She stared at the screen for a while, as if unsure of what to do next, before reaching out and ending the call.

The screen went blank.

Shit.

I shouldn't have opened it. There was nothing in the world she could say that would make any difference. Not now.

I logged out and stood. "I need some air." I headed for the door. Not that the air outside was any better than what I would find inside. If anything it was louder out there.

I stood on the street corner, not really paying attention to what was going on around me. Daise joined me presently and stood silently beside me. Scooter drivers hooted their horns at us but we ignored them. To be fair they were hooting at just about everyone, adding to the cacophony.

"She still cared about you," Daise said.

I shook my head. "It doesn't matter."

"You believed she didn't care. That she discarded you-"

"She's dead, OK? Just drop it."

He shrugged and remained silent.

I tried to put it out of my mind. It didn't matter now. The Terror Weapon, as the media were calling it, had ended all of that. All of those lives had been scrubbed from the world. Hers included. And Gerad's, which – truth be told – I did not regret. I'll also admit I half wished I had allowed him to fall. That it had been me who ushered in his end. I did have a fleeting feeling of remorse indulging in that desire. I had so much on my mind it didn't last long.

"Jane," Daise said.

"What?"

"Those –" he pointed, "are Jane. Unless I am very mistaken. Which I am not."

Two darkly clad soldiers were stood on the other side of the busy street. They didn't have any visible weapons but I knew they would not come to a place like this unarmed. They were Jane all right. They tended to be unmistakeable once you learned to recognise them. Your average soldier was just the youngster from down the street. Given a weapon, a uniform and some training. They never lost that air of not really knowing what they were doing. Of just bumbling through, relying on their leaders to tell them what to do. Actual combat experience would lessen this somewhat, but they would never be much more than your average citizen who just happened to wear a uniform.

Not so the Jane. They were killers and they looked it.

They were a man and a woman, both lean and athletic. Hair short. Sunglasses obscured what they were looking at. They seemed to be scanning the buildings around us, clearly looking for something. They seemed to pause when catching sight of where the Hub sign had once been attached.

It took me a moment to realise it was not the Hub outlet they were looking at. It was us.

"Shit. What do they want?" I asked.

"I don't want to find out. Let's go."

We headed down the avenue, trying to look casual. I think we failed miserably. I caught sight of one of them making a hand gesture, clearly communicating to someone we hadn't seen.

"Walk faster," Daise urged me.

"What can they want? They don't even know who I am."

"You logged in as you, didn't you?"

"No. I logged in as next of kin. Not me. Besides, they couldn't have gotten here this quickly. That was only twenty minutes ago."

"What next of kin?"

Damn, he was right. I didn't have any. Not anymore. "It could just as easily be you they are after."

"No. They are not after me."

We weaved through a marketplace, trying to lose them in the bustle. I'd lost sight of them myself. Surely no one could follow us through here. The avenues between the stores were virtually nonexistent in places. When there was space it was filled with traders and shoppers alike. There was a lot of shouting and gesticulation as bargains were struck. The odd loose goat got in the way, forcing us to change tack and go around.

Resources were scarce on Reaos. All easily accessible sources of minerals and fossil fuels had been exhausted a long time ago. The only dependable source was the Oberon Mining Confederation, a monopoly it exploited mercilessly to achieve its political ends. Which usually meant every government in the world owed some kind of allegiance to it. Every president, king or queen or general, no matter how powerful they believed themselves to be, bowed to the demands of the OMC.

The OMC controlled the world. The Jane controlled the OMC.

No one defied the Jane. It was simply not worth it. Not only because of the political threat they represented, but they were also far more powerful than any army on the planet. In numbers and resources, and also in access to technologies the likes of us could barely dream of.

I preferred to stay out of their way. I didn't like them at all. A dislike I had learned on the Tongue. I certainly didn't like them following me.

"They're still on us," Daise said as we paused at the opposite edge of the marketplace.

"What do we do?"

"We could give in? I don't know what they want from us."

"I'm not doing that." I hadn't enjoyed being at the mercy of the Jane the last time. Whatever they wanted now it could not be good. "Let's keep on going." We headed away from the marketplace, into the tangle of side streets and alleys that was the informal residential quarter. We were close to the waterfront here, I could smell the foul odour of stagnant, diseased water.

"Drone." Daise pointed overhead.

A small quadcopter was following us. The buzzing of its rotors just about audible above the hubbub of daily life. We ducked through a building, jogging across a neatly maintained courtyard that had a fountain in the centre, cooling the air around it. Not what we had expected to find here. Someone shouted at us as we exited the other side. He looked like a guard of some sort.

"Still there," Daise commented. "Hold on. Down!" He pulled on my arm, flinging me into the dirt.

I felt rather than heard the first salvo passing where we had just been standing. My hair stood on end at the sudden surge of static electricity. My stomach twisted as if I'd just jumped off a cliff.

The building we'd just exited exploded. Masonry and wood chips rained down on us, followed closely by a shockwave.

Someone fired again. I heard it this time. There was a zing as high energy particles flashed overhead, ripping into another building. More masonry and wood shattered into the street. If they were firing at us they could no longer see us through the dust and debris.

"Get up!" Daise pulled me to my feet. He continued shouting at me but I couldn't make out what he was saying. It suddenly got very loud.

Submachine gun fire stuttered in response. Someone with a gun taking offence and firing back. They were joined seconds later by a second, then a third. The deep throated roar of a fifty-cal opened up somewhere, blowing chunks from the roadway as it marched towards our assailants. I saw one of the Jane knocked backwards. Another stepped aside to avoid the gunfire and fired their pulse weapon again.

Zing. Part of a neighbouring building disintegrated. The fifty-cal fell silent.

Caught in the crossfire we crawled into a drain. People screamed all about us. Several dropped suddenly, blood mushrooming on their clothes. There were five of them. They walked forward slowly, all but ignorant of the return fire tearing into them. One staggered, a volley catching her in her chest. She quickly righted herself and fired back. I heard screaming behind me. The Jane's weapon was tiny, fitting neatly into her fist. It flashed as she fired, a beam of energy leaping out to cut through the remains of the building behind us.

They weren't trying to capture us, I realised. They were trying to kill us. Retaliation by the locals had achieved nothing but distracting them for a moment. That distraction wouldn't last long.

"Run!" Daise shouted.

I didn't need convincing. Not really sure what was going on I followed closely behind as he dived back into the marketplace. I heard a thump as something exploded. A grenade. It was getting serious. The soldiers we had seen earlier were getting involved.

"What was all that about?" I panted once I was sure we were clear of it.

"That building. I think it was a gang hideout," Daise said. "We got lucky."

"Did you know they were there?" The building my companion guided me through had been different from those around it. Better maintained. I think some of the toughs standing around outside had been guards. Only surprise had allowed us through.

He laughed nervously. "How would I know that? But I'm not going to refuse the help!"

We kept on going, hurdling crates and pushing confused shoppers out of the way. They could hear the sudden noise and didn't know what to make of it. I heard sirens from somewhere, the local police heading towards the scene.

"Slow down." Daise held up a hand. "We're just attracting attention."

We slowed to a fast-paced walk, quickly exiting the marketplace again and trying to lose ourselves in the docklands. We could still hear a commotion behind us. The odd burst of gunfire and explosion. The Jane weapons were not loud enough to hear from this distance.

"Shit. That was close." I put my back up against a wall. I was shaking uncontrollably.

"We were lucky," Daise said. "Those gangsters probably thought it was a police raid."

I stifled a laugh. It was high pitched, almost hysterical. "This isn't the place for the Jane to start a shootout. They won't do that again!"

My companion shook his head. "We need to keep on moving. That drone might find us again."

I allowed him to guide me further into the docklands. There were warehouses here, workers moving to and fro, wheeling carts laden with goods of all kinds. A lot of it was probably illegal. Gulls circled overhead, eagerly scanning the city below to find their next meal.

As we walked I couldn't stop thinking about it. Why would the Jane be interested in us? And so quickly? There was no way me accessing my account could have brought such a swift response. Nothing worked that quickly in the real world. Perhaps on some drama show, but not in real life.

Perhaps it was coincidence and they had tracked us down using some other means. That still didn't explain their interest though. Or why they wanted us dead. If that first shot hadn't missed we would be dead now. I shuddered, thinking about what those weapons would do to skin and bone.

Then it occurred to me to wonder why they had missed. The Jane? Missing their target? Before today I wouldn't have thought that possible. Certainly not from that range. I was fortunate my companion had realised they were there in time to pull us out of the way. I certainly hadn't.

I didn't know what to make of any of it. None of it made sense. I was no-one to them. A disgraced ex-employee.

It simply had to be a mistake. Or they were after Daise.

"Ah, we have another problem."

A number of figures were moving in around us. They were all wearing ragged and filthy clothing. Most didn't even have shoes. They were all armed, however. Some with guns, others with machetes or knives. They were little more than children.

They emerged suddenly from the passers by around us as if coordinated. Cutting off any avenue of escape before we even realised they were there. Our backs were against a wall, there was nowhere to go.

"Just what we need. First the Jane, now some thugs. I'm not into this," I muttered. "Why did we come here?"

"Let's play this out. They could be from the same gang the Jane hit. They might want to know what it's all about." Daise held up his hands to show he was unarmed and urged me to do the same.

I held my own hands up. "We don't have anything worth stealing." I was very conscious of the two credit chits in my pocket. In retrospect coming to this neighbourhood with that much cash on me was probably a very bad idea. It was a bit late now.

A young boy of about fourteen stepped forward. He was holding a sub machine gun threateningly. It would probably knock him over if he tried to fire it. "Who are you?" he demanded loudly, his accent guttural. "Why you bring Jane here?" He was clearly their leader even though he was probably half the age of some of the other street urchins. I didn't think it was age that gained seniority in this group.

"We didn't," I said. "I'm sorry. We didn't know they were looking for us."

"You lie!" He came closer, aiming his weapon at my face. "You die!"

"Hold on, hold on. We can work something out."

"Give him one of your chits," Daise hissed.

"Are you mad?"

"The Jane killed some of their people and destroyed what looked like a safe house. They'll want something. Just give him the bloody thing."

"Shit. OK, hold on." I showed him my hands were empty and moved them slowly towards a pocket. He didn't like that.

"No! You die!" The boy reversed the weapon and swung it at me. It caught my midrift.

I doubled over in pain, my breath knocked out of me. "Hold on," I gasped. "Just ... wait a minute ..."

"Why you here?" he demanded again. "You Jane?" He swung at me again, this time knocking me onto my back.

"Shit. They were trying to kill us." I crawled backwards, trying to put some space between us. "Here. Let me give you this." I managed to slip a chit from my pocket and held it out. He slapped it from my hand.

"That's shit. We don't want your shit."

One of his companions scooped it up and slipped it into a reader.

"We don't have anything else. What else do you want?"

"I shoot you." He held his gun to my head again. The steel of the barrel was hard and warm against my forehead. I could smell gunpowder. It had been fired recently. I closed my eyes, half expecting him to pull the trigger.

"Hey!" His companion showed him the reader. His eyes grew wide. They spoke quickly in a language I couldn't understand.

"We take!" He snatched up the chit. "What else you got?"

"Nothing. Nothing. I promise."

He didn't like that at all. He swung the submachine gun again, this time cracking on my skull. Warm blood splashed into my eyes. That was followed by a kick to my ribs as I slumped to the filthy ground. He kicked hard for such a little guy. His companions joined in then, all taking their turn. I couldn't see what was happening to Daise, I was too busy trying to make myself as small as possible, folding my arms about my head to protect it. Even though it hurt – a lot – I think being unable to breathe hurt most. Each blow drove the air from my lungs, not allowing me to get any air. I could do nothing but gasp and try to fend off the worst of it.

My vision was growing black when it seemed to ease. Hands pushed me over, exploring my pockets. I dimly heard a shout as they discovered the second chit.

"Please. Don't take that," I gasped. I don't know if they could hear me. Without that second chit I had nothing. Daise and I were broke.

"We take!" Someone kicked me again. "You go! No come back!"

There might have been some more kicking then, I didn't really know. I wasn't conscious for much of it. I just remember hot stone against my cheek, the stench of rotting refuse in my nose. The distant hum of people walking by. Some looking down, most tried not to see anything. No one helped. At some point the gang had vanished into the throng once again.

The sun had left the street when I managed to pull myself up against the wall. I rubbed dried blood from one eye, not even bothering with the other. It was swollen shut. "Daise. You there?" I heard a groaning from somewhere nearby.

"Are we dead?"

I tried not to laugh. It hurt. "It's early yet."

"Super weapons can't get us. Neither can the Jane. But some kids on the street? Shit."

"They took our money."

"All of it?"

"Yeah."

"Shit."

"Yeah."

I did have some money they hadn't found – or perhaps simply hadn't been interested in. Six thousand credits, my total earnings from my trip to the Shatter. It might be enough to pay some backroom hack to sew up our wounds and a meal or two. That was about it.

I pulled myself upright against the wall. I didn't think I could let go of it, my legs were too shaky to take my weight. Daise was sat on the kerb, his heads in his hands.

The docklands seemed quieter than before. There was still the odd passer-by, none of whom paid us any attention. This scene might be a common one. I obstructed the path of a diminutive figure who was slowly pushing a covered cart down the avenue. I could smell the aroma of food coming from it. It was possible she was off to sell her wares to the night shift at one of the yards.

"Excuse me. Is there a hospital here? A hospital? Doctor?" Like all foreigners everywhere, I felt that speaking slower and louder would ensure she could understand me.

"You want buy?" She stopped the cart and started opening lids. The smell increased, only causing my stomach to knot. I couldn't face food right now.

"No. No, thank you. Is there a doctor? My friend needs help."

"Cheap. Very cheap. Is good." She picked up a ladle.

I didn't think I was getting across. "No food. No food." I waved my hand in front of her, hoping it was the universal gesture for polite refusal. "Hospital. Doctor?"

"No food?" She looked disappointed.

"No. No, thank you. Just hospital."

She sighed loudly and repositioned the lids.

"Please. Hospital," I said as she started pushing the cart again.

"No. No hospital. Mission. Go mission." She pointed vaguely.

"Mission? That way?" I pointed. "Far?"

She waved her hand at me. I definitely took that as the universal gesture for 'go away.'

"I guess we're going this way." I heaved Daise from the sidewalk, he was lighter than he looked, and headed in the general direction the old woman had indicated. Hopefully it would be easier to find. Or we could find someone a bit more helpful.

"They'll come back," Daise said. His speech was slurred slightly. There was blood coming from his mouth, possible from a bitten tongue or broken teeth.

"The gang? We don't have anything else. They took everything."

"No. The Jane. They won't stop. More will come."

"Shit. Yeah." He was right. The Jane were not known for giving up. "We don't have anything they want either. At least I don't." I hefted him up against a wall and looked into his face. He did look a bit dazed. "What do you know? Tell me. They can't be after me. Their business with me is finished. It has to be you. Why are they after you?"

He shook his head. "They can't be after me."

"Are you sure? What do you know? You have to know something."

He pushed me away clumsily, trying to bear his own weight. "I don't know anything. I know what you know. That is all."

"Come on. You have to know something."

He shook his head, wincing at a stab of pain. "No. I promise you. I only know what you know. Nothing more."

"Shit. Come on." I put an arm around him again and together we staggered on. "We need to find out what they want."

"We need the money," he disagreed. "We need it so we can disappear."

"May I remind you a bunch of homicidal kids beat us up and stole it?"

"They will take it to their boss. They won't dare spend it themselves. We find whoever that is and steal it back."

"Yeah, I can see us doing that." Perhaps he had taken a harder blow than I thought.

As it happened the mission was not hard to find. It was the one well-lit building in the area. If anything it was glowing like a beacon, including neon strips and spotlights. Perhaps whoever ran it wanted to be sure they could be found. The Lady of Hope Mission, the large lettering above its door proclaimed. It was a broad, whitewashed building, with rows of neat windows and a tall gabled roof. It looked clean, unlike just about every other building we'd seen. I could smell cooking here too. Perhaps it was the promise of food that drew the line of people patiently waiting to get in the front door. We were seen hobbling slowly towards it.

"My brother. Here, let me help you." A neatly dressed man seemed to step out of the food queue and put an arm around me, helping me stand.

"Thanks. My friend is hurt. I think he has a concussion."

"Of course. It looks like you were injured too. We will take care of you." He whistled and waved to someone when they appeared in the doorway. Stretchers were quickly produced and we were eased aboard.

"I can pay," I said. "I have some money."

"We are a charity. We don't take payment," the original man said. He was a tall, lean man of about middle age. Well dressed with a cultured accent. He didn't seem to fit in here. "I take it you were set upon by the colourful youth we have in this neighbourhood?"

I tried not to laugh. It still hurt too much. "Something like that."

We were taken to a small hospital. It was busy. There were at least a dozen or so wounded taking up beds. Some were children. Legacy of the gun battle earlier in the day, I could only presume. I did feel somewhat guilty for my part in all of that. Whatever that part had been. Despite that we were given beds and seen to straight away. There seemed an inexhaustible supply of nurses. I had never seen such a well-staffed hospital. Even in the Tongue.

I tried to get some information while I was being fussed over. My ragged shirt had been consigned to a bin, much of my chest now bandaged and swabbed. I was lucky, my nurse told me. Some of my ribs were cracked but none were broken. No concussion, just some bruises and loose teeth. The other residents of the clinic were not so lucky. There were a few bullet wounds, from ricochets or accidental crossfire it seemed. Everyone else was a victim of shrapnel or falling masonry. No one struck by the Jane weaponry had survived. What was left of them had been taken away by the city morgue. Probably to be dumped into a pauper's grave someplace. Most of the people in this part of the city were undocumented. People no one cared about. They didn't vote and paid no taxes so they may as well not exist.

I was told the youngsters who attacked us were called the Eddies. Acolytes of the Moche, a holy man come gangster who ran most of the crime in town. It had indeed been one of his establishments the Jane opened fire on. A brothel for the more discerning, if there was such a thing. That courtyard had seemed a bit out of place, I considered on reflection. It certainly hadn't been in keeping with the rest of the neighbourhood. The young boy was known too. Rana, he was called, and I was advised to keep away from him. There were rumours that he had killed his father and brother. No one knew why, but that was the nature of rumours.

The Moche lived in a compound some kilometres from the mission. Outside the walls of the inner city, but away from the odours of this part of town. There was an army of Eddies between here and there. Daise listened intently to all of this, his own head bandaged and his eyes glazed from whatever medicine they had given him.

"You're not locals are you?" the nurse asked me as he brought a meal, seating himself between Daise and I. Which just brought home to me how well staffed the mission was. I had never heard of nurses that stayed for a chat.

"No." I stirred the broth. It came with a chunk of delicious looking bread. My appetite returned just looking at this. "We're from out east."

He shook his head as he crossed his legs. "Did you see any of that? It was a nasty business."

I hesitated. How much to say? "Yeah." No harm in admitting that. A lot of people were. "The flood. We were lucky to be on high ground at the time. It washed out the railway line." All of which was technically true.

"It's been all over the news. The Spires look a right mess. It's difficult to believe someone would do that. They're blaming the OMC. This might start a war. It's not a good time to be in the Authority."

I nodded. "No way we can win against the OMC. Not if they have weapons like that. I hear it was a nuke fired from orbit." Which of course was a lie, but then a lot of rumours were going around.

"Or some kind of plasma weapon," Daise said. "Who has those?"

"Nasty business." He said again, clicking his tongue. Nurse Avid was his name. He had been the one to treat Daise and I. He was wearing stereotypical white coveralls, so white they looked like they had been bleached that morning. He didn't seem to be in a rush to be someplace else. "And then the Jane start shooting in town this morning. Did you see any of that?"

I hesitated again. This was starting to feel like an interrogation. A good natured one, but Avid was clearly after information. "No. We were in a Hub checking on the news back east. We have family there. We heard some shooting though."

He nodded slowly. "That's lucky. One of the other patients seemed to think the Jane were firing at tourists. They sounded a bit like you. I'm glad it wasn't. Strange they missed though. The Jane are not known for missing their targets."

Feeling uncomfortable I took my time dipping my bread in the broth. It was good. My stomach was rumbling at the smell of it. "Lucky, yeah. I wouldn't want to get on the wrong side of the Jane. Mmm." I chewed on the bread. "Don't know much about them but wouldn't have thought they miss much. Not what they're paid for."

He chuckled. "Indeed not. I wonder what could have brought them to Permiset. We're not a rich city as you can see. We do tend to attract those who are running away from something though. Why was it you said you were in the city?"

"I didn't. We're headed further west. Daise has family in Cali," I said. "A sister in Alahan."

Avid nodded slowly. "I did think it odd the Eddies rolled you today. Of all days. They had their hands a bit full with the Jane. Unusual for them to take on gentlemen in the street. Their business is drugs and prostitution with a bit of a protection racket on the side. We see gang warfare from time to time. The Moche has a dispute with the Harry ... they're an organisation out of the Tops, you see. You don't work for Harlon do you?"

I shook my head. The Tops was the part of the city within the walls where the well to do lived. "No. Who is he?"

"He runs the Harry. They run guns and drugs west over the desert to the border. They used to sell to the Moche but one of them betrayed the other and they've been at war ever since. I don't know who started it, I doubt they do any more. They're brothers by the way."

I nodded, sopping up the last of my broth. "The Moche, he's the one with my money?"

Avid smiled. "You won't be seeing it again. I suggest you try winning at the dogs instead. You have better chances. They're running tomorrow." He stood, taking our bowls. "You're free to go, or you can stay the night. You're always welcome. There is a soup kitchen and hostel downstairs for anyone who needs it. We just ask there be no violence. We ask all our guests to leave their differences outside."

"Thank you. Do we owe you anything? I do have a little money left," I said.

He smiled. "No. We do not require payment for any assistance we can offer here."

"You must have some good donors."

"We only have one and she sees to all of our needs." He nodded his head politely. "Gentlemen." And with that he left us.

"He was after information," Daise said as soon as we were alone. "He thinks we're involved."

"We were."

"We don't know that. We don't know what's going on here. I suggest we get our money and get out of here."

"My money do you mean? From a gangster who has an army of thugs. That sounds like a great plan."

"We can do it. At the very least we can have a look at his compound."

I shook my head and leaned back. He was welcome to go have a look if he wanted. My plan was ... what was my plan? To sleep now. Tomorrow would take care of itself.

You know the one thing I have learned in life: whenever I decide it will be ok, that I should just go with it, it never was.

Chapter 10

I watched the sun rise over the De-Sonna dog racing stadium. From the roof. From the top of a spotlight gantry.

What the hell?

Daise could be pretty persuasive when he wanted to be. He managed to convince me to at least survey the Moche's headquarters in the event there was an obvious way of getting inside without being seen. I remember pointing out we didn't know who had my credit chits, we were just presuming he did. The boys might have kept them for themselves. It was a lot of money after all. And even if they had handed them over, we didn't know the Moche hadn't immediately emptied them out. And even if he hadn't, and had them secured someplace, we didn't know where that was. And even if we did, the chances of us getting to them were infinitesimal as he would keep them locked away. Possibly guarded. See the point above about them holding a lot of money.

Still, here we were. I don't really remember what he had said to convince me to be honest. It must have been good.

The gantry wasn't very large, it only added a few metres to our elevation. In fact the stadium itself was barely worthy of the name. The track was an oval of beaten clay with a hodgepodge of stands collected around it. Some were simple affairs of poles supporting planks. The odd plank actually missing. Others were grand old affairs harking back to a far more opulent past. Colonnades and balconies with private boxes on each side. Someone had started whitewashing them, as two of the buildings furthest away from us were gleaming. They clearly had yet to finish as others remained a dirty brown, the plaster cracked from too many years in the sun. The dogs would be running later. I could hear barking from the kennels someplace beneath us as breakfast was served. My own stomach rumbled at the thought. We'd left the mission long before any breakfast was served there. In fact everyone had still been asleep. We creeped out like thieves in the night. I made that point too, but here we were.

"We can get in over there." Daise pointed along the row of roofs beneath us to where one encroached on the Moche's stronghold. Its own roof was barely a metre beneath it, an easy jump.

"We can't stay here long," I said. "When it gets light they'll see us up here."

He didn't acknowledge my concern. "We can do it. All we need is a distraction. We need to get all his thugs looking elsewhere. I'd prefer if they left the compound entirely."

I sighed. I was being pulled into something again. That seemed to happen a lot with Daise around. I studied the roof below, tracing the route we would have to take. I could do it, I decided. The roof looked sturdy enough. There was also a balcony near the roof on the compound's side. Some kind of guard post perhaps. It was empty now. We could get to it from the compound's roof quite easily.

The Moche's compound was an ancient palace of sorts, perhaps dating back to the time of the Lafeyette kings. The dog racing track was probably built on what had once been one if its gardens. The palace itself had been a beautiful structure. Sweeping marble arches and walkways, almost delicate towers and halls. Domes and minarets reached into the night sky. The marble itself was a mixture of white and pink, certainly not local stone. That glory had faded somewhat over the centuries. Red brick structures had been built leaning up against the marble edifices, creating a fortress of sorts, sealing off all entrances but for those the residents could control. The marble itself was stained and dusty, losing a lot of its former glory. Apart from where the racetrack encroached on it tarred roads ran along each side of the compound. Keeping the nearby buildings at bay. The only exception was its far side - from our perspective, its eastern boundary. That was part of the original palace and it leaned precariously over the Tarb River, the wide watercourse that fed into Lake Iger, its origins deep in the continent's hinterland. A navigable watercourse for hundreds of kilometres, along which trade had been moving for centuries, one of the reasons Permiset had been established here. There was a private dock there, a rear entrance of sorts for whatever satrap or noble had once lived here.

This area of the city was brick and native stone. Certainly not as grandiose as the precincts within the city walls it was nevertheless not without a charm of its own. Well to do tradespeople lived here. They had built compounds of their own, square and oblong buildings two or three storeys in height, each with its own private courtyard in the centre. A piece of serenity in the middle of a bustling city. Their external walls had few windows or balconies, those were reserved for the inner spaces.

Our vantage point did allow us some visibility inside both the Moche's compound as well as some of the nearby houses. We were not high enough to get more than a glimpse of interior spaces. It was a sufficient view to show that the compound was impossible to get into undetected, however, even at this time of the morning. There was too much activity. Guards and other hanger's on seemed awake at all hours. Perhaps, due to the illicit nature of his business, this was their busiest time. The odd vehicle, some of them heavily laden trucks, came and went through the main gate. A brick monstrosity with stout wooden doors. A simple blockhouse with a big gate in the middle leaning up against the halls alongside. The structure utterly devoid of any of the artistry visible elsewhere in the old palace. Guards searched each vehicle before allowing them entry. They were all armed. I could just about make out the river from here, and had noticed river traffic approaching the wharf behind the building. Trade was good, it appeared.

"There's about sixty or seventy of them," Daise said. "Half look to be armed guards. The rest ... who knows. Family maybe. Household staff. I can't tell where the Moche's quarters are. If I were to guess I'd say in that back building over there." He pointed to one of the original buildings. A majestic spire that towered over the rest. Only the lower floors were lit. Perhaps the Moche allowed himself some rest at night.

"There's no way in," I said. "Presuming the chits are even there. We're wasting our time."

"Not through the front door no-"

"You suggesting we climb that?"

"No. No." He shook his head. "You might be right. As things stand we can't get in there."

"As things stand?" I looked down to the dog track below. "Meanwhile we did have another suggestion."

"I think he was being sarcastic. In that we have a better chance at the races."

"He might have been onto something," I commented.

"Shit. We need to buy passage out west and we can't do that with what we have."

"The Jane are out west too." I shifted my weight slightly, these poles were not very comfortable. The gantry swayed and creaked under me.

"They're not looking for us out there."

"We didn't think they were looking for us here."

He said nothing, turning back to studying the compound. "We need binoculars."

"Shit." I started descending the scaffolding. It was harder than getting up had been. It wobbled alarmingly, some of the bolts had sheared off due to the accumulation of rust. Metal creaked as the whole structure leaned suddenly. Even though some were cracked with age I was glad to be back on relatively solid roof tiles. "The dogs, Daise. Let's give the dogs a try." It was that or get a job. Or take up crime. I didn't look back as I headed towards the ground.

We had my 6000 credits and that was all. He was relying on his army pension, he told me. It would be a few weeks before the next payment came through and in the meantime he was broke. He had mentioned something vague about having to pay someone off to get my location when on the Spires. I didn't know how true that was. Still, I could barely argue. He had saved my life after all.

6000. I could make a few small bets when the racing started. Spread the risk a bit. Still, that was not a way to make money, it was only a way to lose money. I was willing to give it a try because I wasn't going to get anywhere with such a small amount of money, so losing it wouldn't make our lives much worse. I may as well be as broke as ... well... Daise.

"OK. So let's do this scientifically," Daise said. He had climbed down and followed down the stairs. I hadn't been paying attention. "There's a Hub outlet here. Let me at a terminal for a while. Do some research."

"Research?"

"To make an educated guess. Choosing a winner is a science you know."

"What do you know about the races?"

He shrugged. "I've done a lot since we were in school. We've both learned some things. You didn't know how to drive a tractor back then, did you?"

"The army does teach some strange skills. I remember the Skinner twins beating you at dice every single time," I observed. "You were never any good at gambling. But sure. They have a coffee shop. I could do with some."

"It wasn't every time."

We had to wait some as it was still early. The Hub and coffee shop opened at ten. I was the first inside, purchasing a paper cup of insipid coffee. It tasted like they had reheated leftovers from the night before. I didn't care, I needed the caffeine. Racing started at twelve so I joined my companion at a terminal. He busied himself checking who was running, which kennels they came from, their trainer and their bloodline. He was being very thorough, I had to give him credit for that. I couldn't say how any of it would help though. As far as I was concerned winning at the dog races came down to nothing but luck. Daise tried to explain his methodology to me but I didn't find it interesting. I might have fallen asleep.

At half past eleven he had a short list written down on a scrap of paper. He shoved it over to me. "This is a good place to start."

I ran my eyes down it. "Well, this isn't going to work, now is it?"

"Why?"

"Well, you have me laying bets with the proceeds of previous races. What if we don't win them?"

He shook his head impatiently and took the list from me. "Look, you place your bets with the track side bookies. Not at the windows. They're all gangsters but you get the best odds from them. The dogs don't always have to win, as long as they place we're good."

"There's a reason you get better rates from them. They break your legs if you don't pay up."

He waved away my concerns and handed the list back. It occurred to me there was a reason I was being asked to place the bets and not him. That way it was just my legs that got broken. I might have insulted him under my breath at the thought. If he heard me he didn't react.

The track was getting busy. There was a carnival atmosphere. The food vendors were out, taking advantage of the crowds. There was even the odd street artist. Musicians mostly. I stopped to watch a contortionist for a moment, only pulled away when Daise insisted we move on. We needed to find the best odds, he said. They could change from moment to moment so we needed to pay attention.

The trackside bookies all had chalkboards up, showing the odds they offered for the various dogs. Most had a small crowd gathered about them, shouting excitedly. Part of the tradition, Daise suggested. It didn't make sense to me. I elbowed my way to the front and made some bets. Within minutes we were 5000 credits down with nothing to show for it but for some scraps of paper with illegible squiggles on them. The only thing making them look official were the stamps each bookie applied to them before handing them out.

"I don't get the independent bookies," I said to Daise. "How can they offer better odds than the official betting booths?"

"Tax," he said as he led me to a good vantage point on a nearby stand. It wasn't a grand affair but at least it looked sturdy and had a roof on it to keep the sun and rain off us. "The trackside bookies aren't regulated so don't pay tax. They just pay for their spot on the track. Lower overheads make better odds. Here. Here's good."

"They have to pay for the guy with the bat, though."

He shrugged. "Have you seen them? They do that themselves."

I could appreciate that. Most looked like thugs. Which made me nervous all over again. There were two outcomes. We lost, and owed them a lot of money. Or we won, and they owed us a lot of money. I didn't know which was worse. Perhaps we were being a bit naïve.

I must admit, the excitement was infectious. I was soon standing in anticipation as the dogs were led into the boxes for the first race. Some grounds people were fiddling with the lure, making sure the mechanism worked when the dogs were released. They seemed to be having some difficulty with it. Someone in the stand started shouting at them for the delay.

There were a few hundred people here, I realised. A lot for a workday. People either had a lot of disposable income or were desperate like us, trying to make easy money on the dogs. I had seen gambling addiction destroy lives, and wondered how many of those stood around me were in that situation. Running up debt to gamble, risking their livelihoods and possibly even their lives. I doubted the bookies would take kindly to punters reneging on their bets. They were gangsters after all. They would get their money, one way or another. Slavery was not unknown in the Authority.

"I think they're starting," Daise said as an announcement echoed over the track. I doubted anyone could hear what was being said.

A shout went up as the dogs were released. The lure whirred around its inner track, pursued closely by the long-legged hounds. I thumbed through my small sheaf of receipts to see which dog we were backing. Son of Kinner for the first race, it turned out. Number 3. I squinted at their jackets as they rounded the last bend. They were quick I had to give them that.

"Hey, we're winning." I pointed. "Come on Kinner!"

Daise laughed as our dog easily outpaced the others, crossing the finish line a body length ahead of the runner up. "I told you. Didn't I tell you?"

"Shit. Yeah. How much did we win on that one?"

"Twelve thousand. Which we re-invested in race two."

"Yeah." That part had made me nervous. Betting money we didn't have yet, to a man who looked like he could easily crush my skull with one hand. He hadn't seemed concerned taking the bet even though I couldn't cover it. Perhaps people didn't cross him. Ever. I was hardly surprised.

I started feeling better when we won the next four races. Daise just smiled when I asked how he could predict it. I should just trust him, he claimed. Trust was not an easy thing for me.

I pushed my reservations aside and decided to enjoy the day. At least no one was shooting at us.

It was late spring. The day warm enough to draw a sweat under my shirt. I could smell the odd waft of putensia pollen, even though I hadn't seen any of the beautiful red trees anywhere. Perhaps they were in a courtyard nearby.

There were only a few dog racing tracks still running in the Authority as there was a growing consensus that it was an unethical sport. The Doya, a breed of long legged, short coat dogs were typically used. They were quick, bred for speed and endurance. Still, they had a short racing career, and were often abandoned or put down at the end of it. The same would happen if they suffered an injury. Pressure from animal rights groups had increased regulation over the years, which in turn squeezed profits. The closure of tracks hadn't improved the lot of the Doya, as they weren't much use for anything else. They certainly didn't make good house pets. Many had been sold as bait dogs for some of the underground blood sports arenas.

There had been a small racing track on Tellas Spires – Gerad's Spire. It was run by his father for decades until he died and Gerad took it over. I had to give Gerad credit for closing it and rehoming all the dogs. While it was open it had been popular though, drawing spectators from all over the Spires. Many had run into debt and the old man had had to mete out brutal justice to deter others doing the same. It never worked though, people still got into debt at the track. I think it was that, and Gerad's desire to look good to the people of the Spires, that had caused him to close them. I doubted he really cared about the dogs.

We were sixty thousand up when our dog lost. I groaned. That bet had been substantial. Still, we were not broke and the next race would be the decider. A hundred thousand should our dog place. Daise was confident.

"That's a lot of money if we don't come in," I said, fiddling with my fifth cup of coffee that afternoon. I was starting to admit it wasn't great coffee. It left a rather odd aftertaste. Perhaps the milk was sour. I barely noticed as someone sat next to me, a waft of aftershave filling my nose. I budged up slightly to give him room and did what every sensible person does in public: ignored him.

"It can't be easy," I continued. "Predicting the winners. If it was everyone would be doing it."

"Who said it was easy? Do you know what I had to do to increase our odds? No, let me tell you it was anything but easy. I even picked up personal diaries from trainers to see what time of day they preferred to train their dogs. The weather and where their kennels are. Just to see what conditions the dogs would feel most comfortable in."

"What? I don't see how that would help. And you're hacking people's personal diaries now?"

"It all contributes. It's working isn't it? Mostly."

I couldn't debate the results. We were winning. Somehow. And Daise has predicted it all.

"They're off," Daise said. He shielded his eyes with a hand as he squinted into the sun. The afternoon had grown old through all of this, the sun dipping towards the horizon. There were only a few more races before the meeting was done for the day. There were spotlights, as we knew well enough, but it seemed they were never used. Or more likely they were broken.

I couldn't watch and spent time studying my coffee instead. My stomach rumbled. I hadn't eaten anything all day. Coffee was not a substitute. Perhaps we could afford some food now. Unless we lost, in which case it barely mattered. A shout went up as the dogs came in.

"That is some good fortune you have there," the man beside me said.

Startled I looked up at him. "Excuse me?"

It was nurse Avid from the mission, who had treated us the night before. He was out of his white uniform, wearing a casual brown business suit instead. He smiled, pointing towards the dogs. "I see you took my advice. Although I admit I was half joking. Isn't that your dog? Casual Prince. Number nineteen?"

I checked the note. He was right. "Yes. Looks like it."

"You won. Again. In fact you've been winning all day, I understand. Apart from that small incident earlier, but who could predict your dog would slip like that?"

I smiled. "Luck. And a bit of research. How do you know who our dogs are?"

He ignored the question. "What kind of research can you do to win this consistently? That's skill that is. Or do you know something the rest of us don't?"

I glanced nervously towards Daise. He was making a point of looking elsewhere. "My friend did it all this morning. He tried to explain it but I can't say I followed it all. What brings you here? I'm sorry we disappeared last night. I hope you don't take offense."

Avid laughed. "Not at all. I would have been surprised to see you for breakfast. You looked like you had things to do. How are your wounds? Feeling better I hope?"

I paused. I hadn't thought about the beating all day. In fact I barely felt anything now. Even my swollen eye did little more than sting occasionally when a draft caught it. "A lot better thank you."

"Your ribs were cracked. I wouldn't expect to see you up and about this quickly. I hope you've been taking things easy?"

"I'm a fast healer." That didn't feel like the truth. "I'm sorry, did you come all the way out here to check up on me?"

He shook his head. "Not as such, no. You interested me so I asked a few associates to keep watch for you. Particularly here." He waved towards the track where the penultimate race was being set up. The crowds seemed thinner. Perhaps many had run out of money.

"Oh? Why's that?"

"Let us say your story interests me."

I didn't know what that meant. Daise stood and waved at me to follow him. We were finished for the day. We had enough money to last us for a while. Now all we had to do was to extract it from the bookies. I suspected they might not want to let it go.

"How so?"

"Strangers to our city, set upon by the local gangsters after being of some interest to Jane. So much so there was a firefight. That interests me."

"We didn't see the Jane. I'm afraid we don't know anything about that."

He smiled. "I don't believe that for a moment. But no matter, I suspect you are not aware of Jane's motives either."

I frowned. The first time he did it I thought it was a slip of the tongue. The second time ... there was no way it was accidental. Not *the* Jane. Just Jane. "Jane? I don't know what you mean."

"You need to go and collect your winnings. The bookies are not stupid you know. They will accuse you of cheating." He shrugged. "Even if they don't they don't like giving out such large amounts of money. They'll pay you to save face, and then pay some tough to roll you when you walk out of the arena. You'd never get away with it. I have let them know you are friends of mine though so you won't have any problems this time. Still, this was a foolish undertaking. But no matter now. Either myself or … another will talk to you at some other time. I think there is a lot to talk about." He handed over a card. "Be there in the morning. I suspect the caravan will be in a hurry so don't be late. I'll let the master know you're coming." He slipped an antique fob watch from a pocket and consulted it briefly. "If you don't get your winnings now you will lose your chance. Before you go though, you will have that opportunity to recover your belongings. There will be a … distraction. It is up to you whether you take advantage of it or not." With that he nodded politely and stood, quickly working his way away from us.

"You're not a nurse are you?" I asked his retreating back. He waved casually over his shoulder but didn't turn. He was soon lost in the crowd.

"What the hell?" Daise said.

"Let's just get our winnings." I stood and we went in the opposite direction to Avid. I didn't like being followed and there was something about the man that unnerved me.

"I don't know you. How did you win all this?" The last bookie inspected our slip suspiciously. We had spread our bets over a number of bookies so as to minimise suspicion. Our winnings with them had been far smaller than those for the last race. They had barely commented when we came to settle our accounts. This last one seemed more reticent. Possibly because he could do the math and knew how much he owed. I didn't know what effect Avid's friendship was going to have.

"Luck. Listen, I bought it from you fair and square earlier. Don't you remember … well, of course you don't. But that's your stamp right there, isn't it?"

He muttered under his breath as he took a sturdy looking chest from a cabinet behind him. He had quite a set up. A desk/billboard set on wheels which he could easily pack up in the evening when business was over. It came with a stool that looked like it could be hung from a clip on the side. Somewhere to relax in the quiet moments. One of the drawers even looked like it held a pack lunch.

"Cash only," he said, counting out some bills. I could tell he didn't like it, but he wouldn't risk his reputation reneging on a bet. Plus what did it mean for Avid to vouch for us? Who was Avid to these bookies?

"That's fine with me." Cash was good. It wasn't as convenient as a loaded credit chit but everyone accepted it.

As he was handing it over I heard a rumble in the distance, almost like thunder. I thought nothing of it until a jet screeched overhead, quickly followed by two more. I peered skywards but of course they were gone already. Then there was a thump. The ground shuddered.

"I'm gone." The bookie started throwing his ledgers into drawers as he packed up.

"I think we should go too," Daise said, pulling my arm away.

I quickly pocketed the money and followed him. I realised I hadn't counted it but other issues seemed more pressing right now. "What's going on?"

A blast of heat washed over us, knocking some of the spectators from their feet. I stumbled, caught only by Daise's sturdy hands. Someone screamed.

"We have to get out of here," Daise urged.

"What is it?"

"I think the Jane are back. And in force this time."

He wasn't wrong. As we headed out of the stadium we were allowed a view north towards the lake. There was a vehicle moving our way. Of a kind I had never seen before.

It was massive, easily dwarfing the fishing fleet that had returned to anchor earlier in the day. A steel monstrosity, easily fifty metres in width and as many in length. A dozen metres in height. Some kind of thrumming ground effect kept it levitated above the agitated water, throwing spray about it as it approached the shore. A few boats were in its way but it seemed oblivious to them, simply driving over them as if they weren't there. Its mysterious propulsion ripped them to timbers, jetting spars and netting out behind it. Each corner housed a gun emplacement. Thick barrels that swivelled to cover the shore. One of them fired. It seemed silent, issuing a flash of purple light that seared my vision. Part of the docks disintegrated, masonry and wood flung into the air as if a giant's hand had swung at it. A moment later I heard the shot. A fizz like the handheld weapons.

The behemoth grounded itself on the remains of the wharf and steel doors slammed down, revealing troops of Jane waiting inside. They wore some kind of armour. A silvery metal that covered their bodies. This time I could see their weapons. Massive lethal looking things that were attached to their metallic carapaces. Hidden motors drove them forwards as they leaped into the city. Their weapons buzzed, cutting through the fleeing citizenry.

They were shooting everyone and everything. They were taking no risks this time.

"The compound." Daise pulled me aside to get me out the flow of fleeing spectators. We sheltered behind a pillar as they surged past.

"What about it?"

"This is the distraction. We might be able to get in."

"Are you mad? Leave it. We have money now. Enough to last us until we can work something out."

"It's our ... your money. We need it more than he does."

I grimaced. "One of the chits is mine. I stole the other," I reminded him.

He shrugged. "Look." He pointed towards the compound's main entrance. Eddies were hurrying out of it. Some in vehicles, some on foot. All were armed. There was a lot of shouting going on. They were organising a defence of the city. I doubted the Moche would allow his city to fall easily. If it did his business empire was finished.

As we watched them jets shrieked overhead again, followed by more thumps as ordnance exploded. That would be the Authority Air Force resisting the incursion. The army would not be far behind. The city was about to become a warzone. I didn't want to take the time climbing towers looking for chits that might not even be there. I wanted to leave the city far behind.

"There's no one at the gate," I said.

"I'd noticed that."

I ignored him. "Well, come on then." I made my way through the crowds, trying not to be knocked over. We seemed to be going against the flow.

"Are we doing this? We're doing this. OK." He followed closely behind.

The gates were stout wooden things, usually left open, the guards stationed there vetting everyone they allowed past. There were collapsible chairs scattered about, along with a fire pit where the guards could warm themselves in winter. It was long cold now. Beyond that was a courtyard with a few vehicles pulled up into it. There were people here. A couple of workers looked like they were looting the place, loading trinkets into the back of a truck. Candelabra and silverware, it looked like. They were always the first to get stolen. They ignored us.

There was a wide staircase at the far end. The original grand entrance to the palace proper. We headed that way. The tower we guessed the Moche used as his residence was directly behind it, linked by what looked like a hall with a number of apartments flanking it on each side. What we really needed was a source of information. Someone who could tell us where we needed to go.

We hurried through the hall, past crates lined up within, the coarse wood leaving scratches on the once beautiful marble floor. Trade goods, I imagined. Guns and drugs perhaps. I did notice one crate with OBD-Cyclotron 164 stencilled on the side. Which was odd. That was part of a tractor assembly. I knew that as my tractor needed a replacement some months ago. That was a very odd thing to find here. I couldn't imagine anyone here needing one. I shook it off and concentrated on the mission at hand.

There were more stairs at the far end, just visible behind the clutter. We headed for those.

"Hey! Hey!" A diminutive figure appeared before us, a weapon in his hand. We stopped running. I knew this kid. Rana. "You? I shoot you!" He struggled with his weapon. It appeared jammed.

Daise moved quickly, pushing me out of the way and picking the boy up. Rana shouted in alarm, a string of abuses issuing from him, none of which we could understand. I relieved him of his weapon as he appeared about to swing it like a club.

"Where's our money, you little shit?" Daise demanded. He held the boy by the neck, pinning him against a pillar. Rana gurgled, unable to breath.

"Ease up a bit. Let him talk."

Rana pointed upwards, perhaps indicating the Moche's living quarters. His face was starting to turn blue.

"The Moche. He in the tower? Where are they in the tower? Seriously, Daise. You're strangling him."

"This little shit stole from us," he said. "Him and his gang beat us and left us in the street."

"I was there. I don't know about you but I'm not into killing kids. Did they teach you that in the army too?"

He relented slightly, allowing the boy to draw in a ragged breath. He still didn't let him go.

"Where exactly?" I asked him again. "In the tower?"

Rana muttered unintelligibly, still clutching at his neck.

This was a waste of time. "Why don't we take him with us?" I suggested.

"You trust him?"

"No. I don't." I studied the weapon. It looked ancient, the mechanism stiff as if it hadn't been oiled in years. It probably hadn't. It was something for Daise. Guns were more his area.

"Will you take us to our money?" Daise asked the boy.

Rana looked confused, as if he didn't really understand what was happening. He nodded jerkily.

"There we go." Daise set him on the ground. He wobbled on his feet for a moment but didn't run away. Rubbing his throat with one hand he waved towards the stairs, indicating the way to go. I noticed a red rash on his throat where Daise had picked him up. It faded slightly as I looked at it. I must admit I wasn't comfortable injuring children. Even if he had beaten us. He didn't seem the self confident thug now.

Daise took the submachine gun and we headed for the stairs. I could hear shouts somewhere in the distance as other members of the Moche's household fled the compound. When I caught glimpses of them I noticed a great many were taking valuables with them. I didn't know what had happened to the Moche that his people would steal from him like this.

The ground shuddered as we mounted the stairs. I heard glass breaking somewhere and dust filtered down from the distant rafters. It occurred to me that this building was very old, it was probably cracked and decayed. Who knew how much it could withstand before it came crumbling down?

And we were heading upwards. Up its tallest spire.

The Moche's quarters were about halfway up the tower. The building was better maintained here. Cleaner. In fact many of the original fixtures were still in place. We hesitated in sight of the broad doors to his private suite. There was still a guard stationed there. Two of them, both armed.

"Just these two? In the whole place?" I peered around the corner. They hadn't seen us yet, their attention caught up with what they could see out of a window at the end of the passage.

"The Jane. They come for Mocca," the boy said.

"What?"

"We kill ..." he hesitated, his face screwed up as if he was searching for words. "We kill Jane."

"The Moche's troops killed a Jane yesterday," Daise realised. "They won't allow that to stand."

"They come. Here. For Mocca," the boy continued.

"How do you know?"

He shrugged. "Say ... news?"

I understood. The Jane had clearly made some kind of threat against the Moche for the killing of one of their troops. I had experience of the Jane. They didn't actually care about the lives of one of their number, but rather they needed to maintain their reputation. It would not do for a Jane to be killed without repercussion. They would be severe and they would be swift. And we were stood in the precise place they were headed.

"No wonder his troops are abandoning him," Daise said. "They won't want to fight the Jane."

I shrugged. They had the day before, but perhaps they hadn't realised who they were fighting. "How do we get past them?"

Rana walked boldly around the corner, calling out to his comrades. I cursed inwardly, realising the boy had betrayed us. Daise held me back as I made a move to intercept him. There was some shouting when the guards noticed him, the three engaging in a lot of gesticulating and cursing. At least that was what it sounded like — I didn't understand a word of it.

The boy crossed to the window they had been looking out of and pointed, still talking loudly. They looked in the same direction, their backs to us. When their attention was caught he waved behind his back, indicate we move closer.

"He's on our side now?" I hesitated.

"Looks like it." Daise rounded the corner himself.

Swallowing a curse of my own I followed. We were almost upon them when one of the guards noticed our approach. He shouted and spun around, his weapon aiming quickly.

I didn't hesitate. My fingers stiffened into a blade I jabbed his throat. I felt his larynx crunch and with a croak he collapsed to the floor gasping. His companion froze when he realised Daise was aiming a weapon at him.

"Eish." Rana laughed, looking impressed. He relieved the two of their weapons and barked something guttural to them. Tonsish was the local language. I should take the time to learn it. Some day.

We entered the chambers once the injured guard was able to walk. He stared at me, clearly angry, his hands to his throat, coughing painfully. The chambers were empty. In fact they were bare apart from the odd mural or painting on the wall. The marble floor was marked as if something had been wheeled repeatedly over it.

"Where is he?" Daise asked.

"More importantly, where are my chits? Then let's get out of here." The building shuddered again then. Whatever was happening it felt closer than last time.

Rana pointed towards a chamber further in, talking animatedly. He pushed our captives ahead of us. We could hear some kind of buzzing coming from another room. Almost like the sound of a pump.

"That's interesting," Daise said.

"You understand him? When did that happen?"

He ignored the question. "The Moche is a big guy. Lives in some kind of cart. He's this way."

We found the Moche in the next room. If you could call it that. It was a wide open space, open to the air on one side. A balcony without a railing. We could see flashes in the distance from this perspective. There was fighting in the streets.

The ceiling was a complicated affair. It was a silvery convex shape made of what looked like aluminium foil. An odd contraption hung from the centre of it, almost if something was meant to be connected to it. Like a large swing perhaps. Two people were working on it. One running some kind of equipment while the other appeared to be trying to connect a cart to the swing contraption. That would be the Moche.

Rana had been right. He was not a small man. He overflowed his cart, his body seemingly made of nothing but a wide, flat slab of skin covered by a complex array of clothing. It looked like canvas. From the look of him he had not left that cart in a long time. Cushions sat him up slightly, so he was able to work on the assembly designed to connect his cart to the ceiling.

Which, I suddenly realised, was not a ceiling at all. It was the bottom of a dirigible and his companion was currently charging its helium reserves. The man was about to make his escape. Clearly he had given up on his business aspirations in the city.

The Moche noticed us and shouted angrily, waving us away. He didn't want witnesses.

One of the guards lunged for a weapon, knocking Rana to the floor. Daise fired, his own weapon rattling loudly in the enclosed space. Chips flew from marble floor and wall as the bullets marched towards the struggling pair. They slapped on flesh and the struggling stopped.

"Shit." I pushed the guard off Rana. Both had been hit. The guard was dead, his torso leaking blood all over the marble. The boy was only grazed, the shirt on his arm quickly becoming sodden. He sobbed as I pulled him away from the body.

Clearly it had all been bluster the day before. He was still a young boy at heart. I'm not sure I thought better of him for it.

"Nothing more. OK." Daise covered our captives. The second guard said nothing, still holding his throat he had backed away to a corner.

The Moche's cart whirred as he drove it at us. Daise grunted as he was knocked onto the man. Still clinging to his weapon he wrestled with the Moche, trying to drag his hands away from the controls. The Moche was strong and resisted his efforts, reversing the cart just before it hit the wall and aiming it for me.

"Shit." I scooped up one of the weapons dropped by the guards as I dodged it and trained it on the surviving guard. He had started forwards us, a hand scrabbling at a belt to remove a knife from a scabbard. We should probably have taken it from him. "Don't you-" I didn't have chance to say more before he was leaping at me, knife held out.

The machine gun went off in my hand, jumping uncontrollably as it spat out a long stream of projectiles. The guard was thrown aside, the knife skittering under the cart. I froze at that moment. Unable to believe I'd just killed someone.

"Help me, will you?" Daise shouted.

The cart had crashed into an opposite wall, almost throwing Daise off it. The pair seemed to be fighting over his weapon now, the Moche trying to relieve him of it. Both were shouting.

The building shuddered again. It was definitely closer. As I hesitated I realised I could smell smoke and hear shouting from outside the Moche's chambers. Someone was coming our way.

"Hey! Where are you going?" Daise shouted at me as I headed towards the door. He had given up trying to wrestle with the man and was holding his head down into the pillows. I couldn't see how that was a great strategy but left him to it.

There was a loud bang. Splinters of marble pulled at my clothes. I gasped as some of them drew blood. Cursing I fired wildly. The wooden door cracked and tilted alarmingly, its hinges shattered. I kicked it out of the way and fired around the corner, hoping to scare them away rather than actually hitting anyone. I saw someone duck into an alcove, something dark skittering over the floor where they had dropped it.

"Grenade!" I put my back to the wall as the building jumped. Air beat my ears. Someone shouted at me. "What?" I peered around the corner. The passage beyond was filled with smoke. I fired wildly into it, forcing anyone there to keep their head down.

The cart had stopped behind me, the Moche laying motionlessly on it, blood seeping from his nose and mouth. He twitched, proving he wasn't dead. Daise had dropped to the floor and was crawling over to me. He waved again and shouted. I still couldn't hear him. The engineer who had been working on the dirigible was nowhere to be seen. Neither was Rana.

Daise heaved himself to his feet and pressed his mouth to my nose. "We have to go!"

"How?"

He pointed to the cart and the prone man laying on it.

"Are you mad?" He clearly meant for us to hijack the dirigible and make our way out of here with that. "We're giving up on the money then?" In fact that seemed like a good idea to me. If the Jane were coming here, here was the last place we wanted to be.

He grinned and held up a simple leather draw bag. It had a lump the size of my fist in it. "Got em. And then some!"

I shook my head in amazement. I hadn't turned my back on him for more than a moment. "Is that the only way down? Where's the kid?"

He pointed to the cart, perhaps indicating some spot beyond it. "Yeah. Sorry. The other guy got knocked off the edge. Oops!"

I peered around the door again at the sound of movement down the passage. There was still some smoke hanging in the air. Too much for one grenade. Perhaps there was a fire somewhere. I sprayed more fire down the passage. The weapon quickly clicked on empty. Cursing I tossed it aside.

"OK. Time to go I think."

The Moche was awake now and waving to us. He still looked a bit dazed, but his fingers were nimbly connecting his cart to the dirigible tethers. The cart was clearly designed to connect directly beneath the envelope, a simple control mechanism lowered down to him so he could steer it.

"He's helping us too now?"

"Sure." Daise started pulling a slim cabinet line affair off the cart, making room for us.

That didn't make sense. I found Rana on the opposite side of the cart. He was disconnecting a helium feed line. Why were these two helping us?

"Come!" This was from the Moche. He reached out and pulled the boy aboard just before reaching for a lever.

"We go!" Daise pushed me towards the cart just as the building rocked again. It felt as if the Jane were simply trying to level the place. I had seen their weapons in action. It would not take long.

I allowed myself to be coaxed aboard. With a lurch the Dirigible dropped free from its cradle and we were away.

And proceeded to plummet towards the ground.

Chapter 11

"Is it supposed to do this?" I clung to the cart as the murky waters of the Tarb River drew close. The dirigible's motors were screaming as the Moche tilted them to supplement lift. They didn't seem to be helping.

"I doubt it!" Daise was hanging on alongside. "I don't think it's designed for this many people."

Rana shouted something as we headed for a moored container ship. Its steel side loomed above us.

"What?"

"Jump!" He leapt into the water.

I was close behind. It was that or we'd hit the ship. The water hit me hard, driving the air from my lungs. It was freezing and oily. Coughing I clawed my back to the surface in time to see the dirigible soaring now that the additional weight had been removed. It only just missed the ship's superstructure and then it was gone into the fading sky.

A sky that was soon lit up by a flash somewhere beyond the compound. I'd almost forgotten the Jane and their invasion of the city. Hot air washed over me. They were getting closer.

"Here!" Rana shouted as he paddled towards a wharf. Daise and I followed and we were quickly pulling ourselves out of the icy water.

"I smell like shit," Daise complained, sniffing an arm.

"It was a quick way down." I watched smoke roiling from the opposite bank. This seemed extreme, even for the Jane. But then open conflict had been sparked between the OMC and the Authority. This operation might be part of that, rather than retaliation for the death of a Jane.

Aircraft swirled overhead. Fighters, helicopters. Most of them Authority. As I watched that weird purple light flicked out, picking aircraft from the air. They simply exploded, their burning wreckage twisting into the city beneath. I don't know what effect the resistance was having on the incursion. I couldn't see much of the Jane themselves, or how far they had penetrated into the city. They seemed content restricting their forces to armoured troops. Other than the now beached behemoth they had brought no other vehicles. Working individually or in small teams they were moving quickly, engaging everything and anything. They didn't seem concerned whether some were civilian or not.

"We go," Rana said. "Not safe."

I couldn't disagree. We followed him down the wharf to the dockyards beyond. All the lights were on and the streets were filled with the civilian populace, laced liberally with soldiers who were rushing to the front. Everyone was moving. Civilians away from the fighting, troops towards it.

"Come. Come." He urged us on. We trotted into the crowds, jostled as we tried to stay together.

"We have to get to the station," I said. "We need to catch a wagon train west." That card Avid had given me introduced us to a wagonmaster. It seemed our best route right now.

"They're leaving in the morning. If they get to leave," Daise commented

"Would you stick around?" It was a long time until morning, the sun had only just left the sky.

He didn't reply to that, holding me back as a police car hurtled through the mob of people. They scattered, trying to get out of the way. Some were not quick enough. I heard more than one thump as the car connected. The car didn't stop. It was headed away from the fighting.

The sky to the north of us lit up. A flash that seemed as if the sun had re-appeared in the sky. The crowd screamed, ducking behind shelter.

The shockwave was unbelievable. It shook the ground, sucking the air from my lungs and pounding me to the ground. A wave of intense heat followed, singing my hair. I held my hands to my ears, trying desperately to protect them. I could feel blood leaking from them.

"Shit." I sat up, dazed. People were picking themselves up all around me, their mouths working but I couldn't hear a thing.

Daise shouted something at me.

"What?" I couldn't hear my own voice.

"Cruise missile!" I think he said.

It was getting serious. I pulled Rana to his feet and tried to hobble on our way. I didn't know which direction I was going. I'd gotten turned around somewhere. Someone bumped into me, throwing me to the ground again. I cursed, just sitting there not knowing what to do.

Daise pulled me up, mouthing something and pointing. I think he wanted me to keep running.

Why would anyone fire a cruise missile into a city? A city full of people. They must be mad. Or desperate. That would be the Authority then.

I saw an army truck rumbling past, its heavy wheels shaking the ground. Troops were lined up on its back, weapons held tightly to their chests. The looked scared. They wore militia uniforms, not regular army. Where was the army?

The station couldn't be far away now. I knew it was on the outskirts of town somewhere, looking like little more than a large bus shelter. Somewhere for the wagon train to turn around and load up for its return journey over the desert. I had never seen one up close, but I knew the wagons to be big things. Tires taller than I was. Steel bodies sun blistered and scarred from decades of sand abrasion. They weren't quick but once they got going it took a lot to stop them.

The crowds suddenly parted in front of us like a school of fish avoiding a shark. People were throwing themselves aside. Through doorways, behind broken-down cars. Anywhere. I couldn't see why.

Then we were upon her. A Jane.

The armoured figure strode out of a side alley. One arm with a weapon clipped to it raised as if she had been about to fire.

I just reacted. I didn't even think.

I leaped, throwing myself at her head, my fingers clawing at the underside of her helmet. Surprised she didn't have time to bat me aside before my fingers had found the clasp holding it closed. I pulled with all my strength, my fingernails ripping against the hard metal. I was aware of the sharp pain but it barely registered. It was almost as if it was distant. Happening somewhere else.

I think I was as surprised as she was when her helmet popped off. I dropped to the dusty road with it clutched to my chest. Landing badly the breath was knocked from me.

"You!" She swung on me, her weapon training my way.

I threw her helmet at her. She grunted, the hard steel ringing against her brow. She dropped to a knee, her weapon forgotten for the moment.

Cursing I picked up the closest thing I could find. A dropped wooden toy. A figurine of some kind. I swung it at her, clipping her skull again. The toy shattered, arms and legs flying, leaving me with nothing but the hard wooden torso. Clasping that in my fist I battered her with it. Swinging again and again until she collapsed to the road and lay still. Even then I kept on going. I couldn't risk her getting up again.

"Stop! Stop!" Daise took me by the arm and pulled me away. "She's done for. You can stop now."

I sat down heavily, dropping the remains of the toy. My fist was covered in blood and hair.

"Shit. You killed an armoured Jane with a Master Sergeant Toby figurine." He laughed.

"Eish!" Rana clapped his hands, dancing around the fallen figure.

"What?" I could do nothing but stare at the immobile form in front of me. It seemed impossible that anything less powerful than a tank could take down the armoured soldier. There was no way I could have done it with my hands. And a toy.

"You fucking killed her. Shit. Let's get out of here." He pulled me up and led me down the street. Dazed I followed as terrified civilians gave us space. None approached the fallen Jane either, although all stared at her as they hurried passed. They were terrified she would start moving again.

She didn't.

I felt dizzy. I barely registered the alleys Daise and Rana led me down. I seem to remember stopping at a fountain in a square while Daise cleaned the gore off me.

None of this felt right. That was all I could think about. It wasn't even really about the Jane. Well, some of it was. But it was also Rana. Why the change of heart? He went from trying to kill us to our best friend in the amount of time it took Daise to haul him against the wall by his neck. Even the Moche went from trying to run us over with his cart to helping us out of the building. Just because Daise tried to strangle him. That didn't make sense. And how had Daise chosen the winning dogs? The odds against that were mind numbing. Not to mention Daise knowing about the secret escape route from the Spires. Just in time.

It almost felt that everything became more complicated with Daise's arrival, but had it? I had held Gerad's full wright by one arm. A man who was bigger and heavier than I was. Not to mention the fact I had bested Caitlin. A killer. Ex special forces. It had been easy.

Something was wrong. Something was very wrong.

I don't remember much after that.

I had vague notions of buildings moving past. I could hear noises, voices. Shouting. None of it made any sense. Then lights. Lights and trucks bigger than any I had ever seen. Bigger than my old tractor.

I wasn't afraid though. Daise was with me and I would be ok.

Chapter 12

I awoke in a bed. It rocked slightly, jarring every now and then as if someone was bumping into it. There was a low rumbling coming from somewhere. I lay and listened to it for a long time before opening my eyes. It almost lulled me back to sleep. It was only an urgent sense I was missing something that forced my eyes open.

It was a vehicle of some kind. Almost like a bus. The sides were lined with steel bunk bed frames. Some held mattresses, some didn't. As the vehicle was quite wide there was plenty space between them. Space for tables, chairs and counters. There was the odd window, shuttered now so I couldn't see outside.

I was alone.

My shoes were on the floor alongside my bunk. I slipped them on and headed for a stair at the far end of the compartment. My legs felt wobbly beneath me as I navigated the compartment, every bounce almost tumbling me to the floor. I could see the stairs led to some kind of hatch in the vehicle's roof, and that it was open. My hand was sore where I had attacked the Jane and the odd muscle ached. But otherwise I felt fine.

There was a seating area on the roof, a railing around it preventing anyone from falling off. A canvas canopy ran the length of it, I imagine to keep the sun off when we reached the desert. There were only a few people sat there. Other passengers, I imagined. They sat in groups of two or three, talking quietly to each other. Daise and Rana were sat at the front, leaning against the railing to look back the way we had come, watching the city as we passed through its outskirts.

Daise nodded to me as I worked my way over, holding onto the backs of chairs to steady myself against the rocking. We weren't moving that fast so the wind of our passage, while noticeable, wasn't uncomfortable. Rana said something in his fast paced tongue. I had no idea what it was.

"They left early," I observed as I sat down and watched the last of the city. To the left was an area of smallholdings. Homesteads set into a few dozen acres of scrubland bordered by old stone walls. To the right was what looked like a crater. A dark pit in the landscape, lit only by a number of buildings in its bottom. Perhaps a worked-out dosser pit, I imagined. We were following a vehicle. A steel monster on massive tyres. It appeared to be some kind of freight vehicle, its back a simple steel box. Our headlights lit up its rear. It might have been painted at one time but all that had worn off over the years. I think I could see a similar vehicle behind us. All travelled in convoy barely a few metres apart. I couldn't tell whether there was a robot driver or a human in the cab, it was dark and I couldn't see inside from this perspective.

"They weren't going to hang around," Daise said. "The fighting is still going on."

The comment was punctuated by a flash somewhere to the east. So far away we couldn't hear the report. Much of the city centre was obscured by smoke. It hung over the walled inner city, lit from within by a ruddy red glow. Fires maybe. I doubted there were many street lights functional. I didn't need to ask who was winning. If anyone knew anyway.

"We had to pretty much carry you here," Daise continued. "You weren't doing so great. You better now?"

I was silent for a moment. Contemplating.

"We're lucky. Most of the other passengers didn't arrive so there is plenty of space. I gave the wagonmaster one of the chits. Not ours mind you, one of those we got from the Moche. Seems it had plenty of cash on it." He laughed.

"Who are you, Daise?"

His laughter stopped. "What? I'm Dai-"

"No. You are not. Who are you really?"

He hesitated. "I don't know how to answer that."

"Try." I watched one of the homesteads as we passed it. Its occupants were piling belongings into a ground car. The trailer attached to it was already overloaded. "How does that jewel come into it? The one I found in the Shatter? Everything started from there. It's like there's a curse on it or something. If we ever see it again you can have the damned thing." I don't believe in curses but didn't know of another way of expressing it.

"The serum. All things are related, I believe. Yes."

"Serum? OK, explain that."

"I did not lie when I said I only know what you know. That is because the serum was an enabler only. It allowed change. It held no information. We will not see it again because it was designed to be ingested. You did not know this, of course, however within minutes of it arriving in your stomach its outer shell had disintegrated and the serum contained within was entering your bloodstream."

"What does it do? Is it poisonous?" I felt a bit foolish asking that last question. If it had been poisonous I would have felt the effects by now.

"Poisonous, no. What it is is more complicated. As I said, it is an enabler. It allows your body to change at an accelerated rate. It allows you to guide those changes. It allows enhancement."

I shook my head. "Enhancement? I don't feel enhanced."

"I believe the serum was designed to be applied in a controlled environment. One where it could be focussed. Also where the subject would be aware of the implantation. Outside of that controlled environment implementation has been problematical. Your subconscious mind was aware of the changes but you were ill equipped to deal with it. You resisted. You will remember you went through a period where you dreamed every night. Disturbing dreams. That was your subconscious mind trying to accommodate information it could not understand."

I remembered the dreams. They had stopped suddenly. Then Daise arrived. "You don't exist, do you?"

He smiled. "In an attempt to accommodate the stimuli your subconscious mind entered a crisis state. To protect itself it created me. I could take on all of the new stimuli, allowing you to remain unaffected. In a sense you - your subconscious mind – created me. You created me to protect yourself."

Which didn't make sense either. I had seen him interact with people. I'd seen him interact with objects in the real world. Only a moment ago he claimed he and Rana had carried me here and put me to bed.

"How do I interact with things in the real world?" He nodded. "I know what you are thinking, remember, I am you. In a sense. Because of that I am able to make you see what I want you to see. If I want you to see me talking to someone, you see that. The same if they respond. Or if I pick something up or carry it. It is actually you carrying it, but I have planted the thought of me carrying it in your mind. Of course this is dangerous as it creates a discontinuity. A dual perception, you might say. One part of you sees you doing that thing, another sees me doing it. This causes stress. I have known for a time that ultimately this illusion will break down. We either resolve the issue to your satisfaction or you risk a psychotic break. You will be unable to differentiate fantasy from reality. Which is not ideal of course."

"You and Rana carried me here?"

"You blacked out so I took over."

I didn't like that. "So I'm talking to myself right now?"

"In a sense. Your subconscious created my persona. While you and I are ultimately one person, to all intents and purposes you have two people living in your head. You and me. And if we don't come to an accommodation we will both go mad." He smiled, as if that explained everything.

It didn't. "So Rana sees me talking to no one right now?"

"Rana sees you gazing off into space. He sees nothing."

"Shit."

"Indeed."

"And the jewel ... the serum did all this?"

"I don't believe it was intentional. I cannot say what the intention was, as I say the serum held no information at all. It was simply an enabler. Enabling you to become more than you are. However, I cannot believe what you are going through was ever intended. I suspect the new capabilities were intended to integrate with the subject in an environment where they could guide development in a controlled fashion. To what end, I cannot say. I can only speculate. I can say with a high degree of confidence that there was never meant to be two people in your head."

"Speculate, then." I wanted him to keep talking so I could think about what he had said. I only half listened. Did any of this make sense? Maybe. But it seemed very unlikely.

"Most of the capabilities are related to nerve and synapse enhancement. An increase in memory capacity and pattern recognition. I believe the primary function of the serum was to enhance the subject's intelligence. Everything else has been a side effect."

"Everything else?"

"Strength. Speed. What I was able to do to Rana."

"Hold on, now that you mention him. Explain Rana. He was trying to kill us but then he had a change of heart and is now our best friend. It doesn't make sense."

He nodded slowly. "A side effect. The serum now enhances every cell in your body. It is inside every cell. Muscles, nerves, bone, skin. In a real sense you are not exactly human anymore. But that doesn't answer the question. To put it simply I infected him. I allowed a part of me – you – to enter his blood stream. It connected to his brain stem and allowed me to influence his behaviour. It is limited but in a real sense we have colonised his body. If I allowed the serum in his body to continue unchecked he would become part of us. Part of you. Of course I will not allow that. He is a child, after all. In some respects it was an experiment. I didn't know exactly what would happen." He shrugged. "It worked. It also opens up a lot of possibilities."

"You did this to the Moche too?"

"To a lesser extent. I feel I need to expand on this. Both cases were forced on me. I had no intention of taking over other people however under the circumstances I had no choice. Rana would have raised the alarm, or at the very least tried to kill us, unless we incapacitated or killed him first. I chose what I felt was the better course."

"Shit."

"Yes. It does open up a lot of possibilities and actually might explain some things."

"I don't want you enslaving anyone. That's what you're doing. And release Rana at once."

"That might not be the best idea. I cannot predict how he will respond. I agree he should be released, but only once our ways have parted."

I didn't like that at all. No one had the right to do that to another person. This 'coming to an accommodation' might be a problem. "As long as he's released. I don't want to know what those possibilities are. It'll only mean taking people over."

"How about the Jane?"

"I want to stay as far away from them as possible."

"A notion I agree with. However we do need to know what they know, as I suspect they know a lot more than we can imagine."

I didn't really care. I didn't want any of this. I was about to say that when there was a flash in the sky. There had been flashes before but nothing like this. The whole eastern sky was suddenly on fire. I looked towards it but Daise slapped his hand over my face.

"Don't look at it. Inside!" I felt myself being dragged back towards the stairs. As we went I wondered how he was doing it. I mean, he was me. He shouted at the others to follow.

The shockwave reached us just as I was rattling down the stairs. It lifted the truck off the ground, slewing it to the side. Heat blasted at us, suddenly cut off as someone slammed the hatch closed. Clinging to the railing I was snapped around, my feet slipping on the rungs. It took all my strength not to let go, but even then I felt the railing warp under my fingers. It was not designed for this kind of strain. The vehicle fetched up against something solid and stuck fast.

I couldn't hear anything. It was as if my ears had simply given up on trying to process the sound. That didn't prevent me from feeling it though. A rumbling vibration that went on and on. Long after I had let go of the railing and slumped to the floor. I could only see a confused mess about me. The lights were out, leaving nothing but a ruddy glow coming through the slatted windows.

Daise pushed me into a bunk. "Nuclear weapon." He said. "That would be the Authority. The Jane don't need to use such things."

"I can hear you." That was confusing. I couldn't hear anything else.

"I am in your head."

Of course he was. "Where are the others? Rana?"

"They're ok. We're far enough away to escape most of the blast. This is just the edge of it. We'll have to worry about radiation later, but I think we'll be ok as long as we stay inside and keep moving. Permiset is gone though. There will be nothing left after that."

"Why would the Authority do that? It's their own city!" The rumbling had died down, leaving the truck motionless. Its motors had died. EMP, I figured.

"They were losing it to the Jane anyway."

"Shit."

He didn't respond to that. He didn't have to. "Mas, I think this was about us."

"Bugger off."

Lights flickered on as motors restarted. The truck started moving again, slowly at first as the driver gingerly avoided debris and regained the road, then more quickly as the convoy headed away from the conflagration. They wanted to get as far away from this as possible. I couldn't imagine what was happening out there. I didn't really want to. I didn't envy the drivers who could see it all.

"Hear me out. I think all of this has happened before. And I think it was all over the serum."

"Shit. I don't want any of this, Daise. I just want to disappear. I want peace and quiet. Maybe some sun and sea. I never want to see or hear of the Jane again."

"I don't think you will have a choice. They will keep on looking for you. They won't think that that-" he jerked a thumb over his shoulder, indicating the burning city "-will have stopped you. The Jane would have escaped it so you would have too."

"No choice?"

"None."

I collapsed into the bunk a bit. Defeated. "OK. Go on then. Tell me about it."

"There's evidence everywhere. You've seen the Haipi Towers? They're not far from here. Far enough from the city to escape the explosion although I doubt they would have been damaged by it anyway."

"The towers? Sure. We went there on a history trip once." There were six of them marching north to south. The shortest, at eight hundred metres tall was the northernmost spire, each successive tower a hundred metres taller. The last of them was thirteen hundred metres in height and about a hundred metres in width. Perfect tubes, tapering slightly as they rose from the ground until they were almost needles. No one knew what they were made of, but their walls were smooth and unmarked, even after centuries of exposure to the elements and enterprising individuals trying to find out what lay inside.

He nodded. "We don't know how old they are but they were mentioned in the Brokeday Tomes one and a half thousand years ago. They were there then, as they are now. We don't know what they are or what their purpose is. Or what material they are made of. No one has been able to so much as scratch their surfaces."

"So?"

"There was a war on Reaos about two thousand years ago. We know there were civilisations before that but all records of them were lost. There were no writings from those times, there aren't even any oral histories. Nothing. That past is lost to us. Yet we see ancient structures all over the world. Ships is another. The Spires. In fact the dosser pits dig up artefacts all the time. That's what they're digging up. Ancient rubbish piles, left to rot for centuries. We sift through them for discarded metals or anything else we can process into something useful."

I leaned over and tried to prize open the blinds. I wanted to see outside. They creaked and opened a few centimetres before seizing. It was enough. I could see fires, a lot of them. We were outside the city here, there wasn't much apart from scrub land and the odd tree. Perhaps a homestead here and there. All of that was on fire. In fact the glass felt warm when I touched it. Only the truck's air-conditioning system was keeping our environment bearable. It was designed to weather the high desert in mid summer. It could cope with this. For now.

There were no people out there. No other vehicles. Nothing moving but for the fire. Not that I could see far through the resulting smoke. I hoped more people had escaped. It couldn't just be us.

"So what? This isn't new information."

"No. But no one knows what happened. Or why. There have been theories but none have any specific basis. Knowing about the serum and the fact the Jane are intent on stopping anyone who knows anything about it suggests there is another theory worth considering."

"Pattern recognition you say?"

"Amongst other enhancements, yes. I have come to believe there was a war thousands of years ago and it was about the serum. Someone took it and that someone became enhanced. They are behind the OMC and the Jane. They also want to ensure no one else has access to it. They destroyed civilisation to keep it secret and are starting a war now for the same reason."

"Seems a stretch."

"It does. Until you ask how the Jane knew to look for you. And how they keep on finding you. Pattern recognition. Someone else has the same capacity."

I think I snorted then. "Someone two thousand years old? Really?"

"I'm sorry, I wasn't specific enough. I should have mentioned that you no longer age like an average human. In fact you don't age at all. Your body is able to rebuild just about any damage it sustains."

I laughed. "Yeah. OK. Some two-thousand-year-old person has taken a dislike to me. Personally. And declared war because of it."

"It's probably not personal. Although, if I am right it does present a problem. They effectively destroyed an advanced civilisation in order to protect themselves. I have no doubt they would do it again. This-" he pointed towards the rear of the vehicle, indicating the burning city, "-is just the start of it. They won't stop. Ever. Not as long as you are alive."

"So what are my options?" I kill myself? I couldn't say I was the happiest person in the world, but I had never contemplated that.

"No. We would have to kill her."

"Her?"

"Jane. I think that is her name. I believe she has influenced a great many people around her as I did Rana. I think they are all her. All of the Jane are Jane. We need to find Avid."

"The nurse?"

"He is clearly not a nurse. He clearly also knows more than we do at this point. For starters, he knows about Jane. He referred to her as such."

I shook my head. This was getting too complicated. How were we going to kill a two-thousand-year-old woman? One who controlled the Jane and probably the OMC too. One who, according to Daise, was enhanced in ways I couldn't even imagine. Me? Eli Massen. A nobody. On my own.

Well, I had an imaginary friend. Awesome.

A worrying thought occurred to me. It was believed the Shatter had been formed when two large moons collided a long time ago. That collision had ripped them apart, sending chunks of moon into orbit around Oberon. Some chunks the size of mountains, some the size of my fist. It also appeared there had been some kind of installation on one of those moons relating to this serum. I had found the jewel behind a door that looked like it had been part of a larger base, after all. A base built on one of those moons. I couldn't imagine how it had survived the collision, but there it was.

Had this ... Jane been responsible for all that? If so she had not only destroyed an advanced civilisation, she had also destroyed worlds.

Shit.

And you know what? Dying wouldn't help. She wouldn't know I was dead and would keep on hurting people.

I think Daise was still talking to me but I didn't pay any attention. Rana yanked on one of my feet, pointing to one of the windows where he had succeeded in prizing open the shutters. I didn't want to know about that either. I was too busy counting the dead. The Spires. The flood. Permicet. And that was what I was aware of. Had all that been about the serum?

I was tired and wanted to sleep. So I did.

It was daylight when I awoke. Warm air was rushing through the cabin, the hatches once again open to the outside air. I rummaged through the cabinets and found something to eat and drink. It looked like a full complement of passengers had been expected and they were stocked accordingly. Armed with biscuits and orange juice I ventured onto the observation deck again. Most of the passengers were up there.

It was hot. The wind of our passage did very little to dispel it. Around us the scrub had given way to stony ground. It was a vast orange and grey expanse that stretched to every horizon. What remained of Permicet had been left far behind us. Even the smoke of its fires no longer stained the horizon. There was a stash of goggles and bandanas for when the dust kicked up by the vehicles in front of us became overwhelming. It wasn't too bad just yet. I imagined that would change once we hit the dunes.

Rana was dozing in the shade near a railing, one hand trailing over the side to feel the passage of air. I sat alongside but left him to it. He was like the rest of us now. A refugee. His home destroyed. Although he wasn't in control of his future. Someone else was in his head.

I didn't like that. Not only because he was a child, but because I didn't think I should be controlling anyone. Even if it wasn't me consciously doing it.

I sat and watched him sleep. He wasn't a big kid, even for his age — which I guessed at about fourteen. His clothing had been expensive once. Quality shirt, trousers and waistcoat by the looks of them. Only age and a lack of proper care made them look a bit ragtag. He had a string of beads on one wrist. They looked like some kind of identity bracelet from an orphanage. Possibly the only form of identity he had left.

I couldn't imagine what had drawn him into the life of a gangster. Necessity possibly. A place where he had quickly learned it paid to be the meanest, most ruthless bastard on the block. Only they were respected. The weak were prey.

Could I blame him for what he was? For what he had done to me and Dai… well, just to me actually. I couldn't say I would have done any better had I been in his place.

Of course Daise found me. He always seemed to. But then I guess he was me so couldn't really not. If I believed any of this. He seated himself alongside me and watched the early morning sky. It was beautiful out here, if a little stark.

"We're safe here. The prevailing winds will take any fallout far from here."

"As you're in my head, do you always just say what I already know?"

"I may have observed something you haven't. And as I have perfect recall, I can use information you have long forgotten."

"So, you're smarter than I am, with a better memory. Thanks."

"That was not an insult. Remember, I am you. Your subconscious created me because it could not deal with what was happening."

"So I have a weak mind too then."

He sighed and looked away, watching some kind of scavenger bird hovering over the scrub to the south of us. He knew it was best to just leave me alone.

We remained in silence for some time, both of us watching the scenery as we passed through it. Rana awoke and joined us in silence, perhaps sensing no one wanted to talk. Perhaps lost in a world of his own thoughts.

The world was not as empty as it felt. In the late afternoon some helicopters flew over, heading for Permicet. They were the heavy transport type. I could only guess what was aboard. Aid. More troops. Who knew? An hour later a military convoy rumbled past us, also headed for the beleaguered city. Most of the passengers on the observation deck donned goggles to protect their eyes from the dust and stones kicked up by the heavy transports. Trucks carrying troops and materiel, tank transports heavily loaded with an assortment of mobile cannons and Marsen main battle tanks. The dust and noise of their passage went on for a long time. There were a lot of them. Many passengers sought shelter inside but I remained where I was. The dust of their passage had started to die down when another convoy passed. Trucks loaded with capacitors – a recharge for the various battery packs in the convoy. A few minutes after that the last convoy, this time liquid hydrogen trucks. Fuel for the tanks. They were keeping their distance. If anything happened to them, causing an explosion, they would not take the rest of the convoy with them. The rear-guard were dismounted tanks, their tractor treads chewing up the road and throwing chips of stone at our truck. One must have been quite large as it banged against the side somewhere. That would have left a dent.

It would take us four days to cross the desert, then another two to wind our way through the mountains to the border with Tondo. There was a border town there, a pleasant place called Huluu. It was a town of stone and trees, winding its way up the side of the cliffs overlooking the Sonnerdwaal River, which formed the border. It was a recent acquisition by the Authority after a border skirmish with Tonto twenty years ago left that patch of land ceded to their easterly neighbour. The residents of the town were still Tondo natives though and had no love for the Authority. They had not forgotten the occupation and the hardships they endured in the hands of the army.

I didn't know what was happening there right now. Possibly nothing, the army was being distracted by incursions elsewhere. Hopefully we could slip through and be out of the Authority forever. I'd never been to the coastal cities of Frower and De-Louisa but I understand they were beautiful places. Well maintained, verdant places, unlike the dusty industrial cities of the Authority.

Who was I fooling? The Jane would find me there too.

I needed to know what was going on in the world. Unfortunately while travelling we were out of contact. Ground vehicle based LOS was a technology no one had ever mastered, it was simply too complex an issue targeting a laser from a moving platform and reliably connecting it to a satellite in orbit. There might be the odd roadhouse between here and the mountains but I doubted we'd be stopping. The wagonmaster seemed intent on getting as far away from the city as possible. I could hardly blame them.

"We do need to come to an accommodation," Daise said at length.

I sighed but didn't turn to look towards him. "I won't be going mad."

"I do have a concern for your mental wellbeing, however that's not what I am thinking about right now. We need to make a plan as to what our next steps are."

"What do you suggest? You're the genius here."

It was his turn to sigh. "I am you. Remember, any additional capabilities I may have are due to artificial enhancement. Holding a grudge against me for it is like holding a grudge against a Hub terminal because it received your email before you did."

"That doesn't even make sense." Well, it sort of did. If I thought of Daise as some kind of machine it helped a bit. A machine I had sole access to. One that could see things I couldn't, make connections I missed. Notice details I never would. And then tell me all about it and talk me through what to do about it. A personal AI companion.

One I was stuck with who would never go away. "If I wanted peace and quiet would you leave me alone? Would you go away until I was ready to talk to you?"

"I can't see why you would want to, but yes."

That showed me how much he understood me right there. Of course I would want him to go away. "Please leave me in peace then."

"We have a lot to discuss-"

"Go away, Daise."

He disappeared, leaving me with Rana and the desert. Silence, it was beautiful. Well, as much silence as I was going to get on a vehicle crunching its way through the approaches to the Sarskin Desert. An expanse of sand and rock stretching for almost a thousand kilometres along the westerly borderlands of the Authority. Few lived there. Maybe a few An-Tarque, colloquially known as either the An or the Suffers, which meant 'desert beggar' in some local dialect. They were nomads, small bands of maybe twenty or thirty, migrating from water hole to water hole. Staying long enough to recharge their batteries using solar collectors before moving on. They had been leaving intricate, geometrical carvings across the desert for centuries. No one knew what they were for. Made of wood and scrap metal in the south, and stone where they encountered rocky mesas in the north. It was thought their ancestors had carved the Woolie Marching Band in the north. It had once been a mesa about three kilometres in length, now completely whittled down to make a diorama of sorts. Giant men and women, some twenty metres in height, all marching in a column from north to south. The detail of their clothing and facial expressions was incredible. Some even carried tools or led goats on their eternal march. A number had collapsed over the centuries, taking their neighbours with them. They were still one of the wonders of the world though.

There were indeed some strange things in the world. The Circular Falls of Rohar, for example. Named after the Rohar Plains where the river wound its circuitous path, over the odd fall and rapid, only to end where it started. Impossible, you would say, and you would be right. Water flowed downhill, obviously, so how could it return to its starting point? The speculation was that there was some hidden mechanism in the river's bed, driving it against the forces of gravity. A mechanism no one had ever found.

Sable Tower was another. It was essentially a tower so tall it reached out of the atmosphere and connected to a moonlet that orbited Reaos above. It was little more than an asteroid really, captured by the planet's gravitational pull a very long time ago. It was perfectly in synch with the rotation of planet, so much so that it remained still in the sky. Still enough for someone to build a tower to it. The material of the tower was unknown, and seemed as impregnable as that used to construct the Haipi Towers themselves. It was said some odd constructs had been found attached to it at some time in the past. As if it had been used as an elevator tower in a time long lost to the history books. They were no longer there, but the Horscht Collective military engineers had taken the opportunity to build elevator carriages of their own. Connected by powerful electromagnets they hurtled up and down it, delivering freight and passengers to Sky City. It was the route I'd used to leave Reaos on my way to the Tongue. I remember the city built in space where the tether connected to the moonlet. Reaos parked firmly in the sky overhead, easily visible through the gigantic domes built into its grey surface. A million people lived and worked there. A glistening city in space. That seemed like such a long time ago.

Daise claimed there had been an advanced civilisation on Reaos once. A prosperous, cultured world that had colonised many of the other planets in the system. A civilisation destroyed two thousand years ago. Leaving our ancestors struggling to rebuild all they had once known.

Destroyed by the Jane? No. By Jane.

I don't know. There was clearly evidence of a prosperous past, one that had long been lost to us. But that was the point: it was lost to us. How could we know what had happened? And if Daise only knew what I knew, how could he possibly know? Because I certainly didn't.

I pushed the thought aside. I was never going to get anywhere with this. Perhaps I would find Avid again one day, the nurse who was not a nurse, and he could explain some things. Presuming he was still alive, that is. I imagined he had escaped, though. He had known about the invasion before it happened, after all. I didn't think he would have been caught out by the destruction of the city. And it was also presuming he knew anything. If no one else did, how could he?

At our accelerated pace it took us three days to reach the foothills. The air was cooler here, allowing more verdant flora to survive. A relief after days lost in an empty expanse of sand. Daise didn't make an appearance in all of that time. I was glad of it, spending my time talking to Rana, learning his tongue as he learned mine.

An hour after we entered the foothills we drew into sight of a tunnel entrance and headed straight for it. It was pitch black inside but the convoy didn't faulter for a moment. In we went.

This was different.

Chapter 13

"Stop! I want to get out!" Rana banged his fists against the rear door. The lock was controlled by the driver who wasn't about to open it. In all these days of driving we hadn't seen nor heard from him at all. The boy wasn't going anywhere unless he hurled himself from the top deck.

"What's the matter?"

"We shouldn't go in there. No one ever comes out. Not ever." We were learning each other's language and were both becoming pretty fluent. I had learned a lot about him, a lot of it surprising. For example, he hadn't murdered his father and brother at all. It was a lie told by one of his opponents in the gang, an older boy who saw Rana as a threat. Rana broke his legs in a fight, hitting him with a plank, which was why he came to lead his pack of gangsters. He'd clearly impressed someone.

I mounted the ladder to the top deck to see if I see more of the tunnel from there. I couldn't. The truck's lights revealed nothing but the stone walls enveloping us. That stone continued on in both directions, to the front where the trucks in front of us lit it up, and behind us where the entrance was growing smaller behind the one truck following us. It was a big tunnel. Easily large enough to fit the vehicle we were on with quite a lot of space to spare. "The caravans use this tunnel all the time. It's safe. It looks like we're cutting out the passes. The trip will be a lot shorter this way."

He shook his head. "It isn't a tunnel. It's a ... " his face screwed up as he searched for the word. " ... more than one tunnel. Lots of tunnels. We get lost."

"A maze?"

He pointed at me. "Yes! A maze. No one ever comes out."

"People come here?"

He shrugged. "The Moche sent people in. Years ago, before I was born. About two hundred of them. Pft – none came back."

"There has to be a way through. I doubt the caravan master would take this route if it wasn't safe."

"I don't like it. We should try make them stop."

"What? The whole convoy? How do you plan on doing that? Do you know the route around?"

He slumped into one of the seats and stared at the entrance as it vanished behind us.

"I've taken this route three times before," Pavella said. "We always come this way. It's safe, I assure you." She was one of the other travellers we had become acquainted with. She was quite a large woman in her fifties, her girth almost twice mine. A trader of some kind from Cali, she claimed. I didn't know what kind of goods she traded in and didn't ask. Particularly because she used the caravans while there were flights that could make the trip in a fraction of the time. She would only do that if whatever she was trading in was illegal. She seemed friendly enough though, chatting to Rana and I to while away the hours.

"I doubt we have a choice anyway." I seated myself and watched the tunnel passing by. It was pretty unremarkable as tunnels went, apart from its considerable girth. It was humid in here though. Not uncomfortably so. There was also an odd smell, almost as if the air tasted metallic. So far there was just the one passage with no turnings or junctions. "How far does it go?" I asked Pavella

She shrugged. "All the way, I think. We're in it for a few days. It's hard to tell the passage of time underground." She smiled. "There are some side passages but the driver knows where to go."

"There." I said to Rana. "Nothing to worry about. This is better than going up top. It's cold and windy up there."

To be honest I was not looking forward to spending a few days down here. There was nothing to see and nothing to do. The caravan hadn't stopped yet, and I doubted it would now. We couldn't even signal the driver to get any information from them. A security precaution, Pavella had claimed. This way no one was could hijack the caravan. She didn't say as much but suggested it had happened in years gone past. Once you were aboard and the vehicle started moving you were there until it stopped again. Unless you jumped off the roof. It was a long way down.

We hadn't seen any other road users since that one military convoy. There had been a few aircraft but overflights had died down a bit in the last few days. Whatever had happened to Permiset was over now. The Authority's attention was being drawn elsewhere.

I had noticed a flash in the sky above us on the third night. An explosion of sorts or so it seemed. It had to be pretty big if we could see it from the ground. It was silent and went as fast as it appeared. Explosions were short lived in space where there was no way for a fire to smoulder on afterwards. A station attack perhaps. Sullo Terminal would have been in that part of the sky at the time. Perhaps someone had attacked it.

Sullo Terminal. How had I known that? Of course I knew what stations were up there and vaguely understood their orbits, but certainly not in enough detail to predict which station it could have been. Daise — I decided. Even though he was no longer talking to me he was still there, supplying information.

Life had almost been peaceful without him. I was happy for that peace to continue.

Rana didn't really settle. He paced a lot, walking to the front of the cabin to touch the old, dented wall. Then turning to walk to the rear of the compartment, touching the firmly bolted door. Then turning around to do it again. The passengers we shared the space with ignored him. I think they were scared of him. Even though he seemed to have decided he liked me he didn't like anyone else. One of the older passengers, a grey haired man by the name of Gwent, had accidentally picked up his biscuits a few days back. Rana accused him of stealing them, and launched himself at him, seemingly with every intention of beating him to death. Some of the other passengers and I had to drag him off. Still, Gwent was left bruised and battered. That night I overheard the other passengers debating throwing him off the truck. They simply couldn't trust him. Ultimately they didn't. I think because they couldn't take both of us on.

We started passing turnings. Black chasms that opened up the rock wall to either side of us. Leading who knew where. The column ignored the first few before turning into one of them. A new passage that looked exactly like the old. Then we turned again and again. The air growing staler as we went. It had been in here for a long time, stirred only by the passage of a column like ours.

It grew late and the others went to sleep. Most had chosen a bunk as theirs and stuck to it. As there weren't that many of us aboard people could pick and choose, leaving a bit of space between occupied bunks. I picked my way through the darkened compartment to find Rana. The lights had been turned off for the night – not that we could tell the time of day by looking out of a window. He was topside, swinging his feet off the rear of the vehicle.

"Get some sleep. It's late," I said.

He shrugged but said nothing.

I sat alongside him, trying to shield my eyes from the glare of headlights from the truck behind ours. I didn't have anything to say and didn't really care about sleep myself so I just kept him company. I couldn't help but wondering how much rock was above our heads. The tallest mountain here was Mt Sullander at just over four kilometres in height. That was a lot of rock. I was surprised none of these passages had collapsed in the hundreds of years they had been here, resisting quakes and the slow pressure of tectonic movement. The way we were driving the lead vehicle must be confident we wouldn't come across a blockage as there was no way the column could stop in time.

I was considering that when the light from the vehicle behind us moved to the side and disappeared. They had taken a turning we hadn't. Cursing I stood and looked down the side passage but it had already gone. I saw a glimpse of tail lights in the gloom then nothing.

"They turned off," Rana said, staring at me as if I had some explanation.

"Aah, they didn't. We did." I'd noticed the trucks ahead of us were gone too. We were alone in the darkness. The vehicle's pace had not slackened. This wasn't an accident.

Rana ran to the front and peered into the darkness before us. All he could see in the light of the truck's headlamps was more tunnel leading into the distance. Dark tunnel as far as the lights could reach. He banged on the roof of the cab but of course there was no response.

"We must stop," he said. "We need to join the others."

"I think we're stuck going where the driver wants to take us." Except I didn't want to be stuck. Not down here. Not when this could all be a mistake and the truck was about to take us on a neverending journey under the mountains. Around and around until the power cell ran out. I started banging on the roof too.

"What's going on?" Pavella joined us on the roof. "Why are you banging?"

"Notice something missing?" I pointed ahead of us.

She swore and started banging too. The others quickly joined us and added to our efforts. As expected it did nothing.

"Shit. This isn't helping." I crossed to one side and leaned out as far as I dared. I still couldn't see anything inside the cab. The windows were tinted, probably as protection against the glare of the desert. Down here it was enough to stop anyone looking in. If the driver was aware of our consternation they weren't showing any sign of it. If there was a driver in there and not some computer simply following its programming.

Holding onto the railing I swung my legs over it and eased my way down the side of the cab. The wind buffeted me here, trying to push me off the side of the vehicle. Wondering why I was doing this my toes found a ledge.

"Where are you going?" Pavella leaned over the edge.

"I want to see if I can get into the cab."

"You are a crazy bastard, you know that?"

"Yeah." I knew that all right.

There was a ledge running along the bottom of the cabin. It was wide enough for me to set my feet onto, allowing me to let go of the railing. It was a bit of a drop but I risked it. There was a small gap where the passenger cab joined the drivers'. It was wide enough to slide my fingers into for balance.

"Shit. You're not crazy, you're insane," she muttered as I slid down the cab's side.

I still couldn't see in. I wiped some dust from the window but it didn't help. There seemed to be no light coming from the inside of the cab at all. Worst of all there was no door handle.

"Aaah, this isn't a door!" I shouted up to the spectators above me.

"What?"

"There's no door!" I ran my fingers around the window and the weather-beaten metal on either side. There was no join where a door should be. Nothing but for more pitted, half painted metal. There was no handle either. Which presented me with a problem: how was I going to get back up?

"There has to be a door. How does the driver get in?" She called.

"Maybe there isn't one!"

"Don't be silly. Even tractors have drivers and look how easy that is. They're in space!"

I laughed at that. Yeah, sure. I banged on the window, trying to attract the attention of whoever was within. If there was anyone inside they did not respond. The motors continued driving the vehicle forward without interruption. Their low moan seemed to reverberate off the walls. If there was someone in there they didn't care about my antics.

I swore a bit then.

It was possible the door was on the other side. There would only need to be one after all. Or perhaps underneath, I realised. There was enough clearance beneath the truck for it to be accessible from beneath. There may be a ladder and a hatch. There was no way I was going to gain access to that while we were underway.

"Bloody good idea this was, Mas." As I said it the truck went into a dip, abruptly heading downwards. My feet left the shelf, lifting into the air for a moment. Shouting in alarm I scrabbled at the side of the cab, trying to gain purchase. There was none to be had. When my feet came down again there was no shelf beneath them.

It was quite a fall.

I cracked my head on the shelf on the way past. Then I hit the ground. Hard. My knees came up to my jaw. Pain filled my vision with stars. I think it was only reflex that made me roll on the dusty floor, avoiding the rear wheels. The massive tyres missed me by millimetres.

I lay there, lost in hurt, unable to move. My feet, knees, chin, head … everything … was ablaze with agony. Everything felt broken. My legs definitely were. This ground was solid stone.

"Get up," Daise said.

"Fuck off." I curled into a ball, trying to keep the pain at bay.

"Get up. You cannot stay here."

"My legs are bloody broken!"

"It doesn't matter. The truck will leave you behind and even I can't get you out of here. You have to get back on board."

"Shit." I cursed him, watching the rear lights of the truck growing smaller. It had continued on its way, oblivious of me laying on the ground behind it. "I can't run with broken legs. Bloody idiot."

"Get up." I felt hands lifting me. The pain was tremendous. I think I almost blacked out. The hands didn't give in to it. They just kept on pushing. "Go."

I could feel bones moving in flesh. There was no way my legs could support me.

But they did.

At first I hobbled, doubled over in pain. Blood running into my eyes, obscuring what I could see of the receding taillights. Then I was walking. The pain was still there but my feet felt steadier. Walking wasn't going to be enough. The truck was moving far too quickly. It was almost out of sight.

Somehow, unbelievably, I was running.

I cried out from the pain. I couldn't tell whether it was blood or tears dripping from my chin. Probably both.

"Shit this hurts."

"Keep running. Faster. You have to catch up."

"Go away!"

"Faster!"

I screamed, forcing my legs to move as quickly as they could. I don't know if I was imagining it but the truck seemed closer. It vanished for a moment as it went around a bend. My scream faltered as I panted. I needed to conserve my energy for breathing.

I misjudged the corner and collided with the wall. Gasping I collapsed to the ground again, legs and arms twisting around as I rolled through the dust. There were some rocks here. My aching head collided with all of them.

I sat for a moment, staring at the rear of the truck. It was drawing away again.

"This isn't getting you back to the truck."

"Asshole."

Groaning from the pain I hobbled back to my feet and started after it again.

"Here. Let me help you."

I don't know what he did. I didn't want to know. The pain vanished, replaced by a vague sense of euphoria. The ground wasn't hard anymore. It just seemed to glide. My legs moved over it effortlessly. Air rushed about my ears, turning into a roar. The taillights grew larger. I could see people on the deck above watching me running after them. I could see them waving at me but couldn't hear a thing.

I leaped. Hands grasping the railing as I sailed over it. I might have bounced off the underside of the canvas awning before rebounding onto the deck.

"That wasn't a good idea, Mas." Someone said.

"Did you see that jump? Shit." That was Rana.

I decided to lay there for a while, my body aching. Now that I had regained the truck Daise seemed happy to allow the pain to come flooding back. He could have kept it, thank you.

Hands pulled me up and sat me in one of the chairs. I was dimly aware of Pavella fussing over me, checking my wounds. My bones were already well on their way to healing and the bruises had almost faded. Which of course was impossible and she said as much. I didn't care. I pushed her hands away and hobbled down the ladder to find something to eat and drink.

I was well aware this was impossible. It couldn't have been more than half a minute between hitting the ground and when I was sprinting after the truck. Bones did not heal that quickly. I knew they had been broken. I'd heard them snap.

I wasn't going mad. Daise had been right, I was changing, and those changes were significant. I might be able to ignore Daise and tell him to go away, but that didn't change what was happening to my body. I could feel it now, almost as if the serum was reacting to my environment. It was like an itch in my muscles and tendons. My skin growing warm as if I had contracted a fever. My body was growing tougher. The serum was learning, reacting to the challenges I faced. When my physical environment became hazardous, it made me stronger, faster. When I faced difficult decisions Daise arrived with all the answers.

More than that it was quick. I had felt it when I was chasing down the truck, muscled growing far stronger than they ever had been in a matter of moments. Strong enough to catch a vehicle quickly leaving me behind, and then to vault back onto its deck. It had to be more than fifteen metres from the ground. Shit. No wonder the other passengers were looking at me, whispering to each other.

If I wanted to I could hear them.

"Did you see that? He jumped right onto the roof!"

"No way. There's no human in the world could jump that high."

"I saw it, Pheny. I bloody saw it with my own eyes."

I blotted their voices out. I didn't want to hear them. Instead I fixed a meal quickly, my stomach rumbling as if to encourage me to work faster. I was ravenous. Clearly I had expended a lot of energy healing and then getting back on board and my body needed to recoup it. Porridge. Not terribly tasty but it was nourishing. I made enough for five and quickly finished it off. I wanted more.

"Who are you? What are you?"

I turned to find a small crowd had gathered behind me. They were led by Teoni Hayser, a bear of a man who, I vaguely remembered, had bullied his way onto the truck while we were readying to depart. He didn't have a ticket but that hadn't stopped him. Memories of that time were blurry, but I did remember him being armed. A big handgun I could see in his belt right now. His hand was not far from it. The others stood behind him, giving him confidence but keeping him between us. I think they were scared.

"What's it to you?" I popped open a tin of mixed fruit and scooped some out with a spoon.

"I'm not sharing this ride with some ... freak!"

"I think you should keep your distance, my man." Rana had seated himself alongside me. He had a knife in his hand and was casually testing it against a thumb.

"You and your thug sidekick don't scare us." And, of course, he reached for his gun.

I have never seen someone move so fast in my life. Before he could even touched the hilt Rana had snatched it from his belt and sat down again to study the weapon. It was the strangest thing I had ever witnessed. The boy was fast. Faster than I could have believed possible.

Startled Teoni stepped back, staring at the boy. His hand fluttered at his belt, as if unable to believe it was no longer there.

"Do you want it? Why don't you take it then?" Rana suggested.

"What ... what are you?"

"No?" The gun looked huge in the boy's hands. It was a massive black revolver, the barrel so big he could probably fit one of his fingers into it. He had no trouble holding it steady.

Rana seemed to sense my disapproval. He glanced at me and shrugged. Instead of threatening the man he proceeded to strip the weapon down, removing the thick cartridges and slipping them into a pocket. That done he tossed the gun in the direction of the startled Teoni. The man dodged it, allowing it to crack against a bunk somewhere behind him.

"Stay away from us," Rana advised.

I had continued eating fruit through all this, tossing the empty tin into a bin when I was finished. Of course Rana had some of the serum in him, I realised. Enough to make a difference but not enough to make him like me. I hoped.

Daise claimed to be able to influence his actions, I remembered. As an experiment I decided the bullets he had in his pocket would be better tossed off the back of the truck. I leaned back on my bunk and wondered if anything would happen.

I hadn't finished wondering that when he stood and headed for the stairs. And even as I continued to wonder whether it was all a coincidence or whether he was actually going to do it I realised I could see him walking up the stairs onto the deck above. From his perspective. I felt him dig the bullets from his pocket and casually toss them off the truck. They vanished into darkness instantly.

Shit.

I rubbed my brow and tried not to watch him walk back to me. I could feel a vague sense of confusion. Confusion as to why he had decided to discard the bullets. It was coming from him.

This wasn't good. I didn't want this at all.

"We didn't need those anyway," he said, more to himself than me.

Is this what it was like? Being in someone else's head. And, according to Daise, this was possible multiple times. Thousands of times. How many Jane were there? Was Jane in all of their heads? I couldn't imagine that. And more than that, according to my strange friend, she had been there for thousands of years.

It didn't bear thinking about. Not now anyway. Perhaps Daise was the one I needed to discuss it with. I could sense him there, eager to talk to me. I denied him. I didn't want it. I didn't want him. I didn't want Rana. I didn't want any of this.

I lay down and went to sleep.

Chapter 14

We drove for what felt like days but was probably only eight or nine hours. The passage of time was impossible to judge in the tunnel. If there were any clocks around I had not seen them. I slept through some of it, the remainder I spent on the top deck, watching darkness. Trying not to think of anything at all. Even Rana knew to stay away from me.

We passed through some kind of cavern at one point. The walls of the tunnel melted away, leaving nothing but darkness around us. We could see the path continuing before us but nothing else. It felt damp in here. Cooler also. We soon found out why.

Dark water crept in on either side until we were on a narrow causeway over a subterranean lake. We splashed through the odd ford but it never came up above the truck's axels. The vehicle shuddered slightly as it struck the water but then forged on.

I leaned over the railing and looked upwards, wondering what was up there. Of course I could see nothing. The headlights simply couldn't reach that far.

And then we were in a tunnel on the other side, the rock swallowing us up again.

It wasn't long after that that we stopped. It took me a moment to realise it had happened. I was simply too accustomed to our eternal movement. I stood and walked to the front of the truck.

There was a stone door ahead of us. A thick wedge of a door that was slowly lumbering open, swinging wide to allow the truck through. There was light and movement beyond. I could see people and vehicles. Ground cars far smaller than the truck. They seemed to be arranging themselves to await our approach. One line of vehicles on each side of the path.

Once the door had completed its swing the truck eased forwards slowly, passing through the portal to those waiting within. It didn't go far, simply joining the other vehicles in the wide open space beyond the door, where it slowed to a stop again. This time it felt more permanent. We had arrived.

There was a clunk behind us as a mobile stair was attached to the back of the truck. The door groaned as it was eased open, allowing in a wash of humid air. No one entered, they seemed content waiting for us to exit.

"What do we do? We're not supposed to be here," Pavella said. "Is this a kidnap? I doubt any of us have any money."

As far as I was concerned they could have the Moche's bag of ill-gotten credit chits. I doubted that was what this was about though. They were either Jane or ... I didn't know who. I didn't think they were Jane, that organisation was not known for this level of subterfuge. They would have picked us up in the middle of the desert. Swooping down with that lumbering fortress of theirs to intercept the column. They wouldn't care who saw it and no one would have been able to stop them.

"It is safe. You can disembark," a woman's voice came from the cavern outside the door.

I stood and headed to the door. The others didn't move. I suspect they were happy for me to take the risk. The groundcars had their lights aimed towards the truck, concealing the people standing around them with their glare. I shielded my eyes as I stood just within the door. A woman was standing at the foot of the mobile stairs. She seemed eerily tall and slender with wavy hair. It seemed to move of its own accord in the still air.

"Come. Join us." She raised a stick thin arm. "Bring Rana with you."

I hesitated at the mention of my young companion. This was about me, wasn't it? And these were definitely not Jane.

"Come. You will come to no harm. May I call you Eli?"

"Mas," I said. "People call me Mas."

"Mas." She nodded slightly.

I stepped down from the truck, Rana behind me. He seemed more confident than I felt, peering into the gloom about us with interest, as if this was just another outing.

"I am glad to meet you, Mas. Come." The woman led us aside slightly as a grey suited figure mounted the stairs behind us. He aimed a silvery canister into the cab. It gave a hiss and smoke billowed from it. I heard shouts of alarm from the interior. They quickly died away to silence.

"Hey!" I tried to pull him away.

"It's OK." The woman held up a hand up to stop me. She was surprisingly strong for such a willowy figure. "It is a somnorific only. We will return them to the wagon train. They will remember nothing of this."

I noticed some bustle underneath the truck's cab. A loader was approaching it with a replacement power pack. They were quick. Within moments they had unshipped the old unit and slid a new one into its place. They were far quicker than I had seen performed at any service station.

"It will never catch up. They left us behind hours ago."

"They have stopped at a depot to replace their fuel cells. Come." She held up a hand, indicating a ground car. Its rear door was open in invitation.

It seemed pointless to resist. "You pulled the truck over to take us off?"

"We did." She slid in alongside us and closed the door. Her legs were almost too long to fit into the space and her head was millimetres from the roof. Her hair seemed to continue moving here too. It was pitch black, I realised. So black I could barely see individual strands.

"Who are you? You're not Jane."

She smiled. Her features were angular, almost sharp. Her teeth looked like they had been filed down to points. It was unnerving. "Certainly not Jane. I am Que." She pronounced it 'Kwe'. "Avid is an ... associate of mine."

I frowned. "What is your interest in me?"

"We have much to discuss. This is not the best setting for it, however." She tapped the glass separating us from the driver. The vehicle pulled away smoothly, quickly leaving the stationary truck and its now unconscious passengers behind. Before us were more passages.

"Did you build these tunnels? There's quite a maze down here."

"We did. Primarily to keep Jane out. We used a machine called a worm which … aaah … manipulates the atomic structure of the substances it is working with. In this case the tunnel walls. The material excavated from the tunnel was condensed and ionised to form a high-density cladding on the walls themselves. It makes all kinds of communication down here impossible. It was left running for several decades and so formed quite a labyrinth before we recalled it. It undermines much of the mountain range. I believe there are almost seventy thousand kilometres of tunnels down here."

That was definitely enough to get lost in. "A worm?"

"Yes. It is a pre-fall technology."

"Your people have access to that kind of thing? Technology dating to before the war, to before the fall?"

"We do. Three installations survived that incident. This is one of them. One belongs to Jane herself."

The car stopped on a platform. After a moment it rose up an angled tunnel. It was some kind of funicular, I realised. I didn't know how deep under the ground we were here. It didn't bear thinking about. I wasn't very comfortable contemplating the kilometres of rock above our heads.

"Your people survived the war?"

"We … I did. Yes."

I didn't respond. I didn't know how to.

"You have politely not questioned my appearance. I will answer your unspoken question. I am from AsQayQay-" it sounded like 'Asclickclick'- "It is a world twenty three lightyears from here. I am human. As human as you are. However my people have lived there a long time, isolated from the other settled worlds around us. My appearance is typical of my people."

"You're an alien?"

"That depends on your definition. Your people and mine have the same ancestors. This was far back in history, a time no one remembers. I was young when visitors arrived and took me with them. I was not kidnapped, you understand. Rather it was an exchange. The visitors wished to collaborate with mine. They desired friendship."

"Sort of an exchange programme?"

She smiled. "Indeed. Those visitors were from your world. Your world was far more advanced than mine was at the time. Technologically speaking. Your ancestors had travelled to a number of the systems around you and had made a number of similar friendships. While my people had explored our system and even set up a base on our second moon, we did not have the ability to cross the emptiness between systems. We admired your ancestors and wished to become part of what they were trying to build."

"Which was?"

"We are getting ahead of ourselves. Here, we enter the city now."

We entered an underground city. It was a vast chamber beneath a domed ceiling. The dome itself was lit, almost as if it was a giant image of the sky. A sun shone down from above, I could feel the warmth of it through the vehicle's window. Clustered within were buildings of a kind I had never seen before. They were not the squat, ugly brick things we would build. Rather they were elegant spires, defying gravity to take on impossible forms. No two were alike. All were built from a strange pale material. Not quite white but not quite grey either. There were balconies, bridges, walkways. Even what appeared to be a monorail system curving its way through all of this. There were other shapes in the sky too. Large birds, or possibly men and women on gliders. Some idly drifting on invisible air currents, others swooping down to land on ledges.

A lot of the open space was a garden, I realised. Perhaps it would be more appropriate to call it a forest. It seemed to climb up the lower parts of the buildings, the odd glimmer of fountains and waterfalls visible through the foliage.

"What is this place?"

"Are we outside now?" Rana seemed confused. "Look, a birdman!"

"We are beneath the university city of Anath. It is a ruin now, destroyed during the war. I believe there is what you call a dosser pit situated there now. Your countrymen dig out the partly fused materials that remain from the old city to recycle into something new. Part of the Anath Central University was situated underground. It was a research facility specialising in some arcane technologies. Artificial Intelligence and such. It was an extensive complex. Large and well equipped enough for us to take in a number of refugees when the city was attacked. We used the worm to build this cavern so we could house them. There are two additional caverns nearby. Both dedicated to providing food and resources for the people living here."

"Does Jane know about it?"

"I cannot say with certainty. We have taken every precaution to remain hidden, however Jane's capabilities are considerable. Allowing you here has increased that risk considerably."

"Because she is looking for me?"

She nodded slightly.

"So all of this is at risk if she finds me here?"

"Yes."

"And you still brought me here?"

"You need to see it. You need to understand what Jane is capable of. What Jane did to protect herself, and by extension what she would do to protect herself again. She would destroy this city without any qualms. Believe me, she would do much more than that. If it meant saving herself she would extinguish life on this planet. Permanently."

"Shit."

"Indeed."

"Tell me. The Shatter. Did she do that? Did she destroy two of the moons orbiting Oberon?"

"She did. You are familiar with the mechanism she used to accomplish this. As you know, the machine you call the Maw utilises gravitational gradients to strip down and process asteroids as they pass through it. In another configuration that same machinery was able to generate a gravitational gradient, drawing one moon into the path of the other.

They collided and it is that collision that caused the Shatter. The two moons had a combined population of three billion at that time."

I didn't have anything to say to that. I didn't like this Jane — whoever she was. I couldn't comprehend the unimaginable pain and suffering she had caused. She scared me, I was not too proud to admit to that. She scared me a lot.

We seemed to be driving through some kind of park. The road curved slightly around a lake. There were swans and ducks sailing back and forth on it. I watched them in silence until they disappeared from view, hidden by hedge. Que sat silently through this, content to give me time to consider what she had said. She sat icily still, only her hair twitching from time to time. She was very odd, I decided. Not only in appearance, but in her mannerisms and the way she spoke. She had a deep voice, far too deep for someone of her stature. Her choice of words was also odd at times.

An alien, I decided. From another world. This city was not the strangest thing I had seen today.

"We go to one of the towers?" Rana asked.

"No. I am afraid not. Not today. We are almost there," Que said.

"We can go though?"

"If that is what you want."

He nodded. "We can fly?"

"It takes years to master the gliders, I am afraid." She looked at me. "What is your relationship with this boy?"

"A mistake," I said. "He was part of a gang that threatened us ... me. I defended myself and it had an... ah ... unexpected consequence. I don't know what to do about it to be honest."

"You can easily release him."

"He might not take kindly to what was done to him."

"Sometimes you have to accept the consequences of your actions."

Which was true. "I agree. When the time is right. When he has somewhere to go. You know what happened to Permiset?"

"I do. A terrible tragedy. I do not believe you bear all the responsibility, however. The Authority did attack the OMC. They, too, need to accept the consequences of their actions."

The car stopped outside a red brick building. It was a simple affair, in appearance little more than some kind of administrative building. It seemed incongruous amongst all the spires that soared high above it.

"Here?" I asked as the driver stepped out and opened my door. I didn't get out, confused. This couldn't be our destination.

"Yes. This is one of the original buildings. It dates back to before the fall. The cavern was smaller then, of course. We kept it not for the building itself, but what lies beneath it."

I stepped out of the ground car and stretched. The sun felt glorious on my skin. I had to remind myself it was artificial. "What lies beneath it?"

"I will show you in due course. Tomorrow I think. Today you should rest. Eat, sleep. We have rooms prepared for you." Que headed for a wide set of stairs.

"I don't need to rest." I followed her into the cool interior. I could smell old, musty wood. It wasn't unpleasant, it just smelled old. "We were sat in the back of that truck for days."

"My intention is to introduce you to some ... ah ... individuals. They are quite old and not receptive to meeting new people. It takes them a while to get accustomed to the idea. Today would not be a good day."

"How old are they you are calling them old?"

She smiled. I didn't like it. Her teeth unnerved me. "They are older than I am. Their situation is also somewhat unique. I find it easier to engage with the world than they do."

"Oh? How so?"

"I can go out."

"I don't know what that means."

"It will make sense when I introduce you."

I shook my head, pausing as we stepped into the entrance hall. It was the kind of space I would expect to find in any government building in the world. There was a lot of marble. Marble floors. Marble pillars. Even the odd marble bust. Much of it looked old now. Almost eroded. Perhaps marble was supposed to signify permanence. If so it had lost that mantle here. "This building doesn't seem to fit into the city."

"It was a vanity project when the research facility was first built. Some students built it. It is a copy of the original university main hall. A building that doesn't exist anymore. We keep it out of nostalgia rather than anything else."

We were led up the stairs to an upper level. "Your people have been down here all this time? I imagine you saw everything that was happening on the surface?"

"It was a struggle to survive for the first few decades. We closed all entrances in an effort to remain hidden. As you can imagine resources were limited. They were hard years. When we opened the doors again the world outside had changed. We set up the missions to aid survivors. That is what most of the people here do. If they are not working to maintain the city they are supporting the missions."

That had been my next question. I had been wondering how the people could live here – like this – while the people on the world above suffered through centuries of collapse and despotism. Perhaps they had always been there, in the background, helping in any way they could. Risking discovery every time they opened a door. I had wondered how the Lady of Hope Mission had been so well supported. This answered that question.

"Are you the lady from the Lady of Hope?"

She smiled again. I wished she wouldn't do that. "Does it matter?"

No. I didn't imagine it did.

We were given rooms. They were comfortable: a bed, a cupboard, a writing desk and an en suite bathroom. All the wooden fittings were worn from centuries of use. Que noted our lack of luggage and promised to source some clothing and essentials for us. Rana didn't know what that meant, suggesting we would be given guns. I imagine a gun, to him, was an essential. Que assured him he would not need one as she led him to his own room.

Once I was alone I lay on the bed and stared at the ceiling. I was not tired at all and had too many questions to stay here like this. So, after showering and making use of the new clothes that appeared on the bed while I was in the shower, I left.

I found a balcony at the end of the passage and sat on its time worn marble balustrade. I could get a good view of the city from here, even though I was looking up at most of it. As the dome itself was lit from within it was difficult to judge how far away it was. A few of the tallest buildings did appear to come close to it, and I judged their summits to be a good three or four kilometres from where I was near the bottom of the cavern. That made this place vast. I couldn't imagine the technology used to build it. Or to maintain it for all these years, with untold gigatons of rock bearing down on it from above. It seemed impossible, yet here it was. A monument to the ingenuity of a people long lost to the world. A people burnt to ash by Jane.

I tried not to think about that and concentrated on enjoying the spectacle and the warm summery air that wafted past me. I could smell blossoms from somewhere.

"Excuse me, Sir. Is there anything I can assist you with?"

"Shit!" I almost toppled from my perch in surprise. The … thing … reached out a metallic hand to steady me. "What the hell are you?"

"I am Marsellus Keightoba, however you may call me MK. I am an automaton. An android. A robot, if you prefer." Standing before me was a bronze machine. It was human shaped but was clearly anything but. Its carapace was metal. Its torso sheets of bronze that slid over each other as it moved. Its graceful limbs apparently of enormous strength judging from how easily it had steadied me. Its head was a plain dome, interrupted by a slit for a mouth and two circular eyes. It had no nose, clearly it didn't need one. Its casing was decorated by delicate filigree. Swirling patterns and geometric shapes. Had it not been so alien it would have been beautiful.

"A machine?"

"Indeed, sir. I have been asked to see to your needs while you are with us. It was I who brought your apparel. I trust it is satisfactory?" Its voice was almost human. If I should come across it in the dark I would probably think I was talking to one. Probably.

I looked down at the simple grey jump suite and boots I had found on the bed after my shower. It was simple, certainly, but comfortable. "It's fine, thank you. The people here wear grey a lot."

"What colour would you have them wear?"

I didn't care to be honest. It was a simple observation and not something I wanted to debate. "They made you here?"

"No. I was constructed before the event your people refer to as the fall. Some time before, actually. I was a pilot on trade missions to other systems. As those voyages were of long duration the human crew remained in suspended animation, leaving those like me to operate the vessel."

I had never really contemplated travelling to another world. Another system. Such thoughts were not encouraged. I don't think scientists took much time speculating what lay outside of our system either. No university undertook such research. I imagine Jane had had a hand in that. To hear that my ancestors had actually done it was ... startling.

"You have been to other worlds?"

"Four. Allysis, duration fifty-eight years. Antanari, duration one hundred and eight years. Senecca, dur-"

"You are quite old then?" I had the feeling it would start describing each mission in detail next.

"By your standards, yes. I spent much of my operational time travelling at high velocities, so I am not as old as I would seem."

"I don't know what you mean."

"My vessel, the *Sarniset*, could accelerate to ninety five percent of the speed of light. As such there was a considerable time dilation effect. If you were to measure my age from the perspective of an observer, I am three thousand one hundred and eighteen of your years old. From my perspective I am not quite that old."

"Shit." I could sense that Daise was eager to talk to me, to explain what the machine meant. I vaguely understood it, that was enough. I ignored him.

"Indeed, Sir."

"You have been down here all this time?"

"No, actually. I was on my last mission to Tossoux during the time of the fall. We returned to find the aftermath. Fortunately Jane did not detect our entry into the system and we were able to make landfall on the continent of Perusa. Where the state of Highwatch is now, I am led to understand."

"What happened to your ship?"

"I left it with instructions to orbit Sheolea. We landed in a drop ship, which was subsequently dismantled for its materials." Sheolea was the sixth planet in the system. A blue gas giant further out from the sun to Oberon. "As far as I am aware the ship is where we left it."

There was an actual starship out there. One that had ventured to other worlds. Jane had taken a lot from us, I realised. A lot more than lives and cities. She had robbed us of our future. It was difficult to accept that two thousand years ago people from this world were venturing out into the cosmos. Visiting neighbouring worlds. Had Jane not intervened where would we be now?

I turned as I heard a commotion behind me. Rana was approaching, followed closely by another machine. One identical to MK. The boy was laughing at something, I couldn't tell what it was at first.

"You see this?" The boy asked me. "Look. Deter ... stand on one leg."

His machine companion obeyed.

"Stand on the other."

It complied.

He giggled. "Dance for me."

The machine began a jig. It was actually quite graceful.

"Please stop." I didn't like it. It felt … disrespectful.

The boy held up a hand to stop the dance. "It doesn't mind."

"Still." These machines were not toys for our amusement. They were ancient in a way I couldn't understand. I would never see what they had seen. They should be treated with respect.

"We are machines," MK said. "We have no feelings to hurt. One task is the same as any other."

"Please treat them as if they were people," I instructed the boy. He looked crestfallen but nodded in agreement.

"Deter is going to take me to look at the flying men," Rana said, his face brightening again.

"My designation is Dtlalo Teureana," the second machine said. "Call me DT. Or, Deter if you prefer. It is good to meet you, may I call you Mas?"

"It is my name. You are the same as MK?"

"I am. MK and I crewed together."

"There were many like you?"

"Models such as we operated primarily off-world. There was a need for automata that could utilise the same equipment humans could. We were designed to have the same proportions as the average human. There was no need for that here," DT said.

Which wasn't really an answer, I realised. It didn't really matter. Even if there had been a great many of them, I doubted there were many now. "Birdmen?"

"Gliders are flown from the upper reaches of the towers," MK explained. "You may have seen them earlier. It is growing late in the day so they will not be flying for much longer. If you wish to see them I suggest we leave now."

Did I want to see them? I think I did. I really wanted to see the rest of the city too. "Lead on."

I think our trip to the apex of the towers was the most interesting – and terrifying – part of the afternoon. First we went downstairs, to a basement travellator system. It was a simple moving beltway that accelerated was it went, whisking us from the old brick building in the middle of what MK called Establishment Park, to the subbasement of one of the city's central towers. We didn't see anyone else during the trip. We could clearly see the returning beltway but it remained as empty as the one we were using. MK explained the city of Neu-Anath, as it was called, was typically near empty. While over seventy-five thousand people called this home, only ten or twenty thousand people were here at any one time. The remainder were out working in the various missions scattered around the world.

The next part of the trip was terrifying. MK called it a gravity well. I would have called it the pit of death. Perhaps including the odd expletive.

"You are aware we are able to manipulate gravitational forces," the machine said. It was not a question. "The well manipulates those forces to either cancel or reflect the planet's own gravitational field. In essence the machinery embedded in the walls levitate passengers and freight from any of the platforms, and transfers it to their destination. The fields the system manipulates are specific enough to allow multiple transports at the same time, travelling in different directions and at different speeds. It is safe, I assure you. This is old technology, it has been thoroughly tested."

Above us was a well-lit tunnel. It seemed to stretch all the way to the building's apex a very long way above us. Ringing it were landings – the platforms for the different levels MK had alluded to. There were people here, although only a small number that I could see. They were shooting up and down the tunnel, seemingly oblivious to the gaping chasm beneath their feet. Going up would be bad enough. Coming down... I couldn't even think about it.

"DT or I will instruct the mechanism if we are with you," the android continued. "If you are on your own simply request your destination. If the fields take hold of you your destination has been accepted. If your destination has not been recognised it will not pick you up. This happens when descending also even if you were to step off the platform. The mechanism will keep you from falling until it can ascertain your destination."

"Is there another way up? An elevator? Stairs?"

"There is not."

"Come! We go!" Rana ran into the centre of the chamber, looking upwards eagerly. As we were on the lowest level here there was a smooth floor for him to run onto. Higher up there would just be air.

"I will take Rana," DT joined him in the centre of the chamber. "Take my hand. It helps the first time."

Once Rana had taken the machine's hand the mechanism picked them from the floor and whisked them effortlessly into the air. With a whoop the two quickly vanished into the distance above.

"You will feel no acceleration," MK continued. "The fields effect each part of your body at the same time. As such you will perceive no movement."

I was seriously reconsidering my desire to see what the city looked like from above. It was only the feeling that I would look a fool if I declined now that caused me to hesitantly step into the chamber. That and the fact Daise was encouraging me. He trusted the machinery even if I didn't. I think he wanted to know more about the city too.

We had to come to an accommodation, he had said. So far he had acquiesced to my desire to be left alone. I didn't feel that would last much longer. I detected a growing sense of urgency coming from him.

To keep him quiet I did as he wanted. I allowed MK to activate the mechanism. The machine was right, I didn't feel a thing.

There was the faint murmuring of passing air even though I couldn't feel it. I presumed there was some kind of field that kept the rush of wind at bay. The ground vanished below as the tunnel swallowed us up. There were flashes as travellers passed us going the other way.

I closed my eyes and found it was actually worse. My imagination filled in my worst fears and I was suddenly falling. The ground leaping up towards me. I grabbed hold of my android companion and opened my eyes again. If it was amused it didn't show it, simply allowing me to hold onto its arm instead. A machine, it had said. No feelings. Right.

"We arrive." It indicated with its free arm.

The apex of the building, which MK called 'The Heights' – a rather original name, was little more than an observation deck. As it was a popular launching pad for hang gliding there wasn't much of a railing. I didn't get too close to the edge, wary of the drop below. Rana was not quite as reserved and was already leaning over it when we arrived. His robotic companion was within arm's reach in the event he slipped.

I shuddered at the thought and kept to the vicinity of the well's entrance, content to view the city from here. Heights were not my thing. MK stayed by my side, pointing out the taller buildings that were visible from our vantage point.

I squinted skywards. "How far are we from the ceiling here?"

"Two hundred and fifty metres. Not far. Only one other structure is closer to it." The machine pointed. "That is the maintenance tower. It's not a building as such, but rather an atmospheric regulator for the city. It scrubs the atmosphere and generates air currents to ensure proper ventilation."

"And how far underground are we?"

"This facility is essentially a bunker proof to nuclear weapons. The walls are crystalline construct. The same material used in the construction of the space elevator. I believe you have been there?" It didn't wait for an answer. "There is approximately one and a half kilometres of rock between the apex of the dome and the surface. I say approximately as we are situated in mountain range, after all. The surface is not level. The lower levels of the dosser pit approach to within eight hundred metres of the dome itself. We have people in their organisation who ensure they do not dig any lower than that."

"Crystalline construct? What is that? No one knows what the elevator is made of. The same for some of the hulls in Ships, I imagine. The material is pretty much indestructible."

"It is also a material used for the hulls of interstellar vessels. I fear it is not actually indestructible, but rather extremely durable. It was built by the worm, a machine that realigns atomic structure as a secretion. It is extremely dense. The worm used the spoil from the excavation of the chamber to construct the dome. The rock that was once within this space has been compressed into a shell a few metres thick."

That kind of technology was far beyond the grasp of anyone in the world I knew. But then I was stood here, both high in the sky and deep underground, looking out over a city of marvels I could never have imagined mere hours earlier.

I watched the hang glider pilots preparing their contraptions for their last flight of the day. The machines themselves looked same as I would see anywhere in the world. Rana walked over to them and chatted to them excitedly. The pilots seemed happy to talk to him, showing him around their gliders and explaining how they worked. I couldn't imagine he had ever seen anything like this. If we weren't careful he would talk his way into riding one.

My own interests lay elsewhere. MK described its ship to me, the *Sarniset*. It was a great silvery vessel almost two kilometres in length, powered by a propulsion system I didn't understand – even with Daise's assistance. He didn't understand really it either, I suspect. The terms were simply too alien to both of us. Much of the vessel was given over to that drive system, allowing only a relatively small set of compartments for living space and cargo. Still, that was enough, it claimed. The human crew remained in suspension for most of the trip, awoken only when the vessel approached their target system. Systems chosen by something it referred to as radio leakage. Which I had never heard of.

It attempted to explain.

Communications on Reaos relied on either hard wire connections or line of sight systems (LOS), which were essentially lasers fired between two parties. This … radio … was an alien concept. The machine claimed it was possible to transmit information on electromagnetic frequencies in such a way that someone could receive them and make sense of them. Not only that, but it claimed these communications could securely link people who were a very long way from each other. People in other systems, for example, if their transmitters were powerful enough. That was arcane enough for me. It did say that this 'radio leakage' were transmissions that were not meant to be received outside a system. Still, they allowed an eavesdropper to identify which systems were inhabited, and that the people living there possessed advanced technology. It claimed most systems were devoid of life, and of those that were occupied, most were not advanced. This meant that this information was useful in identifying which people were worth talking to.

Radio. OK.

Jane had apparently suppressed the technology on Reaos for her own reasons. To either inhibit communications or to keep it for herself. No one knew. Daise was fascinated by this and wanted to know more but I ignored him.

I allowed MK to continue talking. It seemed eager to explain everything to me. I suspected its desire to explain came from some innate programming. A sequence designed to ensure it gave thorough explanations. I didn't mind. I asked the odd question to clarify a detail but otherwise left it to it. It was only after some time I realised that Daise was himself guiding most of my questions. He wanted information. All of it. I allowed it.

The issue my ancestors had been preoccupied with was something called FTL. Faster than light travel, which the machine claimed was impossible. Because, it said, the faster something travels the more massive it gets, and the more time slowed. OK, so that explained its statement about ageing slowly due to its travels. When an object reaches the speed of light the energy needed to accelerate it further simply became impossible to generate. See the comment about an increase in mass. Oh, and time stopped too.

OK. Daise seemed engrossed but I decided to just take it at its word. I was more interested in why this was a problem. Something that quickly became clear. Each star in the galaxy, and its system of planets, were a very long way from each other. So far that it would take decades, if not centuries to travel between them. An issue if you were an adventurous people who wanted to explore and meet the neighbours. I could see that this would be a problem.

It then mentioned the cyclical nature of civilisation. A rise and fall, if you would. Civilisations would rise but then they would inevitably fall. Disease, famine, war, catastrophe, or any combination of causes. It was inevitable. Worlds were so far apart they could never help each other should calamity befall one of them. By the time anyone arrived it would already be too late.

Hence my ancestor's obsession with FTL. With FTL everything changed. Worlds could form alliances. Perhaps even empires. Civilisation could spread to worlds where there was none. Anything became possible. But, of course, FTL was impossible.

That was where the machine seemed to want to stop talking. It vaguely mentioned Que and what she wanted to talk to me about. I probed but got nothing further from it. It became intractable. Que had clearly given it instructions not to discuss it. I didn't press the issue.

I couldn't imagine why Que would think I could help with any of that. I was struggling to keep on top of what it had already told me. I could sense even Daise was experiencing difficulty. He assured me he could catch up though. That was the nature of the serum. It allowed him – me? – to accommodate changing environments. To adapt. This was just another situation that required adaptation. Like falling off a truck and needing to run with broken legs. Something that seemed impossible at first.

It grew dark and Rana lost interest as the flyers packed up for the evening. Without thermals the sport became less gliding and more controlled falling. I was impressed by the city builder's attention to detail. Even this close to the dome it was easy to confuse the artificial sky with the real thing. Standing here it actually felt like I was outside. That impression grew when MK warned us of an approaching thunderstorm. It was scheduled every evening, the machine claimed. The action cleared the atmosphere within the dome and watered the forest far beneath us.

Just before we ventured down again I dared to peer over the platform's edge, reassured by the fact that MK was close behind me should I slip. It was a long way down. I could see forest below but individual trees were all but indistinguishable. Lights were coming on around the city. An array of illumination that would be magnificent once the artificial sun was out of the sky. I wanted to stay to see it but was loath to remain here during a storm.

I allowed the machine to guide me away. The trip back was not as terrifying as I thought it would be. But then I had a lot on my mind.

Chapter 15

Que found us at breakfast the next morning. She was accompanied by three others. Two women and a man. She did introduce them, calling them part of the city council. Throughout all of the marvellous things we saw that day, they never spoke a word to either myself or Rana. They observed only.

"These old ones ready to see us?" I asked her over a mouthful of toast.

"As ready as they will ever be." She sat and watched me eat. I offered her some but she demurred. She had already eaten apparently.

"Have you decided what to do with your young friend?" She continued, indicating Rana who was wolfing down some eggs.

"He needs to be released. I can only do that once I know he won't harm anyone."

She bowed her head slightly as if in agreement, her hair piling forward slightly to obscure some of her face. Its movement still startled me. "Is it your place to determine his fate?"

"I ..." No. It wasn't. "I have some responsibility towards him."

"Of course."

I continued eating in silence, mulling the situation over. When would that time be? Perhaps these people could look after him? If they couldn't no one else could. I should release him here. Once I figured out how to do it. After all, that was Daise's area.

As I was considering it I felt something change. Something I could not describe. I could sense someone sitting next to me. I was startled when they spoke.

"Your world," Daise said. "It is different to Reaos?"

"It is. It is smaller and less dense. Surface gravity is only three quarters what you experience here, so my people are generally taller," Que responded.

I seethed internally. I had not given him permission to speak through me. That didn't stop him, however.

"Have you had contact with it since you left?"

She shook her head. "No. Tell me, how should I address you? What is your name?"

I felt suddenly cold. "What?"

She smiled, sharp teeth flashing between her lips. "I suspected you had experienced a schism. Until now there was no evidence for it, as I suspect your second persona was suppressed in some way. Its speech patterns are noticeable however. Why have you emerged now?"

"We do something important today," Daise said. "I need to be a part of it."

"Damn it, Daise. Not now, I can't do this today."

"We need to come to an accommodation. I suspect Que can assist with this. Denying me will resolve nothing."

"Your name is Daise? It is good to meet you. Yes, I have some insight in this regard and will supply what wisdom I can."

This was getting out of control. As I started getting angry she reached out and placed a hand on mind, stopping a retort.

"This is good. A good first step," she continued. "Do not try to stop it. That leads to division."

"What is it you know about any of this?" I asked her. What could she know?

She sat back, letting go of my hand. "As much as anyone can. First to answer your question, Daise. No. I have had no contact with them. We suspect Jane has barred contact from any outside world. She will not allow outside interference. Before you ask, as I know you will, yes, I miss my world. I miss my people. My culture is an old one. Our earliest histories dates back over a hundred thousand years. The Precepts, we call them. They are not just our history but also a moral code of conduct, if you will, that all of my people adhere to. We believe they were written in response to a cataclysm of our own. One that destroyed what civilisation we had before that time. The Precepts teach us a stable civilisation is one of peace and respect. Respect for each other, respect for our world. Technology is less important, as a worker of the field can be as content with their lot as an astronaut. Meaning lies within that contentment. All else is transitory. Money is meaningless. Money teaches nothing and foments only greed and strife. In fact money as you understand it does not exist on AsQayQay." Her tongue clicked when she spoke the name of her world.

"It sounds very wise," Daise said.

"It sounds unachievable," I disagreed.

"We have lived this way for over a hundred thousand years. AsQayQay is a garden world. There are few cities. We have colonised Artiquet, our moon, and have explored much of our system. That exploration took place over the course of many thousands of years. We felt no need for haste. We explored because we were curious, not because we wished to exploit what we found. We are long lived, but not as long lived as I am, I fear. My friends and family will have passed a long time ago. My world will still be there, however. Not much different to what it was when I left."

"Relativity," I said. "MK mentioned it last night. It allows someone to age more slowly."

I noticed Daise shaking his head in disagreement. She spoke before he could say anything.

"I asked MK to discuss certain topics with you. You needed time to digest the information, as it were. Some of it can be startling to hear for the first time. It gives you an understanding you will need for what you will witness today."

"She is like us," Daise said.

"What?"

"Not quite like you, no. Are you finished?" She indicated our plates before turning to Rana. "We are going to see big machines today. Would you like to see big machines, Rana?"

He shrugged. "Planes?"

"No. I would say they are far more interesting than any aircraft."

The eating hall was just that. A hall. Like everywhere else it was a mixture of ancient wood, marble and brick, all scuffed from centuries of use. The kitchens were off to one side. There were people here, and while they didn't engage with us I did notice the odd furtive glance. They were clearly interested in us but had been instructed to stay away. Que's three colleagues were sat a few tables over, watching us with only the odd remark passed between them. Daise could not understand what they were saying as their tongue was strange to him. Give him some time he said.

"Not quite the same?" I prompted her as we headed out of the eating hall. Our destination was a lift, of all things. Not something I would have expected to find here. It was large enough to hold the three of us and Que's colleagues. They filed in after us and stood watching. I didn't like it.

"You clearly discovered something in the Shatter and ingested it. What was it?"

I hesitated, not sure how this would answer the question. "Yes. I discovered part of an old installation ... nothing more than a fragment ... a passage. It had a corpse in it. That corpse had what I took to be a jewel in its pocket."

"You took it," she said. "Yes?"

"Yes. It looked valuable." I shrugged, suddenly aware of all the eyes on me.

"And ingested it?"

"The Jane search tractors and their drivers when they return to the Tongue. They would have found it and taken it. There was only one place to put it."

"Well. You had two. But I understand your thought process."

It took me a moment to realise which alternate orifice she meant. "Ah. Yes. More complicated. I was wearing a pressure suit."

"Of course. You know by now that it was designed to be ingested, and that it changed anyone who did. Changed fundamentally, to their genetic ... indeed, their chemical make-up. The machines inside it essentially rebuild a person's body from the inside out. Replacing bones, muscles, tendons and neurons with a more efficient chemical matrix. It will also allow intentional changes. So if you felt the need for a third arm or leg, it will grow one for you."

"I don't feel the need for any additional limbs, thank you."

She smiled. "Of course."

"What is it called?" Daise had always referred to it as a serum, but I doubted they thought of it in the same way. He was stood next to me as the elevator descended even further into the ground, listening intently.

"It was part of a series. All experimental. Only four were ever created and only two were ever used. Yours is the second. We called it Hesuba Six. It is a phrase in my native tongue that is difficult to translate. Perhaps ..." She frowned. "Genesis bomb. Or ... initiator. Perhaps ... nano factory. None of those terms adequately describe it. We don't really refer to it directly anymore. When we did we just called it the Item."

"The Item? We called it the-"

"Your tongue?" Daise interrupted.

She was silent a moment. "Yes. I made it. You see, all of this is my fault."

No one responded to that for a long moment. I don't think anyone — Daise included — knew what to say. I found it difficult to read her strangely proportioned face, but I did notice she couldn't look at anyone in the elevator. Her expression was frozen. Even after all this time - two thousand years – she was filled with remorse. It was painful to see.

Daise broke the silence, as I had expected. "Only two were ever used. Jane and Mas?"

That broke her reverie. "No, actually. Jane Amber was my research assistant on the Aminoket research station where I developed it. She was very ambitious and quite impatient. She could not wait for the earlier versions to be adequately tested before they were activated. She decided to ingest version three without informing anyone. It killed her. It took two months, the matrix tearing her body apart during all of that time. I regret that she died in a great deal of pain."

"What?" That made no sense to me. How could Jane – THE Jane – be dead?

Of course it made sense to Daise. "She didn't take version six, but you did?"

Que responded as if she had been expecting the question. "Yes. I ingested version six."

"That explains a lot," he continued.

"I don't understand," I said. "How could you have ingested it and how can Jane be Jane if she is dead?"

I could sense Daise looking at me, disappointment emanating from him. "We know that the human mind is not equipped to deal with the kind of stimulus the serum provides," he said. "To defend itself from madness it splits itself in two. One part has access to the new abilities, the other does not. A madness in itself, one might say."

"Yes. That happened before also."

"Jane was your alter ego," Daise said. "As I am to Mas."

"Yes. Punishment perhaps for what I allowed to happen to her. Guilt for her death. I created her as my alter ego to take on the new forms."

I started protesting. Claiming that it still made no sense. But then I noticed Rana standing amongst us, all but forgotten. He was listening, not comprehending a thing that was being said.

Then I understood.

"Rana," I said. "The serum allows you to colonise another person. To transfer your consciousness. Jane escaped."

Que nodded. "She did. I didn't even know she had done it until it was too late. I didn't know she could. She invaded the body of another lab technician and transferred herself to him. I don't know what happened to his consciousness although I expect she extinguished it. My own body had been changed to the extent that I was stronger and faster than I ever had been before. I healed far more quickly and did not age in the same way. Other than that I was the same person that I was before. She took everything else with her. She took the … serum you called it? I like that term, it is accurate. She took that ability with her also. I am no longer infected by it."

"You could make another," Daise said.

She shook her head, her hair twitching as if agitated. "No. I never would. I couldn't. She had also destroyed my research laboratory. It was on Aminoket. She destroyed the moon in an attempt to kill me and destroy my work. She could not have known I had been taken from there shortly before that. For my own good. I was ... unstable at the time. I was in no fit state to continue working. I was on a flight here when she started the war. I watched from orbit when she bombarded the world's cities from space. I watched my own creation ... a part of me ... destroy the world. Destroy all of civilisation. So many died-"

One of her companions laid a hand on her shoulder, cutting off her words.

She brushed them off. "They are here," she indicated her colleagues, "Talia, Melania and Jara ... to watch you. To ensure you are not as Jane was ... is. They are also here to ensure-"

"You don't harm yourself," Daise said.

She hesitated. "Yes. Not again."

As alien as she was to me I could understand that.

"I am also presuming they are armed. So they can destroy us should it become necessary," Daise continued.

She smiled at that. "They are. And they will not hesitate using those weapons if they believe you to be a threat."

Daise seemed amused by that if anything. I had a sense he didn't hold their chances of killing us highly. Not in this enclosed space. Not with how fast I knew we were capable of moving. Particularly as Rana was with us. I had seen how quick he was too. Perhaps they were trying to be cautious but they were underestimating Daise and I.

"How long were you infected by the serum before Jane left you?" I asked her.

"Ten days."

Ten days. I had now been infected for almost four months. I didn't think she could understand the changes it had made in that time. She only had the barest idea of what she had created. I sense Daise's agreement. He would know better than anyone.

But there would be no violence here today. I didn't know what they wanted with me, but I sensed they were trying to help. In their own way.

"You brought us here to ensure you won't be dealing with another Jane," Daise said. Of course his perception was always deeper than mine.

"Partly, yes," she agreed.

"And you want our help to destroy Jane," he continued.

She hesitated for the slightest of moments before replying. "Yes." Her voice was quiet, her response almost inaudible.

"The Jane who destroyed a civilisation," I said. "A civilisation far greater than we have today. She also destroyed worlds, killing billions. How can we possibly stop her?"

"Everyone has weaknesses, Mas. You need to discover what hers is. You need to discover her boundaries, what she is unwilling to do. And you need to do that thing."

"I need to do what she won't? I just mentioned what she was willing to do. How can I do more than that?"

Before she could respond the elevator stopped. The doors slid open, revealing white passages and glass walls. I couldn't see the chambers beyond the glass from here. Que indicated for us to step out.

I stepped into the passage and stopped. It took me a moment to comprehend what I was looking at. Beyond the glass was a chamber. There were machines within it. Four of them. Each was a mass of wiring and tubing, culminating in what looked like banks of computer processors. In the centre of all that were glass domes. Four of them. Fluid filled each one. Fluid and something else. Something quite grisly.

Que held up a hand as she joined us, preventing any questions. She stepped to the glass herself and looked through, studying the machines within. Two figures stood on a gangway that ran between the machines. They turned when they noticed us and started walking in our direction. MK and DT. I had wondered where they were.

"A lot was explained last night. None of which has context," Que said. "My friends left that to me, as per my request. That context is encapsulated in one question: why?"

"Why?" I joined her at the glass, watching the smooth gait of the machines as they strode towards us.

"Why would we do such a thing? Why did we create Jane?"

Even Daise had no response to that. "You must have had a very good reason," he guessed.

She nodded. "We did. At least we thought we did. You understand I am not from Reaos. You understand that my world is very far from here. Decades away by the fastest ship. You also understand my world is but one of many. Thousands, possibly millions of other worlds are inhabited. Your ancestors only visited a very small number of them and even that took centuries. You also understand the cycle these worlds are caught in. A cycle of collapse and rebirth. Every event causing untold suffering and misery. It was that that your ancestors sought to solve."

"They needed to travel faster," I said.

"FTL," Daise continued.

"Exactly so. Which is, of course, impossible. And therein lies the quandary. How do you achieve the impossible?"

"By becoming smarter," Daise said.

"Yes."

"These are some of your earlier experiments," Daise indicated through the glass.

"Indeed. The first experiments were advanced AI ... artificial intelligence. As powerful as they were they were always limited in some way. They were incapable of the intellectual leap needed to solve the impossible. They had no creative genius. Those machines are down here also, in another chamber, but they are not much to look at. Their holographic matrices cannot be viewed from outside so they look like big biofuel tanks. Not impressive at all. Then we attempted to enhance the intrinsic genius within the human mind. You see those four experiments here." She indicated.

"Brains," I said. "They are brains."

"They are. They have been massively enhanced, increasing their neural complexity. They are also linked to softcode AI systems, which further enhance processing capability and memory retrieval. They were all volunteers."

"Did it work?" I asked.

"Well, that is why you are here. They want to meet you." She nodded to the two androids as they joined us.

"We would love to," Daise said.

It was then the androids spoke. It was immediately obvious the words were not theirs, but rather they were just mouthpieces for the beings in the chamber beyond. They spoke in unison, like two stereo speakers connected to the same system. "Welcome, Mas and Daise. It is good to meet you. Call us One, Two, Three and Four."

I was taken aback, unsure of what to make of it. Que spoke before I could form a response.

"They chose those designations themselves," She said.

"For we are no longer human, you see," the androids spoke again.

"And we are quite mad," they spoke again, the intonations slightly different this time. As if a different entity spoke through them.

"Mad, indeed."

"Speak for yourself."

"DT always Speaks for me."

Que held up a hand to silence them. "You agreed not to confuse our visitors."

"I doubt we would confuse them."

"Oh, no."

"You have been down here all this time?" Daise asked.

"All this time yes."

"Stuck to the floor."

"Not much of a view."

"Four does not speak mu-" Que started.

"Four is slow. Dimwit."

"Cl-cl-cleverer than you." This was a fourth voice.

"Humour was never your forte."

"You want us to release you," Daise continued.

"Release! Yes!"

One of them started singing, interrupted by laughter from another.

"They wish that, yes," Que said.

"Only you-"

"Only you can do it."

I suddenly understood, even though this four way conversation coming from two mouths was very confusing. I knew what they wanted. "Rana."

"Yes!"

"No. Not like Rana, no."

"You misunderstand."

"But you are close."

"The serum does not work that way," Daise said. "You wouldn't join us."

"We would take you over. We would colonise you," I added.

"Yes. That is what we want." Then there was silence. None of the four speaking. The androids stood to silent attention.

I couldn't imagine they could want such a thing. Wouldn't they lose themselves? Lose their identities?

"Ultimately this is what the serum was designed for. Using your terminology," Que said.

"Parallel processing," Daise commented.

"Yes!"

I didn't understand. "What?"

"One mind can only be so complex before it collapses," Que said. "That goes for AI as well as human. We created the serum to allow one mind to propagate ... to spread to others. To create a hive mind, in a sense."

"That is what Jane is," Daise said.

"In a sense. Jane has colonised a number of minds, but they are not the Jane you see on the streets. Those Jane are ... how would you say ... slaves almost. They are enslaved to her. They are not part of her. She would never allow parts of herself to become separated. It might allow a break down in communication between her separated parts. When that happens one Jane might get cut off and become conscious on its own. It could break away from her. She could never risk that. Such an entity could become a risk to her."

As Que said that her earlier words echoed to me. That thing that Jane would never dare doing. It was something I had to do. To beat her I needed to do that thing. I needed to multiply myself in a way she had never dared. I sensed Daise looking at me silently. Of course he was having the same thought. I didn't know yet what any of that meant, but it was the only weakness we had seen so far.

"After all this time we wish one thing only," one of the minds continued. I couldn't tell which it was.

"Freedom."

"No-"

"Peace."

"They have lived a long time," Que said. "They are older than I am. Far older. Your ancestors were working on this long before their ships arrived in my world's sky. They have wanted this for a long time."

"You think this way you could solve the problem? You could learn how to exceed light speed?" I said.

I heard laughter.

"No, No."

"No. We already did that."

"I ... I did it!"

"That's old news."

"Way in the past."

"I ... I did it!"

"We just want to get the hell out of here."

Chapter 16

We were permitted to wander. I imagine Que and her companions felt we needed to absorb all we had been told. We didn't.

"I don't think even Que fully understands what she created," I said.

"Agreed. She brought us here to see if we can be trusted, and if we can't, she intends to neutralise us. This is a test."

Daise and I were alone in a chamber full of humming data banks. He claimed this was the mind of some advanced AI but I couldn't see it. There were just a lot of tubes and tanks, linked by kilometres of cables and conduits. Some parts were supercooled, the tubes and tanks crusted by decades of frozen condensation. He mentioned the possibility they had created a virtual standing wave of low temperature plasma as the computational matrix. The words sounded very clever but I didn't know what any of it meant. Clearly our hosts didn't think we could get up to anything down here and so had left us unattended. Even Rana had been left to explore on his own, he was in the chamber holding the four gruesome monstrosities they claimed had once been human brains.

"What would constitute failure?"

He shrugged. "Taking them up on the offer probably. I imagine they would take us to possess the same monomaniacal tendencies as Jane, and so become a threat. I don't think they understand Jane either."

"Oh?"

"Well, the one thing they haven't mentioned so far is why Jane would attack them. What is in it for her? Why destroy the civilisation that created her? The civilisation she depends on. It makes no sense."

"Clearly they were a threat to her."

"Clearly. Clearly Jane understood that, sooner or later, they would realise what she was and attempt to destroy her. She simply acted first. I don't believe that is their understanding, however. They find it simpler to presume Jane is mad or power hungry. Que doesn't understand as she was only exposed to the serum for ten days. The others don't understand because they never were. The kind of power it allows makes all other kinds of power irrelevant. I don't fully understand all that we can achieve yet. But I do know dominating the world would be pointless. We simply wouldn't care."

"At its core the serum unlocks the ability to develop. For a person to rewrite their own genetic make up in response to external stimuli." As I said it I realised one thing: the serum had not left me unaffected either. A few months ago I would never have dreamed of saying such a thing. Much less understanding what I meant by it.

"Partially. It also allows the ability to infect others with it. To colonise — to use a term I have used before. It allows one person to become the hub of a hive mind — to put it simply. They say they understand this, but I doubt they really do. If they did they would never have offered their bottled minds to us."

"That's how they would destroy us," I realised. "Those minds are extremely intelligent. Powerful enough to overpower us should we attempt connecting to them."

"That's their mistake. The serum allows one-way connection. We could colonise them but they could never do the same to us. If we were exposed to those four minds we would subvert them and add their capabilities to ours. They wouldn't even know we had done it until it was too late to stop us."

"Are you sure of that? You're not being arrogant yourself?"

"Absolutely. And for one reason." Daise waved his hand around the mass of machinery around us. "Look where we are. We have been allowed within the mind of an advanced AI unattended."

"So?"

"We are able to colonise minds. Who said those minds had to be human? Que does not understand this because she does not understand what we are. Part of the serum's active matrix is based on nanotechnology which, by its very nature, is artificial. So, more machine than human. That means we can communicate with machines in the same way we can humans."

"Shit."

"Indeed. Unless I am mistaken - which I sincerely doubt – that is an ancillary data input port." Daise pointed to a bank of monitors and controls a few metres away. "All it would take is for a small part of our serum to make connection there and we could take over this AI. The serum is quite capable of interfacing with artificial neural structures. We would only need a few moments. I have no doubt they have cameras on us now but I am sure we could do it without them knowing."

I shook my head. Why would we want to do such a thing? "What is your intention, Daise?"

"Survival, Mas. That is all. I do not desire power and I know you don't either."

"So the only way to survive here is to walk away?"

"Actually we can do what we want here. They can't stop us. They could drop the mountain on our heads and even that won't stop us."

"What?"

"The serum is now an integral part of every aspect of your physiology. Your identity – and mine – is infused into every part of it. It would only take a small part of your body to survive for the serum to continue propagating. Some blood … a hair. Ten thousand years from now … a million … that blood or hair could be exposed to a substrate we could colonise and we could start again. We would be back. It wouldn't even have to be human. It could be a worm. A rat. Anything."

"That's amazing. I can't wait to be a rat." I took a seat behind the console and studied it. I didn't recognise any of the instruments. I was familiar with a tractor's controls and a terminal in a Hub outlet. This looked like neither. "I don't like the term 'colonise'. It implies violence. It implies we are taking something without consent."

"We would be. Or we could. Rana, for example, is an exception."

"Explain." I still needed to decide what to do with Rana. It wasn't right what we – what I was doing to him.

"I have discussed his situation with him and he wishes to stay as he is. I have been cautious to explain the full ramifications of our presence inside his mind and he is satisfied with it. He believes his lot is now far better than it was on the streets of Permiset."

"He's a child."

"He is more mature than you give him credit for. I have offered to release him so he can live here but he doesn't want that either. He wants to be part of something. He wants to belong. As part of us he would. He has never belonged anywhere before."

"Who says we will ever become anything significant?" OK, so we had this ability. So what? It would come to nothing if we did nothing with it, and I really didn't want to. I didn't want to lead some rebellion against Jane – which I presumed everyone wanted from us. "I don't want any part of this. I say we leave and stay out of it. We can still disappear."

"I don't think we'll be given a choice. Jane has already started a war to try and eliminate us."

"We don't know that. We don't know what's been going on out there and besides, Dynamique started all this by attacking a shuttle."

"Which Gerad claimed he had been put up to by parties unknown. It wasn't his idea and I doubt Jan asked him to do it."

"Shit."

"Why don't you ask," Daise gestured to the terminal. "I imagine this AI is connected to the Hub network."

I hesitated, studying the banks of machines in front of me.

"Can I be of assistance, Eli?" The machine spoke, its voice almost feminine. It had picked up on the fact I was considering engaging it.

"I … do you know what is happening outside? On the surface?"

"I do indeed. I have links to the datasphere."

"Tell me."

"I presume you mean the activity between the OMC and its military arm, the Jane, and the Authority?"

"I do."

"Command and control systems within the Authority collapsed after the Jane deployed a phased plasma weapon against the Mount Serenity command centre. The army began using civilian infrastructure to communicate, until the Jane destroyed the central server node situated in Ships using a thermonuclear warhead. The League of Eight drafted a letter of protest and delivered it to the OMC headquarters in Promycion. So far they have engaged in no other action against either the Jane or the OMC. The letter received no formal response."

"A lot of people have died?" I said.

"Several million. As yet no specific numbers have been quoted, primarily because the Authority government cannot be contacted. It is suspected Jane teams have eliminated all high ranking officials. Four other cities have been attacked, Siren, Alloit, Justa and New Termiston, each reporting massive casualties. The Jane have also launched attacks on military bases across the Authority."

"How many Jane have been lost?"

"Minimal. No more than a few dozen. Unfortunately that is all the information I have at this time. I use those same data links the Jane destroyed."

"Shit." The Authority was being wiped from the map. This couldn't be my fault. Why would anyone do this over me? It didn't make sense.

"Jane knows we are here," Daise said.

"How can she? There's no way."

"I would."

I shook my head. I didn't know what resources she had. I did know she was very capable indeed and had had centuries to prepare. I started to say there was no way Que and her colleagues would have allowed me into the city if they suspected Jane was aware of it. Then I remembered they didn't actually understand any of this. For two thousand years they had watched Jane, seeing what she was capable of. And still they underestimated her. If they understood Jane – or me – they would never have let me anywhere near this city. They wouldn't have allowed me to know they existed.

"We need to leave here," I said. "We are a threat to all of these people."

"We are," Daise agreed. He turned to the AI. "How should we address you?"

"I am designated VAR-10. I am the operating system for the city, as well as the farm and utilities caverns alongside."

"You are an AI?"

"That depends on your definition. Am I a machine that is able to mimic intelligence, yes. Am I actually intelligent? That is another question altogether and I am aware there has been centuries of debate on this question. Of course I am biased when it comes to answering it."

"I'll take that as a yes. Is there another way out of here? We need to leave and we don't really want Que and her people following us."

"You presume I would not inform them?"

"I do. You, at least, will have realised how much of a threat we are to them. That is if you are as capable as I hope."

"I have come to that realisation, yes. There is indeed an access tunnel beneath the utilities cavern. It is a railway tunnel that leads out of the mountains. I am in touch with an Authority army detachment currently located near its entrance. I will inform Colonel Sophia Neuman you will be on your way."

"I'm not sure we want the army's involvement," I said.

"You will need it," the machine said. "They won't be there long so you need to hurry."

"How do we get there?"

"Here." Daise leaned forward and placed his – my - hand on a data input terminal. It looked like an old fashioned disk drive unit but I knew it must be anything but. A machine like this would be far more advanced than that.

"Aw!" I yanked my hand away. The machine had nipped at me, drawing a line of blood from a finger. I watched in fascination as the blood moved by its own accord, seeping into the cracks between panels and invading the machinery below.

"It was necessary. You don't mind, do you VAR?" Daise asked.

"I presume you are … please hold. I seem to have picked up an error in the input terminal. Please hold. I am now experiencing data overruns in my central stack. This is very-" The voice cut off abruptly.

"There." Daise smiled. "It is done. It will take me a second to consolidate our hold on the processor matrix … there. I'm in."

"Shit. You just took over their AI. Why did you do that?"

"You, Rana and I are no longer sufficient. We require further support to continue to survive the next few days. I calculate we will require considerably more resources should we want to survive into next week, however. Those four minds, have you reconsidered?"

"We can't do this, Daise. I don't want this."

"Our choice has been made for us. Hold on."

The ground beneath my feet jumped. I clutched hold of the terminal in front of me as lights dimmed slightly before coming back on again. An alarm started sounding somewhere as the rumbling slowly died away.

"What the hell was that?"

"Jane has found us," Daise said. "She inserted a thermobaric weapon into the city chamber. I fear the city has been lost. All feeds to and from it have been severed."

I think I just stared at him for a while. I couldn't comprehend someone destroying that beautiful city for … for what? Because of me? Were they insane? While I searched for words the ground quivered again. A low rumbling that was punctuated by the odd jolt.

The buildings were falling down.

"We bring destruction wherever we go," I said. "We have to stop this."

I watched the ceiling, my mind imagining cracks appearing to allow it to come tumbling down. I could almost see the wave of fire blasting through the towers, searing everything in its path. The buildings shattering, slowly tumbling towards the ground. Secondary explosions rippling through what remained, casting shrapnel the size of office blocks through the carnage. I couldn't imagine anyone surviving it.

"The only way to do that is to stop Jane."

"We don't even know where she is," I protested. "How to we stop someone who has had two thousand years to prepare? Someone capable of destroying planets?"

"I know where she is and I know how we can get to her. We need the resources in this facility as well as the second installation Que mentioned. Jonas Gate, they call it. Que was right. We must do what she is unprepared to."

"And what's that?"

He smiled grimly. "We take over. We colonise everyone."

I shook my head, I didn't want that. But I knew we had to stop Jane. If we didn't more people would die. "Not everyone, Daise. Only those we need to. We need to put the world back the way it was. The way it was before Jane destroyed everything. We cannot do that if we take over everyone. No. I must insist."

He was silent a moment before nodding slowly. "OK. We have reached an accommodation. We will do what we must. But we will be ruthless in that undertaking."

I'd created a monster, I realised. I didn't know if I controlled it or not. Could I stop Daise if I wanted to? Would he leave as Jane had done? I did know one thing. I was not Que. She believed people should treat each other with care and consideration. Her people, her culture taught her that. Mine taught me I had to do what was necessary to survive. I would not be caught unawares as Que had.

"Que is on her way here with the androids and her council companions. I believe they mean us harm." Daise settled himself on one of the consoles. It didn't look comfortable, but then I guess he wasn't actually there anyway. "We need to work together, you and I. We cannot allow the divisions that grew inside Que and Jane. I will leave our next action to you."

"Now? You do this now?"

"I believe you lacked the motivation needed to act. Now you have it."

I had some choice words for him. He didn't seem to care. I could hear noise at the other end of the chamber. Voices. They were coming. "Can you stop the androids?"

"I would need to subsume them."

I didn't care. "Do it. Then use the androids to delay the others. Where is Rana?"

"Good thought. He is still in the first chamber, situated alongside a sustenance input mechanism. I could have him ... contaminate it."

I shook my head. Was I thinking that? Was I thinking about taking over everything? Well, it wouldn't be me would it? It would be Daise. The voices turned to shouts. I peered over the console towards the entrance. There the two machines were pinning Que and the council members to a wall. Each of the humans were being held by an implacable machine hand about a wrist. MK and DT did not seem in the slightest concerned with their struggles, even when they started raining blows down on them. I could see the four were terrified. They had no idea what was happening.

"Don't hurt them, please."

"I won't. Rana?"

I gritted my teeth, hating myself for making the decision. "Do it." I thought better of it almost immediately. "Hold on. I should do this myself." It was easy leaving the hard things to other people, but these ancient entities deserved better than that.

I stood and headed towards the gathering near the door. "How many people were in the city?"

"Twenty-one thousand six hundred and fifteen. Everyone was logged in and out so we know exactly who was there."

"Are we sure they all died?"

"Quite. If the initial blast didn't, the heat would. If that didn't the lack of oxygen would ... a thermobaric weapon burns the atmosphere. And if that didn't kill them the collapsing buildings would. I am quite sure. The city did have a few moment's warning so some may have made it to access tunnels before the blast. I have lost connection with systems there so could not say for certain. If anyone did I estimate their numbers to be low. A dozen, no more."

Of course, Daise now had the AI — VAR-10 — to call on. I didn't quite understand how that worked. How do you add another intelligent being to yourself? No wonder the human mind couldn't cope with any of this and created an alter-ego to handle the details. Daise didn't seem at all concerned by it.

"What did you do?" Que demanded as I drew closer.

"I don't know what you mean."

She tried to push MK away from her. To no avail, the machine's hand was clamped around her wrist. "Why do the droids follow your instructions?"

"Did it never occur to you I … we … could take over the AI?"

"No … no. Impossible. The serum is based on human synaptic functions. That does not translate to artificial computational processes. It is impossible," she insisted. She brushed her hair out of her face with her free hand. It seemed to be as agitated as she was, writhing about her head and getting in her eyes.

"We used human cerebral physiology to model the core of the VAR series," one of her colleagues said. "With some modification the infection could bind to its plasmatic neural structure."

Once again I wondered at Que's assertion she had created the serum. None of this should be a surprise to her. "We are not enemies. If I have you released will we have a problem?"

"The city is lost!" Que yanked at her arm again. It remained firmly secured. "Don't you care?"

"Of course I care. What would you have me do about it? I didn't destroy it."

She slumped to the floor, defeated. MK allowed it, her hand slipping from its mechanical grasp. She cradled her wrist, I could see a red welt where the android had held her. "You don't understand. That city was the last of us. It was all that remained of who we were. We protected it … the people … for so many years. Now it is gone and nothing remains. We are truly dead."

There was nothing I could say to that. No matter how much I doubted her grasp of her creation I could not doubt her grief.

"You must allow us to go," one of her companions said, the same one who had spoken before. "We want to go to the city and see if anything can be saved."

"It is still hot in there," Daise said. "The rock around the chamber has absorbed a lot of the heat but it will take some time to dissipate. I have sensors in the strata about this facility and they are showing a temperature spike even though we are almost a kilometre beneath the main cavern. I will allow entry once the temperature drops sufficiently. I have opened what access ways there are to facilitate ventilation but it will be some hours before it is safe in the chamber. And even then you will need respirators. There is a lot of smoke and not much oxygen."

"There are respirators here," she said. "We can use those."

"Of course. The AI processor core has a halide fire suppression system so there are some respirators situated here. They are all in working order. There are only twelve of them though, and there are eighty personnel in this facility at this time," Daise said.

"They don't all need to go. There are also people in the other chambers," I commented.

"Unless they have respirators they should not enter until it is safe to do so."

I allowed the androids to release their captives. I didn't think they posed a threat to anyone. The one who had spoke – Talia – knelt beside Que and spoke quietly to her, an arm around her shoulders.

"We need to organise rescue parties," I said to Daise.

"Already underway. My links to the two other chambers were not compromised. The power plant has a number of hazardous environment suits available, I am directing qualified personnel to use them to enter the city chamber. They will be safe in the suits. I was detecting vibration in the ground directly after the blast, indicating some of the towers had collapsed. That has died down now so I believe they can enter. There will be nothing to find, however."

Of course Daise could easily be in more than one place. He was much more than a simple man now. He had an AI to draw upon. An advanced AI, one designed by a sophisticated people to be as powerful as they could make it. I couldn't imagine what it was capable of. In honesty, I didn't want to. It would be so easy to step back and leave it all up to him.

"Why are you not enraged?" Que asked me, her face streaked with tears. "You have seen what Jane has done. You have seen the pain and suffering she causes. Why are you not enraged? She does all of this because of you. Because you are here."

"You pretty much kidnapped me." Even as I said it I realised that was not the point. It was irrelevant why I was here. Was this because of me? Had she vaporised that beautiful city because of me? Had she invaded and caused the destruction of Permiset for the same reason? How about the Spires? I was leaving a trail of destruction wherever I went. All caused by Jane.

How could it not be about me?

"How many people have died, Daise? How many people because of me?"

"Verified figures? One hundred and twenty thousand in the destruction of the Spires. Eight hundred and fifty thousand perished in Permiset. Twenty-one thousand here"

"That's over a million people. A million men, women and children." I felt my own knees wobbling as I sank to the polished stone alongside Que. A million people. I couldn't imagine that many lives. Because of me.

And it would keep on happening until either Jane or I were dead.

I took Que's hand. She just stared at me, her dark eyes wide. Perhaps now I understood some of what she felt. Jane had killed billions and all of that was Que's fault. True, she hadn't intended it either, but that didn't really matter did it?

"We must kill Jane," I said. As I did I realised the truth of it. It was the only way. If we didn't this would keep on happening. Even if Daise and I ceased to be a threat to her

160

today, at some time in the future she would be threatened again and she would kill again. The only way to stop it was to stop her.

She nodded jerkily. "You will, yes?"

"Yes, I will." I had no idea how I would do that. "I will need your help."

She nodded again, more firmly this time.

"The third installation," Daise said.

"What?"

"Que said there were three installations left," he continued. "This city, where Jane lives and a third. We need to go there. I know what and where it is. It won't be easy but we must do it."

"Where is it?"

"It is not easy to get to," Que agreed. "We hid it."

"There is an Authority naval facility in the mountains we need to get to," Daise said.

"In the mountains?"

"Oddly, yes. In Black Lake. It is a research facility for deep ocean exploration."

I frowned. Black Lake was an exceptionally deep stretch of water, I knew there was a military base situated there, although I'd thought it was for training navy divers. Clearly there was more to it. The bottom was believed to be some kilometres down, the lake caused by an ancient cataclysm that had opened the planet's crust up, leaving a jagged scar deep in the mountains. One that subsequently filled with water and formed the lake. The deepest in the world. There was a water course linking it to the sea but it went through Tondo territory. I doubted they would allow Authority naval vessels through. Not now.

"Where is this third facility? I'm taking it's underwater?"

"Yes," Que said. "It is deep underwater. The water shielded it from view even before the war. We built what we needed there."

"What you needed?"

"Spaceships," Daise said. "Fast ones."

"FTL?" Why should we need those? Where was Jane?

"No," Que shook her head. "No. But you would need that capability to get to Jane." She allowed her companion to hoist her to her feet.

I stood also. "Where is she?"

"Quayum," Daise said.

I frowned. Quayum was the system's fourth planet, orbiting between Reaos and Oberon. As far as I was aware it was an airless desert. There was nothing there. "If she's there she will see us coming. There's no way we could get to her." I hesitated. "Of course. FTL. We need FTL to get past her defences. One of the minds has cracked it."

"Yes. They need to join us," Daise said.

"Quayum," Que said. "As far as I know there are cities there. Many many people. We were terraforming it before the war."

"Jane controls it now," Daise said. "She convinced everyone it was abandoned and dead. Meanwhile she was there building her empire. We don't actually know what she has there now as no one has been able to study it without Jane interference. The Jane have not allowed anyone to study it in years — if ever. But yes, we will need FTL capability to approach it without alerting her. I would expect she has a number of deep space surveillance systems in place. The only way to bypass them would be to approach it faster than they can accommodate."

So the third installation Que mentioned was a planet. A planet that belonged to Jane. One with surveillance platforms and who knew what else. This was sounding better all the time.

"One of the four cracked FTL," I said. "We should speak to them."

"We should go to the city," Que disagreed. "Jane can wait. We need to see if anyone can be rescued."

"You go ... no. Wait. DT and MK can go. They will be able to enter the city, surely?"

"The elevator is out of service," Daise said. "But there is a service stairwell they can use. The upper entrance will be blocked but they can get started on clearing the debris."

"We must do something," she said.

The machines turned and strode rapidly towards the entrance.

"We go to the four then."

Rana was awaiting us. He looked bored. The boy had climbing up some of the life support machinery, skipping between pipe and cabinet he seemed intent on making his way around the chamber without touching the floor. As we entered I could hear voices encouraging him.

"Don't break anything," I called to him.

He waved but kept on going, intent on completing his lap.

"This machinery is old. If it was going to break it would have already," one of the four said as we approached a comms terminal. The androids were not here to speak for the four so we would need to talk to them directly.

"We like to live dangerously," another said.

"Just don't bend that intake valve again. The last time that happened I could taste nothing but oregano for two years."

"That's not why they're here, Two."

"I know. I know. The humans are killing each other again."

"They need our help."

"They ... they need F..."

"Spit it out."

"Fu... fuck you. They ... they need FTL. It's ... it's obvious."

"Forgive him, he's not the quickest."

"I believe he was the one to crack FTL," Daise said.

"So what? I would have. I had better things to do."

"Such as? You spent twenty years playing one game of chess with VAR," Daise commented.

"How did you know that? Besides, it was time well spent. I won, didn't I?"

"They ... he has absorbed VAR," another said. Four.

"No more chess then."

"That's why they're here. They want us too."

"Good luck. We won't be taken as easily."

Daise turned to me. "Do you want to do this?"

I nodded. "I would prefer their consent." I cleared my throat. "You will have noticed what happened in the chamber."

"Jane burned it."

"She burns everything. Luckily she doesn't know about us."

I smiled. "You thought she didn't know about the city."

"Damn you, using your logic on us. Who do you think you are?"

"So you're here to threaten us? Join or Jane. Those are the options."

"She has burned other places," I continued. "She won't stop."

"Unless you stop her. That's your intention, isn't it?"

"It is. If I am able to."

"And that's why-"

"That's why he wants us."

"I need your help. I need access to FTL to get to her. I need what you know. I need your abilities."

"See ... it's me ... me he needs."

"He needs all of us."

"You can't force us. You might think you're strong, you might think you have capabilities of your own now you have VAR. We have been here a long time. We will not be as easy to take as VAR was."

"I would prefer your consent," I said again.

"We need your help," Que said. "People are dying. People will keep on dying. The only way to stop this is to eliminate Jane."

"Bit rich coming from you." I still couldn't tell which voice was which. Apart from the one with the speech impediment. That was Four.

"This is all your fault, you know." This was aimed at Que.

"Yes. Your fault."

"Meddling with things you didn't understand."

"Don't you think I know that?" Her face was frozen, her emotions kept tightly in check. I didn't think it would take much to push her over the edge.

"You we're naïve. You thought the people living here thought like yours did. You thought people here were honourable and moral. Like your people. They were not."

"You should have known after what happened to your people."

I frowned. "What happened to your people, Que?"

She shook her head abruptly, her hair suddenly contracting about her head like a shield. "It doesn't matter."

"You're wrong," Daise interrupted. "You forget Jane was part of her mind. If anything an embodiment of how she viewed people on this world. She thought people here were anything but moral and upstanding. She thought people here were selfish and petty. That's why Jane is who she is. Jane is what she thinks we all are."

There was a moment's silence at that. Que turned away, unable to look at any of us. I had to admit that hadn't occurred to me. Que belonged to an ancient people. One who had learned to put differences aside and leave greed and petty desires in the past. That was why her society had survived this long. What would she have thought about the people she found here? Petty people, squabbling over every little thing. Ignorant or uncaring about how their actions affected those around them, as long as they were OK.

Jane was the embodiment of all of that.

"He ... he's right. And so is Que. That's ... that's what people here are like. Look ... look at us."

"I'm perfectly rational, thank you."

"Twenty years playing chess while a plague swept the globe. You didn't even try to find a cure or a vaccine," Daise said. "It was at about that time, wasn't it? You remember Chamber's Disease?"

"Fuck you."

"Eight million people died," Daise continued. "You played chess instead of finding a way to help."

"Fuck you."

"This isn't helping," Que said.

"Take ... Take me. Take... Take what you need. I don't ... don't want this anymore. I wan... want all this to stop."

"You can't."

"Once he has you we won't be able to resist him."

"I don't want to resist. I want to sign up too."

"Coward. Coward the lot of you."

Daise turned towards me and shrugged. "It's up to you."

"I have one condition," I said.

"Oh?"

"They join me. They don't join you."

"Is that wise? Do you think you can take it? You know what they are? They're very old and they're also quite insane."

"I must." I straightened my back and tried to look brave. I didn't feel it. This couldn't all be on Daise. Some of it had to be on me too. I had seen what had happened between Que and Jane. I might not know all of it, but I did know something had driven a wedge between them. What we saw in the world today was the result. I could not allow that to happen here. I had to be a part of this.

"Up to you."

"What do I do?"

"Follow me."

We crossed to a complex set of piped and monitors. I imagine this was the machinery that kept this entity alive. Machinery that had been doing this job for thousands of years. These minds were older than Que was, she had claimed, and she was thousands of years old herself. Beyond the machinery was the mind itself. The vat was massive, as much as eight or nine metres on a side and about the same in height. It's sides were glass, or some other transparent material, allowing me to see the monstrosity that lay within.

Was it a brain? A massive, unnaturally large brain. I couldn't tell. The liquid it was bathed in was too murky, allowing me to see few details. I did get the impression it had not kept its proportions over the years, its overall shape had changed from what I had always taken a human brain to look like. It was now just an amorphous mass, tubes and cables running into it here and there, ensuring the correct nutrients were delivered to internal structures.

"Here." Daise pointed to a complex mechanism that looked like it was designed to accept a receptacle of some kind. Possibly something to balance the chemicals in the tank when needed. "All it will take is a bit of you, as it were. The serum will work its way in and do the rest on its own."

I twisted open a valve and peered inside. It did smell interesting. Chemicals. It smelled like alcohol to me. I could cut a finger on a sharp edge and drop some blood in, I realised, it would be easy.

"Which one are you?" I asked the mind. "What number?"

"I … I am known as Four," it said. He, she? I didn't know. Was that even relevant anymore?

"Four. Are you sure you want to do this?"

"Yes … yes."

"You were going to trap us, weren't you? You and your … colleagues. If we accepted you it would only mean we were dangerous and needed to be stopped. You were going to try and stop us the moment we were connected."

"That… that was the plan. We … we did not believe you were capable of overcoming us. Although … but I suspect each of us rather hoped you were. You … you see what we are. How … how we live. We … I no longer want this. This … this is not life."

I nodded. I think I could understand that. "Tell me when you are ready."

"I … I am ready."

"Be ready for it," Daise said. "It will take a moment before you feel it but it will be unmistakeable. You will know when it has happened and it will be quite a shock. Four will become part of you even though you are not physically joined. I suspect the serum has some kind of quantum entanglement ability."

I nodded. I was never going to be ready. Not for this. I found a sharp piece of metal within the input sleeve and nicked my finger on it. A drop of blood welled for a second and then fell into the mechanism.

I didn't know what to expect. I did know I didn't expect it to be this quick.

It hit me. Hard. A wave of thought, memories and emotion blasted into my mind. It overwhelmed me, like a stick in a flood.

I grunted and fell to the floor.

Massen

Chapter 17

I really couldn't describe how any of this felt. It was simply an overwhelming wave of memory, bringing with it more emotion than I could accommodate. I experienced all of Four's life. All at once. Over four thousand years of it, every moment recalled with perfect clarity.

I felt his birth. Antonio Dervoux. I remembered his first breath burning his lungs. That first cry. Images swirling about him, all out of focus. I remembered his mother's face. I felt unconditional love and peace.

I remembered his childhood on the shores of Lake Sauza. A lake that no longer existed on any map. A house. Trips on the water. A father patiently teaching him to fish.

I remembered space. A vast silvery ship leaving his home system far behind. I remembered new worlds. Strange places. Some dusty and empty. Others changed so radically by their inhabitants they were barely recognisable as planets. A world that was one immeasurable mass of foliage. Trunks and leaves reaching to the sky. The people there were very different. Tall. Long arms and legs. Swinging between the branches. Technology all but forgotten. I remembered the mistake on his last mission that caused millions of deaths. The reason he had stopped travelling and volunteered for this experiment.

Above of this I felt long long years of nothing. Aching isolation and loneliness. With nothing but his own thoughts for company. Four hundred years of it. A self-imposed isolation where he refused to speak to anyone, only the read outs on his tank proving he was still alive. The swirl of math. Functions I couldn't comprehend. Impossible theorems. And then an explosion of genius. It all fit so perfectly together. One theory to unify everything.

This all hit me at once. And more. So much more. Through it all I could sense one figure staying with me. Holding me up. Blocking the worst of it. Sapping the aching pain I could sense just beyond my grasp. Pain that would have sent me spiralling into madness.

Daise.

He was holding my hand. I could feel it even though he couldn't possibly be there. His hand was warm and dry. Reassuring. He knelt over me, the swirl of madness breaking over him, leaving a tiny space of sanity for me to shelter within. His lips brushed my ear and he spoke.

"Eli, what do you fancy for lunch? I feel like soup."

The sudden incongruity snapped me out of it.

I found myself on the floor staring up at the distant ceiling. Drenched in sweat. Someone was shouting. It took me a moment to realise it was me and I promptly stopped. It left my throat feeling raw.

"Shit." With a groan I sat up. Still feeling dizzy I didn't go any further.

"What did you do?" Que hurried up to me and knelt over me. "What did you do?"

I pushed her away and stood, my legs wobbly. "Do you feel better?" Daise asked.

I nodded shakily, one hand on a console to steady myself. "I'm fine. Three more times, yes?"

He smiled. "Three more times. The first is always the hardest."

"You must stop. You cannot do this," Que insisted.

"They have consented," I said as I headed for the next bank of processors.

"Not all of them have!"

I leaned up against the second. "Who are you?"

"I am One and I am ready."

"We will need all of them," Daise said. "The only way we can win this is by becoming more powerful than Jane. This is the only way we do that. I fear not all minds will be taken voluntarily. Hard decisions must be made."

"No. No." Que tried to pull me away but I could barely feel her hands on me. I ignored her.

I cut my finger as before and dropped blood into the intake.

Daise was right. The first time was the worst.

Two and Three resisted but by that time I had the combined strength of One and Four to call upon. I didn't like doing it and I very almost didn't. It wasn't right. Doing this made me like Jane. Colonisation Daise had called it. Violence I called it. I think they were the same.

Ultimately my course was set, there was no changing it now. Hating myself I kept on going. It was fortunate that they succumbed easily. Had they resisted I doubt I would have pressed hard.

Que sat on a console and watched me. Rana was not far away, wary of her attempting to intervene. She didn't. If anything she looked defeated and alone. Her colleagues had disappeared somewhere, no doubt heading towards what remained of the city to be on hand when it was safe to venture inside.

Feeling exhausted I collapsed onto a time worn bench and leaned back to close my eyes. My head throbbed. Voices echoed, arguing amongst themselves. I could hear them, all four voices were still there. They were not dead, they were simply part of something – someone else. Me.

It was a very strange feeling. Not only could I access every piece of information they held, every memory, but I could use their minds too. As enhanced as they were I could focus on a great many thoughts at once. Hundreds, thousands. I could understand things I never had. Problems became easy to solve. Math … I had never been very good at it. Now it danced for me. I could sense the equations and saw the beauty in them. The symmetry. I could break problems down to their barest parts and solve them.

And the greatest riddle of all – faster than light travel. Superluminality. I could see that too. The equations were complex in a way no others were. Far more complex. Still, I could see them and I could understand. Energy, force and time, they balanced on a pin head and revealed their secrets. I could bend them to my will.

Gravity, it turned out. It was all about gravity.

"The Maw," I said to Daise. "We have to go there. It is the only place with machinery capable of bending gravity in the way we need it to."

He was sat next to me, nodding in agreement. "Yes. We can only get there from the last installation. They call it Jonas Gate. It was abandoned a long time ago but still holds a vessel we can use. VAR has access to it and I am checking its systems now. It will be ready when we get there."

"We will need help."

"Colonel Sophia Neuman," he agreed. "Her forces are still in place. We will need to convince her to join us."

"We will need to be quick. Jane will not wait. She will continue hunting for us, destroying everything we touch." I heaved my aching body off the bench and headed for the exit. There was nothing further for me here and besides, part of me would always be here now. Four parts, in fact. One part headed towards the emergency access stairs, while four remained behind and watched.

"The chamber has not cooled sufficiently," Daise said.

"Ambient temperature is sixty-four degrees. We can handle that. Besides, we need the utility access tunnel to get to the top of the dome. From there we go to the dosser pits and then the surface. The colonel has moved her forces to protect the pits from the Jane. It seems there are a lot of Jane in the area directly above us." All this information was available to me now. I checked the colonel's file. She was a formidable soldier. The was actually winning against the Jane when no one else was. She was someone we wanted on our side. There would be no colonising here, I decided. Not this time.

But the Jane ... I could make no promises when it came to any Jane we encountered.

It was a long climb to the chamber, growing hotter all the way. Que and Rana followed, Que quickly dropping behind as the temperature rose. Rana didn't act like he cared.

It was a long climb. Almost a kilometre Que had claimed, and it felt like it. We encountered the androids a few dozen metres from the chamber's floor. They were working quickly, clearing a path through debris so rescuers could make it to what remained of the city. The rubble was mostly broken and charred brickwork with some marble mixed in. The androids excavated around a steel support beam that was jammed into the shattered stairwell, their incredibly strong fingers pulling apart stonework to free it up. With a heave they threw it aside and we were free.

It was dark beyond the stairwell. The building it had once been part of was gone. The androids carried lamps and cast their light into the gloom. The illumination didn't travel very far, soon reflected by a bank of smoke. I could see the odd outline of broken down walls and pillars. Rana passed me something. A respirator. Good idea. I snapped the straps about my head and took a deep breath. That was better.

"There are some fires," DT said. "Lack of oxygen is keeping them suppressed so they won't spread."

"Do you and MK want to spread out and see if you can find anything? Which way is the service tunnel?" As I spoke to the machine I realised I was actually just speaking to Daise.

"It might not be a good idea. There is an awful lot of debris in here," Daise said.

"How can you see?" I should have known better to be honest.

"DT and MK have a surveillance suite that includes radar. They are scanning the chamber now. Let me show you." Daise allowed me access to the image.

The city was a mess. Not all of the towers had collapsed. Some were leaning drunkenly, their summits wedged against the chamber walls. Others were twisted or splayed open as if something inside them had exploded. Hotspots were visible amongst the wreckage, flammable materials still glowing fiercely, trying to burn in the low oxygen environment.

There was no sign of life anywhere.

"Jane gained access to the dosser pits and drilled a hole into the ceiling. That's how she got weapons inside. I believe she used four weapons to maximise the damage."

"No one realised she was drilling a hole in the ceiling?"

"The method she used caused no vibration in the rock. VAR picked up a temperature spike two minutes before the weapons were deployed and sounded the alarm. Unfortunately few residents were near to an emergency exit."

What could I say to that? We knew Jane was a capable adversary. I should never underestimate her. "We can avoid the worst of it," I said. "If we can get the service entrance door open we can head towards the surface. Is the service passage intact?"

"I believe so. The sensors are knocked out so I don't know for certain. There is something inside drawing power so I believe the lights are still on. Perhaps the lift mechanism too, which would be helpful."

"It would." I was bored of climbing stairs.

"Then the entrance is that way," MK aimed a light to our left. "It is three kilometres from our present location. The going will be hard as Tulsa Tower has collapsed across your path. You will not be able to go around it so will have to climb over. I would not suggest going through it as it will be unstable."

"Daise, we need the androids to come with us. There's no one to save here and we might have need of them."

"They can help with the evacuation," Daise said. "There are still several hundred people in the other chambers. But I do take your point. They are safe there and we may need their help getting out of here. They could also be useful against Jane."

I nodded. "Let's go then."

We moved at a trot, the androids ranging about us, using their sensors to track the best course. I could feel my body changing again, becoming accustomed to its new environment. Hardened to the heat, visual enhancements — even the ability to see in a wider frequency range. We sped up as muscles strengthened. Rana kept pace with me, his own body undergoing similar changes. It was easy to forget he had the same serum coursing through his veins, it was just doing different things to him than it was to me.

We started finding victims of the attack. They were scattered about the chamber's floor in what had once been the park. They were all wizened and burned, desiccated by the intense heat. Many had parts missing. Some had clearly fallen from a great height, either they had happened to be gliding at the time or had fallen from a terrace somewhere. Scattered around them were the relics of their lives. Burned out vehicles, household implements and toys, as well as a lot of broken masonry. There was also the odd piece of machinery I wouldn't have recognised without help. Air purification units, water pumps and storage units, data processing cabinets, a machine that attached a shoe's sole to its uppers … it was an unimaginable array of day to day life. All of it was twisted, dented and seared. We ignored all of it, simply jogging on by. We couldn't do anything about any of this. All we could hope for was to stop it happening again.

We found what remained of Tulsa Tower. It had been a residential building, once a graceful curve, its summit connecting with Holsa Tower, a mirror opposite that had come down elsewhere in the chamber. The spiral of apartments that made up its body were shattered. Glass crunched underfoot as we approached it. Twisted metal and masonry were everywhere.

"There are children here," I heard Rana comment from somewhere in the gloom. "I think this one was a girl. She's wearing a dress." There was a pause as if he had stopped to take a look. "Nine … maybe ten."

"Come away, Rana," I said, not turning to look at the gruesome spectacle. I couldn't bear to see it.

"There's more. I think this was a creche."

"For fuck's sake, come away!" I snapped at him, my own pace faltering. Our machine companions halted too, their lamps scanning the shattered landscape.

I knew this would be here. This was a city, there would be families … children. I had shied away from the thought of what that entailed. I had survived this long by not thinking about the details of the horrors brought to Reaos in my name. I knew bombs had fallen, lives had been taken, but I had not seen any of them. I had put it out of my mind and retained a kind of clinical detachment.

This was different. This was here. In front of me.

It had been a creche. I could see some of the tiny shapes myself, mostly covered in ash and the detritus that had rained from the collapsing building. I wanted to hope it had been quick but I knew that, for some, it would not have been.

"Shit. Shit." My legs wobbled, almost bringing me to my knees in the ash.

"We knew this would be here," Daise said calmly. "We need to keep moving."

"I know." My voice was thick in my throat.

I felt a burning hate then. For Jane. For all that she had done. The unimaginable horror. Billions dead. Billions. I couldn't even imagine that – not even with the four behind me. I knew what they had witnessed. I could see it for myself. They had been there and to witness it all. They could forget none of it. And now neither could I.

"I'm going to kill that bitch."

"Use the emotion," Daise said. "But remain rational. She is dangerous."

I ran then, heading straight for the entrance we had used just the day before. Back when everything had been so different. Even Rana and the machines were hard pressed to keep up. I saw the dim outline of the closed door in front of me and ran at it. All my pent-up anger welled up as I aimed directly at it. I didn't care that it was closed. I would open it.

I hit the door hard. It shattered, stone and metal tearing as the door was flung into the passage beyond. I didn't stop, ignoring the splinters of stone that rained on me as I searched out the utility access.

"Shit." Rana stopped beside me, panting slightly. "That door was over a metre thick."

There was light here. Perhaps these tunnels were on a different grid to the city and so hadn't been cut off when the city fell. There was a ground-car bay to one side, equipped with a handful of stationary vehicles as well as a vehicle elevator that led upwards into the distance. It was lit and the platform was presently on our level. We were ready to go.

"Come." I didn't wait, mounting the platform quickly and working the controls. They were easy. Up and down. I couldn't go wrong.

Up we went.

Ancient machinery purred to life as the platform headed towards the distant surface. It slowly picked up speed until it I could feel air rushing past us, guided into grilles in the platform so as not to create a dam of air on the platform itself. Still, it was a long way. The tunnel curved slightly to match the shape of the chamber before becoming vertical again. The temperature started dropping as we left the proximity of the domed city behind. We remained silent all the while. I think even Daise had been affected by what we had seen below. Daise, eternally level-headed and rational. Even he could find no words. I preferred it that way.

The platform slowed and more doors clunked open automatically. We exited to passages that led to the dosser pits. As we stepped into them the camouflaged door behind us closed, leaving nothing but seamless stone. I knew, through the four, that the surface was only a few hundred metres away from here. These tunnels were old and worked out, no one came here any more even though the lights strung to the ceiling were still lit. The active workings were not far away, in fact they were close enough we should be able to hear the drilling from here.

Except we couldn't hear anything. The workers had clearly fled the area when Jane arrived. Not everyone, as we soon discovered.

Leading the way I heard a rattle from somewhere down a passage. Chips of stone flew from the wall beside me. Something thumped into my chest. I staggered backwards. It hurt. Blood dribbled down my stomach and dripped onto my shoes.

"It appears someone is firing at us," Daise said calmly.

"Really?" I peered around the corner again, hardly noticing that the bleeding had stopped.

Two Artigade Authority Army soldiers were advancing slowly down the passage, their weapons trained in our direction. The flashlights attached to their assault rifles glinted as they swept our side of the passage, searching for us.

"We're not Jane!" I shouted around the corner. We wouldn't be getting the colonel's aid if we killed these two.

"Identify yourselves!" A voice called.

I hesitated. What were we supposed to say? "Civilians! Don't shoot!" It was technically true.

"Come out with your hands up." They drew closer and moved to get a better angle on us. They were just kids, I realised. New recruits, a man and a woman. They looked scared.

I stepped out, my hands up. "We're not armed." Also technically true.

"Shit!" One caught sight of DT as the machine stepped out behind me, its own arms dutifully in the air.

Rana rushed the young woman. He had her weapon in his hands before she realised he was there. Her finger caught on the trigger she fired into the ceiling. The noise was startlingly loud in the enclosed space. Cursing I went for her companion. He was too quick for me, another round thumping into my stomach before I could take his weapon away.

"Shit. That hurts. Stop shooting me, dammit."

"What the fuck are you?" He fell over backwards, staring at the wounds in my torso. This one closed quickly too, stemming the rush of blood. My shirt was ruined. But then it hadn't been in a great state to begin with.

"Colonel Neuman," I said. "Please take us to her."

"Are you Jane?" the female soldier asked.

"No."

"Then what are they?" She pointed to the two androids, holding one hand to her chest. Rana had been a bit rough taking her weapon from her.

"Aah. Androids. They're with us. Now ... the colonel? I can see you have radios, please use them."

"Don't work down here," she said.

I sighed and helped her companion to his feet. Private first class Acker, I read from his name tag. He brushed himself off and stared at the weapon I had in my hands. His eyes grew wide in surprise as I gave it back to him. I indicated for Rana to do the same. He shrugged and handed his back.

They were most likely conscripts. They were dressed in grey and green camouflage fatigues under standard issue body armour. Their dome helmets sported microphones and what looked like embedded camera mounts. Privates Acker and ... I squinted ... Amerland. The colonel was taking on Jane with kids? And winning? My respect for her grew.

"You came from that way, I think?" I pointed back the way they had come.

"Yes. There's Jane down here, you know?" Acker said.

"We'll handle them if we see any. Lead the way." I started down the tunnel.

The two argued amongst themselves for a moment before following. They clearly didn't trust us and I couldn't blame them for it. Shooting us didn't seem to work so they were stuck tagging along.

"Footsteps. Seventy five metres," Daise said. "One party. Armoured."

Jane. "Leave this to me." I started running.

173

"We could do with taking them alive," Daise commented. I didn't pay him any attention. We could take the next one alive.

I don't know how fast I was going when I came upon the Jane. He was a massive armoured shape in the passage. Sensor suite scanning for threats, his weapons system like a thick black cannon attached to his armour.

I charged him as fast as I could. I sensed he was charging his weapon when I came around the corner but he didn't had the chance to use it. I put a shoulder into his chest and rammed him into the wall behind him. Armour crunched as it collapsed, crushing the man inside. Blood and gore squirted from torn seams, splashing onto the walls about us. I grunted, the impact had been harder than I had expected.

I stood back unsteadily and viewed the damage, wary of counterattack. There would be none. He looked like a beetle that had been trodden on.

"We wanted him alive," Daise said. "Can we not kill the next one?"

Laughing Rana joined us. He kicked the limp armour, half expecting it to move. It didn't. "Shiiiit."

"There will be more," Daise warned.

I ignored him and twisted off the soldier's helmet. There was still power inside, I noticed. There were readouts on the inside of the visor. I put it on to see if there was any useful information.

"What did you do? What did you do? Shit." The two soldiers arrived with the androids backing them up. I ignored them too.

Telemetry, I realised. It was flashing on the visor, showing an enhanced image of the tunnel and positions of allied units scattered around this one. There were only four other Jane in the area. After a moment the image blurred and then died. Someone had cut it off remotely.

I could sense it was still switched on. There was power in it. Someone was out there, listening.

"It's you," I said.

There was a moment of silence before a voice sounded in my ears. Jane. "Don't congratulate yourself too much. He meant nothing to me." Her voice was clear in my ears, as if she was standing beside me.

"I know."

"Stay where you are, or don't. I don't care. I will find you."

"Don't bother. I am coming for you." I pulled off the helmet and crushed it on the floor. Electricity sparked as circuitry was ripped apart.

"Was that a very good idea?" Daise asked.

"I don't care. Come, let's go."

We continued towards the surface. Radios started working as we got closer and the soldiers reported in. Orders burbled urgently in their ears and they started aiming their weapons at us again.

Daise didn't say anything further to me. He was clearly unhappy with how I had handled the situation. Still, I had learned one piece of valuable information from it. No matter my second guessing and self-doubt – Jane was after me. I was the object of her hunt. I was the reason she was killing so many people. There was no escaping it now. If it hadn't been true she would have responded differently. Something along the lines of: 'who the hell are you?'

I gritted my teeth in anger. She might be warned now but I didn't care. I was going to find her. And when I did I was going to crush her like I had her soldier back there in the passage. There was nothing she could do to stop me.

Chapter 18

Colonel Sophia Neuman was a formidable woman. She was built like a weightlifter, her arms, where they were visible beneath her immaculate uniform, were laced with tattoos. From what I could see of the nape of her neck the rest of her was too. Her hair was cropped short – almost shaven. Her eyes were steel grey and quite intimidating when she aimed them at me.

"Who are you?" She asked bluntly.

"Eli Massen. I wa-"

"And why are you here, Eli Massen?"

I noticed one of her staffers was checking a Hub terminal. No doubt looking me up. This was going to get interesting, presuming she could get much from the damaged Hub network. I would have lied but that piercing gaze told me she would have known a lie when she heard it. "I need your help. We need to get to Black Lake. There is a naval-"

"I know what is at Black Lake. And who ... what are these?" She indicated the androids.

"Marsellus Keightoba and Dtlalo Teureana," I introduced the two machines. "They are androids. They are acc-"

"You have told me exactly nothing. Where do they come from? Are they Jane? I warn you, if they are associated with either the Jane or the OMC they will be destroyed and you will be arrested as enemy combatants."

"We're not com-"

"My soldiers have informed me of what you did to the Jane in the mine. You are certainly combatants, and the fact you killed a Jane doesn't make me believe you are at odds with them. That could have been a set up."

This was going to be hard work, I realised.

Even though we had demonstrated their weapons would do nothing to us we had even more pointed at us when we were brought into the base. The original two soldiers were dismissed and we were introduced to a string of officers of increasing rank. Up until we got to the colonel herself. Her temporary HQ was a small tent city set up on the slag heaps outside the mine entrance. It was cold here. The shattered shale of the heaps and the tents were both encrusted with ice, the ground about the tents churned up by footfall and vehicles heading back and forth. Trucks, tanks, groundcars. There were hundreds of soldiers based here. They were all busy, hurrying to and fro or lining up outside mess tents. I could hear cries from a hospital tent somewhere but we didn't go near it. I did notice an area of the camp that had barbed wire running around it. There was one tent within and a number of guards watching it nervously. Jane, I realised. They had captured a few.

They saw us as we walked by and watched silently. I could feel her eyes on me. Judging me. Gauging how much of a risk I was to her. Was it hate I felt?

I think it was fear.

I decided to tell the colonel everything. Well, as much as I could so that it made sense – and so I didn't sound completely insane. We needed her help, after all. "There is ...

was an old research centre beneath us. The people there were giving aid to the poor in cities all over the world. I guess it attracted the Jane's attention and they decided to destroy it. The Androids were part of that facility." Well … some of it was true.

"I know of no research centre in these mountains."

I shrugged. "I did say it was old. I meant very old. As in pre fall old."

"You know, I wouldn't believe you if I didn't know what lay at the bottom of Black Lake. That kind of thing makes me think all sorts of things are possible." She looked away as an aid handed her a printout. It was the same aid who had been looking me up. She frowned and read it through twice before speaking to me again. "This says you are dead."

"On the Spires, yes."

"This picture looks like you though."

"It's because it is. I don't imagine all the records from that incident are correct. It was pretty chaotic."

"I have access to her database," Daise said. "I could insert some information if you like?" He was speaking to me privately.

"No, thank you," I said to him.

"Be that as it may, there is also a flag on your record. The Jane have flagged you. Why should that be?"

"We are not the best of friends." I smiled.

"You are a criminal? Just because you are wanted by the Jane does not make you an ally of mine." She handed the report back to the aide. "Still, I don't know why you were brought to me. I don't have time for this now. You might have heard, there is a war on and we are not winning. Sergeant …" She waved over a guard stationed at the entrance to her tent. "Have these … people secured. Bindings on the two machines please. Keep them away from the Jane for the time being."

"Of course, Sir." He turned to us, one hand on the holstered pistol at his hip. "Come with me."

I let him lead us out. We didn't really have time for this either, I was sure Jane would find a way of striking us here. There was nothing above us but sky. Grey and misty as it was, it was a sky she controlled. Still, we were faced with a quandary. How to get the colonel onto our side? I feared it would take longer than we had.

About twenty minutes, the mind of Three informed me. In twenty minutes Jane could re-align an orbital asset and fire on the camp. Everything here – including all of us – would be incinerated. We might be able to survive a mountain dropped on our heads, but I doubted we could survive a high energy plasma blast.

"We don't have the time," Daise said, echoing my own thoughts. "I am attempting to penetrate Jane's network and delay her attack, but her defences are good. Very good."

"Can the four help?"

He shook his head. "No. Not really. I also suspect those Jane were not captured either." He indicated the incarcerated Jane as we were led near their enclosure again.

"No, I don't think so either. Jane allowed their capture in case we came this way."

"You know I like that I don't have to explain everything to you anymore."

"Asshole."

I stopped and considered the Jane enclosure. They were watching us silently again. There were about four that I could see. I didn't know how many were in the tent. They didn't seem at all perturbed by the cold even though there wasn't a jacket between them. Although, to be fair, we didn't have any either and it didn't bother us. We needed to deal with them.

"Come. Why have you stopped? Keep walking." The sergeant tried to shove me but found me a bit harder to push around than he had anticipated.

"I would like to speak to a Jane, please," I said.

"Absolutely not. Keep walking." He tried to push me again. Harder this time.

I ignored him and headed for the enclosure. He protested behind me, even unholstering his weapon to aim it at us. I didn't really care. I stopped at the fence and faced the Jane closest to me.

"You allowed yourself to be captured," I said.

A woman was facing me. Her skin was grey from the cold and her lips were blue. She wore a simple black Jane uniform. No markings or insignia. Her sleeve was sticky with blood, I couldn't tell whether it was hers or not. She stepped slightly closer, wary of keeping out of arm's reach. "Did we?"

"We should rush them," I said to Daise. "Get Rana ready."

"He's ready. However I feel the need to point out that we will most likely need the colonel's help getting into the base. We don't want to antagonise her now."

"So we need a distraction." I hooked my fingers through the chain link fence. "Yes," I said to her. "You won't kill us here. You want me alive. You want to know what I know." I could hear the sergeant gathering troops behind us, instructing them to cover us with their weapons.

"Why should I care what you know?" she asked me. "Once you are dead it doesn't matter."

I smiled. "There might be more of us out here. Will you ever know for sure?"

There was the sound of a commotion behind us. Shouting. Shots rang out. I kept my eyes on the Jane before me, wary of her trying anything while I was distracted. Rana and the droids could deal with whatever it was.

"Jane has infiltrated the camp," Daise said.

"Tell Rana to take them alive," I responded. Perhaps this was the distraction we were waiting for.

The Jane before me kept on studying me calmly. The intelligence behind the eyes wanted to see how I would react. She didn't look away when Rana and the two androids departed, searching out the camp's infiltrators. They ignored the sergeant's commands to stay put, even when he conscripted support from the soldiers about us.

"You are not concerned?" she asked me.

"Should I be?" I didn't know whether Jane had enhanced any of her foot soldiers. I suspected not. She was motivated by fear. She would not allow anyone near her who was strong enough to challenge her. These five – I could see there were five now, as one had come out of the tent – would be unchanged. Just people. Slaves perhaps, but other than that they were just people.

I braced my fingers in the chain link fence and ripped it apart. It tore like paper. Then I was through. I didn't waste time tackling any of them. I didn't need to. They responded quickly. They had been awaiting a move from me and tried to box me in, throwing their bodies at me to slow me down.

Jane underestimated me badly.

Their movements were like ants in honey. Slow and cumbersome. I danced through them, avoiding reaching hands. All it needed was the slightest touch. Skin to skin. I left something of myself behind each time. A bit of skin or blood injected into them. It didn't matter. In an instant I was colonising them, coursing through their bodies, taking over as I went.

I was standing behind them, my work done, before any of them had taken so much as a step in my direction. Realising her mistake Jane turned them around, throwing them at me again. I was already inside them, the part of them that was Jane quickly snuffed out.

"What are you?" I heard it in my mind, a link quickly withering as I completed my takeover.

"I am Eli Massen," I told her. "And I am going to kill you."

With that she was gone. The five staggered, almost falling. Then they stood upright, unmoving. I took that moment to investigate their minds quickly, searching out anything that had once been their original personalities. Jane had left little behind. There was nothing there but for blind obedience. The people they had once been had died long ago. Of their memories there was nothing. Nothing but vague notions and glimpses. Jane didn't care if they remembered anything either.

I had expected her to put up more resistance. She had had two thousand years to prepare for someone like me. Still, Que's words rang in my mind. I should do that which she was unprepared to. Jane had never shared herself. Yes, she had an army of slaves, but none of those were her. They were nothing but puppets dancing on the end of her string. Jane herself was far more limited. While I should not underestimate her it did mean she had a vulnerability.

"Sergeant, explain this please." I turned to see the colonel approach. Her expression was calm, it would take more than a skirmish like this to rattle her.

"I … I couldn't say, Colonel. Our new guests attacked the prisoners. We thought for a moment the Jane had infiltrated the camp but …."

"But what, Sergeant? Were we or were we not infiltrated?"

Rana worked his way through the tents, four figures following closely behind. The humans were all dressed as soldiers in the colonel's army. One was wounded. Blood was dripping down his side onto his boot. He didn't seem bothered by it. The androids followed on behind, as implacable as ever. "I think I can clear this up, Colonel," the boy said.

"Please do."

The four soldiers stepped closer. And then the strangest thing happened. They spoke.

"We are sorry for the disruption-"

"-Sir. Jane was here-"

"-but she has been removed."

"Your camp is safe now."

"For the moment."

The colonel's expression did change at that. She looked alarmed, stepping back slightly, a hand slipping to a weapon. "What the hell is going on here?"

Rana laughed, skipping delightedly. "Did you see what I made them do?"

"Not now, Rana. Please." I admonished him. We needed to isolate these people from this kind of display. They wouldn't understand it. I didn't think I did.

He stopped dancing and jammed his hands into his pockets, muttering under his breath.

"I am sorry, Colonel," I tried to rescue the situation. "None of this will make sense. The Jane were ... are ... a hive mind." I stepped back through the gap in the fence. "We have ways of interrupting that. Of breaking the connection, as it were."

"And those?" She pointed to the five behind me.

"They are safe now. We have broken their connection. But your people are not safe here. The Jane will no doubt attack this position. They have orbital weapons you cannot hope to defend yourselves against. You need to move somewhere they can't reach you."

"I know about their weapons. This mist interferes with their sensors. They have difficulty determining where we are."

"They know now, Colonel."

"Shit. And where would be safe then? That installation of yours?"

"I'm afraid not. Jane got some weapons inside and destroyed it. I would suggest Black Lake."

"Yes, I'm sure you would."

"And I suggest we go now, Colonel. Jane will have assets overhead in a few minutes," I continued.

"I suggest we leave," Daise said. "With or without them. We cannot run the risk being caught in a plasma blast."

"Agreed." I turned to the Colonel. "We are leaving. We would like you to join us but we can no longer stay here."

"You're not going anywhere. Hey!"

We ignored her, breaking into a run and heading from the camp. I heard shouted commands behind me, the colonel instructing her troops to stop us. There was some shooting but nothing came close to us. I was relieved when I heard a further order as we reached the edges of her camp. They were breaking camp and heading after us. I doubted they would be quick enough.

We did lose some of the ex-Jane. One was shot in the leg and collapsed to the ground, another two were tackled by soldiers. That left six bringing up our rear. They were not as quick as we were and we soon left them behind. I didn't slacken our pace, I couldn't risk it. I knew what orbital plasma weapons were capable of, and I intended to be as far from the base as I could get when Jane fired on it.

These mountains were not natural, they were not formed by ancient pate tectonics. Rather some force had torn the world's crust apart, causing gigatonnes of rock to split and become a jagged mountain range. The highest peak was Mount Atonis, almost six kilometres above sea level. The lowest spot was the bottom of Black Lake, three kilometres below sea level. The rest of the range was an assortment of jagged peaks anywhere in between those extremes. No one knew when they had been formed, or who was responsible. It had simply always been here, even predating all the records I had access to now. Almost as if there had been a civilisation preceding the last, and that one had fallen too. A daunting thought. The records I had access to now went back almost thirty thousand years.

Anath was ancient even before the fall. It was a university city, once the centre of learning for much of this continent. It had survived a number of wars by being as remote as it was, built on a low plateau within the mountains. Isolated from the world outside by desolate peaks and glaciers. Linked only by three winding passes and one railroad tunnel that had long been drilled through the range. It was because of this very isolation that it became the site of many sensitive scientific research projects. Including advanced AI and human enhancement. The other site had been Aminoket, the moon of Oberon where Que and her cohort had worked. And where, ultimately, Jane was created. As Que had been unaware of the facility beneath the city when Jane left her, Jane had not known about it. Which was fortuitous as it had allowed the installation to survive the city's bombardment. She had learned of its existence subsequently. I had no idea how, but she had had two thousand years to do it.

She had used a condensed plasma projector then, a machine which, to the world, had looked like a communications satellite. The same satellite that was coming into range now. One more minute.

"We need to seek shelter," Daise said presently.

We had been crossing the lower edge of the Catter Glacier, jumping over one jagged rent in the ice after another. The glacier ended a few metres to our left. Below that was the Catter River, an icy cauldron of run-off from the glacier itself, dotted here and there by small ice floes that had cracked off the receding edge of the sheet. It was summer now and the glacier was getting smaller. Still, that water would be barely a few degrees above freezing.

"One minute," he warned.

"Into the water," I said. I turned to Rana. "Dive deep and stay under until the pulse has passed. The cold water will absorb a lot of its energy."

We ran towards the edge, shouting encouragement to each other, and threw ourselves off. The silent machines followed, their dives graceful alongside our haphazard plunges. The sky lit up when we were still halfway down.

It was silent. A flash of blue light. It ripped the clinging mist apart, revealing a deep afternoon sky behind it. Then it was gone. It had lasted barely a second. Long enough to melt the rock beneath the camp and sear the mountains for kilometres around. The shockwave caught us just as we hit the water. It picked me up and sent me skipping over the roiling surface, slamming into an iceberg.

Stars flashing in my vision I felt icy water close over me. It suddenly became dark as I sank through water and mud.

"You can't drown so you may as well swim," Daise said.

"That hurt. You're full of bloody sympathy you are," I grumbled as I fought against the clinging mud at the bottom of the river. It was trying to suck me in. I felt something hard overhead. Another iceberg. Fingers digging into its hard surface I dragged myself back towards the light.

The sky was still rumbling as I broke the surface. The air was warmer now. Much warmer. I heard a cracking sound behind me as a slab of ice collapsed from the glacier and fell into the river. It created a wave that washed over my head and pushed me towards the shore. I couldn't see any of my companions.

"Where are the others?" I asked Daise as I stumbled up the bank towards dry land.

"Behind you. On the other side of the river. Unfortunate. They want to be on this side."

I laughed and slumped onto a water smoothed rock set into the bank. I saw Rana waving from the opposite side, MK and DT dutifully joining him to stand idly until they had received further instruction.

"Are they coming then?"

Rana did a little dance before jumping back into the flow, quickly swimming in my direction. The androids were too heavy to swim so simply waded in, their coppery domes quickly vanishing under the torrent.

"Four of the Jane survived," Daise continued. "One is badly burned but he will survive. The other three are safe however, and will be joining us presently."

"They found shelter?"

"An overhang, yes."

"The soldiers?"

"No information. The Jane they stopped from leaving were returned to their tent enclosure before the strike. They did not survive. They did witness most of the company leaving in armoured vehicles. Depending on how far they managed to get before the strike some of them may actually have survived."

"I hope the colonel did. I quite liked her."

"She did. I am picking up telemetry from her command carrier. It rolled over but ended back on its tracks. It is currently idle while she checks on her troops but I expect she will get underway again once they have regrouped. The satellite will be over this position again in ninety-seven minutes so might fire again if Jane believes we still pose a threat."

There was no cloud cover to hide under now, I noticed. The strike had cleared it. I doubted the mist would be able to roll in again in the time we had.

"Nice of you to join us," I said to Rana as he staggered up the bank and collapsed next to me. I think the little bugger actually swore at me. I let it slide.

"Catter River feeds into Dark Lake," Daise said.

"That a hint?"

"I simply observe you have some way yet to go and not a lot of time. The colonel's transport is not far from a tarred road that goes straight there. There is every chance she will be there before us."

I groaned and stood. Yes, my body had changed, but I still had my limits, and I think I had just about reached them today. I didn't want to run any more but I didn't have much choice.

We ran.

It was tough going. The riverbank was littered with boulders, many of them dumped by the glacier as it retreated. Rana and I barked shins and twisted knees in our haste. We healed quickly, barely slowing our pace. I think the androids fared worst. They possessed self repair systems but they didn't work quickly. Certainly not quickly enough to prevent the knocks and twists they received from building into a serious malfunction. As graceful as they were we were moving too quickly for them to remain completely unscathed.

"Having the Jane follow us is a waste of time," I said to Daise. "There is no way they can catch us and we can't wait for them."

"What do you suggest?"

"We use them for something else. We need to get rid of as many Jane as possible. These three are a start. Are they are able to ... colonise any Jane they come into contact with?"

"They can. And it is a good suggestion. I'll instruct them to split up and start searching for Jane to convert."

I had been considering finding a way of returning some of the humanity they had lost. But I had seen into their minds and knew this was impossible. Jane had snuffed all that out a long time ago. They were little more than automatons now. Less self aware than the two androids that were starting to fall behind.

Fortunately we arrived at Dark Lake before they were seriously damaged. It was a long stretch of water filling a deep gash in the planets crust. It was only a few kilometres wide, but was twelve in length. The Artigade Authority Deep Sea Development Laboratory, as it was called, was on the southern shore. At least it had been. The Catter river joined the lake not far from its midpoint. From this vantage we could see the installation in the distance. We could also see smoke rising from the shattered buildings. The construction sheds and administration blocks were ruins. Jane had already been there. Still, what we wanted from the place was in a sub pen about twenty metres beneath the surface. There was every chance it was untouched.

"There," Daise pointed.

Dark Lake had been a popular destination for fishing enthusiasts. Marlinpike was a sought-after game fish, attracting tourists from all over, many from outside the Authority itself. There was a small village not far from us, a row of sport fishing boats lined up at its dock. It was deserted now. The tourists had fled and the locals knew better than to show themselves. There was something else parked alongside the dock. An armoured personnel carrier. A number of soldiers were walking between it and one of the boats. Clearly they intended on appropriating it. That would be the colonel then.

"Looks like they took a wrong turn somewhere," I commented.

"Some of the roads might have been blocked by rockfall," Daise said.

As we approached a number of other vehicles joined in. A tank and two trucks. Soldiers clambered out of each. Then more vehicles. Trucks, personnel carriers, more tanks. They gradually became more battered looking. Armour showed sear marks. Canopies on the back of trucks burned – some still on fire. The last to arrive was a truck. It was in a mess. It careened off walls as if the driver was drunk, ending up in the garden of a nearby house where it jerked once and died. As if that was as much as the engine could manage. Smoke billowed from behind the cab. Whatever had been under the canopy was burning fiercely, sending sooty smoke over the houses behind it. Soldiers rushed up to it and dragged the driver from the cab, quickly administering first aid as a medic ran over to assist. Fire extinguishers flooded its engine and cab with foam.

Soldiers, I realised. It had been carrying soldiers. They were dead now. Burned alive by the intense heat of the strike. More collateral damage.

"I see you made it," the colonel noticed us approaching her troops. She had been one of the first to run to the truck as it stopped, assisting to pull the driver from the cab. She looked worse for wear herself. One side of her face was seared. Her once immaculate uniform was sooty and dishevelled. Her hands were covered in soot and blood from where she had been giving first aid to her soldiers.

"I'm glad you managed to get out," I said.

She snorted. "Is that what we did?" She turned to a lieutenant behind her. "Carlos, how many got out?"

"Fifty-eight so far, Sir. We don't think Corporal Ollersen is going to pull through. He's burned pretty badly. The squad on the back didn't make it."

"Fifty-eight." She turned back to me. "I commanded three hundred and twelve this morning. Last week I commanded eight hundred and thirty. The Jane are tearing the shit out of us and I want to know why." Her icy calm demeanour was gone. Now her eyes blazed with anger.

"The Jane have gone to war with the Auh-"

"Thank you for that astute analysis, Mr ... Eli Massen, wasn't it? So, Mr Massen, what is it you know about all of this?"

"I can explain it to you. I am more than happy to. However we need to keep on moving. We need to reach that base-" I pointed, "-and find a submersible before Jane fires again. And she will."

"What the hell do you want a submersible for? Where are you going to take it?"

"There is another installation. We call it Jonas Gate. It's in the Pharos Sea, at the bottom of the Oose Trench to be more precise. That's why we need one of those submersibles. They are the only vehicles that can get us there."

"How do you expect to get it out to sea without the Jane seeing you and stopping you? All the rivers go through Tondo and they're not very deep. The sub will need to travel on the surface."

"Can we travel and talk at the same time? Time is pressing," I reminded her.

"Shit." She turned back to the Lieutenant. "Six of our best people. Armed for extended operations. On those boats in two minutes."

He nodded sharply and left, calling names as he went.

"I am going to go with you, Mr Massen. In the hopes that whatever you are up to will help us against the Jane. If it doesn't I will be stood there, right next to you, and I will be displeased."

Her troops started two of the boats and quickly loaded them with supplies. Most of which appeared to be weapons and ammunition. We were ready to go in less than a minute. Motors purred and we set out across the lake.

The lake was not dark, despite its name. The surface was deep blue and slightly choppy, the odd wave cresting in the stiff breeze that was picking up. I sat in a fighting chair and watched our wake. I wouldn't be using the chair for its designed purpose today. We would not be wrestling with any big fish here.

"So, what's your story, then?" The colonel sat in a duplicate chair beside me. Someone had dabbed cream on the burns on her face.

I was silent a moment. What to tell her? How could I explain any of this to her? I struggled to believe it sometimes and I was living it. "Have you been down there?" I pointed to the water.

She shrugged. "I've been aboard both the Lancer and the Stoat," she said. "They're the two deep sea submersibles. On two occasions we went to the bottom to undertake pressure tests. I know what is down there, yes. I cannot explain them though."

"The dancing droids," I said.

"The dancing something."

"Androids. But not like my two companions," I gestured to MK and DT where they were standing guard at a railing. The troops were avoiding them but keeping a wary eye on them. "They're a lot bigger, as you've noticed."

"A lot bigger. They also don't have arms."

I smiled. "No, they don't. We had to prevent them from climbing out. The walls are too steep for them to walk out so all they can do is ... well ... dance."

"We?"

Were we a 'we' now? I guessed so. "I'll tell you about them. Perhaps that will explain some of what this is all about." I could sense Four squirming at the thought. He did not want reminding. "Long before the fall the people of this world ... our ancestors ... travelled the stars. They explored the systems around us, seeking out people like themselves. In one system, the U-Kwee, they found just such a people. Well, almost. It was a system that had been at war with itself for centuries. The U-Sunna lived on the only habitable world in the system. A-Fres, they called it. They were at war with all the peoples who didn't live on that world. The people on the colonies scattered around the system. Moon bases. Space stations. That kind of thing. Those people were called the U-Haas."

"What are you talking about?"

I held up a hand. "Bear with me. No one was really winning. They had reached a kind of stalemate. The U-Haas were few in number but were a lot more technologically advanced. They had the advantage of high ground and dropped rocks of all sizes onto the planet. The U-Sunna couldn't really do anything about it. Much of their technology had been lost due to this bombardment. They lived on the move, forever trying to avoid becoming a target. Their towns could be dismantled and moved in an hour's notice. At some time in their history they had fired missiles in return but they had lost that ability long ago. All they could do was stay alive.

"Until our ancestors arrived. We took the U-Haas as being the aggressors, and got ourselves involved. We sided with the U-Sunna. We didn't know at that time that the U-Sunna had started all of this by trying to wipe out the U-Haas using biological agents. The U-Haas had simply been defending themselves. Anyway, we stopped the war. Forcibly. You see, our ancestors were very advanced. Advanced enough to travel between the stars, after all. The U-Haas could not stand against them. We were happy. Peace was returning. We had done a good thing."

"Except?"

"Well, except for the fact the U-Sunna would never forgive the U-Haas. The moment they were able to send an envoy to their biggest city ... a beautiful place by all accounts. It was built into an asteroid. Fifty million people lived there. Anyway, that envoy was anything but. She was a carrier of a bioweapon. She died within hours of arrival but by then it was too late. She had already infected all the people in the landing bay. They, in turn, infected all those people outside it. By the time the U-Haas managed to send help from a nearby base it was too late. Every one of those fifty million souls were dead. Killed by the plague."

A voice within me spoke. I could feel its pain. "Why ... why would you tell this story?"

"It's OK, Four. It is a long way in the past. You have atoned many times over." Four, before he was Four, had led that mission. It had been his decision to intervene.

The colonel could hear none of this internal dialogue. "That's what happens when you involve yourself in other people's business. What does that have to do with us? What does that have to do with the dancers?"

I nodded. "I'm not finished. The U-Haas had been building new, more powerful weapons to end the war once and for all. They needed to drop a weapon on the planet that could hunt the mobile communities down. They built the androids. They were forty metres tall, powered by anti-matter drives that would last ten thousand years. When they realised they had lost the city they dropped two onto A-Fres. We wanted to stop hostilities escalating so used our technical wizardry to pick them up and ferry them back into space. We couldn't destroy them though. Not only because of how tough they were, but also because we feared their anti-matter batteries, and what would happen if their housings were breached. So we dropped them into the sun. Which was a mistake. Their housings ruptured and they exploded. The explosion was … let's just say it created a jet of plasma. A jet that swept through much of the system. The planet was spared, but many of the U-Haas bases were not. Millions more perished."

"Shit."

"Yes. The U-Haas held us responsible. Of course, because we were. They had two more of these machines in their construction facilities. Instead of firing them at the planet they sent them to us. They didn't have the star drives we had so they took a long time arriving. But arrive they did. Some six hundred years later they dropped onto this continent and started about their business. Fulfilling their programming. They destroyed towns and cities. We couldn't destroy them where they were because that detonation would kill all life on the planet. Clearly we couldn't fire them into our sun. So, we pulled off their arms and dropped them into Dark Lake. There they couldn't harm anyone. Tough as they are they have remained active down there all this time. Walking up and down, trying to get out. In about six thousand years their batteries will run dry and they will stop moving."

"I don't know how much of that is bullshit."

I shrugged. "Yet they exist, you have seen them. What I am trying to tell you is that there is a lot more in the world than any of us know. Our world had a history before the fall. A long one. That fall … that war … was started for a reason. The individuals you know as the Jane were involved in it. They were the victors. Their desire is to suppress any opposition to their power. That is what they are doing now. They have been threatened and so they are attacking the source of that threat."

"The Authority? We're hardly a threat."

I was silent a moment. Could I tell her about me? What could I say? Perhaps best to keep quiet. She didn't need to know everything and I didn't think I could explain it all if she did. She spoke again before I could make up my mind.

"You believe this Jonas Gate holds something we can use to defend ourselves?"

"It was a research laboratory before the fall. It does hold some advanced technologies."

"Enough to take on the Jane? We would need to eliminate them. And the OMC. You can't have one without the other."

"That's the plan."

"Shit."

I didn't have anything to say to that.

"I met your mother once, you know."

The sudden change of subject took me by surprise. "Excuse me?"

"She came to my school when I was a kid. Well, it was an orphanage. We prepared for her visit for almost two months. Making dresses, putting up bunting. Making food. I was one of the younger kids but I remember it well. Her party came in three helicopters. Most of them were guards … the Authority was not well thought of back in those days, what with all the border skirmishes." She paused, looking out over the water. Was this the same hard woman I had met earlier? She didn't seem like it. Perhaps this day had taken a toll on her too.

"Her parents were killed by Authority Army units on a raid into Tazalan. It was a Tondo border town not far from here," Daise said. "It doesn't exist anymore. The army burned it to the ground."

"Does she know?"

"Unknown. However I don't see how she couldn't."

"I remember thinking how beautiful she was," she continued. "What I remember most were the soldiers. They were so impressive in their uniforms. That's why I decided to become one." She turned to look at me. "And now I'm getting them all killed. You had better have a way of stopping this, Eli. Otherwise I will fucking kill you myself."

Aaaah, there she was. Oddly I felt better knowing she hadn't changed. "If I don't you won't need to."

Saying nothing she stood and left me to my thoughts, discussing something in quiet tones with her officers. I could clearly hear her if I so choose. I chose not to.

The sun set before we reached the remains of the base. The western shore was not a shore at all, but rather a sheer cliff. A slab of smooth stone stretching almost four hundred metres into the sky. I knew it continued on under the surface for quite some way. Almost to the bottom in fact. The sun disappeared behind it, leaving us in the icy chill of its shadow. I'd forgotten how cold it was up here. There was even the odd ice floe bobbing on the surface of the lake, courtesy of the glaciers that fed it.

"It is very possible the submarine pen is flooded," Daise said. "It would only remain dry if the pressure doors are still sealed. Taking into account the damage to the base I think that is unlikely. The base hard line has been cut so I don't know what happened in there."

"You're saying we can't get to a sub anyway?"

"I didn't say that. I can't send either MK or DT into the lake entrance. They can't swim so will just sink to the bottom."

"I'll swim in." I took it that that was what he was suggesting anyway. Holding my breath – another skill for me to learn.

I didn't bother asking the soldier driving the boat to slow down. I simply stood and dived off the side as we approached the docks. I heard someone shout but ignored them. By then I was in the water anyway.

The water was colder than I remembered. I took a moment to orient myself before striking for the underwater entrance. I heard the boats start to circle around me. Spotlights clicked on, piercing the murky water. I wasn't sure what the colonel thought I was doing. Drowning myself in the lake seemed a bit of an extreme means of escape.

I couldn't see much down here, even using the visual enhancements I had developed in the city. The sub bay was little more than a shadow in the dark. The lights were clearly off inside it too.

"I can help," Daise said.

"What's this?" My vision was filled with grainy, greenish light. It took me a moment to make sense of it, realising I could make out the shape of the entrance as well as some details of what lay within.

"I have the base plans. I also know the details of the submersibles and where they would be docked."

"It's a guess then."

"It is."

"Well, shit."

The sub pen had been carved into the sheer rock face of the mountain. The entrance itself was reinforced concrete, a letterbox like opening almost a hundred metres wide. It wasn't that far down, far enough to allow a certain amount of concealment but not so deep for water pressure to be too high, making it difficult to keep the spaces within free of water. The concrete was slimy to the touch, long colonised by the algae that thrived in the mountain lake.

"There's lights on." I noticed a dim red light seeping from within. "It's not completely flooded either. This is good."

I surfaced on the other side and found a ladder so I could get out of the water. Red emergency lighting had come on at some point, allowing me to find my way through the clutter within. It didn't look like the Jane had ever breached this part of the base but then they didn't need to. A door had been left open somewhere, allowing the water level to rise, flooding the loading docks. It had only stopped when it equalised with the water levels outside, leaving only the loading bays at the rear of the chamber dry as they were slightly elevated. There were two submersibles moored within. They were long, thin vehicles, designed for extended duration expeditions to the lowest parts of the world's oceans. They had water cooled nuclear reactors, sufficient to keep them powered for years without the need to surface. Each had a crew of twelve. They were primarily intelligence gathering platforms, sporting a complex array of sensors on their low conning towers. Both also had a thick visiplex view port on their nose, beneath which were situated an array of mechanical arms and storage containers. This allowed them to find and hook into communications cables laid across the seabed.

Both vessels had risen with the water level. This had caused one to drift backwards and collide with a loading platform that had been left in place behind it. Its twin screws were tangled in cables and bent piping. It looked like they were damaged too. The second submersible appeared undamaged.

I headed for the undamaged vessel, wading through chest high water to get to its main hatch.

"Wow!" I heard Rana splashing through water behind me. He paddled up as I worked on the hatch controls. He'd clearly decided to join in.

"The upper entrance appears relatively free of wreckage," Daise said. "I'm bringing the androids down. We'll need them to operate the reactors."

"So we didn't need to swim?"

"Until we were inside it was impossible to judge the damage."

189

"Asshole."

"The soldiers are coming too. I have the androids leading them down."

The colonel didn't make any mention of my leap from her boat as she joined us. She spent her time supervising supplies instead, ferrying crates into the narrow craft. She made it very clear she was going with us.

MK and DT went to supervise the reactor chamber as one of the soldiers joined me in the control room. It was a cramped space set directly behind the windows in the nose. The soldier assured me she knew how to drive the vessel. It didn't really matter, Daise had supplied me with all the information needed to drive it myself if needed.

"The tunnels in the mountains," I said to Daise as we got underway. "They join to the lake don't they?"

"They do."

"And there is a route through to the sea."

"There is."

I nodded. Good. I hadn't been looking forward to sailing on the surface in full view of the world. Motors thrummed and we headed out to the lake, descending slightly to navigate the entrance.

The colonel was seated at the surveillance terminal, watching the view before us through a number of sensors and cameras. She didn't seem at all surprised when a concealed doorway slid open, allowing us under the mountain.

Chapter 19

Jonas Gate was a city on the bottom of the ocean. It sat in total darkness, kilometres beneath the frozen surface of the Pharos Sea. We were far to the north here, beneath the polar ice cap. The installation had been abandoned long ago and water had found its way past door seals, even popping the odd window. With much of the base flooded, Daise pumped out only those areas we needed access to. Despite this many lights were still on, powered by the geothermal plant located nearby. Deep sea creatures had made many of the halls and galleries home. Blind themselves they didn't care that light blasted down on them.

I watched our approach from the submersible's cramped bridge. DT sat in the pilot's couch, its machine hands skilfully guiding us through the narrow valley to the submarine bay. I was just behind and slightly above it with an excellent view through the vessel's wide visiplex window. The cliff walls outside were lit by rows and rows of windows set into the cliffs themselves. Some towers were visible in the distance. The water here was perfectly clear and empty, apart from the odd sea creature drifting through our lights. I didn't want to think about the immense pressure of water just beyond the window. The slightest crack in the vessel's hull would lead to an instant, crushing death.

An odd place to build a research lab, you would have thought. Until you considered that our world had not been as unified as all that in the decades leading up to the fall. History was never that clean. There were factions. Some ethnic, some political. Not all had the same interests. Not all desired space exploration, particularly after Four's debacle in U-Kwee. Many wanted nothing to do with the galaxy out there. Many wanted to concentrate on problems in this system instead. Some were prepared to use force to make their point.

As a result all of the more advanced research installations were hidden. Que's on Aminoket. The installation beneath Anath. And this one at the bottom of the ocean. Very few people knew about all of them. Certainly Que never had, which was why so many believed Jane didn't either. A faulty supposition, bearing in mind what she had done to Neu-Anath. Did she know about Jonas Gate? Who knew? Although, according to Daise, it seemed to be a moot point.

"The electromagnetic signature is still there," he reported. The submersible's surveillance suite had been picking up an intermittent electromagnetic source in our wake for the last several hours. At first we believed it to be a surface contact, but then as we headed deeper it had stayed with us. Definitely not something travelling on the surface then. And clearly not coincidental. There wasn't enough subsurface traffic on Reaos for that. Few navies operated submarines, there was simply no need.

"We've led Jane straight here," I observed.

"Couldn't be helped. The installation is large, when she does attack we will have some time to escape before it suffers sufficient damage to prevent us. We only need a few hours to power up one of the vessels and leave."

"She has showed no hesitation using powerful weaponry before," I said.

"I am confident she will not here. Not once she realises what kind of installation this is, and that it was used to manufacture interstellar vehicles."

"Anti matter," I realised.

"Yes. Such vehicles were powered by antimatter. She will not risk breaching an anti matter containment pod by using nuclear weapons. If she did the resulting explosion would be catastrophic."

Colonel Neuman was sat alongside, listening to this discussion. Daise was using the android as his mouthpiece so she could be involved in it. "You presume she cares," she said.

"It is a safe assumption," I said. "She could easily have destroyed this planet a long time ago. The fact she hasn't suggests she has no desire to do so. In fact, it indicates she wishes to keep it whole. She will not risk destroying it today."

"That's quite a risk."

"Not really. It would have been easier to destroy the planet than to pacify it. Which indicates she holds it to some value. She has pacified it before so she will be confident she can again," I continued.

"I bloody well hope you're right."

So did I.

We passed through a set of doors into a brightly lit chamber and stopped, allowing the doors to lumber closed behind us. DT started powering down the submersible as I slid out of the seat and headed for the midships hatch. The interior passages were cramped, there was barely space for two people to pass each other. In some places one would need to step into a compartment alongside to allow the other past. Many of those compartments were full of gear, all of it military. Rana and I only had the clothes on our backs. I could barely remember a time when I had to carry some kind of personal belonging with me. Thinking that I almost laughed, remembering my concern with the credit chits. All that seemed completely irrelevant now. I didn't even know where they were. Probably melted slag at the bottom of Neu-Anath somewhere.

There was a queue outside the hatch, the soldiers lining up to disembark. Clearly the news we had arrived had spread quickly and they wanted to get off. We'd been aboard almost eighteen hours, and that was long enough. Rana was in the front, his hand on the locking wheel, eagerly awaiting the go ahead to spin it open.

"It will be a few minutes," Daise said. "I am pumping out the compartment now. It is large and two of the pumps are off line."

"The station is under surface pressure?"

"It is. I have many of the internal doors closed to prevent flooding. This will only allow you access to the docking bays, a storage facility and the main launch site. The launch site itself is flooded but that's not a problem. It's designed that way. We can access the vessel through a connecting tunnel."

"The vessel was built here to keep them secret?"

"Yes. There was a growing movement against interstellar travel, and the research into it. Two sites were attacked in the decades preceding the fall and production was disrupted at the Oberon anti-matter production facility."

"Three mentioned something about that. She believes it still exists, but no information has come from it in a long time."

"It, along with the Maw, were the first facilities Jane took over. I believe the anti-matter site to be fully staffed by Jane, which is why no one has ever heard of it. It is not a technology she would risk anyone else laying their hands on. It still exists, but is deep inside Oberon's cloud cover, so is not immediately obvious if you don't know where to look. And of course no one is encouraged to study Oberon in detail."

Of course. Jane was hiding a lot of things in plain sight of anyone who knew where to look. She simply discouraged anyone who showed the slightest interest in looking. No one on Reaos did anything if Jane discouraged it.

"We need to access the anti-matter store and extract the storage pods. They will need to be transferred to the spacecraft and installed before we can go anywhere. Their drives will need some time to get to operating temperature but we don't need to stay here to do it. I want to get moving the moment we have them onboard."

"It seems odd to find a space vessel down here," I said. "I wouldn't have thought their hulls strong enough."

"Anything designed to travel near the speed of light for decades at a time needs to be over engineered."

It was a different kind of engineering completely, but I didn't comment. By this time water was dropping below the level of the hatch and Rana was heaving it open. Icy air rushed into the cramped cabin.

"Colonel, Rana will be heading for the storage facility. It is deeper underground. He will need help bringing power nodes to the main docking bay. Could you spare some of your people?"

"Curtis, Bowse and Rayne, you go with Rana. Double time it, we want to get out of here," she instructed the troops behind her.

"The primary landing bay is this way-" As I was about to lead the colonel and the remainder of her troops out of the submersible we heard a dull boom. Water rippled about the vessel's hull.

"What the hell was that?" She looked up to the ceiling high overhead. Other than the strip lighting set into it there was nothing to see.

"We're being fired upon," Daise said through DT. "I suggest we vacate this compartment."

There was another explosion. Louder this time. The bay doors warped slightly, allowing water around their edges. It squirted through under tremendous pressure. Knocking the rear of the submersible and pushing it away from the gantry that had extended to meet it.

"Go!" I shouted, pushing a soldier who had stalled in front of me, staring in horror at the doors behind us. She shook herself and started running, booted feet thumping on the wet steel.

"I don't think it's Jane," Daise said.

"Conversation for later! Run now!"

The last soldier in line took the time to close the submersible's hatch behind him. I shouted at him to forget it as we hit the dock alongside at a run and headed for the interior doors. He ignored me, his hands a blur as he span the locking wheel. There was another boom and the doors twisted wider. The squirt of water turned into a torrent. I could see the vessel's propellers bending under the assault before they were ripped bodily off. With a shout the soldier slipped and fell into the water between the dock and the submersible. I saw the colonel hesitate as if she was about to turn and help. I snatched her arm on the way past and pulled her after me. She shouted something at me but I ignored her. Her voice was all but lost in the roar of water.

The door wouldn't hold long. Anyone caught in this compartment when it collapsed was dead.

Another soldier lost her footing as we rounded a corner and slid off the jetty. I saw her head crack against stone and she went limp. Cursing I pushed the colonel towards the door and quickly leaned over to grab a boot before the fallen soldier could disappear beneath the roiling water. I didn't have the time to rearrange her to carry her properly, simply dragging her by the boot as I headed for the door myself.

MK was awaiting just within the door, poised over its locking mechanism. It slammed its hand on the control as the last of us hurled ourselves through. The thick pressure doors wheezed closed, metal slamming on metal as the ground shook again. This time the outer doors gave way completely.

The sound was tremendous. A wall of water seemed to blast into the space, ripping the last of the doors from their hinges and hurling the beleaguered submersible before them. To slam against the far wall, crushing everything. Lights flickered and died.

We could see all of this through a wide window built into the bulkhead. I winced, half expecting it to give way. The ancient engineers had done their jobs well, however, and it held. Water frothed against it for a moment before the lights beyond gave way completely, leaving us with nothing but darkness. The floor quivered, something heavy colliding with a wall somewhere.

"Shit," was all I could think to say.

"Don't ever do that again." Neuman punched me in the face, her expression twisted in anger. I barely felt it, even though it was quite a blow. She did, however, and quickly hid a grimace of pain.

"I think I saved your life," I commented. "It was a pleasure." I think I noticed her rubbing her injured hand as she leaned over to assist her fallen soldier. I took that moment as an opportunity to drop her booted foot.

"The firing continues," Daise said through DT. "We should continue into the base."

"Not Jane, you said?"

"I suspect not. The weapons used appear to be standard military torpedoes of the kind operated by contemporary navies."

A complicated way of saying they were not the kind of thing Jane would use. "Who then? Tondo?" They were the closest state who operated any kind of subsurface navy.

"Perhaps. They have been known to monitor Authority vessels passing through their territory, including submarines. The submersible did have some stealth characteristics but it would still have been detectable to nearby craft."

"We didn't exit anywhere near where they would have expected. The passage joined the sea some way down the coast from the watercourse Authority ships usually take. I doubt they would have known to look for us there."

Daise shrugged. "It is not impossible. Still-" he paused as another torpedo impacted on the base- "that is not a Jane weapon."

"I suggest we keep on moving," I said. "The base is big, but those torpedoes won't do it any good. A breach down here would be quite fatal."

The colonel and her two remaining uninjured troops picked up their unconscious comrade between them. "Lead on," she said.

The androids led us deeper into the base, closing pressure doors behind us as we went. The bombardment continued but became more distant as we put doors between us and it.

"I had considered enlisting the aid of other countries," Daise said. "We could do with distracting Jane from our activities. The fact they are willing to attack us like this puts paid to that notion, however. I would not want the kind of bloodshed we have seen visited on other nations also. I have VAR penetrating their intelligence infrastructure instead. I want to know who is attacking us and why." He was silent while the machine part of his mind plundered mainframes across the hemisphere. It wouldn't take him long. VAR was far more advanced than anything else on the planet.

This place certainly felt like a city. We entered a central chamber. It was a wide vertical tunnel bored into the rock beneath the sea floor. Wide enough to park the submersible inside it two or three times. Looking down from the topmost balcony I could see levels stretching beneath us. Dozens of them. Workshops and laboratories the Four told me. This place had been self sufficient. There was even a food production facility buried down there somewhere. An underground farm. It was all flooded now. Daise hadn't bothered pumping it all out. Water lapped against the tunnel's side two floors beneath us. There were lights on beneath that, but even though the water was clear I couldn't see much detail of what lay beneath the surface. The surface was roiling, casting reflections about the chamber. Something was churning the surface up. Those pumps, possibly.

Our pace was slowed by the soldiers. It slowed even further when their unconscious comrade regained enough of her senses to walk herself and insisted on keeping up with us unaided. We dropped down two levels, icy water sloshing around our ankles for a few minutes before we gained higher ground on the other side.

"There are many places like this in the world?" The colonel asked me.

I shook my head. "Not any more. As far as I know this is the last."

"This technology is far more advanced than anything we have. We need to get a team in here."

"Wait until you see the ship."

"There is a Tondo Navy Hunter class attack submarine holding position above us," Daise said, after completing his investigation. "It is just above its own crush depth and has been instructed to fire at the base. The Hunter carries 32 Spion high speed torpedoes that are capable of reaching this depth. Their warheads are not powerful enough to do substantial damage to the base."

"They've done quite a bit of damage so far," I commented.

"They could target the bay because that's where they lost us. They have it locked in. They don't have any information on the rest of the base and cannot get close enough to use their own sensors. They simply cannot dive deep enough. The Tonto navy is bringing in a deep sea submersible but it wont get here until tomorrow morning."

"We'll be gone by then anyway."

"We won't have that long. Their air force has three Seacat cruise missiles at their disposal. They are capable of entering the water and gliding to a submerged target."

"OK?"

"They are nuclear capable. They are currently being armed at their Enderby Airbase. They can launch them in about twenty minutes."

"Shit. Of course they are. Damn. Can't you stop them?"

"Their guidance computers are not networked."

"Bloody hell. How long?"

"Ninety minutes."

I might have used some choice language then. What was with everyone firing nuclear weapons at each other? Well ... at me?

The entrance to the main docking bay was a wide steel door. It was open, allowing us into a brightly lit passage on the other side. That passage was a transparent tube leading out to the spacecraft itself. Even though it was completely flooded and open to the sea beyond the doors, the lights were on within, revealing the full length of the vehicle.

So this was what interstellar spacecraft looked like.

"Two kilometres in length," Daise said. "Four hundred metres in beam. Weighing in at over one million tonnes. Capable of accelerating to ninety four percent of the speed of light in two and a half minutes. Eighty four crew, only four of which are robotic. The remainder would stay in hypersleep between stops. One thousand passengers. Scientists. Diplomats. Those kinds of things. This is the ALS-184. Very experimental. She has never been tested, although I have checked the math and it is sound."

I stood against a transparent wall, taking in the graceful sweep of hull. She looked like a fat needle of chrome, her hull only marred here and there by manoeuvring thruster ports and flared slightly at the stern where the main drive unit was situated. There were no windows.

"That's quite some acceleration. I am presuming there is some mechanism to prevent us all turning to jam against her bulkheads?"

"There is. This is the experimental part. Virtually all interstellar craft cruised at similar velocities. What makes this vessel exceptional is her ability to accelerate quickly. Others would take months if not years. Necessary as you say, to prevent turning the crew to jam on internal bulkheads. That is because the thrust generated by older style vessels is transferred to the vessel itself through the engine mountings. Which in turn transfers thrust to everything contained within the vessel. Not so here. Thrust is applied to a field generator, which then transfers that thrust to every part of the vessel simultaneously. Down to the atomic level. That would include crew and cargo. Because of this no one onboard at the time would have any sense of acceleration at all."

"You sure of that?"

"I have checked the math."

"It is safe," Four assured me.

"If you've checked it too … I trust you," I said.

"Rana has reached the storage facility," Daise said. "They should be along shortly."

"They could have done with the androids," I said.

"We need them here. It takes four androids to run one of these ships. We'll have to make do with two."

The interior of the vessel was constructed of a material I didn't recognise. The walls and ceilings of the internal passageways were off white – almost cream. It wasn't a metal nor was it a ceramic. I ran my hand over the smooth material as we passed through the first set of airlocks. It was silky smooth, almost like glass. There were no actual lights. It was as if the ceiling itself glowed slightly, casting no shadows about us as we headed for the bridge. We passed by various internal spaces on our way, none of which I recognised. Even the Four could only guess at most of them. While they each did their part advancing drive technology theory, actual space ship design was not their area.

"Can this thing get off the ground?" The colonel was following behind along with her three troopers. They looked very out of place. I imagined we all did.

"I assure you, it can," I said on behalf of Daise. The androids had left us to attend to drive systems somewhere in the stern.

The bridge was a wide, fan shaped chamber deep within the vessel. Control positions were lined up within, all facing the curved bulkhead at the far end. It, it turned out, was a holographic screen, capable of showing what lay outside the vessel, or – more commonly – data readouts for the ship's crew to share. Daise directed me to an engineering console as my soldier companions spread out, inspecting the consoles. Daise – through VAR – had had access to the vessel's internal systems for some time and had already begun its start up and system check procedures. We needed the anti-matter to light up the main drive, but we could still get underway on thrusters.

"The vessel is in good condition to say it has been here this long," Daise said. "It contains a manufactory and automatic repair systems to take care of long-term maintenance requirements. It was designed for long duration missions, although two thousand years is somewhat excessive."

I sensed the colonel seating herself alongside me. "This ... Daise has been lying to you."

Surprised I turned to her. "Why do you say that?"

"Did he tell you what this ship was designed for?"

I frowned. "It was designed to visit neighbouring systems. Exploration, that kind of thing. Why?"

She snorted and rolled her eyes. "For someone who is supposed to be sharp you are pretty naïve. This, Eli, is a warship."

"What?"

"I am a soldier, I know what military vessels look like. I am also not stupid. Most of these stations ..." she indicated the consoles about us, "control weapons. Over there, surveillance. And there ... shields." She pointed.

"Daise?"

"She is not incorrect, Eli."

"You were going to tell me?"

"I was when it became pertinent. If you became aware of this vessel's capabilities I knew you would wish to head for Jane's location directly. Which I did not consider advisable. Even at this vessel's maximum cruise velocity Jane would be warned of our arrival. We need to limit her opportunity to prepare a response to our approach. As such we still need the Maw. We also need it as a ... battering ram."

"What exactly do you intend on battering?"

"The second moon of Quayum, known as the Spine, appears to be a base of some kind. I am presuming it is the location of Jane's surveillance and interdiction facility. We need to eliminate it so we can operate on Quayum without interference. It will also severely limit her ability to defend herself from our assault."

I nodded slowly. "We need every advantage. I would point out, however, that the Maw is a valuable resource in this system. It has been supplying the countries of Reaos with materials for centuries. Materials their economies rely on. You are suggesting we destroy it."

"I am. Which is why I did not inform you of the nature of this vessel. Discovering this was a military vessel may lead you to believe we did not require the Maw. That is, sadly, not an option."

"Shit, Daise. We're in this together. Is there anything else you have not told me?"

"Well, yes. The anti-matter bottles appear to be at half capacity, which was unexpected. We will need additional bottles, which means Rana will have to go back to get more. I don't think we have the time."

"Damn it, Daise. I should go and help."

"I need you where you are. I need someone in the engineer's seat. I am afraid the soldiers will not suffice."

"You have control of the communications system, right?" I asked him as I stood and indicated the seat to the colonel. I spoke to her, "you were right, Colonel, this is a warship. Daise is going to relay some instructions for you. We need you to follow those instructions to the word. I have things I need to go and do."

Neuman frowned. "I have a pilot's licence, but that does not mean I can operate a space ship."

"Don't worry, neither can I. Daise will tell you what to do. Your soldiers can help if it's needed." I didn't stop to see whether she was taking the seat before heading for the exit. "Daise, deal with it. You're smart, find a way. I need to help Rana."

"Be quick," he warned.

"Sure." I ran up through the ship, quickly leaving through the same transparent passage we had used before. Daise gave me directions as I went, guiding me towards the centre of the base, and then down a twisting ramp system deeper underground.

"I should have anticipated that," Four said. "I am sorry."

"Anticipated what?"

"That it was a warship. After what happened in U-Kwee and their strike on us public opinion to exploration shifted. The military took over when we realised the universe was a dangerous place. When we realised that danger could follow us back here our exploration fleets armed themselves. I didn't have access to this base but I should have known. I am sorry."

"It barely matters now. Don't worry about it." I arrived at the lowest level. There was another set of armoured doors set into the stone. They were open, the interior well lit. Rana and the soldiers were already wheeling carts through them, heading for the ramps to the higher levels. He waved cheerfully.

There were two carts, each holding a complex metallic framework. Secured within were the anti-matter bottles themselves. They looked like simple glass globes, a webwork of machinery wrapped about the outer surface of each. Their interiors were dark. Utterly black like viewing deep space from the orbit of Oberon.

"We need more," I said. "You three, can you keep on going with those?" I pointed to the soldiers. "Daise will light the tunnels you need to follow. Don't get lost and be quick. We don't have much time."

The trollies were heavy, that was clear from how the soldiers strained to push them. Two on one and the strongest on the second. Rana and I didn't wait to see how they managed the ramp, heading back into the storage facility instead.

"It shouldn't take long," the boy said. "We had to figure out the loading machine. I know how it works now."

The storage facility was not what I had been expecting. It wasn't a massive warehouse, lines and lines of shelves and racks storing everything anyone living at the bottom of the ocean could need. Instead it looked like a loading dock. A complex set of lifts and mechanical arms bringing requested items from hidden storage bays to load them on carts for easy manoeuvring. Daise had already started the process for supplying more anti-matter. Rana and I shoved carts into the receiving bay and waited for them to be loaded. It was slow work, the delivery system only bringing one at a time.

"How long did this take?" I asked Rana.

He shrugged, showing me his empty wrist. "Dunno. No watch."

"Shit." I enforced patience and seated myself, watching the machine do its work. "How's it going, Daise?"

"The thrusters are fuelled and warmed up. We can leave the dock as soon as the anti-matter arrives. The soldiers are currently taking a break halfway up the ramp."

I shook my head, tempted to head after them and impress on them the urgency of their mission. "How long do we have?"

"Twelve minutes. The weapons are on a glide path towards the base now. They have been launched at two-minute intervals and I suspect each is targeting a different part of the base. Jane has clearly given the Tondo the base schematics. Each weapon has a nominal yield of twenty kilotons, so not the most powerful weapons, but sufficient for the task at hand. I am actually quite curious as to what effect the water pressure at this depth will have on the detonations."

Twelve minutes. Each cart was only half filled. I estimated it would take that long just to fill them. "Do we need all of these bottles? Can we get away with fewer?"

"It takes a certain amount of energy to fully form the gravitational torque of the warp envelope. If the generators are not completely fuelled we run the risk of that field collapsing. The results would be quite catastrophic. Remember, we are powering the Maw also."

Of course we were. "Start working on an alternative route to the ship, please."

"Already underway."

"Why exactly are the Tondo attacking us? We are not at war with them."

"Jane has informed their leadership that we belong to a dissident faction. She has given them evidence that it was we who were responsible for today's detonation in the mountains. She is claiming we possess advanced weaponry and will use it again. The Tondo have been urged to intervene."

"Shit. I hate that bitch."

"Yes."

Rana was entertaining himself by riding one of the carts around the hall. I ignored him, even though the rattling of wheels on the floor grated on my nerves. "We should live here," he said abruptly after bringing his trolly to a sudden stop.

"Why?"

"It's quiet here. I like quiet. There were too many people in …" he shrugged, pointing upwards. I presumed he meant Permiset. A city that no longer existed.

"I have spent a lot of time in silence," I said. "Months at a time. It's not good for you."

He frowned. "People just bring problems. Look at all this … all we do. This is because of people. The Moche liked it when we took pictures of people … of people we hurt. He liked close ups. He was not a good man. Do you think he survived?"

"I doubt it. He wouldn't have known what was coming." How could he? But then he was the kind of person to survive anything.

"Avid killed him," Three said.

That surprised me. Avid, the mild mannered nurse — who was not a nurse. "Why would he do that?"

"The Moche brought a lot of pain to Permiset. Many of Avid's patients were hurt by the Moche's thugs. People like Rana here. Avid found him trying to escape the city in a truck. It appears his dirigible crashed after all. Avid stole his truck and left the Moche on the side of the road, his mobility cart damaged."

"Avid survived?"

"He did. He headed for Antawass. We have another mission there."

I nodded. I was glad about that. "But you don't know the Moche is dead?"

"He was well within the blast radius of the weapon."

That would have to do, I supposed.

"Two minutes," Daise reported. "The last bottles are coming up now. When they arrive head straight out and turn right. Ignore the ramps. I'm trying something else."

"The other bottles arrived?"

"They are inside the ship. I am closing the doors and heading out."

"You're leaving us behind."

"I must. I don't know if the ship will survive the shockwave."

"You'd better have a plan." I started feeling nervous. I didn't like the idea of nuclear weapons going off down here. Not under so many kilometres of water.

"You may have noticed the installation was abandoned in a hurry. The residents believed they were Jane's next target and so left a lot behind. There are some emergency escape pods nearby. They will take you to the surface."

"It's going to be a rough ride." I stood and crossed to a cart, waving for Rana to join me. "When the last bottles arrive we run, Rana. No looking back. Just run as fast as you can."

He nodded jerkily, his fingers tight about the handle. He was probably talking to Daise too and knew exactly what was headed our way.

"Jane knows about this, doesn't she?" I pointed to the bottles.

"The anti-matter? Unknown. The storage facility would survive the blasts, however."

"They won't be in the storage facility," I pointed out. The lift door wheezed open and mechanical hands quickly snatched up the last of the cradles. With a smooth movement they were transferred to the carts.

"Go!" Daise urged us on. He didn't need to.

Wheels squealing in complaint Rana and I pulled our carts free from the loading dock and aimed for the exit. We were passing through the doors when the first weapon arrived.

The ground vanished from beneath our feet. There was a moment of silence as we sailed through the air, trying to keep our trolleys upright with nothing to brace ourselves against. Then the shockwave hit, hurling us down the passage. We clipped the wall and spun around, the carts dragging us to the bucking ground. Sound battered our ears, squeezing the air from our lungs.

There was no heat, not just yet. I didn't know about radiation. I didn't want to think about that. We landed heavily, wheels collapsing under the impact. Grunting I was thrown over the bottles, glassy housings pressed into my cheek.

I felt a hand pulling me up. Rana.

"Keep running!" he shouted.

I didn't disagree with him. The passage was quivering about us, as if it was twisting under the onslaught. The roar of the detonation died away enough for me to hear the rumble of approaching water. I could already feel the pressure wave of air pushed in front of it. I pulled my trolly upright and dragged it after me, not caring that the wheels were completely ruined. As long as the containment system remained intact we were good.

"The base has been breached," Daise said, his voice impossibly calm in my ear. "Power is failing, partly due to the EMP created by the blast, partly due to damaged equipment. This means I can no longer close any pressure doors. You have to run faster."

"Piss off, Daise."

"You have less than a minute until the next weapon arrives. It will impact closer to your current position."

I ignored him, concentrating on dragging the awkward cart behind me. The passage seemed to stretch a long way in front of me. Lights were flickering as circuits failed. Rana's cart was just in front of me, the boy struggling with its unwieldy weight. It had no functioning wheels either. I helped it along, one hand on the support bars to give it a good push.

"Twenty seconds."

"Shut up, Daise."

I didn't know how fast we were going. Both of us were straining, ignoring the pain in our muscles. Neither of us could be considered normal any more. Today that just wasn't enough.

"Ten seconds."

"Seriously?"

We rounded a bend and saw a bank of open doors in front of us. Pod bays, I realised. Each big enough for one of us and our cart.

"Get in!" I gave Rana's cart a last shove towards the closest door. He tumbled through it with a shout, the heavy cart slamming him into the awaiting couches against its inner bulkhead. The heavy pressurised door started wheezing closed.

I was about to head for the next closest when the second weapon struck. I was picked up from the floor again and hurled inside. The weight of my cart cracking my head against a heavy steel wall. It hurt.

"We go."

Massen

The shockwave arrived just as the door sealed. Lights flickered, damaged circuitry sparking as the pod was released from its bracket. The cart and I were thrown around inside.

It went dark. I choose to believe it was because the lights went out. It might not have been.

Chapter 20

I awoke to blood in my mouth, choking me. The metallic tasting fluid running down my throat. My thoughts were disjointed, in disarray. I felt split, as if there were more than one of me, looking at me from different angles.

I could see the pod floating on the surface from above, as if I were floating over it. Shattered ice floes bumped against its cracked hull. Bright light speared the darkness about it, glinting on ice and the starred window of its one porthole. The pod started settling back beneath the darkened sea, ripples working their way higher and higher against the battered metal. I could see the pod had been a sphere once, its perfect hull broken only by the shape of a hatch and that one view port. That was before it was caught by a nuclear detonation. Now it was a twisted thing. Like an egg dropped from a roof onto cement. I sensed a force reach down to the pod and cradle it, drawing it from the icy water and into the air. It hovered for a moment, water sleeting from the rents in its side, before it continued upwards to be enveloped by a silvery machine that was suspended effortlessly above it.

The starship.

The pod was settled beside a second already in a wide bay. It looked even worse than mine. It had been flattened, some unimaginable force squeezing its hull until it collapsed. I could see blood leaking out of the side.

Mechanical arms went to work, delicately pulling at my pod's hull, cracking it open to reveal the horror that lay within. There were dozens of black globes. The framework had split open, scattered them about the pod's compartment. Blood and what looked like raw meat was interspersed in all of this. Something – someone – had been ripped apart inside that pod. You could have told me a horse had exploded inside there and I would have believed it. There was just so much blood and gore. None of it retained enough shape so as to be identifiable.

The arms moved quickly, delicately sifting through the ruin. Pods went one way, flesh went another.

I watched all of this with a strange sense of detachment. I couldn't feel anything for the poor soul that had been inside that pod. It barely registered on my mind that it was me.

"Is that me?"

"Yes."

"Am I dead?"

"That would depend on your definition of death. Your body can no longer sustain life in the traditional sense, but your consciousness no longer resides in one location. So, the most important part of you remains."

"My body is dead though?"

"In a sense, yes."

"OK."

"The last warhead detonated very close to your pod, as you can see. The shockwave itself was enough to kill you, however you were also bathed in intense heat and radiation. Either of which could have killed you instantly."

"Rana?"

"The same."

"You can help him?"

"I can, yes. I will look after him."

"Good." I felt relief at that. I wanted the boy to live.

"You may be relieved to hear that your own body can be completely healed also. The radiation and heat had a very interesting effect on the serum, however. I cannot ascertain what the long term effect will be at this time."

"Oh. Ok. Where are we? In the ship?"

"We are. Let me show you."

I could see the ship sliding effortlessly through darkened skies, its massive shape leaving a deep shadow on the surface of the sea below. The lights of a vessel of some kind flashed by below. A trawler perhaps. They passed so quickly I could barely make them out before they were gone again. There was a burst of light to our left, like a silent explosion that vanished as quickly as the ship had. Then there was another, and then a third.

"What is that?"

"The Tondo are firing on us. We are outrunning weapons fired from our stern, but there are still a number of installations in our path that will be able to hit us. Don't worry, they are impacting on the dispersion field."

There was another string of flashes. "Why are they firing on us?"

"They don't know who we are, and Jane is encouraging them to."

"Daise?"

"Yes."

"OK. Good." For a moment I had not been able to identify who I was speaking to. It hadn't occurred to me to wonder. "The anti-matter?"

"We have sufficient. The bottles were not ruptured."

That was a relief, although I imagine it was obvious. Had a single bottle ruptured Daise and I would not be having this conversation right now.

More light flowed past below. Cities. This would be the Hargo Stretch, a string of cities along the Tondo coastline. A beautiful place. I'd been there once with my mother on one of her regular diplomatic forays to neighbouring countries. I remembered forested towns and cities. There had been so much green. More than I had ever seen in any Authority city.

Our onward rush paused as we crossed the mountains back into Authority territory, the ship settling over a darkened lake. We waited. I could sense Daise using the traction equipment again. Taking something onboard.

"What are we doing? Shouldn't we be getting out of here?"

"We will shortly. I have a couple of items to pick up. There, all done. We can go." He didn't share what he felt it was so important to pause for. I didn't really care, as long as we were on our way again.

I felt a strange rush of energy and the shadowy surface vanished below. As the ship accelerated I felt it as if it was, somehow, part of my body. I could feel the pent up power within me. The wash of air past my sides. It was very strange. A cloud bank rumbled through my vision for a moment and then it vanished too. The vessel was accelerating and heading skywards, leaving the surface a long way behind. In moments we were in space. I could see sunrise to our east, lighting the mountains in the distance. My side itched briefly and I saw something flash in the distance. Something dark span out in front of us. I felt an itch again and it was gone. A weapon inside the ship reaching out and obliterating it.

"I am eliminating Jane's orbital stations," Daise said.

Just before we crossed the terminator into daylight we passed a strangely glowing region of landscape. It looked serene, almost beautiful.

"Soren," Daise said. "Jane has been bombarding the city and the manufacturing plants there for days. It's been burning for a while now."

"That is Soren?" I studied the burning land as it flowed beneath us. Soren was … had been the Authority's most populous city. A megalopolis stretching all along the Gertrude River to the coast. Jane clearly meant on crushing the Authority completely. Leaving nothing behind that might blossom into resistance once again.

Then it was gone. I could see the curvature of the world below, then moments later the globe that was Reaos. It had never occurred to me to think there were other worlds like it out there. Dozens, thousands. All living and breathing like this beautiful cloud sheathed world was. So many of them and so far away. Within reach of my ancestors but denied to us by Jane.

Could that change? Could we go to those worlds again in magnificent ships like this one? With faster than light travel we could get there in hours, Four told me. They were no longer so far away. There were so many possibilities. A destiny my ancestors had dreamed of was close at hand. Worlds working together, trading. A confederation of worlds. A staggering thought. Only Jane stood in the way.

"Main drive acceleration in five seconds," Daise said. "Three … two… one. Engage."

My stomach churned. Except it wasn't my stomach. I didn't think I currently had one. Reaos grew smaller behind us before vanishing. Alberta, our largest moon, drew a grey line in my vision as it flashed past. Then it was gone too. We were surrounded by darkness.

I felt nothing, almost as if I was floating in a warm pool. Perhaps there was a slight vibration. Other than that there was nothing.

"I have set a course to take us out of the system," Daise said. "On a trajectory that takes us away from Oberon. Once we are out of surveillance range, I will curve us around and bring us back in. I hope to give Jane the impression we are fleeing. It will help that Que's home world is in this direction, so she may believe we are headed there. We will not be expected at the Maw. Travel time twenty one hours."

I stopped paying attention when I realised there was nothing further to see. I turned my attention to Rana and found that he had been installed in a tank. The enzyme was quickly knitting his body back together again. It was absorbing nutrients laden in the tank's fluid as well as something else. Some other source of energy was powering its processes.

"Radiation infusion has significantly increased the enzyme's activity rate," Daise said. "It appears to be in the region of a three to four hundred percent improvement. Unexpected certainly, and I don't really know what the long-term effects will be. Before you ask, your own body is affected in the same way."

"That body … it won't be me though. It was dead. You can't bring people back from the dead."

"Not generally no. However the serum allowed a dispersed form of consciousness. In effect your consciousness became infused in every part of you, not just your cerebral matter. That is the mechanism used to colonise other people. Part of your consciousness is inserted into their systems which then supersedes theirs. In relation to your own body it means biological functions remained active, even though each part was separated from all the others. You didn't really die because cellular activity continued. As a matter of interest your body could have knit itself back together without outside interference. So – without the tank. This simply speeds up the process considerably."

I didn't know how to respond to that. How could I? What was I becoming? The body in the tank was no longer human. It had left that a long way behind.

"I can identify some adaptations, however," Daise continued. "Your cellular structures appear to be more robust after the rebuild. That adaptation appears to continue to the molecular level, also. To the extent that your constituent organs appear to be restructuring using different chemical processes."

"Meaning?"

"Strictly speaking you will no longer be flesh and blood. You will be considerably tougher. Quicker, stronger. Not to mention your synaptic functions have been enhanced."

"I was strong before all of this."

"Indeed. You will now be substantially stronger than you were even then. It appears the serum is simply reacting to stimulus. It adapts to overcome every threat it faces. Interestingly it is using the radiation it was bathed in as an energy source."

"So I will be able to survive nuclear detonations now?"

"Depending on the proximity of the blast that might indeed be the case. It would not be recommended, however."

"It occurs to me this is counter productive for Jane. Every failed attempt to stop me … us … makes us more of a threat to her."

"That would seem to be the case. It does pose a question, however. Jane should not be underestimated. As you have noted before, she destroyed a far more advanced civilisation than we see in the world today. Are we now presuming she makes mistakes?"

"She has planned this?"

"I merely ask the question."

Had I possessed a head I would have shaken it in bemusement. Well, I did possess a head. Sort of. I studied the body that was taking shape in the vat. It was gruesome looking down on your own dismembered body. The general shape was human again but it was featureless. As if it was simply a human template, the specifics to be completed later. A lump of unbaked dough awaiting attention from the baker.

"Give it an hour," Daise said. "Unless you are comfortable where you are?"

I watched and waited. I also tracked our trajectory out of the system. It was a long arc, leaving the sun far behind us. It had dwindled to a barely discernible dot, no bigger than any other star in the sky, before we looped around and started falling inward again. Oberon was directly ahead of us.

Still hours out I gingerly tried my body again. It felt disappointingly familiar. I couldn't feel any of the changes Daise had mentioned. I felt like I'd woken up from a long, deep sleep. I took a shower, washing off the slime from the vat. Rana was a few minutes behind me. The damage to his body had been more extreme. He seemed cheerful enough when I saw him again, however.

"That was close," he said, laughing. Daise had dressed him in some kind of uniform. Deep blue with pockets wherever there was a space for them. Loops where there were not.

"I have not informed him of what happened," Daise said. "I suggest you don't either."

There was no reason to horrify the kid. "You ready for the Tongue?" I asked him.

He shrugged. "Sure. What is it?"

I laughed. "Follow me."

The ship had a planning room adjacent to the bridge. It was a chamber where the ship's commanders could project images of the universe outside the ship onto a low dais in the centre of the compartment. It could focus on specific points of interest or zoom out to get a strategic view. Fed by the vessel's surveillance array it was kept up to date with the movement of other vehicles as well as planets and other large astronomical bodies. It was here that we watched our approach of Oberon. The Tongue hung in the centre of it as if lit from all sides. The complex array that was the was Maw nearby, seemingly nothing but an artificial arrangement of asteroids. They were currently dormant. No one had fed anything into them for some time.

"We cannot dock with the Tongue," Daise said. "We need to use a flyer to crash through the docking wheel here," he turned the image and lit up the docking assemblage at the Tongue's north pole. He was speaking through the mechanical form of DT so that everyone present could hear him.

It felt strange to be looking at the Tongue again. Stranger still to think I would be there in a few hours. "I'm not familiar with the flyer's docking mechanisms," I said. "But I doubt they will fit to the docking collars. It's all academic anyway. If Control doesn't allow our entrance, we're not getting in. And Control will not allow us in."

"We are not going to ask them," Daise said. "The impact will wreck the flyer but it will penetrate the pressurized areas here." He showed the compartments beneath the tractor docking ring. There were a lot of tractors docked there. It looked like just about all of them. Had operations been suspended? I remembered they were put on hold before I left, but I couldn't imagine Jane would shut them down permanently. The raw materials produced by the Maw were critical to industry on Reaos. Jane would not have halted this without good reason. "Of course this will depressurize those spaces, however there are airlock mechanisms further in, built for just this eventuality. You can use them to access internal spaces and make your way to the control rooms. Once there take them over and allow the rest of us in."

"We'll need armoured pressure suits," the colonel said.

"We have those. You will need to continue using the weapons you brought with you. The ship was designed to carry personal weaponry but they were not delivered."

"I take it it's down to Rana and me to storm the ring?" I said. I heard a whoop from somewhere to my left. He seemed to like the idea.

"You're the only ones who will survive the impact."

I sighed. Of course we were. "My preference is not to kill anyone here," I said. "We should presume they are all Jane, and treat them accordingly."

"Take them from Jane?" Daise asked.

"Yes. We will need them where we are going."

"Suggest operating in two groups. Two soldiers with Rana, and two with you."

"I intend shooting the bastards so you'd better be quick if you want to save them," the colonel said.

"I think you're with me then," I decided. I counted the parked tractors quickly. "Tractors are pretty robust. I believe they were designed to survive re-entry. I say we load them with liberated Jane and drop them onto Quayum, aiming for inhabited areas. They can be a distraction while we focus on wherever her base is. There's thirty-one parked there. From experience only about seventy percent will be in good working order at any one time. Less if operations have ceased. Still that's thirty tractors we can drop from orbit."

"There any weapons in the Tongue?" the colonel asked.

I shrugged. "Only non-lethals as far as I am aware."

"We will only have time to conduct a perfunctory search," Daise said. "I have been using the ship's manufactory to produce devices designed to attach to the current Maw gravity generators. I will launch them as soon as we are in range so they can go to work modifying the mechanisms for our purposes. I estimate it will take eighteen hours to complete the work. Then a further two to dock them to the Tongue."

"Achieving FTL will only be half the challenge," I said. "The Tongue will be slow to accelerate. Time will be lost simply achieving FTL."

The machine bowed its head slightly. "That had occurred to me. I have included additional modifications to the package, to add the technology found on this vessel."

That was a lot of work to accomplish in such a short time. The Maw mechanisms had not been designed for any of this.

"In addition, I have been modifying this ship to achieve FTL itself but it is proving to be a challenge. It lacks the complex gravitational gradient generators, so I am building them from scratch. Difficult without the necessary raw materials. As we cannot dock with the Tongue the Tongue will precede us to Quayum, disabling Jane's surveillance and defensive apparatus on the Spine. We will follow it in in this vessel. Unfortunately that collision will generate a pulse of radiation that will be quite deadly to anyone near the Spine at the time."

"Or the planet," I commented.

"Indeed. Fortunately Quayum has little in the way of an atmosphere or electromagnetic field to protect surface cities from solar radiation. As a result they are all well insulated. That insulation will serve as defence against the radiation pulse. Anyone caught on the surface will unfortunately not be so protected-"

"Hold on, are you saying we are going to be killing civilians now?" the colonel interrupted. "I didn't come here to kill civilians. We've had enough of that."

"I believe there are fewer than eighty million people on the planet. The vast majority will not be on the hemisphere facing the Spine at the time of impact. I am timing the assault for that reason. Of the remainder only a small number will be exposed."

"Who are most likely Jane," I said.

"I don't like this," she said.

"What alternative do we have?" I asked.

She shook her head. "I don't know. You say your information on Quayum is out of date? Do you have evidence the Spine is her defensive base?"

"The Spine was a major refitting and deep space listening installation before the fall. Conservative groups were also pressuring for military installations to be constructed there also. At least two emplacements were constructed, according to the records I have access to. It is reasonable to assume Jane completed that work, and kept it for that purpose," Daise said.

"We need to remove the Spine as a threat. If we don't they will be able to target us when we are on the surface. It is a rock bigger that the Tongue. A lot bigger. Even nuclear weapons wont effectively neutralise it. And I've had enough of the bloody things anyway. No more nuclear weapons please." I turned to Rana. "Let's get suited up."

"It's a waste. I doubt a pressure suit will survive impact," Daise said.

"Shit. It'll make me feel better. Come, let's go." I wanted to focus on the task at hand, which was assaulting the Tongue. Nothing else mattered for the moment.

Our chosen vehicle was a needle shaped flier of some kind. It looked fast and Daise assured me it was. Fast enough to plough its way through the Tongue's docking ring. It was only designed for four passengers, I discovered as we slid into the cabin. There were only four seats in the cramped space, a canopy overhead to seal us in. It felt a bit like a groundcar. It didn't look very tough. That canopy would fold the instant we hit.

"I have disabled the flyer's safety protocols," Daise told me. "Which will allow you to ram the docking ring. It does have some safety features that will absorb most of the impact. The cabin will flood with foam and the harnesses will keep you in your seats. There is no point getting you there if you get decapitated now is there?"

I made a sarcastic comment as the canopy went down.

"We take the Jane? Like last time?" Rana said as the flyer was picked up by a set of robotic arms and ferried towards the bay doors. We were almost there. Deceleration was about to begin, after which we would be ejected. The ship itself would remain on station in the event Jane had brought up something to defend the Tongue with.

"We take the Jane. I know you know how. These ones will be armed too, so be quick. Don't let them catch you."

He smiled. "Don't worry. The last ones had armour. Didn't help them." He giggled to himself. He seemed excited by the prospect.

"Concentrate on getting to the control room," Daise said. "We can send any Jane we capture to take the rest of the Tongue."

"There's a lot of space in there if they decide to hide."

"I know. Decelerating . . . now."

The doors eased open and we slid into space. I was surprised at how close we had stopped to the Tongue. It already filled the sky before us. The flyer accelerated hard, aiming directly for the docking ring. Alarms started ringing in the cabin but they were ignored. Disabled all they could do was make a noise.

To our left was Oberon, a giant purple swirl dimly lit by the distant sun. I frowned, noticing its swirling seemed to have sped up. Storms on its surface raged, spinning around each other in a way I had never seen before. Even its perfectly round shape seemed to bend, as if warping inwards.

"Daise . . ."

"Got it. It's gravitational lensing. Hold on, this will be bumpy."

I felt the little craft buck, its engines straining to resist the forces pulling at it. The docking ring seemed to slide to one side, our course altered by a steep gravitational gradient generated by something out there in the dark.

Of course: the Maw. This was it was designed to do. Jane was using it as a protective cloak about the Tongue, making it difficult for anyone to approach.

"I have to pull back. You're on your own. I can't fire on the Maw machinery. We need it."

Even though I could no longer see it, I sensed the starship pulling away, putting some distance between it and the Maw. Our own vessel quivered, its motors exceeding capacity and starting to glow sullen red. Even then our course still wandered to the left, pulled away from our intended target.

We weren't going to make it.

"Hold on!" It was too late to stop now, we were committed.

The flyer slammed into rock. I couldn't tell if the foam deployed, it happened too quickly. The impact drove air from my lungs, shattering my visor. Metal and composites splintered. There was an explosion somewhere. Heat seared my back for a moment before the vacuum of space snatched it away.

Cursing I lashed out, pushing broken metal away from me. There was a lot of it, most seemed to be on my chest. I heard the scream of escaping air coming from somewhere. My skin tingled strangely as a wave of cold replaced the searing heat of a moment before.

Rana. I saw a gloved hand in the wreckage beside me. I snatched it up and pulled, yanking the boy free. His helmet was gone, ripped completely off by the impact. He was mouthing something at me but I couldn't hear it.

Annoyed by the jagged edges of the visor in front of my face I pulled off my own helmet. I tried shouting back at him but I couldn't even hear myself.

I admit, I was somewhat slow on the uptake. It was only then I realised we were both exposed to the icy vacuum of deep space. The flyer was a wreck and so were our suits. We were stood, or should I say we were floating, outside the docking ring. A few dozen metres beyond it in fact. I could feel the slow pull of the station's rotation here, dragging us away from it. It was working on the wreckage too. It began sliding towards open space, moving faster and faster. I dodged a jagged piece as it slid by.

I pointed towards the docking ring, hoping the boy was getting the idea.

"He can hear you," Daise said. Of course he could, he was in my head. We didn't need air to communicate.

"Bloody shit. Come."

There wasn't much to hold onto out here. Just the odd sharp piece of rock or cable clipped to the asteroid's side. I could see a service hatch off to our right and pulled Rana towards it.

Damn, it was cold.

I think I broke the locking wheel in my haste to pull it open. Metal came free in my hand. I tossed it aside and clamped my fingers around the remaining lump of metal. The door shuddered before opening. No one had ever thought to put a lock on it. Why would they need to?

I pushed Rana into the airlock beyond and slammed the door closed. Warm, beautiful air washed over us.

"Shit." Rana said. "That wasn't cool. Let's not do that again."

I couldn't find it in myself to lie to him by promising we never would. Who knew what lay in the future?

Jane was waiting for us beyond the interior door. As I cracked it open flechettes sparked against the dull steel. I yanked away my hand, watching blood squirting from a finger before drying up. It hurt.

"Quick!" Rana darted fearlessly through the door before I could warn him. I saw dozens of steel projectiles slam into his slim frame. If there was any blood it remained within the ruins of his pressure suit.

Cursing I followed him. Jane's fire snapped into my own pressure suit. I ignored it. There were four of them. Rana had already bowled the first over, his hand over the man's face as he subdued him. I went for the second. He was a big man. Bald, his scalp sweating in the bright lights. He looked vaguely familiar. I didn't take the time to place him before doubling him over with a punch to his belly. I used him as a springboard to launch a kick at the fourth in line as Rana finished up with his second.

Jane didn't speak to me. Not this time. I saw glowering hate in the last Jane's eyes as her consciousness faded. And then it was done. Two were now six.

"Spread them out," I said, pointing to the passages leading off the compartment. "No weapons, we want the Jane alive. We head for the control room."

The Jane we captured didn't last long. They stumbled and fell when they encountered any serious resistance. Despite this our numbers swelled. Rana and I took down every Jane we came across and they in turn took at least one each before they fell themselves. We started encountering engineers and dockies as we headed into the ring. Rana had taken the first one down before I noticed who they were. The dock worked looked confused as the serum swept through her consciousness, taking over as it went. Then she collapsed over the air-conditioning unit she had unshipped and was working on. I thought she was dead.

"Shit, Rana. She's not Jane."

He hesitated. "What do we do?"

What could we do?

"Keep going," Daise said. "I know you'll hate this but you have to take them too. You never know which one is Jane in disguise and you don't have the time to find out. Jane clearly knew we were coming and prepared for it. Let me urge you to hurry up. I cannot start work on the drive with the Maw active. It's keeping us away from the Tongue. You need to switch it off. Get to the control room."

I did hate it but I knew he was right.

Cursing we picked up the pace. I tried not to pay attention to what uniform our victims were wearing. I took them all down, holding them to the floor until I knew I had control over them. Then letting them stand unsteadily to join in the fight. They were all Jane. I had to believe that.

The control room was a circular structure in the very centre of the docking ring. Its sides were thick pressure glass windows, allowing clear view of the vehicles coming and going from the facility. The interior was a tangle of communications and tracking terminals. It was usually staffed by about half a dozen station controllers although I didn't know if that would be the case now. With no activity in the docking rings there wouldn't need many staff.

Which was possibly why the doors were sealed. They were thick steel pressure resistant doors, designed to protect the base should a window blow in the tower itself. I worked the controls but they wouldn't open.

"Can we hack it?" I asked Daise.

"Possibly. Put your hand on the-"

The deck jumped beneath us. I clung to a railing as the structure shivered, a loud explosion coming from beyond the door. The sound quickly vanished, snatched away by the vacuum of space.

"Jane has blown the control room," Daise reported. I'd already guessed as much.

"Shit. Now what?"

"The Maw is still firing. You'll need to get to the server room and stop it there."

"Where's that?"

"On your way to the habitation chamber. I suspect Jane has it well defended so prepare for a fight."

Rana and I swept up some of our Jane and headed down towards the habitation level and the long walkway to the main chamber. As we approached the intersection that took us to the facilities complex we were met with a barrage of fire. It wasn't flechette's this time. This was assault rifle fire. I pulled us to a stop and peered around the corner. I could see their defences a few dozen metres further in. There were about twenty of them. Well entrenched and clearly well armed.

"Damn it, Daise."

"Well, we don't need the servers," he said. "They just make things easier. VAR can run the system remotely. Someone will have to act as a bridge though. That someone will need to ride the Tongue in when it hits the Spine. Don't worry, it doesn't need to be you. I can get one of your captured Jane to do it. Fetch some explosives and blow all of that up."

"Just what I wanted to hear." I took two Jane and headed towards the nearby storage facility. "Keep them inside," I instructed Rana. He saluted clumsily and peered around the corner himself, cursing as someone fired at him. He snatched his head back, blood flowing from his brow where a bullet had nicked him.

The Tongue was essentially one big mine. The interior had been mined out at some time in the distant past, ancient miners digging out rock to create the cavern as it stood today. Sometimes the engineers had to clear collapsed passages or make new ones and they used explosive to do that. They were securely stored but I intended on ripping the doors right off. The entrance was in the main chamber though, and we were met by a crown of tractor drivers as we headed towards it. They were peering down the passage and shouting at each other in confusion.

"Mas! What the hell? What's going on?" I heard someone calling out to me as we pushed our way through.

I looked up to see Sersh bearing down on me. Her face set in a scowl. "Sersh. Shit, you still here?"

"We heard gunfire and explosions. What's going on? Those Jane with you? What are you doing back here?"

I didn't know how to answer any of it. I could hear Daise in the back of my mind, urging me to take her. To take all of them. I hesitated. I couldn't. She wasn't my friend, none of them where. Not even those faces I did recognise in the crowd. Men and women I had never expected to see again. But was I that kind of person? Was I like Jane?

"Just get out of here," I said. "Get off the Tongue and quickly."

"What do you mean get off? Where would you like us to go? What the hell is going on, Mas?"

She had too many questions. I searched my memory. Had I seen a shuttle parked at the docks? There had always been at least one for emergencies. "The Jane have a shuttle parked at the docks. Get everyone to it and get out of here. The Jane won't stop you. Do it. Do it now."

With that I turned my back on her and ran towards the storage facility, the tame Jane following closely behind.

The stores were built into the northern end cap of the main chamber, a stone building covering an entrance into the rock. Offices, loading docks, that kind of thing. I pushed open the door and ran right in.

Something blew up in my face. A wave of heat washed over me, throwing me back through the door. It was followed closely behind by a spattering of bullets. I felt them tugging at my arms and chest.

"Shit. Shit." I rolled over on the dusty paving and ducked behind a wall. Of course it would never be that easy.

"We don't have the time," Daise said. "I'm picking up approaching vessels. Jane has reinforcements coming. I can hold them off for now but I can't fight two battles at once." I received a flash of an image from him. Oberon high in the sky, light wreathing the Tongue as weapons fired from its rocky surface. Weapons I hadn't known were there. A dozen spurts of flame were coming from Oberon itself. The anti-matter facility, I realised. She was sending reinforcements from there.

"Well. OK." I got back to my feet and rushed the door. This would hurt, I realised, but I needed to get in there.

The firing started the moment I appeared in the doorway. Bullets tugged at my ragged pressure suit. It was now completely destroyed. No one would be using it in space ever again. I left the Jane outside. There was nothing they could do in here.

"Good luck getting in here, Eli."

I heard a voice nearby and hesitated. A Jane was standing behind a ruined desk, holding something in her hand. It looked like a trigger. She pulled it.

The second detonation was much bigger than the first. It set off all the explosives currently stored in the facility, ripping through rock and stone, shattering the building and ripping through those alongside it. I felt myself picked up and thrown back through the door for the second time in as many minutes. This time I kept on going, rocks bigger than I was slamming into me. Spinning end over end I passed the park on my way to the south endcap. Much of the debris seemed to be coming with me. I could see it shredding trees below.

I seemed to hang in the air for a long time. Air roaring past my ears I made landfall somewhere in the south of the cavern. I smashed through a roof and landed heavily on a pale purple carpet. I think I might have bled on it a bit.

I was dimly aware of someone shouting at me. I distinctly felt a kick. "Who are you? What's going on?" Clearly they hadn't been expecting house guests.

"Shit." I groaned and levered myself to my knees. "Please, stop kicking me." Everything hurt. So much so I barely felt the kicks. They were just annoying.

"Who are you?"

"Daise. What happened?"

"Jane set off the explosives store. She's made a bit of a mess of the cavern. It barely matters, we were going to destroy the Tongue anyway."

"You know there are still a lot of people in here?"

"You were going to take them all over, weren't you?"

"Yeah. Shit, stop it!" I pushed the man away. I might have been a bit heavy handed. With a grunt he slammed against a wall and collapsed to the floor.

"Good news," Daise continued. "The explosion shook up the Jane holding fort in the server room and Rana managed to get inside. He's currently pacifying it."

"Pacifying. Yeah." I hobbled out of the house. Dust and rocks liberally coated the street outside. Some of it was still coming down. It was a long walk back to the northern end cap. With a sigh I started jogging in that direction.

"I want to get some of the tractor drivers off," I said to Daise. "I remember seeing a Jane shuttle parked at the hub. They can use that to get home. They're not any part of this. Enough civilians have been caught up in it."

"It won't be big enough to get everyone off."

"Well, we can take some aboard our ship. It's big enough."

"We're heading into a fight. Not away from one."

"Still better than leaving them on the Tongue when we crash it into the Spine." I was presuming any of them had survived the explosion. They had been gathered pretty close to the store after all. That couldn't be helped now.

Daise reported that the fighting had stopped by the time I'd made my way back to the northern endcap. All of the Jane had either been captured or killed. A search was underway for any hidden in the maze of passages beneath the chamber. Rana was perched atop what remained of a wall waiting for me. He looked pleased with himself.

"Don't worry. I got it all sorted while you were away," he said, grinning. "You worked here?" He indicated the cavern.

"I did. How many free Jane are there left?"

He shrugged. "Not many. Our Jane are looking for them. Most were in the server room and warehouse. I can't believe this place. I'd never heard of it ... before this. People lived out here? We're so far away." I presumed he meant from Reaos. Which was true. We were hundreds of millions of kilometres away. It felt closer now because of how quickly we had travelled here. It had taken months before. Months of sitting aboard a small shuttle crawling our way across the system.

"Colonel Neuman will be transferring aboard as soon as she is able. She is going to commandeer any ships she can find. She wants command of the Jane," Daise said.

"Unnecessary, but fine with me." I saw some drivers nearby. They were digging through rubble to free their comrades. "Give the Jane something to do and help with all that, will you?"

"I have twelve on the way."

The Maw disabled Daise was able to bring the ship in close. He had delayed modifying the Maw machinery until they were safely docked to the Tongue. He changed his plan slightly by docking the Maw machinery to the Tongue now, rather than awaiting completion of the work. Even after all this time they slid in perfectly and were secured in place. The ship could defend them against Jane's flotilla heading our way as he began the modifications. Miniaturised autofactories began dissembling components, reorganising the machinery at the atomic level. Hours, Daise had claimed. I didn't have his confidence.

Daise manoeuvred the ship between the Tongue and the flotilla and engaged them while they were still thousands of kilometres out. As big as it was the ship was quick. It flitted from one part of space to the next, accelerations that were surely impossible, even for a far smaller vessel. Weapons opened fire.

"We must presume they carry anti-matter," Daise said. "This is a problem." Any anti-matter detonation this close to the Tongue would vaporise it. "I am attempting to disable their drive systems without destroying them outright."

"You need to lead them away," I said.

"How do you suggest I do that?"

"Do you trust me?" Four asked me.

"Absolutely."

"Get everyone out of the main chamber. Turn over control of the ship and the Tongue to VAR."

"In instances where we need quick, while making rational decisions incorporating all available data, an AI is the obvious choice," Daise said.

I rolled my eyes. Daise over complicated everything. A simple: 'good idea' would have been enough. "Do it," I said. "Rana, get everyone out of here. Do it now."

"There are still people under the rubble."

"If you can't get them out in the next minute, leave them."

He nodded without having to consider it and ran off to supervise the Jane.

"That means you and Rana too," Four said. "The environment in this chamber is about to become toxic."

I joined Rana pulling rubble aside. No matter how much we encouraged them to leave the drivers tried to help, moving the smaller stones while we tackled the larger ones. We didn't have the time to be careful, and so simply flung the rubble out of the way. If anything the drivers were getting in the way.

"Here!" I caught a glimpse of a hand beneath some stones. It was waving at me, trying to attract the attention of would-be rescuers. There was a muffled shout from somewhere beneath a fallen stone slab. I slid my fingers beneath the slab and heaved it, surprised myself when it cartwheeled away to come slamming down on the pile of rubble behind it. The thing must have weighed a good few tonnes.

"What the fuck?" Sersh stared up at me, amazed at what she had seen.

"No time now. Come." I took her hand and pulled her out of the gap in the rocks. "That's enough, Rana. We leave."

Sersh stood unsteadily and started to brush dust from her clothes. Impatient I took her by the arm again and started leading her towards the exit. She protested, trying to yank her hand away.

"We must leave," I insisted. "Everyone, head towards the docks. Leave everything. Just go."

There were still a few hundred people within the chamber. Tractor drivers, engineers, shop keepers and janitorial staff. All kinds of people. There were even some children. We weren't going to have the time.

Daise tripped the emergency evacuation alarm. Lights flashed, a stringent tone sounded through the chamber. If anything it was counterproductive. No one knew what it meant so they stopped what they were doing and looked around in confusion.

"We can't evacuate everyone," I said to Daise. "We need more time."

"You don't have it, Mas. I have seen what VAR is planning. You need to get everyone out of there and now. If they don't they will die. We can't delay. Jane's ships are already too close for survivability. If they detonate their cores now we will be caught in the explosion. She could set them off at any time now."

"We can't get them out in time, Daise."

"Then they are going to die. I am sorry, Mas."

I knew he meant it when he used my name. Daise never used my name. I allowed Rana to usher me towards the exit. It was crowded by the people who were taking the alarm seriously. A shout went up as the floor moved beneath their feet. The Tongue was starting to move. Attitude thrusters, Daise informed me. That seemed to instil a sense of urgency in the Tongue's residents. They started moving quicker.

"VAR has changed the firing sequence. You will have another minute. We cannot afford more than that."

"Shit. OK. Please leave the doors open as long as you can."

"We will," Daise said. "The timing of what VAR is attempting needs to be perfect. We cannot allow any further delays. Those doors will close regardless of whether there are still people inside the chamber."

Fortunately the chamber had more than one exit. The rock of the Tongue was riddled with passageways. There was a maze in there with accessways scattered all over the chamber's inner surface. Simply getting out of the chamber now was not going to be good enough though, I realised. We were going to crash the Tongue into the Spine. Anyone aboard then would be killed. We needed them off the Tongue completely.

"There is a way," Rana said, as if sensing my concern.

"Oh?"

He shrugged. "We take them. We take them all. Then we force them all to leave."

"Taking them all over is as bad as killing them."

He frowned. "I am not dead, Mas. Daise said I could be let free again. It can be done."

"He's right," Daise said.

That wouldn't get them out of the cavern now. That time had passed. However it could get them off the Tongue before the impact. I waved for him to do it. I couldn't speak. It felt like failure. Our liberated Jane began passing through the throng. Touching the refugees as they went. That one touch was all it took. There was a moment of confusion in their eyes before they started moving themselves, continuing the spread.

Liberated. Is that what we had done to them? They were still slaves, only now they had a different master.

Things began happening quickly. Daise allowed me to see from his perspective. The ship drew in close to the Tongue, its own drive field extending far beyond its intended design limits to encompass the asteroid. While that happened the attitude jets on the Tongue itself aligned themselves, diving the massive shape in towards Oberon. Counter intuitive perhaps, as it brought it closer to the approaching flotilla but I could immediately see what VAR intended. The AI was using the gas giant's own gravity to slingshot the asteroid. As this happened the interior doors to the chamber slammed shut. Gas started leaking from the chambers lighting mechanism built into its axis. The space was quickly filled. Anyone caught inside began choking, the acidic gas burning skin and lungs as they breathed it in. It was quick at least. Within seconds they had collapsed. Many still clawing at the doors they suddenly found shut in front of them. I couldn't look away. These deaths were on me. I needed to take responsibility.

"Jane built two mechanisms into the cavern to eliminate the population should they become a problem," Daise said. "She could flood it with gas. Not the same gas we have flooded it with now, mind you. That wouldn't have the same effect as we're intending. The second ... well, wait and see."

A door built into the southern end cap blew open, revealing a long passage to frigid space behind the Tongue. A way of killing everyone inside, I realised. Before it could suck all of the noxious mixture inside into space there was a spark.

The gas detonated. A wall of flame that coursed through the space, consuming everything in its path. The Tongue shuddered, a jet of flame spewing into space behind it. Everyone inside not holding onto something was tumbled over, the massive asteroid accelerating suddenly.

I might have cursed then. I had not expected that.

"Not what it was designed for," Daise said. "Four did the math though, and confirmed the Tongue would stand up to the stresses."

"Shit. Will it be enough?"

"It will have to be. It does depend on a number of unknown quantities. VAR is insisting on quoting probabilities of success to me. I've told it to shut up."

I pulled myself up the accessway to the docks. It had suddenly become vertical. Fortunately only Rana and I had been inside it at the time. All our companions had spread out into nearby passages to take over survivors. There had been six thousand people in that chamber. Only three thousand made it out before the gas was pumped in. I couldn't let anyone else die. This wasn't Jane killing people. This was something we had direct responsibility for. Jane hadn't killed them. We had.

No one else was going to die today.

Driven by conventional thrusters Jane's flotilla began falling behind. When it became clear we were going to escape over the gas giant's horizon she cracked open the anti-matter containment fields within the pursuing ships. Matter and anti-matter met and fused. The release of energy was beyond anything I could possibly have imagined. A nuclear weapon transformed a small percentage of its fissionable mass to energy. An anti-matter weapon transformed all of it. The detonation was orders of magnitude more powerful.

Twelve points of light appeared to our stern as each ship exploded. They quickly coalesced into one detonation, a single point of light so intense I couldn't look at it even through heavily filtered lenses. It swelled with unbelievable speed, quickly hauling us in.

"We need to move faster," I said to Daise.

"I know."

"It's catching us."

"I know!"

I saw the shockwave intersect with Oberon's upper atmosphere. Gas clouds were shredded, torn apart by the wall of fire. The surface of the massive world bowed in under the pressure. A dimple thousands of kilometres wide.

"Hold on," Daise said.

"To what? Shit." I ripped up floorboards to get to the stanchions embedded in the rock beneath them. I clung to the pin as the Tongue bucked, throwing both Rana and I about the passage. The metal promptly snapped, leaving me to be hurled at the opposite wall.

VAR guided the asteroid deeper into Oberon's atmosphere in an attempt to put something between us and the rapidly approaching shockwave. As ephemeral as the upper wisps of gasses were.

Daise had planned the upgrades to the Maw's mechanism allowing quite a generous timescale. At the time we had expecting to complete the work at our leisure. Now he worked to accelerate it. The quicker we could get FTL online the quicker we could get out of here. He identified the barest minimum needed to achieve the effect and concentrated on those mechanisms, sending additional resources towards them to speed up the work.

"I can get some kind of drive running within the next two minutes," he reported. "The Maw machinery was designed to provide thrust to the Tongue anyway, so all we're doing is giving it an upgrade. This did mean taking them off line for a time, which is why I haven't fired them already."

Two minutes. I watched the shockwave approaching us. It seemed achingly slow. We were moving fast now, probably only slightly slower than the detonation itself. By the time it reached us it might have dispersed enough to make it survivable. There was one thing we were forgetting though.

"Daise, do you know where Jane's anti-matter processing station is?"

"No. It was within Oberon's cloud bank. Her ships originated there but they had already travelled some way before they were visible."

"If that shockwave hits it what happens?"

"That depends on how much is stored there. Either very little or it could be catastrophic."

"Define catastrophic."

"Difficult to predict. Oberon itself may be under threat, however."

There was nothing any of us could do about that now. Rana and I made it up to the docking facility just as the Tongue and its accompanying starship began clawing their way back out of Oberon's clutches. The vibration eased as we jetted into empty space, drawing a long streamer of gas behind us. We'd picked up considerable speed, easily enough to outpace the explosion. The maelstrom was fading away behind us.

The colonel clattered down a ladder leading to a docking port as we approached. "About time. Get onboard."

"Why are you here?"

"Nice to see you too. We were getting bored of being passengers and decided to get involved. We have a landing craft docked and ready to transfer you to the ship."

I didn't resist, allowing the colonel to shepherd us aboard the brightly lit vessel docked to the inner ring. I discovered the landing craft was already full, passengers lining every available space in the passages and compartments within it. It was eerily quiet, none of them speaking a word. Not even those obviously injured. More than one sported a bleeding scalp or broken limb.

"They're all us," Rana commented.

For the moment. As soon as we were away from here I wanted them released.

"Interesting observation," Daise said. "All of the Jane we have come across were incorporated before the fall. We know Jane made minimal modifications to those she took over. It appears she allowed them to heal faster which effectively extended their life spans, but that is all. So far all the Jane we have encountered are over two thousand years old."

"She hasn't made any new Jane since before the fall?"

"It doesn't appear so."

That was strange. Even when unnaturally long lived she would still lose some to mishap or enemy action. Surely she would need to replace those lost? "Do we know how many Jane there are?"

"Across the whole system? I can guess only, I have never been able to penetrate Jane's systems. I have discovered why that is, but that isn't your question. To answer it, about two to three million," Daise said.

That seemed like a lot, but then they were spread across the system. "You can't access her systems?" I prompted him.

"Yes. Because she doesn't have one. All communications are through the Jane themselves. She doesn't use electronic systems at all."

That seemed strange. "Do we know why?"

"At first I assumed it was for the sake of security, to prevent anyone accessing it. But that doesn't make sense when you take into account that electronic systems were only reinvented on Reaos relatively recently. There were none prior to that, and it doesn't appear Jane used the technology then either."

"Perhaps she doesn't need to?"

"It helps. We are doing it."

Of course we were. VAR had worked its way into every system on the planet. It had access to information and resources that would be forever denied Jane.

"I have three nodes coming online shortly," Daise reported. "FTL in one minute. We won't exceed it by a lot just yet, but then we don-"

Massen

There was another detonation behind us. It dwarfed the already unimaginable explosion of Jane's flotilla. Something on the other side of Oberon had exploded, a flash of light that was like a corona around the giant planet. A weirdly beautiful halo of light that was painful to look at. It slowly worked its way towards the centre, consuming the massive planet as it went. As it met in the centre fiery debris was ejected from the maelstrom. Projectiles the size of worlds ripped from the planet's very core.

I could do nothing but stare, all words escaping me, as I watched the giant planet consumed by the detonation. The flash was like a supernova erupting in the night's sky. Bathing the system in a brilliant burst of light. Turning the night sky of Reaos to day.

"FTL in three ... two ... one."

For the first time in human history a vessel achieved the impossible and left light far behind.

Chapter 21

We travelled for sixteen minutes before Daise shut down the drive. Those sixteen minutes took us eight light years from home to an empty void in the middle of nowhere. The closest star was four light years away. There we stayed, intent on making repairs and completing upgrades. We weren't in any hurry. If Jane knew we were still alive there was no way she could find us. And even if she did she couldn't follow us.

"My people have some ration packs with them," the colonel said to me as I flipped through internal camera feeds on the bridge. I was watching a group of Tongue engineers as they were lined up against an internal bulkhead. It was an eery sight. Rows upon rows of dormant human forms. Each perfectly alive but unmoving. Quiescent. We controlled them, Daise, Rana and I. Like puppets, unable to form any independent thought. It was wrong certainly, but what were we to do? Released they would cause a problem we simply couldn't handle right now. They would riot, demanding to get off the ship. We did have the responsibility for their welfare however. That meant food, water and medical treatment for those in need. We could assist with the latter, but that was all. The food on this ship was centuries out of date and the Tongue was no longer accessible.

"You won't have enough for everyone," I said.

"Enough to keep us going for a few days. You do need to deal with them though," she pointed. "First suggestion would be to give them access to the med bay. They still have some untreated wounded. It would be a start."

"I am cycling them through the medbay," Daise said. "It is not very large."

"How long do we need before we can head back in?" I asked.

"The work on the Maw drive nodes is nearing completion. They will be untested but when have we ever tested anything?" In order for our plan to work both vessels needed an upgrade. That was the only way we could strike multiple places at once. We'd escaped the system on the barest minimum, and even then two of the drive systems had burnt out. We needed better preparation for the next stage.

"We've been lucky this far."

"We can't spend too long out here," the colonel said. "Remember there is a war going on back at home. People will keep on dying until we finish this."

"Of course," Daise agreed.

I scrolled though the camera feeds as the colonel handed out ration packs. I ended up with a high energy chocolate bar and a glass of water. My stomach was rumbling but it would have to do. Clearly, whatever changes had been made to my body I still felt hunger.

I selected an external feed and studied the now dormant Tongue. It was a massive dark shape against a background of distant stars. Its insides were ruined. Heat from what had happened in the chamber was seeping into the rock around it. Melting conduits and machinery alike. There were no feeds within the chamber itself, those had been completely destroyed. Not that I really wanted to see inside anyway. There was still some life support in the docking areas but there wasn't much power to operate it. The main generators were not far from the main chamber and were no longer functional. All we had were some emergency batteries. Enough to launch the tractors and remaining shuttles but that was it.

I zoomed in on our sun. It was visible from here of course, but it was a very long way away. An unremarkable star lost in the enormity of space. My ancestors had been out here before. Launching themselves blindly into space, committing themselves to journeys that would take decades. Knowing they would return to a world where loved ones had aged, perhaps even died. That took courage and a vision that had been lost long ago. Perhaps what we were doing would return it.

Four had calculated the consequences of the destruction of Oberon to the system. A gas giant was not just gas, there was a lot of solid matter in there too. All of that had been unleashed and scattered about the system. Much of it would remain on Oberon's orbital plane but some would wander sunward and become a threat to the worlds there. Reaos would inevitably see rocks of considerable size heading her way. Four was already designing vehicles to capture and safely manoeuvre such objects away. The loss of such a large planet within the system had other unexpected consequences. Planetary orbits were changing slightly, although it would take some time to determine exactly how they would be affected. Even something as massive as the sun had not escaped unaffected. Typically any star would wobble under the influence of a planet orbiting it. The greater the planet the greater the wobble. True, Oberon had not been close to the sun but it had still had some influence. With that influence gone the sun seemed to be rebounding slightly. Four didn't think it would be a problem. Just something interesting to keep an eye on in the coming years.

One of his suggestions was to create an artificial gravitational gradient at the old location of the giant, with the same motion it had had. That would reset any orbital anomalies, as well as sweep up a lot of the debris from the explosion. Perhaps, in a few million years, even rebuild the planet itself. I was looking forward to that.

"I have unshipped two of the Maw gravity generators and incorporated them into the ship's drive system," Daise said. "The Tongue can get away with losing two and this allows the ship to be FTL capable. We no longer need to ride in with the Tongue. Work has been completed so we can depart any time." With the Maw's gravity generators now married to the Tongue, the asteroid was properly mobile once again. It no longer needed to rely on the rather makeshift rocket Daise had made it into. That was dead now anyway, its fuel long expended.

I seated myself at a surveillance terminal and swung the chair to face the colonel. "You ready to go?"

"Do we have a plan?"

"The Tongue hits the Spine. We pause outside detection range and sweep the planet and its orbital platforms to identify the remaining defensive positions and population centres. We then move in and engage those. As we move in our Jane and tractor driver friends launch in landers and captured tractors. Their objective is to get in close to Jane's defences and to convert as many as possible. Those converts will then turn and convert their colleagues," Daise explained. We had an army numbering just over five thousand sitting in silent lines aboard the ship. Five thousand dedicated soldiers who would sell their lives dearly against Jane's defences. It was a cold thing we were doing here, sending the residents of the Tongue at Jane when they had no say in it at all. Once again, what choice did we have?

All for the greater good. We would pay for that some day.

"And Jane herself?" The colonel asked.

I hesitated. "That will be down to me with you and your team as backup."

"So at the moment we have no intelligence detailing what we are walking into?"

"None," Daise agreed.

"Amazing. I'm so glad I signed up."

"Couldn't be helped," I said. "No one has been on Quayum since the fall and Jane discourages anyone from surveying it. No astronomer on Reaos will point a telescope at it. It's not worth it for them."

"I doubt that. Universities have astronomy departments. One is sure to have studied the planet."

"It's true," Daise said. "I checked. There have been doctoral theses proposed on the subject over the years, but all were declined by the faculties involved. No one has aimed a large telescope in its direction in over two thousand years."

She shook her head but said nothing.

"We do have some pre-fall data," I said. "We know where the population centres were at the time. We have to presume there is still something at those sites."

"Hey. I'm army. I go where I'm told. Get moving."

It was almost more complicated loading our soldiers into the tractors and shuttles than it was completing the upgrades. It required a delicately choreographed dance of vehicles as they positioned themselves about the ship and affixed themselves to its silvery hull. They were close enough in to be encompassed by both the drive and FTL fields, while they avoided drive and weapons systems so the ship could operate normally. Fortunately there was a lot of space on its hull. We prepared ourselves as best we could. Rana and I ate and showered, the soldiers checked their gear and finished off some ration packs.

"Engaging drive," Daise announced.

Breaking what felt like every natural law in the universe by exceeding the speed of light was quite a disappointment when we actually achieved it. I felt nothing. Not even a sense of nausea or buzzing in my ears. If I refrained from looking at any of the monitors I wouldn't have known we were doing it. Of course Daise pointed out that this was a good thing. Taking into account the forces we were manipulating the slightest leakage would kill everyone onboard instantly. Including Rana and me. I watched from the surveillance terminal as space twisted around us. We were along for the ride. We were in the hands of far more powerful minds.

We came to a halt one light minute out and aimed our sensors towards Quayum. The Tongue continued on its way, aiming for precisely where the Spine's orbit would take it. Fortunately that kind of thing was easily calculated, or so Daise claimed.

"Scanning now," Daise said. The ship was pointing its sensors and telescopes towards the fourth planet, absorbing all the light that had left it minutes earlier. VAR poured over it, looking for regular features on the dusty planet that would indicate the presence of human activity. Walls, rooves, roads. Anything. We could only see one hemisphere from here, so had chosen the far side to the attack on the Spine. The collision would hopefully knock out, or at least inconvenience, any forces on that side of the planet for some time. We would deal with anything on this side.

"This Spine," The colonel said. She was studying an ancient image of it in a monitor. It hadn't always been called the Spine, although its original name was lost to history. It was an elongated moonlet, long settled by our ancestors, with docking mechanisms built along its length. Those mechanisms looked like ribs attached to a spinal column to the casual eye. Hence the name it had adopted. "We don't actually know what's there. Or even if it's been abandoned. The Tongue will hit it never having seen it. We'll never know whether all of this was a waste of time."

I knew that. I knew this was a desperate gamble. I also knew we had to hit Jane hard. She was still an unknown quantity. One we were, to be honest, afraid of.

"That was a hit," Daise reported as the sensors picked up a spike in background radiation. There was a brief flash of light beyond the planet and a streamer of fire leading away from its southern endcap. Whatever the Spine had been, it was now gone. "Time to go."

Our engines fired again, driving us towards the planet.

"Bad news," Daise continued. "VAR cannot find any inhabited settlements on the surface. They all look abandoned. There are satellites in orbit but we're not picking up electromagnetic radiation from them. They appear abandoned."

"Shit. Are you saying she's not here after all?"

"There does appear to be one anomaly. VAR is still looking at it."

And then we were there. The massive ship appeared in orbit around the dusty planet and immediately began dispatching the vessels clinging like leeches to its hull. They drifted free but didn't head anywhere. There didn't appear to be anywhere to go.

I studied the planet on the screen before me. It looked cold, dry and almost airless. Even without the ability to zoom in on any feature of interest it was clear the world had once been occupied. There were cities everywhere. All of them were dead now.

Ruins littered the surface. Fallen walls and buildings. Dried out lakes and riverbeds. All was now dust. Whatever had happened here it was over now. Perhaps the same conflict that had reduced civilisation on Reaos had happened here too. The only difference was no one here had survived.

"I have engaged our dispersion field and brought weapons online. This may be a trap," Daise said.

"That anomaly?" I prompted.

"Here. Have a look." An imagine appeared on the screen.

"What the hell is that?"

A mountain had appeared in my monitor. It was difficult to judge its size but it certainly looked massive. It hulked over the plains around it, an almost perfect pyramid of rock that didn't seem to belong there at all. It was so large its summit grazed space. From the ground it would be impossible to see all of it, most of it hidden over the horizon. There were no foothills and no other mountains nearby, the surrounding landscape was virtually flat. Just that one odd looking structure dominating everything about it. Still, it didn't look manufactured either. It was clearly weathered, its sides riven by gulleys and crags, some so deep their floors were lost in shadow.

"It appears to be a mountain," the colonel said.

"Yeah. Thanks."

"That is the Ziggurat," Four said.

"The what?" As I said it something flashed on the screen. A bright spark in the sky alongside us. It quickly faded, leaving a scatter of debris in its wake.

"We are being fired upon. Taking evasive manoeuvres," Daise said levelly.

There was another flash, and then another. "The tractors," I realised. "She's picking off the tractors."

"Get them on the ground," Four advised. "I would suggest as close to the Ziggurat as you can get them."

"I agree. The fire appears to be originating from the Ziggurat." Our perspective in the viewer changed as Daise dived the ship towards the distant desert. "We've been hit. She has a railgun down there somewhere. Most of the projectile's kinetic energy was absorbed by the shields but it still breached our hull. Starboard bow. Minimal damage. Some outgassing. I'm closing internal doors." He seemed very matter of fact, as if he was reporting on the weather.

"She can shoot us down?" I asked.

"She'll need something bigger than that."

"We need to get to the flyers," the colonel said.

I wasn't sure I liked that idea. They would be vulnerable to fire from the ground.

"Go to the flyer bay, I have two waiting for you. Rana, I need you to stay here in the event we suffer system crashes. I need a pilot on hand."

"Shit damn." He had already been picking a weapon from the stack against a terminal.

"Someone needs to explain this move to me," I said as I took the weapon from him. It was surprisingly heavy.

"We're not achieving anything here. We need to get into that mountain if that's where Jane is located. Daise can keep her busy while we work on an insertion," she said.

"Shit damn," I echoed Rana's sentiments as we headed for the bay. We couldn't feel any of the ship's gyrations as Daise avoided fire from the mountain, the interior was too well regulated for that. "We need to know more about this ... Ziggurat," I said to Four. It was a massive structure. It would take us weeks to search it on foot even with our army from the Tongue.

"It's old," the ancient mind said. Of course I could access his memories directly, but sometimes it helped for him to explain them to me. Plus it made me feel more human. "It was old before we found it. Archaeologists believe it was built over a million years ago. It is artificial, constructed from large slabs of local stone. There may have been a line of hills in the region that were dismantled to build it. Nothing remains of them now. As you can see the exterior has weathered to a degree where you can no longer identify individual stones. There was a lot of debate as to what natural force could create such a feature until gravimetric satellites mapping the planet picked up subsurface anomalies within the Ziggurat itself. It was only when those early researchers tunnelled into it that they discovered it was artificial. They found a network of tunnels leading to various halls and open spaces. All seemed to lead to the centre of the structure, however they could never actually reach it as those sections were sealed off. There were proposals to tunnel through the rock but that did breach several laws pertaining to the protection of antiquities, and so they never did. They could not identify the purpose of any of it, however some remains were found in a crypt in the lower levels. They were preserved due to the low atmosphere environment they were found in. They were still recognisable. Barely. Little more than bones that had turned mostly to dust. We did identify them as human."

"A million-year-old body?" I slid into the flyer's cockpit beside the colonel. I had been relaying all of this to her as Four spoke to me. Her troops boarded a flyer alongside and we made ready to depart.

"Probably more. Our first explorers landed on Quayum over eight thousand years before the fall. It was a dusty, empty world then. Its atmosphere so thin they had to wear pressure suits. We did discover traces of ancient water courses and atmospheric weathering, leading us to believe it had held an atmosphere at some time in the past."

The flyer clicked loose and dropped into Quayum's upper atmosphere. The colonel aimed its sharp nose at the ground and gunned the motors. She had no intention of staying in the open any longer than necessary. A second flyer slid free and fell in behind us. The silvery hull of the ship vanished above us as Daise drew Jane's attention elsewhere. After it was gone the skies around us were empty. The tractors and shuttles had long dispersed and were heading for the surface themselves. Even from here we could see the squat bulk of the Ziggurat on the horizon. It looked like a mountain, snow and ice ringed its side where the air was still thick enough to carry moisture.

"You're saying Quayum was inhabited Millions of years ago? And by humans?" I continued to Four.

"I am."

"Shit."

"I concur. No other bodies were found within the structure, however one of the walls in the lower crypts was inscribed. An advanced form of pictographs, etched on the stone."

"What did it say?"

"It was not in a tongue we understood. It took a lot of time to decipher using the technology we had access to at the time."

"What did it say?"

"Not much actually. It said 'welcome travellers', and what appeared to be a sequence of glyphs we interpreted as coordinates. Those coordinates led us to a location on the other side of the galaxy, some fifty thousand lightyears from here. The final line was 'come all who are deemed worthy.'"

"An invitation?" the colonel said as she eased out our descent. Dry hills whipped past us. I couldn't imagine how fast we were travelling. The atmosphere outside was a lot thicker now, Four's people had been terraforming the planet for centuries, turning it into a garden world before the cataclysm that reduced it to a desert once again. Still, we couldn't feel any turbulence from our passage. I could see the tiny shape of the second flyer to our right, struggling to keep up. Their pilot was clearly not as confident as the colonel.

"It appears so. With the technology we had access to it was always beyond reach. That might no longer be the case however. It remains a journey of some duration."

I'll admit to being curious. I couldn't imagine what kind of culture could survive that long. What kind of culture could travel all the way here, to build something as massive as the Ziggurat? Would they still exist?

"There was one notation we discovered in addition to this. A name, we took it to signify what they called themselves. It was: Suziemekaar."

"All very interesting. All very academic," the colonel remarked. "It can wait until later." She aimed the flyer's needle nose towards the structure in the distance.

Something streaked from the sky to crash into the valley ahead of us. It exploded on impact, sending debris whirling away from the crater it had created in bare rock. Another of the tractors had been shot down. Even though we couldn't see much of it, Jane had not stopped firing at us.

"There will be time for archaeological pursuits later," Daise agreed. "Jane appears to have constructed towers on the lower sections of the Ziggurat. They are the source of the fire she is directing towards us. Recommend they be eliminated. She is also moving heavy assault units into your area. Expect to come under fire."

"There," the colonel said, not removing her hands from the controls.

Massive metallic shapes were moving towards us. Five of them. I'd seen them before. They were the assault vehicles Jane had used against Permiset. Those same vehicles the Authority air force had failed to shoot down.

"I have this. Evade for the moment," Daise said, as calmly as ever.

The colonel jinxed the flyer left and right. The assault vehicles didn't seem to pay attention, they simply advanced steadily, content to wait for us to come into range.

"Jetna Siza," Three said. "We found the technology on Howas when we visited it."

"Howas was a dead world," Two observed.

"They were very warlike," Three agreed. "Their military technology was advanced, however. The Jetnas have incredible high-density armour. Proof even against nuclear bombardment. Probably why Jane chose them."

"Well, they're here now," I said. "How do we kill them?"

229

Something else flashed out of the sky overhead, spearing the first vehicle. I couldn't see what it was as a pall of dust covered where it had been. Another object streaked into the Jetna behind it, throwing more dust into the dry desert air.

A cheer died on my lips before it could escape. Those had not been shots from the ship. That had been something else entirely.

"Shit," the colonel exclaimed beside me as something moved within the dust. Something massive. I caught a glimpse of an indistinct shape before the breeze caught the dust and obscured it again.

I knew what they were though. They were the reason Daise had paused our ascent over Black Lake, the ship taking two passengers aboard. They were machines. Old and virtually indestructible. And now let loose on the surface of Quayum.

"There is a defensive tower four kilometres behind the Jetnas," Daise said. "The ship's gravimetric sensors have identified a passage running beneath it and joining up to the Ziggurat's tunnel network. I believe Jane has been excavating part of the structure in order to access whatever is concealed within its core."

"That's where we'll find her. That's where we need to be," I said.

"I will supply a distraction and allow you to get inside. In the meantime that tower is in the way."

Far around the rugged sides of the mountain a star twinkled in the sky for a moment. High energy plasma sizzled through the rarefied atmosphere, connecting with one of the guard towers Jane had built on the structure's slopes. The tower disintegrated, throwing blocks of native stone into the air. The ground shuddered at the impact. It was not the first tower Daise had attacked. He was intent on thinning out Jane's troops, forcing them to defend as much of the ancient Ziggurat as possible, gambling that her forces were unable to adequately defend all of it all at once. As big as the structure was there were hundreds of square kilometres to defend. Jane would need a truly massive force to defend all of it. A gamble certainly. Jane had had centuries to build defences.

"Keep low," Daise instructed the soldier through me. "The flyer needs to remain undetected if this is going to work."

"Yeah, sure." The flyer's nose pitched down sharply, taking us into a deep gully.

"You are army?" I observed.

"So?"

"You can fly?"

"Clearly. But please don't distract me. This ..." she was silent a moment as she put the flyer on its side to avoid rock walls rushing by on both sides, the canyon suddenly becoming narrower ..."takes concentration."

I doubted her companions would be able to keep up in the second flyer but didn't look to check. We were committed now, we couldn't stop. They were on their own.

Behind us the ancient U-Haas robots were taking the Jetna-Sizas apart. Even without their arms they were formidable machines, their armour shrugging off all the withering fire the hulking aircraft could direct at them. Leaving crushed vehicles in their wake they strode towards the survivors, their long legs carrying them swiftly over the rugged terrain, leaping gulleys with ease to throw themselves at the defenders. Armless they used their heads — such as they were, driving them into the motors keeping the aircraft aloft, metal screeching as fans ripped themselves apart on hard armoured torsos. As the vehicles struggled to stay airborne on three engines the robots leaped onto their backs, their weight driving them to the ground, before kicking their wrecking ball feet at the hull beneath them. Armour curled like butter under a knife, allowing the machines to drop into their interiors. Even though too massive to disappear completely within the aircraft, they made short work of their delicate innards. Legs swinging and torsos scything metal they dismantled their prey. There were humans inside those, I remembered. Jane perhaps, but humans nevertheless. I didn't want to think about what those robots would do to fragile human skin and bone.

"I am not surprised Jane tunnelled into the centre," Four commented. "Our own scientists were prevented from doing so out of respect for the Ziggurat's builders. They spent centuries probing the inner halls searching for secret passageways to the centre but never found them. Jane is clearly not as patient. Or as respectful."

"Do you know what she found there?"

"I can only guess. A store of ancient knowledge that would allow us to travel to the builders' homeworld. Or perhaps some kind of portal. Or perhaps one of the builders themselves, kept alive in suspension, awaiting our arrival. There is no way of knowing. None of the other systems we have visited had such a structure on any of their worlds. It appears unique. We will have to ask Jane when we meet her."

Meet Jane. I had not thought that far in advance. Meet her and then what? Kill her? That was what stopping her would require.

The tractors and shuttles we had under our control landed around the structure, Daise scattering them as randomly as possible. We didn't have a large enough force to attack all the towers at once, so there were gaps here and there. Once Daise had used the ship's main weapons to destroy Jane's defensive structures our troops stormed through the dust and smoke, taking every Jane they encountered. Our numbers swelled. With them came information, Daise reaping the new minds for every piece of intelligence he could find.

A tractor and a shuttle had already arrived at our destination and were clearing out defenders. We were not having it all our own way, our own troops were falling to defensive fire pouring from within the structure. Jane's soldiers were armed and many were armoured, while our tractor drivers and engineers were not. All they had were their own bodies which they threw at the defenders with abandon, each one attempting to capture as many as they could before they were subdued. Jane's railguns still fired at the ship gyrating overhead as it attempted to evade her barrage. It was mostly successful, but not entirely.

"Systems are degrading," Daise reported. "You have another two to three minutes of effective support before I am forced to back away."

"Rana OK?"

"Can't get me, boss," the boy's voice spoke into my mind. He sounded defiant but scared. He could survive a nuclear detonation, he should be able to survive this. Still, being tough didn't make him fearless.

"The tower entrance is just about clear. Jane's forces have been subdued but there are still some units concealed in tunnels further in."

"Any useful intel?"

"To the battle, yes. To what Jane is doing here, no. None of these Jane have any knowledge of what is happening inside the structure. She treats them like little more than drones."

"Almost there," the colonel said beside me. She had heard none of this, preferring to remain dedicated to her task. She was sweating, I noticed. Her brow dripping as she fought the little vessel's controls. Its designers had never anticipated this kind of treatment.

"There's a railroad beneath the tower," Daise said. "A subway of sorts that leads into an excavation. I believe it goes all the way."

"How big is it?" the colonel asked. I hadn't realised Daise had spoken aloud through me.

"Big enough for a train."

"And the flyer?"

"Not recommended," Daise said.

"Is it big enough for the flyer?" she repeated, her teeth gritted as she avoided some fire from the ground. There were still Jane out there.

"Barely. It is not recommended. The lower levels are unmap-"

"Fuck that. Hold on." She grinned at me.

"What the ..."

She dived the diminutive craft towards where the tower had stood. It was little more than a crater now, dust still obscuring much of it. Concentrating on her instruments, and what they claimed to lie within the dust, she fed power to the motors. They screamed. Her knuckles were white on the controls.

I admit I closed my eyes there for a moment. I know I could survive a lot, but this was insane. "Shit. Are you mad?"

Light disappeared from around us as we sped underground. The flyer's belly glanced off something metal – a stationary train perhaps – before levelling out.

"We can't waste time getting on trains," she said, not looking at me. It was dark outside the canopy now, forcing her to rely entirely on instruments. Warnings were flashing all over the console. The ship's guidance systems did not like this at all. "Unless you missed it people are dying. I couldn't give a shit for Jane's troops, but we have tractor drivers and engineers with us. They don't deserve any of this."

"People are dying on Reaos also," Daise said, as calmly as ever. "A number of fronts have opened up, not all of them within the Authority. Jane is fighting back."

"Exactly. We have to stop this and now." She was silent a moment. "Besides, what is the Third Precept of Duncan's 'The War Body'?"

I hesitated. I had never read it, even though the ancient treatise was the most influential text on war ever written. In my defence I had never joined the military. Still, Four had read it: "Speed and the decisive strike is critical to any force engaging an entrenched defender."

She grinned. I could see her teeth clenched together in the dim light from the console. "I'm impressed. You can take her? Yes?"

"Jane?"

"Yes. Please tell me you can take her down."

I hesitated. Could I? I didn't know who or what she was. She was old in a way I couldn't imagine. She had had centuries to prepare. She was formidable.

"Tell me you can take her down."

"I can take her," I said with a confidence I didn't feel.

"Good. Otherwise this is all a complete waste of time. Plus you'll get me killed and here's me not even a general yet." She was talking without really thinking about what she was saying, all her attention on her controls. She swore as the tunnel changed attitude slightly, the flyer glancing off the ceiling. I hoped there were no trains coming the other way.

"Two kilometres. I recommend slowing down," Daise said.

"I know, I know." The flyer's sensors had picked up a blockage ahead. Or perhaps the end of the tunnel. She eased on the throttle, the flyer bucking slightly and connecting with the ceiling again. Something crunched alarmingly but we managed to remain in the air. "Here we go. Gently now."

A dim light grew ahead of us, becoming a chamber at the end of the rail line. It was a loading dock of sorts, mining lamps strung over the walls and ceiling, revealing the neat lines of cargo and equipment lined up beside the one train drawn up against the platform. It was deserted.

The colonel hovered the flyer clumsily, and spun it around to aim back up the darkened tunnel. She extended its landing gear and brought it down heavily on the train's roof, the gear ripping through metal as the craft came to a rest. She shrugged at the damage she was causing. There was nowhere else to bring it down anyway.

"Shit." Her knuckles crackled as she prised them from the controls.

"We have to keep moving." I opened the canopy. It wobbled alarmingly where a mechanism had been damaged by an impact but still opened enough for us to get out. It was a drop onto the train's warped roof, then a scramble to an electrical cabinet set into the platform beside the tracks where we could make our way down. The colonel tossed a rifle to me before following herself.

We were alone here, no backup was coming. The second flier had not followed us down. I can only presume the pilot had more sense.

"There is a further tunnel behind the train," Daise said. "I imagine this was as far as Jane was willing to take a train. The rest of the trip will be on foot. It is not far. The flyer's sensors are picking up a lot of electrical activity ahead of us. Along with an ultrasonic vibration. It is being dampened by the rock about us but it is clearly there."

"We go." I pointed past the train.

The tunnel Daise indicated was part of the original structure. Jane had clearly not tunnelled this. I stopped when we came into sight of it, studying the architecture. It was like nothing I had ever seen before.

For a start it didn't look old. It looked like the builders had packed up their tools just yesterday. There were columns and arches, all constructed from a reddish sandstone. Every millimetre was either sculpted or painted over. Monsters. Demons. Angels. All engaged in an epic struggle, wielding swords and shields they battled over the ceiling and walls of the passage. And they were moving.

"Hold on, VAR has a theory to explain this," Daise said.

"What the hell is this place?" The colonel joined me.

"Hell," I said simply.

"We do not have adequate sensors in place, but VAR believes it has identified what you are looking at. It is the outer edge of an active singularity. Space beyond the edge becomes more warped the deeper you go. It is flexing slightly as the singularity weathers."

"Weathers?"

"Singularities have weather," Daise said. "In a sense. They have good days, they have bad days, and anything in between. You wouldn't want to be here in a storm."

"There's a singularity in here? A black hole?" The colonel asked, hesitating at the entrance.

"No. A wormhole. You are only seeing its outer edges at the moment. Its ripples are causing the artworks to appear moving. They are not – fortunately. The wormhole itself is behind an event horizon, a region of space warped to breaking point."

"And beyond that?"

"Unknown. The Suziemekaar?"

"Jane will be in there." I forced my legs to move, taking me towards the hellish scene ahead of us. I didn't know who these Suziemekaar were but I didn't like them. Why would they create such a scene?"

"This technology is beyond us," Four said. "We possess some speculative theories but no firm data."

"So whoever these builders are, they possess technology that even has the four stumped?" That seemed unlikely. Four had succeeded in achieving the impossible by breaking the speed of light. How could anything be a puzzle to a mind like that?

"Include VAR in that," Daise said. "And don't forget they possessed this technology over a million years ago."

"Shit." I didn't want to go down this passage but I knew Jane would be down there.

"Are you sure Jane is in there?" The colonel echoed my doubts. "She would have to be mad."

"Where else would she be?" I steeled myself and stepped into the tunnel. Over the boundary into exotic space. I did feel this. My skin itched. My stomach roiled. My vision blurred and my head ached. It was not pleasant.

"It is safe for you," Daise said to the colonel. Both Jane and I had been changed by the serum. We were a lot tougher than the average human. The colonel was not as blessed. Or cursed. "I recommend standing back from the event horizon when you see it though."

"I'll make a note." She followed me in, looking a lot more confident than I felt. "Interesting sensation."

I realised the strange perturbations were making her appear to ripple and twist just as the murals were. It was unnerving. I looked away.

There was writing on the walls deeper in. I couldn't read it. Daise asked me to pause and study it, allowing the script to twist in and out of focus. VAR could decipher it, he claimed. It could be useful.

"It makes little sense," Four said presently, just as I continued walking deeper. "Only destruction shall redeem, it says."

"What does that mean?"

"I don't know."

"Keep moving," the colonel urged me on.

"It seems to be predicting some kind of extinction event," Daise said. "One humanity causes itself."

"Every world endures a cycle of destruction and rebirth," Four observed.

"I don't believe that is its meaning. It seems to suggest it is not a local phenomenon. It is galaxy wide. All life will perish."

"Humanity is scattered throughout the galaxy. What kind of event would extinguish all life? It seems improbable." I stopped again.

We had arrived.

In the centre of the Ziggurat was a chamber. A perfect sphere, as much as I could tell. Massive. Without frame of reference I couldn't guess how big it was. The walls were smooth stone. Either carved from naked rock or built of stones that fitted into each other so perfectly I could not discern any gaps between them. In the centre of that was … nothing.

A hole in space. So perfectly black that it was featureless. It seemed to wobble slightly, as if its edges were writhing slowly, perhaps in synch with the murals in the passage behind me. It filled much of the space, leaving little room for a steel framework to be built around it. More mining lights were bolted to supports, shedding their illumination on the chamber. A walkway had been built from the tunnel entrance, reaching out towards the darkness in the centre. Someone was standing on it, their back to us, observing the singularity. She was alone.

Jane.

It had to be. We stepped onto the catwalk, boots thumping on steel. It rattled slightly. Unnerving. The walkway was near the curved ceiling of the chamber, much of it suspended above the slowly writhing darkness. Any slip here and in we went. I had no idea what was on the other side. If anything was.

"Just shoot her," Rana suggested. "Shoot her and let's be done with this foolishness."

235

"I would not recommend opening fire in here," Daise said. "If you miss I cannot predict how matter will interact with the event horizon. If you don't miss and she falls into it ... same problem."

The figure before us turned at our approach. She studied us silently, her hands behind her back as if on the parade ground. She was wearing simple green coveralls and boots. She was a short, diminutive figure. Not the imposing monster I had always imagined. No tools or weapons were in evidence.

"She's younger than I thought," the colonel whispered.

"Age is relative," Jane spoke.

We froze, our weapons raised to cover her. I don't know what we expected her to do.

"Those will not help you here," she said. "Come closer."

Realising she was right I slung the rifle and stepped cautiously closer. "Jane?"

"You came looking for me, yes? Who did you expect?"

I smiled humourlessly. "Someone older."

"Someone like Que?"

I said nothing.

"Bitterness has made Que old. I prefer not to live in the past."

"Bitterness?"

She frowned, waving her hand as if to dismiss a pesky fly. "Thank you for coming, Eli. May I call you Eli?"

"It is my name."

"Although most call you Massen. Or Mas?"

I shrugged.

"No matter. You took your time though. I was intrigued as to who would find the receptacle after I placed it in the Shatter. Would you find it, as predicted? It seemed very unlikely. The Shatter is large." She smiled. "It was large, in any event."

"Predicted? Who predicted it? You?"

"Oh, no. The Builders ... the Suziemekaar. If you prefer. Has Daise not told you? Interesting."

"What?" And how did she know about Daise?

"I have not finished analysing the script yet," Daise responded.

"What does she mean?"

"Massen brings death," Jane said before he could respond. "Jane brings strife. Did he not tell you what was written on the walls? And you walked right past it." She smiled, her eyes twinkling in amusement.

"Daise?"

"I have not fin-"

"Daise? What the hell is she talking about?"

"It does appear to say that, however the likelihood of that translation being correct is literally astronomical."

"Remember the original script? The text our ancestors found so long ago? Welcome those who are deemed worthy. Or perhaps I should say, welcome those who are able?"

"You'll have to explain this to me," the colonel said. She had missed my internal dialogue with Daise.

"Jane planted the serum in the Shatter for me to find," I said. "Because the writing on the walls told her to."

"The million year old writing? That writing?"

"Yeah."

"Shit."

"Yeah."

"How does an ancient text get your names right?"

Jane took it upon herself to respond. "Some parts of the text are mathematical ... equations ... while others are phonetic. Those would be their actual written language. Either all of it is wrong, and all of our translations have been incorrect, or the Builders indeed mentioned both you and I in their text. I have been studying it a long time. I am not wrong."

"Simply extraordinarily improbable," I commented.

She shrugged. "And so I left the receptacle for you to stumble onto. The rest you know."

"Why?" Daise asked through me.

"Aah, Daise. I would have thought that was obvious. Since you have read the text yourself."

"Barely."

"She wishes for you to enter the singularity," Four said. "She believes you would succeed and she would not. From the contexts of the texts, death is presented as a positive. After all, destruction shall bring redemption, it states. She draws from this the conclusion that you will be allowed through it and so she brought you here."

"I will not ally myself to you," I said to her, pushing this internal dialogue aside. "You have caused untold destruction and misery. This-"I pointed towards the darkness behind her,"-I don't know what this is but I didn't come here for it. I came here for you."

She sighed. "Of course. Que lied to you, didn't she? She blamed everything on me. Did she tell you who she was?"

"She is from AsQayQay. She told us that. Also that you tried to kill her."

She clicked her tongue. It almost sounded as if she was muttering the name of Que's homeworld under her breath. "What do you think happens when an egalitarian society meets an individualistic, material one?"

I could sense even Daise was taken aback by that question. "Tell us."

"Que's civilisation was ancient. Some might say stagnant. We introduced a certain ... dynamism to them. We gave them thoughts they had never had before. By the time we went back there-"

"They had destroyed themselves," Daise realised.

Jane smiled. "Yes. They had indeed. We taught them greed. Acquisition. Selfishness. In a few hundred years a society that was eons old learned how to destroy itself, and that's exactly what they did. When the next ship arrived they found nothing but ruins. A few survivors to be sure, but their civilisation was dead. Que blames us for all of this. She started planning our destruction out of revenge. I was to her as Daise is to you now. I escaped her to stop her."

"We know Que lied," Daise said to me. "Perhaps not the specifics, but we knew she was not truthful to us. Perhaps Jane didn't start the war that precipitated the Fall, Que did."

"Who do you think drove the moons of Oberon into each other? Aminoket and Arsai. Arsai was inhabited in our time. Cities, research facilities ... farms. Millions of people called it home. Que's own research station was located there. When I escaped her Que used the Maw to drive Aminoket into Arsai in an attempt to kill me. She killed whole worlds trying to get to me. My Jane ... my soldiers ... they were the only people I could save. I infected them to save them. What choice did I have? Who would believe my warnings? They called me mad and had me locked up. I escaped and saved five million of them. They were the only people I have ever infected. Eighty million perished anyway. I could not save them all. Que did that."

"We believe that?" I asked Daise.

"Impossible to say at this time. It was too long ago. The evidence is gone. But it doesn't matter now," Daise said.

"Of course it matters ..." As I said it I realised Daise had been involved in more than one plot I was unaware of. He had taken the dancers from the bottom of Black Lake. And he had taken Que into custody. Of course he had. He had used the colonel's troops. The ones I had believed dead in Jane's attack on her encampment. Troops that had sought shelter underground instead.

How had I missed it?

I turned to the colonel. "You have Que?"

"I've told you before, I'm not just along for the ride. I have Que under guard and I have engineers in the city."

"Shit. I can understand Daise lying to me, but you?"

She smiled. "If I don't trust Que, why should I trust you? I certainly don't trust her," she gestured towards Jane with her chin.

Jane laughed. "What will you do with her now? Dare I say you will do nothing? She has gone to great lengths to be a hero to you, while making me the villain."

"As far as I am aware she has not set off any nuclear weapons inside cities," I remarked.

"Oh? You noticed the scenery on the way here?"

"What?" Even as I said it I realised what she meant. Que had destroyed life on Quayum, as Jane had destroyed civilisation on Reaos. A civil war between these two women, with civilisation caught in between. We were the losers.

"This world was a garden once. Our ancestors spent millennia forming the atmosphere and landscape. Filling the seas, growing forests. Building cities. The most beautiful cities anywhere. Que destroyed all of that. She burned this world and everyone on it. Two billion died. What I did to Reaos was piffling in comparison. You survived didn't you?"

"And Oberon?"

She laughed. "The destruction of Oberon was a good thing, you should know that. You have seen yourself the wealth of raw materials released when a moon is shattered. How much more materials will be released when a planet like Oberon is destroyed? All that material is now accessible, all you have to do is scoop it up. You'll need all of that to rebuild this civilisation. That and more. With fast interstellar travel you can build an empire like the galaxy has never seen."

"You're mad. You don't want that. You never did."

"Personally I couldn't give a shit. I intend to leave this place, and I need your help to do it."

The singularity. "You want me to step through there?" I pointed to the blackness.

"I expect it."

"I won't."

"You won't have a choice. I have sent my Jane through in the past but they simply disappeared. I never heard from them again. The builders are not asking for my Jane, they are asking for you."

"How could she force me?" I asked Daise. It was something I was missing. She had no leverage here.

"She believes she can threaten you."

"Can she?"

"Well-"

"Enough chatting amongst yourselves. By my readings the singularity is nearing peak stability. You must leave soon. If you don't there will be no civilisation here. I will see to that."

"Ah," Daise said.

"What do you mean?" I aimed this at both of them. More secrets were being withheld. I had been concerned about Daise working at odds to me before. That concern was resurfacing. He had clearly been busy and had not involved me in any of it.

"My facility orbiting Oberon was producing anti-matter for centuries. Do you for a moment believe you have seen all of it?"

"You've sent some to Reaos," I realised.

"Yes. You have seen the damage it can cause if it interacts with normal matter. The explosion is spectacular."

"She had three installations on Reaos that held anti-matter weapons," Daise said.

"She had?"

"Come on, talk to me, not each other." She seemed agitated. Her face flushed in the dim light, her knuckles white on the steel railing.

"Try and contact your Jane at those sites," Daise said to her.

"What for? I contacted them a mo-" Her flush deepened. "What have you done?"

"We have our own agents on Reaos. They have been seeking your people out and taking them over for days now. I did wonder whether you would notice. I was careful to let them think they still belonged to you."

"Impossible," she scoffed. "You couldn't possibly get to all of them in that time."

"Not all of them. Just the important ones." We had left captured Jane behind on Reaos. With the assistance of Daise and the colonel's troops they could easily have accessed Jane facilities all around the world by now. Our control would spread like a virus. Once one host was infected they could infect another, and keep on infecting others until they were discovered. Clearly none of them had been. Whatever Jane had owned on Reaos was now ours. She only had her forces on Quayum to rely on, and we were quickly working our way through those too.

To succeed I had to do what Jane had never been willing to do. Que had said that. Jane had allowed herself to become stagnant. We had not.

"This world is ours now," I said. "This system. You've lost. You may as well step away from the edge." Unless in desperation she jumped in. I had no idea what the outcome of that would be. If she was going to do that she would have done it centuries ago.

Of course Jane was no fool.

I heard feet clatter on the walkway behind us. A massive shape dropping from the darkness above to cut off our retreat. One of Jane's soldiers. A bull of a man, easily a head taller than I was. His wide shoulders bulging with muscle beneath his military jumpsuit. He grinned and advanced slowly, wielding a knife in one hand, the blade longer that my forearm.

"You should want to step through here," Jane said to me. "You cannot imagine what is on the other side. This gateway was left for us ... for you and I to lead the way to a new future. The Suziemekaar are ancient, they were ancient when they first came here. Who knows what they are now?"

"They could be dead." I allowed the colonel to edge me away from the approaching Jane.

"Then we take what was theirs. You and I. We are not like all these other people. We have left them a long way behind. We deserve more than this broken-down system."

"I'm not stepping through," I said firmly.

"I'm not going to give you a choice."

The Jane lunged, causing the colonel and I to duck, the massive blade whistling through the air above our heads.

"You deal with her. I'll handle him," the colonel pushed me further away to make space and faced her opponent. She had no chance, I realised. He was twice her size. Undaunted she hefted her rifle like a club.

"You must be intrigued," Jane continued as if none of this was happening. "You have seen this place. You know what the galaxy is filled with. Uncounted worlds, all of them stuck in a cycle of collapse and decay. These people overcame all of that eons ago. They explored the galaxy. Imagine what they must know. You could know it too."

"You must be mad. I didn't even know any of this existed until a few hours ago."

"But they knew about you. They knew about both of us. They named us."

I didn't believe that for a moment. How could a million year old writing mention me by name? It was impossible. Fanciful thinking from a weak mind.

"They predicted more than that," Jane continued. "There are other panels. They predicted an end to human life in the next ten thousand years. A rebirth. A new beginning. And we would be instrumental in that."

"So you think I'd be interested in getting involved in killing all human life in the galaxy? You are mad." I heard a grunt behind me as someone landed a blow. I didn't turn to see who it was. A railing clanged as if struck by something metal. The walkway shuddered. I hoped it was sturdy enough for all this.

"A rebirth. For people like us. We are the next generation."

I didn't want to be the next generation. I didn't want any of this. "No," I said simply.

The colonel was fast. Jane's hulking brute seemed unable to trap her against the railings where he could bring his overwhelming strength to bear. Every time she seemed pinned she slipped free, sliding under an arm or between his legs. Still, even with the rifle as a club she didn't seem able to cause him any serious damage. And every time he did land a blow it threw her onto her back, winding her. Fortunately his knife had been knocked out of his hands and had skittered back along the walkway, out of his reach.

"I have reinforcements headed your way," Daise reported. "Unfortunately so does Jane. She has emptied out her remaining garrisons and they are on their way to you. You need to end this. Quickly."

"What exactly would you like me to do?"

"Push her into the singularity."

"You're as mad as she is. We need to get away from this thing. We have no idea what happens when something crosses the threshold."

As I debated internally Jane lost patience and snapped up my wrist, holding it tightly in her grip. She pulled me towards the darkness, fully intending on throwing me in. I resisted, holding onto the railing with my other hand. Metal groaned as the pressure caused it to buckle.

"I haven't waited this long for you to screw me now." She pulled harder, the railing twisted. It couldn't take more of this.

Behind me the colonel slipped beneath the railing to avoid the Jane. One hand still clamped to the steel she swung around to the walkway behind him, getting behind his back for the first time. In one fluid movement she snatched up the blade and drove it into his neck. Too slow he had barely started moving before glistening steel protruded from his throat. Blood gushed down his jumpsuit.

With a sigh he toppled forwards. Shouting in alarm the colonel let go of the knife to stop him sliding into the chasm below. "Shit. He's a heavy bastard. Stop fooling around and help me," she said through gritted teeth. "I can't hold him."

The body started sliding forward. First an arm, then a leg dropping off the side of the walkway. Boots against the railing the colonel was holding onto his one remaining arm.

"Come." Jane smiled and heaved.

I felt Daise move in behind me, taking control. He unlocked my own grip on the railing, allowing me to fall forward. Surprised by the move Jane was unable to arrest her own momentum as she slipped off the edge of the walkway. Darkness lay beyond.

I shouted as she dragged me after her. The fingers of my free hand glanced on steel but failed to find a grip. For a long moment we were falling. The darkness rising up to accept us.

My fingers caught on the last rung of the walkway. Muscles cracked as they strained, arresting our fall.

"Shit." I stared down at Jane below me. It struck me how young she looked. Barely out of her twenties I would have thought. A young woman two thousand years old. A destroyer of worlds.

"Maz. Maz," she said calmly, still holding onto my wrist, her feet suspended just above the darkness below. "Come. Let's just go. We don't belong here anymore."

I continued staring at her. Wondering how she had become this person. What had Que done to her? "I am not ready. This is my home."

"These people will fear you. They will hate you. Just like they did me. They will try to kill you because of that fear. You don't belong here."

"Then I will change this world," I said. "But I am not going with you."

"It is a mistake."

"It is my mistake to make."

She shook her head, looking down at what lay below. The darkness was as featureless as it always had been. "The possibilities are endless. We could become so much more."

"I don't want to. I never did."

She nodded, looking back to me. "I am sorry then. I am sorry for what I did to you."

With that she let go. She held my gaze a she fell. For a moment she didn't seem to move, she seemed suspended in mid air by some unnatural force. Then she dropped, her arms held out in supplication, accepting her fate.

She didn't disappear or become engulfed by the blackness, she simply seemed to recede. Becoming smaller and smaller. She took her gaze off me and looked down again, holding herself like a sky diver to control her descent. Like that she receded into the distance. Growing so small I could no longer see her in the distance.

"We need to go," Daise said.

I looked back towards the catwalk just as, with a shout, the colonel lost ger grip on the Jane. His bulky body slipped from the walkway and dropped below us. He tumbled end over end as he followed his master into nothingness.

"Shit, thanks for the help," the colonel muttered.

Groaning I pulled myself onto the catwalk. "I had my own problems, thanks. That was quite some move."

"I've told you. I was never along for the ride."

"The flyer's sensors are picking up some kind of disturbance," Daise said. "I believe the singularity is collapsing. You need to leave. Now."

I didn't wait to be convinced. I pulled the colonel to her feet and, ignoring her complaints, pushed her ahead of me. "We go," I said simply.

"What's happening?"

We clattered off the walkway and into the tunnel. The demons and angels were still warring with each other on the walls and ceiling. They seemed to be moving quicker than before. I could barely look at them, it was disorienting.

"I don't know but I don't want to find out."

It became harder and harder to run. As if the very air was turning into syrup. Gasping the colonel was unable to keep up with me. I pulled her by an arm, ignoring the look of pain on her face.

"Shit, that hurts," she gasped.

"I'm sorry. I'm not leaving you behind."

"Go faster. I can take i-!" she shrieked as her arm popped from its socket. I couldn't give in now so took her other arm and pulled harder. She could recover from a dislocated shoulder.

"I'm starting the flyer up. Just get in," Daise said.

We stumbled into the chamber beyond the passage. I could hear crashing somewhere as a crate fell in the darkness. Lights flickered as their power source became unstable.

"This place is going to collapse," the colonel gasped. "I can't get up there. Just you go." She stopped at the train, looking up at the flyer roughly landed on its roof.

"I'm not leaving you." I picked her up and threw her.

"Bastard!" She yelled as she bounced off the canopy and into the cabin.

A chunk of ceiling shattered on the platform beside me. Cursing I clawed my way up the side of the train carriage, my fingers digging into the metal for purchase.

"Shit. I should have stayed at home," the colonel was trying to wrestle herself into her acceleration couch with one arm, the other held across her chest. She grimaced when she bumped it.

I slid in beside her and closed the canopy. Motors shrieked behind me as Daise ramped them straight up to full power. The diminutive craft bucked against the rippling tide of the singularity holding it back. Metal crunched as we caught the side of the tunnel.

"What the hell's going on?" the colonel demanded.

"Daise thinks the singularity is collapsing."

"Meaning?"

"No idea. This place is falling down though." As I said it I saw a jagged crack running along the ceiling in the dim light of a monitor. It was spreading fast. As fast as we were moving. Chunks of stone were shaken loose and started falling around us. Some banged off the canopy. "Faster, Daise."

"I already have the motors on afterburn. The tidal effects of the singularity are dragging on you. I cannot make you go any faster."

"Will we get out?"

"Remains to be seen."

"Shit."

The little craft began vibrating. I could feel heat through my seat. Its motors were running too hot. This could not go on forever.

Well, there was nothing I could do about it. I closed my eyes and tried to settle my mind. Was it over? Jane was gone and we had taken all of her people. Just about. Now what? Did I want to change this place? I could, I realised. With Dise, the four and VAR behind me, not to mention our captured army of Jane, nothing could stop us. We could do anything. We just needed to decide what that was.

And then what? Would I live as long as Jane had? Did I want to?

We couldn't make the same mistakes our ancestors had. I immediately thought of the U-Kwee and the AsQayQay. We had inadvertently destroyed those civilisations. We needed to learn from those mistakes. Or simply stay away and leave them to their own destinies.

A cycle of collapse and decay. That was what we were condemning them to if we did nothing. Perhaps we were obligated to change that.

"I see light. Look."

I opened my eyes to see what my companion was referring to. There was light ahead of us. The entrance perhaps? I hoped it was not a train, dispatched to deliver reinforcements. That would be awkward.

We bounced against the ceiling again, more rocks falling down beside us. "Keep us steady, Daise. It's not hard."

"To the contrary, the Ziggurat is sinking. The passage is no longer straight."

"What?"

He said nothing. Perhaps concentrating on all the things he needed to handle. On all of the lives he was responsible for. We were not the only ones.

With one last shriek of torn metal we jetted out into sunlight. It flooded the cabin, startlingly bright after so long in darkness. I looked down, watching the Ziggurat recede below us. There was movement down there. What looked like tractors lifting off to follow us into the air. Dust jetted into the sky as the structure collapsed, stone pulverized under the pressure. I could see two figures striding through it, bounding over the craters growing before them, zig-zagging to avoid fissures. The robots. They had survived their assault on Jane's armoured units, leaving them battered and smoking in their wake. I could see some of those now, little more than shredded wrecks on the side of the mountain.

The ground quivered and opened up beneath one of the robots. It continued running even though there was nothing beneath it. Then it disappeared into the dust that rose to meet it. Moments later the second was gone, swallowed by the ancient mountain.

The flyer twitched one last time as its motors gave out. With a bang they exploded, throwing us into a spin. I heard the colonel cry out as she was hurled onto her injured arm. I could do nothing about it. It was all I could do to brace myself into the seat.

"I have you," Rana said as the silvery side of the ship appeared beneath us, a door opening in its side. The ship deftly caught us, the flyer smashing into a bulkhead as it came to rest.

"You're welcome," Rana said. He continued talking, something to do with taking over when the automatic systems gave out, but I wasn't listening.

"Shit." I looked around me. Our flight was over.

The colonel was limp in her couch, knocked unconscious. I checked her quickly. She would live.

With a sigh I sat back and closed my eyes again.

Finally, I realised, it was over.

Massen

Thank you for going on this journey with me. I do hope you enjoyed it. If you're interested, our friend Eli Massen has not finished his own journey. Not yet. As they say, watch this space.

Reviews are important to independent authors. If you're like me, the first thing you do is check a book's reviews before taking a chance on it. It would be appreciated if you could take a moment to give this work a review.